THE LAST DROP

The Last Drop Series

ANDREA PERNO

To: Laurel
Hope you enjoy
this story !

Andrea Perno

CONTENTS

Chapter 1

I stare at my reflection in the bathroom mirror, hardly recognizing myself. My dark, crew-cut hair is growing out all wrong. Even at sixteen, there's a rough haze of stubble along my jaw and across my upper lip. I'll have to shave before reporting. I balance my armpits on the tops of aluminum crutches and rake my fingers along my scalp, watching my hair stand on end from sweat. It would feel amazing to splash cool water on my face and rinse the dirt from my skin, but those days are gone. Water is too precious. The sink basin is dry and coated with a layer of sand and dirt like everything else in the house. I turn the knobs anyway and pretend water fills the basin before reaching for the powdered bathing substitute and electric shaver. I need to look and smell presentable today. Dad and Jeremy are returning from overseas. My older brother, Jeremy, won't care what I look like, but it wouldn't be *acceptable* for the son of a prestigious military commander and esteemed biochemical engineer to have even one hair out of place.

The thought of their return brings a nervous anxiety, which I try to evade by pressing the electric shaver into the cleft of my chin, daring the blades to cut me. I don't want to think about what my father will do if this mission failed too. No one on base will tell me anything substantial, but rumors say diplomacy is out the window. It explains why recruitment numbers are through the roof and why Jeremy doesn't want me along for any missions. Thanks to him, I get another few weeks off before recruitment officers force me back into basic training. "Only had three days left, now I'll have to start all over. Least you could've done was waited until I finished basic," I whisper at the mirror.

For just a moment, as the last bit of facial stubble falls into the sink, my reflection takes the form of Jeremy's face. Striking blue eyes, prominent jaw line, he's only two years older than I am, but all I'd need is a good haircut and we'd be twins. Sighing, I shift weight off my broken leg to ease the throbbing pain. The heavy plaster cast encasing my left upper thigh down is a cumbersome reminder of Jeremy's loyalty and love, however misguided. He was only doing what he thought was best, the only way he knew to keep me on base, but he had no right.

"You're a smart kid. You don't have to be a grunt. Stay put. Go to class. Get your ass on the flight list outta here." His voice fills my head as if he's standing in front of me. But the flight list is a joke. Commanding officers like to dangle the hope of being hand-selected for space settlement in front of students and soldiers as motivation. It works...mostly. Everyone wants out of our military base, Asik. Off Earth. I'm guessing I'm the exception. I don't hold out much hope of a successful space settlement even though people rumor that habitable planets are out there. If we can't fix what's wrong with our own planet we're doomed no matter where we wind up. Jeremy would be pissed to know that I requested transfer out of space academy, though. Too bad. He doesn't get to choose the life I lead. Brothers are supposed to protect each other. I'm supposed to be watching his six out there. Instead, I'm stranded here nursing a fractured femur. *Jerk!*

I finish shaving and attempt to move quietly past my other brother and sister's bedrooms. The uneven metallic clomp of my crutches on the linoleum floor is less than subtle. Thankfully, neither of them wakes. I'm not in the mood to deal with Jace's overly optimistic ten-year-old banter. And my older sister,

Caileen, has been more than nurturing to whatever needs and limitations she now thinks I have, whether physical or mental. I'm just not up for it.

I trudge past my own bedroom door and slip into Jeremy's room. Grabbing clothing off the floor, I tug on a pair of digitized camouflage trousers and a tan T-shirt. It feels strange to put on and lace up only one steel-toed boot, but with it on, my feet are nearly equal in weight. It's almost like my leg isn't broken in three places and the cast is gone. Until I shift my weight and the bones grind mercilessly. Gritting my teeth against the pain, I reluctantly hunch back down on my crutches. Before plodding out of the room, I grab my Corridor Access and Readout Display Device, or as soldiers call it, the CARDD, from the bedside table. As quietly as I can, I maneuver down the narrow hallway toward the front door.

"A bit early in the morning to be leaving, don't you think?" My mother's quiet accusing voice from the kitchen table makes me cringe. It was too much to hope I'd get out of the house without having to talk to anyone. Mom hasn't slept right in nearly a week since she learned Dad would be coming home. I should've known she'd be sitting up. I look longingly at the front door, but instead move into the kitchen. Mom rises to flick on the wall light. Still in her nightclothes, her long hair tangled in a messy braid. Deep purple rings under striking green eyes accentuate her anxiety.

"Sorry, Mom. I just need to—"

"It's okay." She waves a hand so I don't have to finish. I shoot her a confused look, but she ignores it. "Give them this for me." She opens a cabinet beside me and pulls out a small black book bag. It feels light, empty, except that the contents shift with a quiet rustle as I sling the bag onto my back. "Don't be gone long. I don't know what time your father is coming home.

We need you here today."

I nod and kiss her cheek. "I'll be here."

"You're a good boy, Avery. Jeremy will be so proud to know you're doing this." She hugs me tightly around my neck before letting me go and settling back into a chair at the kitchen table.

I latch the front door behind me and take a deep breath. *I've been so careful. How can she know where I'm going?* I try to shake off the nervousness that's now invaded my stomach. It's early and the sun hasn't risen yet. The odd off-color orange glow is just beginning to emerge over the repulsive concrete walls surrounding Asik's military base. For just a moment, the light coming over the wall blends with the sand and dirt, drifting against the concrete and the barrier is gone. What would it be like with no walls? My hands grip the lower handles on the crutches a little tighter. *You know the answer to that question.*

I watch the sun rise a little more and the wall defiantly comes back into view. Instinctively I scan the area before clumsily navigating the steep set of cellar stairs next to our house. No one is around. Not that anyone would be able to see or hear me anyway. One of the advantages of Dad being a commander is we get officer housing on base. It's a little better than the cookie-cutter neighborhoods where the houses are so close together you can hear your neighbor snoring at night. Our home is at the edge of Asik, tucked right into rolling sand dunes. The houses of other military families are not far from ours, still within sight, but we're afforded a little more privacy.

At the bottom of the cellar steps, I punch in a code and a huge metal door swings inward. I lean the crutches against a counter and sling the backpack down. Yanking the pull chain attached to the hanging light, I quickly rummage the shelves sliding canned goods toward the bag. I grab a little bit of everything, including cans labeled fruit, beans, and the like. I snatch a gallon jug of water from our reserves and drop it next to the bag with a thump. I'm about to reach for a second gallon but think better of it. Our water rations look surprisingly low and there will be two more bodies tonight. The water supply should be greater with Dad and Jeremy gone and I rack my brain trying to think if I've been using more water than normal. I quickly give up. The sun will be up in an hour and soldiers will be making their rounds. I need to be finished by then. One gallon will have to be enough. I hobble back to my crutches and start shoving supplies into the backpack. It's only then that I notice the strawberries freshly packaged in a suctioned airtight bag.

"Christ, Mom," I curse under my breath and cast a cautious glance over my shoulder even though the heavy lead door is closed behind me. I shove the bag deep inside the backpack and bury it with the other supplies. No wonder our water rations look low. It would take nearly all of Dad and Jeremy's rations to grow fresh fruit like this. Where did she even get the seeds? If the government knew she was using water rations to grow food without a permit, she could face jail time, even be exiled from base.

I'm contemplating destroying the fruit when a satisfying thought pops into my head. What a kick in the face it would be if the government knew food grown on base without a permit was being smuggled directly to the outsiders they refuse to provide rations to. Mom's subtle act of defiance suddenly feels liberating.

I throw the backpack over one shoulder, clomp up the steps and cut through the drifting sand in our backyard toward the guard tower. It's about a mile and a half hike to the barrier at the edge of Asik where the south guard tower stands. During the day, the hike would be brutal, especially on crutches, but the sun isn't up and there's still a comfortable chill to the desert air.

When I'm a few paces from the tower, a hostile voice hisses from inside my pants pocket, "Can you move any slower?"

I grumble and yank my CARDD from my pocket. Bruce's flushed face on the screen is annoyed.

"Shut up, Bruce. You'd be slow, too, if you were crippled. Just have the gate open."

"You sure you want to do this? Jeremy's due back in like—"

"Shut up. I can do it."

"Fine. You better make it fast, gimpy. Patrol goes out in half an hour," Bruce says, pushing a button on the device so the gate dematerializes.

"Right." I shove past him and head straight across the room, around the center security desk to the gate directly opposite the one I came through. It's the only other barrier between the military base and what lies beyond. Bruce grabs one of my crutches and I nearly eat floor trying to keep my balance on the polished marble.

"What the fu—"

"Dude," Bruce snaps, his dark eyebrows knitting in frustration. He presses a handful of letters into my hands. "I've got people out there, too, remember?"

"Right. Sorry." I dip my head but keep moving. I should show more respect. Bruce was my superior at the beginning of basic. He, his father and twin brother, were summoned away right at the beginning of training to lead a mission in Brazil. Bruce was the sole survivor. He still refuses to talk about what went down out there. His uncle is the only one who really knows. He raised a big stink about what happened to Bruce, but it only got him kicked off base. That left Bruce alone with no other family members aside from an elderly grandmother with severe dementia. The only reason he stayed was so she'd still have family ties to the military and a safe place to sleep. She'd be thrown out in a heartbeat if he left. The decision to stay has weighed heavily on Bruce. Now he's just another rifle-carrying body on base that will occasionally turn a blind eye to what I'm about to do. Hell, Bruce practically begged me a week ago. Jeremy would be the one to do this kind of reckless stuff, but with him gone…Bruce and I both know it's illegal, but we also both have people on the outside now.

My teeth grind thinking about it. It's a death sentence beyond the walls since the military controls and distributes food and water. Only essential personnel working on base get any aid. It's just one of the messed up ways people are forced to work for the army. They don't even need to instate a draft. Just leave people without water beyond the gates for whatever act they deem defiant. It's a simple matter of survival.

"You get me a vehicle?"

"Already out there," Bruce says, punching in code on his CARDD. The gate at the other end of the room disappears, revealing a tan dune buggy. I pass Bruce my crutches, hop into the driver's seat and prop my bad leg up on the frame. A large brown box on the passenger seat lets me know Bruce isn't the only one trying to get supplies to outsiders. I point to it and raise my eyebrows.

"Like I said, you're not the only one with people on the outside. But patrol won't look the other way for long, so move your ass."

"Thanks." Sand spits behind thick rubber tires as

I gun the engine toward the sprawling city, which is emerging from the sand dunes in the distance.

It only takes me a few minutes to hit what used to be Main Street. Now the road is just a bit of cracked asphalt covered with dirt and sand. Walls of trade buildings, restaurants, and shops are eroded and desolate. I crank the wheel right and spin up an alley hung with heavy opaque plastic tarps used to keep out the blowing sand. Batting the plastic away with one hand, I drive straight through a blue plastic tarp into a building that used to serve as the Army Federal Bank. Outsiders use the AFB's locked vaults as a safe place to sleep and store supplies. I know I'll find Aunt Sara and Uncle Jim here.

Killing the engine, the vehicle skids to a stop near the center of the room. It's eerily silent. All but one of the florescent light panels above me is burnt out. The remaining one flickers with a nauseating strobe. Outside, a distant helicopter's blades cuts the air with an unnerving chopping sound. I resist the urge to check my CARDD and see if it's arriving or departing. *Maybe it's Jeremy and Dad. I need to make this a quick trip in case it is.*

A soft click behind me makes me flinch.

"Hands above your head, kid." A raspy voice coughs at me.

"Put the gun down, Jim. It's Avery, for God's sake." I recognize Aunt Sara's voice. She and a small group of men with rifles and handguns step out of the shadows. Uncle Jim lowers his weapon, but it's clear he doesn't trust me. By the look on his face, I'm not sure he even recognizes me. His swollen red eyes dart from Aunt Sara to me, to the men around him and back again. He's not the same strong man who served for my father a year ago. Now he's gaunt, confused and breathes with staggered, labored breaths. Jim, caught in an explosion during a mission in the Middle East, breathed explosive material laced with titanium. The metal tore his lungs apart and reduced him to a severe asthmatic with heavy metal poisoning. The Army investigated and faulted Jim for the explosion. No longer fit for any military duties, he and Aunt Sara were removed from base. Mom tried to convince Dad not to approve their removal, but he wouldn't give in. Mom's never forgiven him.

Aunt Sara throws her arms around my neck and kisses my cheek. I try to ignore how bony and frail her arms feel. I quickly pass her the backpack and gallon of water but she hands them behind her to someone and hugs me again.

"How are you? How's your mother? You look well. Jace and Caileen, are they well? Jeremy, will he be coming back soon? Have you heard anything?"

She's asking too many questions all at once. At the mention of Jeremy's name, butterflies swarm in my stomach. I look beyond Aunt Sara. Dozens of faces peek out from the shadows of the room, waiting with bated breath to hear if I've heard anything. All seem anxious to hear if Jeremy will be back soon. That's really the only question they want answered. Suddenly I feel very guilty. I didn't bring enough food or water. Not for *all* of them. Jeremy would've brought twice the supplies. He should be here, not me. It was stupid to think I could carry the torch for him while he's gone.

"I'm sure he'll be back in no time." I hand her the box in the passenger seat and tell her I have to leave right away since patrol will be going out shortly. She looks disappointed, but wishes me well and presses a folded paper into my hand.

"For your mother," she says.

"Right, I'll make sure she gets it." Aunt Sara hugs me one last time.

The tires on the dune buggy squeal as I tear out of the AFB. I punch the plastic sheeting out of the way angrily. It was stupid to think I could make any kind of difference for them. Those supplies won't last them a day. I'm not even sure how they're still alive. Good thing Jeremy will be back soon. I slam the gas pedal to the floorboards and feel the dune buggy surge as it skips and dips through the sand. My cast bounces painfully on the metal frame but right now, I welcome the excruciating lightning bolts of pain zinging through each broken bone. I'd do anything to get Uncle Jim and Aunt Sara's desperate, starved, sunken features out of my head.

I'm back at the south guard tower, watching the gate dematerialize in minutes. Bruce is waiting for me and hands me my crutches. "What is it?" he asks, reading my sour look.

"Nothing, there's just a lot more of them than I thought."

Bruce nods. "Did you give him my letters?"

"Aunt Sara will make sure he gets them," I say, walking around him to the security desk so I can punch in for my two-hour shift.

Bruce puts an arm up to stop me. "Nope, not today. Commander Zimmerman just pinged me looking for you."

"What?"

Bruce shrugs. "I tried to tell him you weren't part of space training anymore, but he wouldn't hear it. He said to send you his way when you checked in."

"Great," I groan.

"Hey, you should be happy you're still being

considered. You have a shot of getting out of here."

"You're starting to sound like my brother," I grumble, entering code on my CARDD that will call a transport vehicle. "You know what? Forget it. I'll drive myself," I say, swiping the code away with my index finger. I hobble back through the gate and throw my crutches into the passenger seat of the dune buggy. Bruce shoots me a look of disapproval as I violently shift into high gear. It's a thirty-minute drive across base to the space agency. I intend to do it in fifteen. I don't have the time or the patience today to deal with Zimmerman's space training nonsense.

Despite Zimmerman directly contacting Bruce, no one seems to know I'm coming. When I drop Zimmerman's name at each checkpoint, none of the security officers can get him on his CARDD to verify his appointment with me. With no response from Zimmerman, getting through the checkpoints is a nightmare. I've been deleted from the space roster so none of my retinal or fingerprint scans work. All my access data has to be re-installed on my CARDD as if I'm a brand new cadet all over again. By the time I make it to the fourth and final security checkpoint, I'm fuming. *So much for a quick trip!*

Sweaty and exhausted from hobbling around on crutches and waiting for security to process my request for access to this part of the military installation, I gladly welcome the rush of cool air from the pressurized chamber doors leading into the building lobby. I shut my eyes and linger between the doors, letting the air dry some of my sweat. When I open my eyes and cross the threshold, Jeremy is leaning nonchalantly against the lobby desk at the center of the room, chatting with a female receptionist. My stomach hits the floor.

Chapter 2

The woman behind the desk sees me enter and blasts me with the charming welcome look she's trained to give everyone who walks through the door. Her pause makes Jeremy turn.

I want to disappear, fade into the walls, and be sucked away like the air in the pressurized doors. I'm not prepared for him to be here. We regard each other in stoic silence and a surge of suppressed anger rises. How can he be standing here in the lobby chatting with the receptionist like he wasn't gone for several weeks? Doesn't he know I had to take care of Mom, the kids…everything? I'm not supposed to be in Asik, I was supposed to go too. I huff out the breath of air I've been holding and release the death grip I have around my crutches.

Jeremy cocks his head and gives me a stupid, yet oddly comforting, half smile that I've been missing for weeks and my anger fades. My brother, my best friend, and a person I can truly trust. He's here again, alive. Everything is going to be okay. I'll never tell him how much I missed him, or how glad I am that he's back. Instead, I give him a disapproving scowl and look him up and down. His skin is a deep reddish brown from sun exposure and multiple bruises in various stages of healing decorate his face and arms. A nasty gash on his temple is bound to scar from poor stitching. He sees me looking at it and presses a hand over the wound.

"Just a beauty mark in a few more days." He chuckles.

Three fingers on his hand are missing fingernails and I don't want to think about how he lost them. "Beauty mark, my ass! Christ, Jeremy! What the hell happened to you?" I say, crutching my way to him.

"Long story." He shrugs and closes the distance to meet me.

We throw our arms around each other in a massive, bone-crushing hug. Jeremy grabs my upper arms and thumps his forehead against mine. "I missed you, kid."

"I could've gone with you. If you hadn't paid off Robertson to drop me from the rappel tower you wouldn't have had to miss me."

"You want to look like this, too, huh?" he says sarcastically.

"Ah, I bet 'you should've seen the other guy.' Am I right?" I try to make it sound like a joke, but Jeremy doesn't crack a smile. He looks off into the distance like he's thinking hard about something and his fingertips dig painfully into my arms.

"You didn't tell anyone what Robertson did. Did you?" Jeremy pulls me away from the front desk so the receptionist won't hear.

"No...no way. That would get him thrown out."

Jeremy sighs with relief and loosens his grip. "Robertson's a good man. He wasn't supposed to tell you."

"He didn't have to. I found my mission papers crumpled in your room. You know, opening someone else's mail is a federal offense. I just happen to accidently break my leg right before being assigned to the same operation as you? Bit of a coincidence, don't you think? You're lucky there wasn't a full-blown investigation. It could be your ass on the outside with Aunt Sara and Uncle Jim."

"I did what I had to do to get you back on track. But you're supposed to stick with the space agency. Seriously, what's gotten into you? Working security?"

"Until my leg is good enough to complete basic."

Jeremy sucks in a frustrated breath and looks at the ceiling. "Do I have to break your other leg too? You know how many strings I had to pull to get you here—"

"I didn't ask you to do that. You need me to watch your back. Christ, Jeremy, you look like Frankenstein. Mom's going to freak when she sees you."

"Watch my back? So you can get hurt too? Maybe even killed? Who will that leave to take care of Jace and Caileen and Mom?"

"Caileen could—"

"Caileen could what? I nearly got killed out there. If I die, if you die...people are being killed, Avery. No one has a good solution to this mess. No one wants to give up the rights to their water. They don't even want to share. Shit is hitting the fan over all this. Look, Jace is too young for recruitment. Caileen would be the only other person who could sign up so that the family could live on base. Can you picture her in basic? Boy, I bet she'd be the perfect person to go out and shoot people. You aren't even fit to do that."

My teeth grind in opposition, but I know he's right about Caileen. Basic training would eat her alive. She wouldn't have the guts to shoot someone. It has to be me that stays behind.

"Look, I know you're against the space program, but it's our best bet. You think it's bad in Asik? You think the outsiders living just beyond our walls have it bad? I already talked to Bruce, so I know you've been out there..."

"Bruce? You've talked to Bruce? How long have you been back?"

"A few days."

"God, Jeremy. A few days! What the hell! Does Mom know? When were you going to tell us?"

"It doesn't matter. Probably won't be staying here

for long anyway with the way things are going. Look, what matters is you get back on the space settlement list."

"Why's that so important to you? What aren't you telling me?" I yell at him.

Jeremy glances at the receptionist who's beginning to eye us suspiciously. "Stop shouting," Jeremy whispers and walks me farther away from the lobby desk. "If you're chosen, the rest of the family gets to go. Don't you get that? Look, if you knew half the shit that's going down right now you'd be begging to leave."

"If it's so damn important to you, why aren't you trying to get on the list?"

"You think I haven't?" Jeremy gives me a pained look. He's easily smart enough and he's in great physical condition. It makes no sense. Zimmerman should be standing on his head to have a person like Jeremy. Then it hits me.

"Dad didn't approve it?"

"I'm his right hand man." Jeremy scoffs. "If he only knew, right?" Jeremy's lips curl in a devious grin and I can't help but smile back. He's opposed pretty much everything Dad's put in place. Jeremy doesn't support recruiting hundreds of men to use for missions and he helps sneak food to the outsiders. By how smoothly things went with this morning's supply drop, Jeremy's got a whole crew of people on base working covertly against our father.

"So, if you're his right hand man, you must know what's going to happen next."

Jeremy runs a palm across the top of his shaved head. "Let's just say our trade didn't exactly go as planned." He sucks in a breath and gives me a serious look that makes my stomach drop again. "This is why you need to get your act together. Today! The shit storm is coming and it won't be long until it hits home."

Jeremy is about to say something else when his CARDD squeals wildly. He takes it out of his pocket, glances at the screen, then quickly slides it back into his pants. He looks past me. His nostrils flair and his jaw bulges as he clenches his teeth.

"What is it?"

"Nothing you need to worry about." He flashes what he thinks is a reassuring smile and pulls me in for another hug. "I'll be by the house to see everyone tonight."

"What about Dad?" I can't keep the nervousness out of my voice.

"Tell Mom not to worry. I'm guessing he's going to be tied up for the foreseeable future."

I try to ask him another question but he won't hear it. "Tomorrow, where are you reporting?"

"Here," I grumble.

Jeremy pushes me out of the hug. "Don't sound so sour about it, kid. People need you here. Besides, it will be easy as pie to get to this checkpoint now that your data is in the system again. Zimmerman will be waiting for you tomorrow. Don't be late." Jeremy gives me a wink.

This was his plan all along. He set it up with Bruce and had him lie about Zimmerman wanting to see me. He probably even had Bruce plant the seed on purpose that it should be me to make the supply drop to the outsiders in Jeremy's place. That way Jeremy can be sure I'll pick up where he leaves off if he's killed.

"You set this up. You set me up."

"Not set up. Set straight. Everyone has a purpose. When I'm gone, this is your purpose. Take care of the family any way you can. If that means sneaking food to them, you do it. If that means working somewhere you don't want to, you suck it up and do it anyway. Family is everything. When a member strays, sometimes you have to pick them up and literally put them on the right path again."

"You really believe you can do that? Think you can do that with Dad?" I say sarcastically.

"I'm still working on it."

"Yeah? What if I don't believe it will work? What if I think the space program is bullshit? What if we make the same mistakes on another planet?"

"Relax, kid. You'll do the right thing. Don't let them make the same mistakes." Jeremy cups the back of my head in his hand and pulls my forehead to his. "Listen to me very carefully. Bad things are going to happen, sooner than you think. Jace and Caileen, people are going to need hope. This building that you're standing in right now, this is hope. Whether you believe it or not. Now get home." He slides away from me to the exit but then turns back around. "And another thing, I better not see your name on the security roster again. I'm serious. I'll break your other leg too." He smiles and takes off at a jog through the door.

When he leaves the room, it's like he's shipping off overseas all over again. He takes everything with him. I want to run after him, follow him wherever he's going, but my body feels heavy and my legs feel weak. The only thing keeping me from falling on my face is my crutches. Looking down at my feet, the ground seems much farther away than it should. I take a few deep breaths to calm myself. *Do the right thing? I don't know what the right thing is.*

I look over at the receptionist. She isn't smiling anymore. I give her a halfhearted wave and hobble out the exit toward home.

When I get back to our house, Caileen is trying to

corral Jace. He's flitting around the house, swiping a dust rag across surfaces in a way that sends more sand and dust into the air than onto the cloth. Mom is buzzing around behind them, barking orders.

"This house has to be spotless before your father gets here."

I see Mom's nervous anxiety and go to her. "Mom?" She turns to me and what's left of the color fades out of her face.

"I got the call. They're coming home tonight. The house, it's not ready," she says nervously and starts to give another order.

"Mom." I touch her arm. "Mom, it's okay, it's only Jeremy tonight," I whisper.

She whips her head in my direction.

"It's only Jeremy," I tell her again and watch relief spread across her face. She sighs and drops down on the living room couch exhausted.

"What about your father?"

"Jeremy doesn't think he's coming home. Not for a while."

"Why isn't Dad coming home?" Jace pipes up. I didn't know he was listening.

"He's…got important business to take care of, sweetie," Mom says soothingly.

"Oh. I wish he was coming home. I miss him." Jace doesn't hide his disappointment.

Caileen and I exchange a glance. We've done our best to make sure Jace has as little contact with our father as possible. The mere fact that Dad's hardly ever around is a blessing. Jace barely knows the man and we intend to keep it that way.

"Come on, we have to get the rest of this house clean," Caileen says, swatting Jace's butt with her own dust rag. Her distraction incites a playful war with Jace loping after Caileen, swinging his own dust rag.

"So you saw Jeremy then? How is he?" Mom asks when Jace is out of the room.

"Fine," I lie and give her a hug. "I better make sure those two don't make a bigger mess, huh?" Mom tips her head in acknowledgment. I just can't bring myself to tell her that Jeremy looks like hell. It wouldn't change anything anyway.

For the next four hours, we clean the house regardless of Dad coming home. It's just something to keep Mom occupied and not thinking about him being in Asik. When missions go badly, Dad has a way of taking it out on Mom…or anyone within striking distance. Not this time. Caileen and I have planned it out. If things start to go badly, she'll distract Jace and take him to the cellar. They can lock themselves inside and set a security code so no one can get in from the outside. Jeremy and I will take care of Mom. But Dad won't be coming home, I remind myself. Nothing bad will happen.

The sun is just beginning to set when Jeremy arrives. Just as he said, he comes alone. Mom is overjoyed to see him, but hovers about his head, analyzing each bruise and cut. She orders Caileen to fetch the medical kit and won't hear a word from him until she's had a chance to properly address his injuries. Jeremy sits patiently and tells pleasant stories to Jace and Caileen about the people he met overseas while Mom dabs medicine on his face. He skillfully avoids any questions Jace asks about how he got cut up by weaving harmless anecdotes about animals and clumsy accidents. I can't tell for sure if Jace buys it all, but Caileen and I "oooo" and "ah" at appropriate moments and Mom lectures him about trying to be more careful.

The rest of the night consists of eating a less than appetizing MRE style meal, swapping stories and playing games that Jace invents out of household items. Jace loves to invent riddles and challenges and watch people solve them. It's like old times before basic training, before Dad became a power-hungry commander in charge of all of Asik and Jeremy started going on missions with him. It's good to see Mom with a smile on her face again. Jace and Caileen's playful banter makes everyone laugh and, for a moment, everything is right in the world. I wish I could freeze time.

Unfortunately, no such technology exists to freeze time. Jace and Caileen tire quickly. Mom shuffles them off to bed and kisses Jeremy and I goodnight. She looks exhausted. With all of her children safely home, perhaps tonight she'll get a decent sleep. I hear the click of her door close and the squeaking of rusty springs as she climbs into bed. I follow Jeremy to his bedroom and flop down on his mattress.

"Like what you've done with the place," he says, glancing at my clothing strewn around his room. When he left, his room slowly, subconsciously became my own. He pulls a pair of jeans off the lamp and lets them fall to the floor, before sighing and settling onto the bed beside me.

"I missed you, too, kid," he says knowingly and punches me in the ribs. I punch him back and bite the inside of my cheek to keep any kind of emotion from showing. I want to ask him a million questions about what happened while he was gone and what's going to happen now that he's back. Instead, I keep my questions to myself.

We lie shoulder to shoulder staring at the ceiling until sleep finally finds us.

Chapter 3

"Get up, now!"

The voice seems far away like it's part of a dream. Then an excruciating blast of pain surging up the left side of my body wakes me like I've just been set on fire. I hit the ground hard, my cast bouncing painfully on the floor. I force my eyes to adjust to the shadows swinging at each other in the darkness.

"Where is it?" My father yells.

"What do you want?" Jeremy yells back. I can see his form in the darkness dancing just out of Dad's range. In the background, I can hear muffled voices. Mom's telling Caileen to take Jace somewhere. Light, little footsteps are running toward our room. *Oh God, Jace can't come in here, not now.*

I scramble onto my crutches and hurry to the door. Jace is already turning the knob. I make it to the door just as he's pulling it open and shove him backward into Caileen's arms.

"What's going on?" he screeches.

"Get him out of here," I warn Caileen. She has her arms around Jace, demanding that he comes with her, but he's focused on the voices shouting in the bedroom.

"Is that Dad? Dad!" he yells, trying to rub the sleep out of his eyes and go toward the voice.

Caileen covers his mouth and tries to drag him backward, but he's a bigger challenge than we thought. "Jace, you have to go with Caileen." I try to reason with him but he's only half listening.

"Get them out," Mom pleads.

"Do what she says, Avery!" Jeremy shouts.

"Tell me where it is!" Dad yells again. Something

in the room hits a wall and shatters.

I don't want to leave Jeremy alone with Dad, but I know Caileen can't take Jace by herself. The two of us quickly guide him out of the house and down to the cellar. He's only half-awake and doesn't fully understand what's going on, but with the two of us leading him, he complies more willingly. "Caileen wants you to help her plan a game. Plan it out so when Jeremy gets up in the morning all of us can play it together," I tell him as we make our way into the cellar.

Jace looks at me like I'm crazy. "But it's still dark. Mom's going to be mad we're up. It's still bedtime."

"No, Mom said it's okay. In fact, she wants you to build your most challenging game yet. We have to keep Jeremy's mind sharp before he leaves again you know." Caileen adds.

"Leaves, he just got home. I'm tired. What's going on?"

"Keep working on him," I whisper to Caileen and quickly change the inside access codes.

"You're not going back up there." Caileen grabs my arm. "You can't."

"I have to help. When I leave, you press this button. You hear me? Military police will be here in minutes." I point to an emergency call button on the access panel.

"Avery, don't."

"I'll be right back. I promise." I shove through the door and push it shut behind me. Climbing the stairs in panic mode on crutches is horrendous. I trip over myself several times and nearly plummet down the full flight twice. When I reach the top of the stairs the shouting and pleading is getting louder and coming from behind the house. I edge my way around the side of the house and peer around the corner.

Mom's clinging to Dad's knees, her long, dark

hair tangled with sweat and tears.

"No, Daniel," she sobs. "Please don't do this."

The motion-activated floodlights at the back of the house illuminate Dad's face, adding to his crazed expression. He's got a rifle and his face and clothes are spattered with blood.

"Please, not him," Mom begs.

Daniel refuses to look at her and raises the butt of the rifle in the air. She shrinks away from the threatened blow, sobbing.

I'm about to turn the corner and go to her, but then I see Jeremy kneeling on the ground. He catches my gaze and shakes his head ever so slightly, telling me no.

"He's the only other person that has access codes," Dad says, stepping away from Mom. He doesn't seem to notice Jeremy's communication with me.

Jeremy is crouched on the ground, struggling to get up. His right eye is bloody and beginning to swell shut, but he holds his head proudly. Dad must have struck him repeatedly with the gun. Blood oozes from the ruptured stitches on his forehead.

"How could you do this to me?" Dad asks. A look of anguish burdens his handsome features. He leans down so that he's nose to nose with Jeremy. "How could you turn on your own family?"

Jeremy scowls. "You've lost sight of what's best for this family."

Dad slams the butt of the rifle into the side of the Jeremy's face. The blow breaks several teeth and knocks him onto his side in the dirt.

"Look what you made me do! I don't want to hurt you. Just tell me where you put it," Dad says.

Jeremy struggles back into a kneeling position and regards him with a look of defiance. Dad's hands tremble as he raises the gun to Jeremy's chest. My heart is hammering wildly and I'm not sure what I should do. Dad shakes his head, and his tone softens a bit.

"It doesn't have to be this way. Tell me where you put it. We can still fix this." His finger wavers on the trigger and beads of sweat glisten on his brow. "We can save them. All of them. Think how great it will feel to say you saved the world."

"Save the world? The one you poisoned?" Jeremy spits a wad of blood and teeth into the sand. "That's a fucking joke," he growls.

"We could do it…together," dad pleads. "All you have to do is tell me where you put the case."

"I don't have your fucking case!"

"Liar!" Dad turns away, refusing to look at Jeremy. "He's not going to help us. He's been against us from the beginning," he tells Mom.

"No. That's not true," she cries.

He turns back to Jeremy. "I want you to be a part of this. Think how amazing it will be to finally fix something. But I can't have you stand in my way and ruin everything. I *can* do it on my own. I'll make it again. But it'll take time. Millions of people will be dead before it's ready. Their blood will be on your hands."

"Shut up," Jeremy mutters.

"This is your last chance. Are you going to continue to stand in my way?" Dad raises the rifle square to Jeremy's chest.

"As long as I'm still breathing," Jeremy snarls.

"Daniel. No. Please!" Mom weeps.

"Dad! No!" I scream and struggle through the sand toward them.

Bang! A flash of white-hot light erupts from the rifle and blows a hole in Jeremy's chest. Dad flinches backward as the sound echoes across the vast expanse of desert.

A sob rises in my throat and my knees are suddenly too weak to hold my body. My crutches snag in the sand and tumble down. "No! Jeremy!" I can't take my eyes off the shocked expression on his face.

"Oh, God," Dad curses under his breath. He looks down the barrel of the gun in shock. He lowers the tip of the rifle and looks pleadingly at Mom.

"I'm so…I—"

A mournful, hysterical sound rises up from Mom.

Jeremy's body topples sideways and Mom howls. As the sound of the gunshot dissipates, her broken sobs mingle with the sickening gurgle coming from Jeremy as he gasps his last breaths.

Jeremy's lips peel back in a malicious smile. Blood dribbles from the corners of his mouth. "What is it like," he chokes out, "to know you will die by one of your own weapons?" He chuckles, which sends more blood running down his chin and onto the red, dusty ground.

At Jeremy's words, Dad raises the gun again. He looks away, squinting up at the sky like he's in pain.

He looks back at Jeremy and shakes his head. "You have to tell me where you put it," he begs. "So many people are going to die."

Jeremy's smile turns into a grimace. "That's what you wanted," he chokes, and his eyes become glassy and unfocused. He smiles again as if he's thinking of a fond memory. "But remember…water is—"

Dad shoots Jeremy again, this time in the head. I look away and throw up into the sand.

When I look back, Mom is crawling toward his lifeless body. Sobbing, she gathers him into her arms. She raises her lips from his head to mutter accusations at his killer.

"How could you? How could you?" She gently

rocks his body. "My son, oh, my boy…he was your son," she sobs. "He was your son!" she screams.

Dad strides past her.

"You're a monster!" she wails.

He flinches at her words and freezes. Then he turns slowly to look at her. Dad tries to hide his regret.

"He took it, I know he did."

"And now you'll never get it back. Murderer!" she spits with disgust. "He was our son." She rocks his body back and forth.

Daniel grinds his teeth and his features turn to stone. "I guess it's a good thing we've got two more. Avery! Jace!" Daniel yells. He turns in the direction of my sobbing. Sirens and flashing red and blue lights are coming toward the house, but he acts like he doesn't notice.

"Come!" he yells.

Chapter 4

No! Don't kill him! My eyes shoot open, and I bolt upright in my bed, clutching my chest. Breathing heavily, I wipe beads of sweat from my forehead. It's been two months since my father killed Jeremy. I relive his death every night.

There's the sound of muffled crying coming from somewhere nearby. I listen for a moment to be sure. The sound is hollow. Muted. Jace, my ten-year-old brother, is undeniably crying. I rub the sleep from my eyes and curse under my breath. Gripping the sides of my dirt-covered mattress to control my breathing, I try to pull myself together. The reoccurring images of a gun going off repeatedly, my brother Jeremy falling dead, dust rising around the feet of Jace and Caileen and me as we run to safety, blur and fade as the nightmare passes. But it's not just a nightmare—it's a nightly reminder of the war and how very real it is. I'm forced to relive the memories that come relentlessly each night despite the handfuls of sleeping pills I swallow. The war is real. I can't escape. None of us can…except in death.

I press my palms into the sides of my head to stop the pounding and focus on the wall in front of me. I linger on the cracks caused by the bombings, tracing them with my eyes. Jeremy was right. The shit storm had been coming. It came just a few weeks after Jeremy's death. And now my home is practically gone, blown apart and reduced almost entirely to ash and rubble in the war over water. A small, well-prepared underground bunker built into my home is the only reason I'm still alive. *Alive? I wish I were dead.*

Everyone around me is dead or dying from an

unknown virus. *Virus.* I look over at the Hazmat mask on the ground next to my bed. I should be wearing it to protect me. It hasn't helped my mother or my sister, though. I give it a sharp kick across the room and watch it bounce off the wall. A puff of dry dust and dirt rises around it as it skids across the floor. Our family is falling apart. Jeremy is dead. My father is gone. He disappeared just after he murdered Jeremy. The screaming sirens and police cars, they took him away. Away to where, though? That's the real question. The investigation into Jeremy's murder was very hush, hush, and we haven't seen or heard anything about Dad since the murder. Everyone on base, even Bruce, acts as if nothing happened. If there's any type of justice left, Dad's dead.

Dead. The simple, four-letter word bounces around in my head with more meaning and less meaning than ever before. My mother and sister will likely be dead soon, too, and there's nothing I can do to prevent it.

I swing my feet over the edge of the bed. The heavy steel-toe boots I refuse to take off my feet make a loud thump on the floor. My feet and ankles ache for release, but I don't know when the next bomb will drop and I'll have to run. I stand tentatively, allowing my full weight to shift onto my bad leg. I took myself off crutches earlier than the medical personnel on base recommend. Mornings are still rough until the stiffness fades. I grab one crutch and shove it under my armpit for extra stability, as I push my way through the blue tarp that serves as a makeshift doorway to my room.

Down the hall, the hunched form of my brother is sitting at the foot of Mom's bed, sobbing uncontrollably. As I draw closer, I see the dried paths his tears have cut through the layer of dust on his face. His little body has long since stopped producing liquid.

Keeping watch over a dying family is taking a toll on him. He doesn't try to hide his emotions anymore like I do.

Jace doesn't acknowledge my presence, but he knows I'm in the room. I watch his shoulders convulse as he sobs, and I'm not sure what to do. I've never been good at providing comfort and support. Not like Caileen. She would do a better job. She would know what to say, how to handle this. *This isn't fair. We're too young. How do I fix this?*

I look across the room to Caileen's bed. It's pushed as close as possible to the last intact window in the ruined shell of our house. She's watching us. There's still life in her eyes, but her breathing is labored and erratic. I can tell she wishes she could find the strength to get out of bed and help. Days of fighting the virus has left her body weak and crippled.

I walk to her bedside and brush a sweat soaked strand of hair off her face. Leaning down I kiss her forehead. "Don't you dare stop fighting. We still need you." A sob rises in her chest. "Shhh, rest. It's going to be okay. You're going to be okay." Her sob turns into a cough as she tries to respond and a dribble of blood seeps from the corner of her mouth. A feeling of panic punches me in the gut. *She's not going to live.* Using a corner of my T-shirt, I wipe the blood away. Caileen's face fills with concern. Her eyes dart back and forth between Jace and me. "Don't worry. I'll think of something. I'll take care of him. I promise," I whisper and run the back of my hand down her cheek. I turn away from her so that I won't lose it. She can't see that I don't really know how to handle this. I walk over and place a hand on Jace's shoulder. It's the best I can think of to do for him. My touch causes deeper racked sobs as he tries to pull himself together.

"They're getting worse, Avery." Jace manages to

say, as he breathes slowly to calm himself.

I turn my attention to our mother and look for signs of rise and fall in the chest. Her breathing is slow and methodical as if every breath is calculated and full of effort. But, the rise and fall is there. Her hair is gray and thinning, gone entirely in places and her rich-green eyes are red from ruptured blood vessels. A small trickle of dried blood outlines the base of each nostril. She doesn't have much time left either. I hope today is her last. Unlike Caileen, there's no life in her eyes, but I lie and say, "Her color looks better today."

Jace looks up from his perch. I can tell he's searching my face for the lie. I hope he can't see past the failed attempt at hope in my expression.

"I can't get her to even look at me today. It's not fair. You and I aren't sick. How come they are?"

I shake my head. "I don't know, Jace."

"You think someone will come and we can get Mom and Caileen moved up on the hospital list?" He scans my face hopefully.

The hospital, the last medical visit came with half a dozen men in white Hazmat suits. Each mask they wore bore the hospital's square blue emblem with a red cross. All they left with were vital signs and blood samples. No words of hope. No possible cure in sight. In fact, no communication at all aside from, "Give me your arm. If you try to remove the bracelet, there will be extreme consequences."

I look at the complex looking metal bracelet on my arm. This newfound form of torture has a needle that jabs our wrists and takes our blood samples three times a day. We're probably being scanned for infection. Any second now, Jace and I could be next on the infection list. Supposedly, a group of hospital personnel comes and takes the very sick for close study and treatment. Apparently, Mom and Caileen, who have barely moved, let alone eaten in two days, are not sick enough.

"Maybe," I say. "How about we let them rest for awhile? We can go get them something to drink."

Jace nods and we exit the bedroom through the blue tarp and go down the steep set of steps to the cellar. We called it the cellar before the war since that's where we kept all our emergency supplies—canned goods, water, batteries, medicines, generator, etc. All the things you would need to survive a war. Well, to survive it physically.

Now that the war has officially come to Asik, we don't call it the cellar anymore. Now it's the dungeon. Caileen screamed for days in the claustrophobic space as the bombs dropped around us, the air raid sirens blaring wildly. It took three days of silence and no bombs for us to emerge from the dungeon. Even now, standing at the lead-filled metal door knowing there's life-sustaining food and water on the other side, it's hard to open and enter.

I punch in our seven-digit code and listen as the security locks disengage and the door slides open.

Emptiness illuminated by sterile fluorescent light awaits us. I hear Jace crumple to his knees next to me and realize a second after he does so that we've been robbed. Nothing remains in our cellar. What was left of our water supply is gone. Perfect rings of dust on shelves are the only indication that anything used to be on them. So dehydrated, Jace can't even conjure up more tears.

Just as I reach for the handle to haul the enormously heavy door shut and block out our horrors, there's a scuffling upstairs and a frantic hissing voice.

"Avery, hurry! They're coming! Hurry! Get out!"

Jace and I race up the stairs to see a sweaty, frantic, slim boy with disheveled, sandy-colored hair poking out at odd angles beneath the straps of a Hazmat mask. Fear lacing his aqua green eyes. It's Sheol Cultchanter. He lives five blocks down from our house. He's panicked and running through a gap in the wall, which was blasted down by shockwaves following the bombings. He doesn't even make it one hundred yards before he's down. He's flailing uncontrollably under the electric shock of Tasers. The electricity immobilizes Sheol long enough for the hospital workers in white Hazmat suits to come through the rubble and inject something into his neck. His movement stops instantly, and Sheol's aqua-green eyes turn glassy.

Military personnel step forth, dressed from head to toe in white uniforms stained with a mixture of dirt, dust, and possibly blood. One crouches next to Sheol's fallen body and examines his metal wrist bracelet.

"Soldier 97 accounted for. Get him on the truck." His stern, muffled voice comes from behind his Hazmat mask. He lets Sheol's arm fall lifelessly to the ground and steps out of the way as two military men haul Sheol's body up and heave him roughly into a nearby vehicle.

Through all of this, Jace and I are standing behind the corner of the wall Sheol ran through. Shock sets in. What are these men doing? Aren't they supposed to be providing help to the wounded? Why is Sheol running from them? Why are the hospital workers collecting people who are clearly healthy when so many people are sick and dying from infection?

Grabbing Jace's arm, I pull him behind me out of view. I watch a hospital worker pull out a CARDD and run a finger over the illumined screen. He pauses for a moment before addressing the man who ordered Sheol to be put into the truck.

"Soldiers 134 and 135 should be located just over

there," he says, gesturing to the pile of rubble that used to resemble a wall in our direction. I curse under my breath and try to think of where to run. Before I have a chance to say or do anything, Jace falls to the ground behind me with a low-muffled moan. Taser darts are sticking out of his side and two men are advancing on us quickly. Without thinking, I reach down and rip the darts from Jace's body. I grab his arms and drag him through the hole Sheol ran through. We run right into the waiting arms of four soldiers who open fire on me with their own Tasers.

One set of darts nails me square in the chest, while the other finds its home in the right side of my rib cage. I collapse to the ground. As my body twitches from the electrical tremors, I force myself to roll over so I can see Jace. He's motionless beside me. A pair of hospital workers are hovering over him, jabbing him with needles, and reading information on his metal bracelet. Jace's eyes are lifeless and unseeing even though they're wide with terror. I try to reach for him, but my muscles won't respond the way I want them to.

There's an intense pain in the side of my neck, and I feel myself slipping into unconsciousness. I struggle to stay awake against the drugs coursing through my bloodstream. As my vision blurs and separates, I see two metal gurneys with bodies covered by white sheets. A strand of my mother's gray hair falls from beneath the sheet. A loud explosion makes the earth tremble beneath my body. Dust rises as what's left of our home implodes, and then everything fades to black.

Chapter 5

I feel disconnected and nauseous as my vision slowly comes back into focus. *Not dead yet* I think, trying to lift my head. I can't move. My head is strapped down. My arms and legs are strapped down too. A large man dressed in a blue medical-looking suit hovers over me. I catch a brief glimpse of his eyes—iridescent gold irises—as he shines an impossibly bright light in my eyes. I blink violently to escape the pain and shock of the illumination.

"Pupils are equal and reactive." The doctor's voice is gentle and matter-of-fact. Beeping sounds let me know information is being recorded.

"Jace?" My voice comes from me rattled and cracked. Hoarse, as if my vocal cords haven't been used in quite some time. "Jace!" I yell this time. If I'm not dead then it seems a logical thought that he's alive too.

"Avery!" I hear Jace's voice clear and crisp. He doesn't sound like he's in pain. A brief feeling of relief washes over me and I struggle against the restraints to try to look for him. "I'm okay!" he yells. "They won't let me in until you've been processed!"

Processed? I feel a needle prick the inside of my elbow, and I go rigid as the pain and heat from whatever was injected floods my bloodstream. The pain is excruciating. Squinting down, I try to look at my arm, but all I can see are tiny black-and-white dots. My eyes don't seem to want to adjust properly.

"It hurts," I tell the man through gritted teeth.

"The pain you feel is part of reversing the cryogenic sleep. It will pass quickly," he says.

The pain doesn't pass. I want to thrash and jump,

scream and run, all at the same time. My vision becomes more disjointed. Flashes of light and color come crashing in wave after wave. Then the flashbacks come. There's my mother's voice yelling something unintelligible at me. Then there's Caileen's voice, quiet and comforting. An image of my father standing tall in the desert, dressed in his digitized military combat uniform, calmly commanding a group of young, recently recruited soldiers to execute thirty captured prisoners while I watch from the sidelines.

My muffled screams fill my ears, and then fade to a buzz. I feel another needle force its way into my arm, and the colors and noise are replaced by dizziness as the world around me fades back to black and I slip into unconsciousness once more. I don't fight the feeling this time.

The next time I wake, I simply lie still. As if I could move, anyway. The pain I felt before is gone. I listen to the sounds surrounding me. There's the annoying beep that announces my heart rate. The low droning buzz of some sort of machinery I can't identify and the quiet sounds of conversation between hospital workers.

"Check," a familiar voice says. The voice sounds both close and far away at the same time.

"No, make that checkmate," Jace says.

"You know, you could let me win one once in a while," says another familiar voice.

"If I let you win, you'll never learn how to play the game. Or actually get good at it," says Jace.

The voices seem closer to me, just off to my right side. I struggle to open my eyes and find that it takes much more effort than it really should. Slowly they crack open, and I shift them from side to side. To my right are two familiar faces. Jace, looking no worse for wear, is sitting across a squat white table playing chess with Sheol. I try to turn my head in their direction and notice with pleasure that I'm no longer strapped down. I give a little groan and let my head fall to the side. *So stiff.* I wonder how long I've been in this position.

"Avery, you're awake!" Jace is on his feet and at my side in an instant. "You had reactions to *all* the inoculations for Panacea. We weren't sure you were going to wake up before we land."

"You've missed a lot," says Sheol, reading the confused look on my face.

I clear my throat and attempt to speak. When I do find my voice it sounds raspy, not my own, as if my vocal cords have been coated with gravel.

"Panacea?"

"It's our ticket to salvation," Jace says matter-of-factly. "Panacea is the new planet. It has a military base with everything we need to survive. We're going to find a cure for what's making everyone on Earth sick. Then we can go back and fix it. Mom and Caileen will be all right."

Jace is getting more excited now as he recounts everything he's been told so far. He's searching my face for acknowledgement and support, but it only makes me think he's been brainwashed. He doesn't seem to realize that what was left of our home in Asik was blasted to bits. I watched Caileen and Mom taken away on gurneys covered with white clothes. Dead.

Should I tell him? Would it make a difference if he knew? Mom and Caileen are already gone. There's nothing on Earth left to save.

I feel a lump forming at the back of my throat, and choke it down. There's no sense in losing it in front of Jace. Trying to think about anything else, I reach up to stretch my arms. The metal wristband is still attached to my arm, and there's an array of tubing emanating from the back of my hand that's installed to machines both above and behind the hard, gray table I'm lying on.

"How long have I been asleep?" I ask.

"You have been in cryogenic sleep for two years, four months, six days, and eighteen hours," says the doctor with gold-colored eyes. "You have been in a coma in this hospital bay for an additional twenty-three days, twelve hours." His voice, coming from seemingly nowhere, makes me flinch. For someone who is easily six foot, seven inches and built like a linebacker, he should make more noise when he moves.

He approaches my bedside and asks for my wrist. Knowing it's probably best not to piss off a giant, I hand it to him willingly. He presses a button on the side of my metal wristband, and like magic, all of the liquid feeding tubes retract into coils attached to the surrounding machines. I feel a familiar stab of a needle along the underside of my metal band and realize my blood is still being sampled.

The man examines the bracelet and says, "Soldier 134, Avery Evericon. Eighteen years old. Inoculations complete. Vitals stable. Cleared for orientation."

Eighteen years old. Just yesterday, I was sixteen. That means Jace is twelve. I glance over at my brother. *He doesn't look twelve.*

While the doctor takes notes on a small holographic pad, I take the opportunity to get a good look at him and my surroundings. The man is remarkable looking, from his long, jet-black, spiral-ringlet hair, to his eyes, which are different from anything I've ever seen on Earth. His skin is the most outstanding. It's pale white, almost translucent and perfect-looking with no freckles or wrinkles from desert sun exposure. *Who is this person?*

There's a small rectangular-shaped name placard

surrounded by the familiar blue and white symbol of hospital workers pinned to his shirt.

"Lupète?" I read it out loud. It sounds crisp and of Spanish decent as it dances off my tongue, pausing only briefly at the accent over the middle "e."

He stops taking notes and meets my eyes. I look away as a jolt of his electric gaze shocks me to my core. Not painful, but powerful.

His voice is gentle and soft. *"Interesting. You are one of the first here to pronounce it correctly."*

Even though Lupète's lips don't move, I hear his voice in my head.

Did that really just happen? Did he speak to me…in my mind? I shake my head, thinking I must be completely insane.

"Are you feeling okay?" the man asks out loud. He seems calm and collected, like nothing just happened.

I imagined it then, him talking in my mind. I put a hand to my head at the throbbing pressure that is suddenly present.

"Yeah…guess I'm just having a hard time waking up," I say cautiously.

"I suspect you will feel better in a few days. It takes time to adjust from cryogenic sleep." He narrows his eyes as if he's thinking hard about something. Then he turns his attention back to his holographic screen. "The next orientation is scheduled in two hours. You will go," he says, walking away.

I watch his back for a long minute and then look at Sheol and Jace. Sheol is standing over the chessboard, examining it with a perplexed look on his face. I know he won't find his mistake unless Jace points it out. He's too good at games of logic and strategy.

Jace, ignoring Sheol, is bouncing up and down on

his toes in front of a small oval window that's about three inches too tall for him to see out. I groan and shift my feet over the side of the bed. Every muscle is stiff and weak, leaving me feeling like I've been mugged or trampled.

I stand up to walk over to Jace but immediately sit back down. My vision blurs with nauseating flashes of light that form fragmented images. A television screen in my kitchen is showing crops bursting into flames, and Egypt announcing war on Sudan to control the Nile River. There are street riots, hordes of army soldiers in training and space cadets marching, a mission letter with Jeremy's name. *Jeremy.* The very thought of him brings flashes of his murder, the gun going off, his gurgling last breaths. "No more," I growl and press the palms of my hands to the sides of my head.

"It's better not to fight it," Sheol mumbles.

"What?" I say, squinting at him.

He shrugs. "The memories. Your brain's been suspended for over two years. It has to re-adjust. You'll remember all the crappy things first."

"Why?"

"Bad stuff sticks with a person longer, I guess."

"It figures. There's not much good stuff to remember anyway," I grumble.

Sheol nods and goes back to examining the chessboard while I keep trying to force the memories not to come. I struggle to my feet and plod over to the window Jace is looking out. Being a solid foot taller than him, I have no problem seeing outside. There isn't must to look at, just a never-ending sea of blackness. Though know we must be on some sort of rocket or ship and moving at an incredible speed, I notice no movement. I stare into the pitch-blackness of space in complete disbelief that I'm here. I did everything

Jeremy said not to do and I'm still here on this ship headed for God knows what. After Jeremy died, I assumed my fate would be at the end of a gun. That I would never leave the desert…except maybe in a body bag.

I try not to think about death because it automatically makes me think of Jeremy again. I try not to think at all, just void my head and stare into space. When that doesn't work I look down at Jace. He's bouncing up and down on his tiptoes with a goofy grin on his face. There's so much that he doesn't know. Life was so difficult. Caileen, Mom, Jeremy, and I, we all tried to spare Jace as much as possible. Being born in the midst of a brewing war, growing up on a military base, being forced to do whatever the government says, never knowing if you're going to ever see members of your family again when they leave on missions…it isn't easy.

Now Jace is twelve seemingly overnight. He's just four short years away from basic training. I heave a deep breath and look outside again. Maybe it'll be different where we're going. But I know nothing about this Panacea place. I should've listened to Jeremy and never gone back to working security after his death. I should've been studying with the space academy, learning everything there is to know about Panacea. Instead, I spent my time opening and closing the military gates for approved personnel and using Jeremy's intelligence access codes to see if I could find out anything about Dad's disappearance. Unfortunately, there was no record of a trial, a jail sentence or even an execution. All I found before the people running the intelligence databases got wise to me logging on with my brother's access codes was a small amount of information about Jeremy's missions. He and Dad were running some sort of trade operation, exchanging experimental devices for water from other countries. It's how Asik was able to survive after the great lakes bordering our military base dried up. Without those weekly shipments of water, I don't know what would've happened.

Thinking about the water delivery trucks makes me cringe. A vivid memory of outsiders rioting and being run over or shot while trying to intercept the water trucks splashes in front of my eyes. The outsiders, Uncle Jim, Aunt Sara, they didn't stand a chance against the advanced weaponry of soldiers working on base. And then there were the orphans arriving at our gates.

I look away from the ship's window and take a deep breath, willing the memory not to come. *Let it happen. Sheol said to let them come.* There's a metal railing running the length of the wall in front of me that's waist height. I gratefully grip it and brace myself as the orphans' whimpering cries make my ears ring.

The orphans came about six weeks after my brother's murder. Mom was still inconsolable. She stopped crying, but resigned herself to sitting on the floor in front of an open window that she refused to let anyone close. The heat would pour into the house and she would just sit there and sweat, refusing to drink, a tattered family photo clutched in her hand. The photo was taken years ago when Jace was still an infant. It was one of all of us together, smiling.

She would sit, mutter, and worry at the photo with her fingers until the faces were all but worn away. If anyone tried to talk to her, she would get a wild look on her face and start muttering, yelling, or screaming verses from the Bible. Her verse of choice was Luke 16:24.

"Father Abraham, have mercy on me, and send Lazarus to dip the end of his finger in water and cool my tongue, for I am in anguish in this flame!"

Caileen was beside herself trying to help Mom, and we often resorted to calling the military infirmary on base to have someone come to the house and sedate Mom.

I don't know what was worse for her—losing a son in such a brutal way, knowing that the man she loved was the killer, or worse yet, that my father escaped without justice.

While my mother became a mere shell of herself, Caileen took charge of the household. She did her best to care for us and try to make sure Jace never knew the whole truth behind Mom's hysteria.

I wasn't much help. I was walking through life like a ghost, dead inside, just going through the motions. I still believed that at any moment Jeremy would show up on base from some far-off mission saving the world. Here, home, happy, and with us. But it never happened like that. To get through the days meant eat, sleep, drink, work, and hope to survive to see better days.

I and four other men around my age were manning the front gates of the military facility. Our job was a very simple one—only allow government-approved vehicles in and out of the base.

The day the orphans came, we were waiting for a water delivery. A member from each household in Asik was gathered on the inside of the gate, waiting anxiously for their rations. With the riots shown on television each night, the atmosphere in Asik was tense. People formed an unwavering line behind the designated soldiers. Each soldier was armed just in case a fight broke out. Water always came every week. But that day was different. The truck was late. In its place came the outsiders.

Nothing in our training prepared us for the

families of outsiders who brought their children that day. Dozens of desperate parents appeared through the hot, dusty, desert haze that surrounded the base. Many of them came carrying the lifeless bodies of their children who were too dehydrated to walk. Without a word, they carefully laid the bodies of their children at the foot of our gate and backed away, vanishing in the haze as quickly and as quietly as they arrived. The frantic, mournful sobs of toddlers still haunt me.

No one knew what to do. There was total disbelief at the final, silent protest from a hopeless people.

Without thinking, one of the young men on duty with me threw his rifle to the ground and opened the gate. He walked out to the children and scooped up the child closest to the gate. She was a young girl, no older than three years old. The life was gone from her and she hung limp in his muscular arms. He took his water canteen from around his neck and dribbled a few precious drops into her mouth. It was futile. She was already dead. Consumed with grief, the man rocked back onto his heels in the dirt, cradling her lifeless body to his chest. He gently laid her in the sand and motioned for the rest of the children to enter the gates. He scooped up another child who was still alive, but unable to walk.

The rest of us started to put down our rifles to help gather the children when a booming voice spoke over our town loudspeaker. Each subdivision in Asik had a tower with a loudspeaker to warn us of desert dust storms and potential bombers.

"Put down the child!" the voice said. I can still see the disbelief in the soldier's eyes as he defiantly carried the child toward our gates. He was promptly shot in the head. The child, covered in the soldier's blood, tumbled to the ground.

"No one else is to enter!" the voice said. The gate

controls were mechanically shut, leaving dozens of orphaned children and one dead soldier on the outside.

A rebellious murmur erupted from the crowd waiting for their water. A riot broke out as people rushed the gates. The crowd got out of control just as the air raid sirens began to blare around us. The sirens were the only thing that quieted the angry mob. We had been drilled never to ignore the sirens that indicated bombs. When whole countries fight to survive, you never know when you're going to become a target. Only a third of the population respected the sirens that day. Others perished for the children, as explosions shook the ground around us.

As the memory of the orphans fades, flashes burst in my eyes of feet running, me tripping over my crutches, screaming, and grabbing Jace's arm and hauling him to the cellar. I grip the railing a little tighter as if I'm gripping his hand. My brother's high-pitched voice somehow pierces through the onslaught of unwanted memories.

"I *said*, do you want me to come to the orientation with you?" I barely hear Jace beside me. I'm too lost in my sadness over the death of those helpless children. Distraught by the destruction of home and the longing I have to see Mom and Caileen again, alive.

Jace grabs my arm, and I automatically go rigid. Looking down at him, his face is so young and filled with hope and excitement. Selfishly I want to tell him all that I know. He knows nothing about Dad killing Jeremy. He doesn't know that I watched the whole ordeal and didn't do a damn thing to stop it. A part of me wants to crush him so I can have someone to share my pain. But as I look at him, I can't bring myself to do it. He doesn't need to know. Things will be different where we're going. They have to be. Maybe Jeremy was right and this place is our best option. Even if we never see Earth again, at least Jace will get to live what's left of his childhood with normalcy and peace.

"Why are you looking at me like that?" Jace asks.

I shake my head and clear my expression. "I—"

"Orientation. You need to go to an orientation. We're going to land in a week, and you've been asleep through a month of orientation. You missed weapon training, agriculture, history of the planet and…" He trails off, trying to remember all the information he was supposed to cram into his little brain over the last few weeks. "You've missed a lot of stuff!"

Sheol steps forward. "Jace, why don't you meet us in the mess hall? I'll wait with Avery while he gets dressed."

"Okay. See you there. I'm meeting someone in a few minutes anyway," he says enthusiastically and sprints out of the room.

"Who's he meeting?" I ask.

"Got me. He's not afraid to make friends, though. He talks to just about everybody whether they want to talk to him or not. Come on, get dressed, I'll show you around. Not that there's much to see," he adds under his breath. "I have combat training in an hour."

I look at Sheol. He's not the slim, nerdy boy that I knew on Earth. He's gained weight and looks strong and muscular. Though his body type and build are different from Lupète, I can't help but notice a similarity in the muscular structure. I look down at my hands and arms. My body looks about the way it feels—weak and thin. The skin falls loose over my bones with little muscle. Even Jace looked fit and well.

Sheol notices me taking in my own state of affairs and echoes what Jace said, "You've missed a lot, man. You've got some catching up to do."

"And apparently I've only got a few days to do it in?" I ask.

Sheol shrugs. "I'm guessing you can make up some of the training when you get to the planet. Next time, don't be allergic to everything."

We leave the small, white sterile hospital room. Besides me, only one other person with wicked-looking purple hives remains.

"What happened to him?" I gesture over my shoulder as we head for a small, white portal I assume is a door.

"Dumbass tried to eat the purpural," Sheol states with disgust.

"Not an edible plant?"

"Yeah…pay close attention in Planetary Agricultural training," Sheol says.

As the automatic sensors in the door trigger with our presence and slide open, I look over my shoulder to Lupète one last time. His golden eyes are following me with a look of utter curiosity. The same electricity as before forces me to lower my gaze. Turning away, I follow Sheol out the door.

Andrea Perno

Chapter 6

As the doors click shut behind us, I realize how grateful I am that Sheol and Jace are here with me.

I pause in front of the door. "Thanks. I mean, thanks for...you know, taking care of Jace. I couldn't...I would ha—"

"Don't worry about it." Sheol shrugs. "You guys are the closest thing to family I have left," he says with a lopsided grin.

On Earth, Sheol and I were merely acquaintances. The same age, but we ran in completely different circles. Aside from an occasional class together, and the fact that we lived on the same military installation, we could've been strangers. Family doesn't seem like the right comparison. Nevertheless, I'm thankful for his company. I know how hard friends are to come by.

"You know," Sheol continues, "you, me, and Jace are the only people who got picked up from Asik."

"How many people were left behind?" I ask.

"No one else survived...no men, at least. They said in orientation that several quarantine centers were set up to try and save some of the infected, but most died in the bombings."

My mind swirls as I try to reconstruct our hometown and the day our military base was attacked. The awful wailing sound of children left behind fills my ears. There's the gunshot killing the young soldier. Then I remember the air raid sirens. I was running with Mom away from the gates to gather Caileen and Jace. We got down to the cellar and went into hiding for days as the earth shook in chaos. There should've been more warning before the bombs fell. As one of the few places left on Earth to receive water deliveries, it was only a matter of time before we were attacked by another country. But our state-of-the-art weapons detections systems should have alerted us long before the sirens did. It was as if the detections systems had no idea that bombs were being deployed.

We emerged from the cellar to find our home and town leveled except for random buildings standing eerily intact, untouched by the bombs and shock waves. Mom and Caileen fell ill within days of leaving the cellar. I don't remember seeing any other people from our town until the hospital personnel showed up. Jace and I were so preoccupied with taking care of Mom and Caileen that if there were other people wandering the rubble, we didn't notice them. Is it possible that not one other person survived the chaos in Asik?

"Here we are. The closest thing to home we have on this ship," Sheol says, interrupting my thoughts.

We're standing under a hand-carved wooden sign that reads, *Barty's Tavern.*

The doors slide apart, and I'm hit with the most amazing smells imaginable. My mouth waters.

I take in the dimly lit room. A large S-shaped bar flows gracefully around the oval room. Simple triangular lights hang down from thick wooden beams in the ceiling, emitting a soft yellow glow. There was a place like this on base, but it wasn't as warm and inviting. It had an enormous stockpile of the most awful-tasting beverages. Dad took me there once before I started basic training. He made me drink a bottle full of the foul amber liquid. When I couldn't finish it, he got angry, dragged me to the door and shoved me out into the street. I threw up for hours after that. I never went back into the building.

Sheol slaps my shoulder. "Come on, let's get a drink. You have to be thirsty," Sheol says.

At the mention of a drink, I suddenly notice how dry my mouth feels. I'm immediately desperate for water. "I don't have money," I say as we ease our way between round wooden tables toward the bar.

"Don't need money here. Think of it like an all-inclusive vacation, except we didn't have a choice in destination."

We take seats at the bar, and Sheol orders us two glasses of water. *Water is life*. I think the slogan in my head.

The water appears as if from out of thin air. It's crisp and clean-looking, not murky and full of particulates like home. I pound it back in three massive gulps. Sheol chuckles and slides me his glass.

"You sure?" I look at him suspiciously.

"They'll bring us more." He holds his hand up for the bartender.

I look at Sheol's glass in my hand. *Don't be greedy. We have to make it last.* Mom's words echo in my mind. Water comes so easily here and I'm so thirsty that I push her words out of my head and drink.

After my fourth glass, the bartender brings a pitcher. I drink half of that too before I can focus on anything else.

"What're they eating?" I point to a table close to us. A group of men are dipping spoons into a soft, white substance that is quickly turning to liquid.

"They call it ice cream." Sheol shakes his head and scrunches up his nose. "I don't like it. It's too cold."

I nod, acknowledging his words while I watch them eat. I always pictured space food as crappy, frozen, shrink-wrapped meals. Or perhaps food fed from tubes. Or maybe even like the food we had in Asik.

Since I was five years old, we had nothing but

canned and processed foods meant to be stored, saved, and consumed in times of emergency and war. The government gave each home in our community a three-month stockpile. Every month they would send more. Mother used to share our cellar contents around town with families that had more children. Our father hated it, but the government never accounted for families with large numbers. Each household was given the same rations.

Here I see waiters pass by with heaping trays of fresh meat and whole vegetables. Not like the kind that comes in cans. Not chopped, blended, pureed, or mashed.

Sheol must notice the drool practically running down my chin. He picks something called a wood-smoked bacon burger, and orders four of them.

"What's a burger?"

Sheol smiles. "Trust me, you'll love it."

I almost cry when a server puts them in front of us moments later. The aroma is powerfully delicious.

He laughs. "They have food down to a fine science here. You won't go hungry." With food and water resources plummeting on Earth, I wonder what it took to make this kind of meal possible.

I happily grab a burger that is quite possibly bigger than my head and greedily dig in. The food is perfect. Juicy. Cooked just right. At least I think it's cooked just right. I can't remember the last time I had meat that wasn't ground up and packaged into tiny cans meant to satisfy a day's hunger.

I don't slow down my eating pace to question the food's source further. I've finished the second burger as Sheol passes me a third.

"You might want to ease into it a little bit after you finish that one," Sheol tells me. "The steroids and growth hormones they add to the food to bulk us up will bind you tighter than a python's death grip."

"That explains why everyone here looks like body builders," I say.

Sheol rolls his eyes. "You haven't even had combat training yet. You won't look like a concentration camp victim for long, the way we get worked."

We both go back to eating, but I feel suddenly nauseous. Combat training is still a thing on this new planet. In fact, while I spend a few minutes people watching and eavesdropping, most of the conversations are about combat training. Men show-off bruised eyes proudly. *Just like home.* Others are talking about people they haven't seen on the ship and some are speculating what the new planet will be like.

I'm about to ask Sheol what goes on in combat training when I spot a smug-looking Jace sitting at a gaming table near the corner of the room. He has a crooked up-to-no-good grin on his face, and his arms folded across his chest as he leans slightly back in his chair. A small crowd encircles the table. Nudging Sheol's arm, I gesture in Jace's direction. Sheol's joking attitude snaps to concern.

"I told him to leave Clesandra out of his games," he mutters, getting up from the bar. Trying to act casual, he heads in the direction of Jace's table. I follow.

We approach the table but maintain a safe distance. I sense Sheol has become very protective of my little brother. Jace has that impact on most people when he's not annoying them with questions, or trapping them into playing one of his games.

A smile tugs the corner of my mouth when we get closer to Jace's table. I recognize the game. Jace used to call the game a "quest." The victim, in this case, a disgruntled-looking girl, would have something of value taken by Jace. To get the object back, the victim would have to play for it. One time, Jace took all of my clothes and hid them in the desert behind our home. I had no choice but to play.

At home, the quest could extend for hours with multiple levels of clues, riddles, and physical challenges. I smile, thinking about how creative Jace is. A mastermind of engineering, he probably would've been an architect on Earth.

The three-foot tower is built from wooden rectangles. Playing cards are haphazardly placed between the slats of the makeshift wooden beams, which are balanced in perfect harmony on top of three tin centerpieces. The magnificent tower looks like it took a solid hour to engineer.

The game looks straightforward. Remove the cards without toppling the tower. The girl has managed to secure but one of several cards in the tower. It's impossible not to grin at her misfortune while I wonder what Jace took to get her to play.

Her face reddens with anger as she nearly burns herself on the lit candles in the tins trying to remove one of the cards. Then it occurs to me that this girl is not accustomed to Jace's clever games meant only in fun. For safety sake, I size her up.

She's tall, just under six feet, nearly eye level with me. I won't be much of a match for her in my current condition. Her piercing green eyes compliment olive-colored skin. Her long, black hair is French-braided down to her mid-back. Her body is muscular and fit. She's athletic. She's the most gorgeous woman I've ever seen.

While I'm still gawking and pondering an appropriate plan of action, Sheol casually glides up to Jace.

"Aren't you late for agriculture class?" Sheol asks.

Jace frowns.

"There's not going to be an agriculture class to go to if I don't get my knife back," the girl grumbles and makes an attempt to remove a card from the tower.

"You took her knife!" I burst out. Everyone knows you don't mess with weaponry. Not that I can imagine that this girl would be allowed on the ship with a weapon in the first place.

"Beat it, Sleeping Beauty," she spits back in my direction. "You ain't a part of this."

"Give her back the knife," Sheol growls.

Jace grins mischievously. "Relax. She'll get it back when she completes the quest."

The girl rips her hand away from the tower again, shaking it furiously and cursing under her breath. The tempting card she was going for is propped loosely in the center of the tower. It's just far enough above the candle flames so it won't burn.

"I told you! Not with your hands!" Jace's voice has an annoying high pitch. "You can only use the tools on the table. Follow the rules!"

"My hands are the only tools I need," she says and makes another stubborn attempt at the card. Again, she burns her fingers and yelps in pain. The crowd grows larger, gawking at her. She pauses to look around, then glares at Jace. Hatred and anger flush her cheeks. Again, she makes another failed attempt at the card.

Her face purples with rage. "This is impossible!" She raises a hand to smash the tower.

"Wait!" I yell before it's too late.

She pauses in mid-swing. Her lips curl back in a growl. "Move."

"If you wreck it, you'll have to start all over. You don't think he'll give your knife back just because you knock it down, do you?"

A small shred of understanding and reason crosses

her face for a fraction of a second before her expression turns cold and heartless. When she speaks again, it's at a volume only I can hear. "If he won't give it back, I ain't stopping with the tower."

"He'll give it back. You just have to play it his way." I extend a hand to her. "I'm Avery, by the way."

She doesn't take my hand. Instead, she looks at me like I'm crazy, her eyebrows furrowing, and her forehead wrinkled.

"Clesandra," she grumbles, still refusing to shake my hand.

The crowd around us is silent as we size each other up.

I let my hand fall to my side. "Are you at least going to let me help you?"

"Avery, you—" Jace starts.

I shoot him an annoyed look that makes him pout and fold his arms across his chest. He mumbles something under his breath, but I ignore it.

"Clesandra?"

She'd probably rather kill me, but eventually she says, "What ya got in mind?"

I relax slightly, realizing I'm not going to get pummeled to death...at least for the moment. I shoot Jace an, *I'm going to kill you later*, look. Then turn my attention to the tower and the table. Not much is provided. A drinking glass half filled with ice water, two straws, a used paper napkin, and a set of silverware. The tower itself has four remaining cards inside. The one that Clesandra was going for is the most tempting. It looks as if you could get two fingers inside and pluck it right out. That isn't the case, though, because it's balanced carefully above the candle flames. The other three cards are built into the tower rather than just tucked in as an afterthought.

I decide to attempt the card Clesandra was aiming

for. I use a spoon and carefully fill it with water from the glass. Expertly sliding the spoon past the wooden blocks, I extinguish the flames. The crowd murmurs in acknowledgement of this approach. Clesandra makes a move to reach in and retrieve the card, but I knock her arm away.

"No hands." I carefully echo my brother. Clesandra's face contorts and goes red with rage at not only being outsmarted but knocked aside. Her hands ball into tight, white knuckled fists. I pause, waiting for her to lunge at me. When she doesn't, I return my attention to the tower.

I snatch one of the straws and rip up a small piece of paper napkin. Wadding the napkin up in my mouth, I make it into a tight ball and load it into the tip of the straw. I carefully line the straw up with the center of the playing card and force all the breath from my lungs. The sticky, wet bullet shoots out from the end of the straw and hits the target dead center. The card is blasted straight out of the tower without hitting a single wooden block on the way out.

The crowd erupts with applause and laughter. Resisting the urge to gloat and repeat that it *can be done* without hands, I turn my focus to the other cards. They will not be as easy to remove. There's no way to shoot them out without hitting blocks and potentially collapsing the tower. I slowly circle around the tower like a vulture circles prey, looking at all angles. I see no way of removing them without removing some of the wooden blocks first. It would be almost impossible to remove blocks without destroying the balance of the tower, so I decide to have a look from above. I inch a chair close to the table, careful not to bump the wood.

Standing on the chair and gazing straight down I see the answer. The cards were not built into the tower, they were carefully dropped in from above. They balance precariously on the edges of the wooden blocks. If I can lower something down to nudge the cards off their blocks, there's a chance they'll fall straight down through the tower and land on the tabletop, easy enough to slide out with a fork or knife. I raise my eyebrows at Jace.

"I would've made it harder if I knew you were playing." Jace scowls.

I stand precariously on the chair, leaning over the tower. "Hand me the glass of water," I command.

Clesandra hands me the glass. I carefully drip water over the tower onto the cards. The first card pops free and glides to the tabletop below. I gloatingly smile in Jace and Sheol's direction. Just then, the unthinkable happens. The remaining ice in the glass shifts and tumbles down on top of the tower. I catch some of it as it falls, but I'm unable to prevent a few pieces from crashing down on the blocks. I watch in horror as small cubes tumble through the tower, releasing invisible shockwaves that act as mini-earthquakes through the wooden blocks. The tower shudders. A support beam above one of the tin centerpieces buckles, about to collapse the tower. My breath catches in my throat. A flash of metal comes from the corner of my eye, and the tower slowly sways to a stop without toppling.

I pull the cup away from the top of the tower. Clesandra has wedged a butter knife against the support beam. We regard each other in stunned silence. She nods at me to continue pouring the water. My hand shakes as if I'm diffusing a bomb. This time I hold one hand over the top of the glass so no ice can pass. I allow only a small trickle of water to pour onto the tower. The cards pop out and fall to the table below the tower. The crowd erupts with cheers as I slide them out from below with a fork.

"Game over, Jace," I say.

Jace pulls a small silver tube from his back pocket and holds it out to Clesandra.

She pulls the butter knife from the tower and drops it to the floor. The tower collapses, spilling blocks haphazardly and she grabs the tube from Jace's hand. In an instant, she has him choked in a headlock. People around us gasp. Sheol and I take an offensive stance, ready to rush her. The tube in Clesandra's hand has magically burst open to reveal a six-inch shiny metal blade that glows florescent blue around the edges. She holds it close to Jace's face just above his cheek.

"Take something of mine again," she gestures in my direction with the tip of her knife, "and Sleeping Beauty will be collecting your body parts from around the ship."

"Let him go!" a booming voice from across the room commands. A tall, muscular man with dark skin stands in the entrance of the tavern, looking strong and powerful.

"The commander," someone whispers in awe.

A few curt whispers from other people die down and the room falls silent. The commander takes a few calm steps forward. Those closest to him fall back.

Clesandra's teeth curl back in anger as she shoves a choking and sputtering Jace roughly in my arms.

"Report to the command room now," the man orders.

Clesandra spins on her heel, and with her head held high, strides defiantly out the door.

"You, too, Soldier 134," he says.

I don't try to hide the confusion on my face. I look around the room, hoping that someone else has the same number. Finding no one, I look down at Jace's face no longer purpled with strangulation.

"You okay?" I ask him. He nods and sniffs. A trickle of tears is forming at the corner of his eyes. "Try to stay out of trouble, Jace." I look away, worried if I say anything else a flood might ensue. I pass him to Sheol, who pulls him in and protectively wraps one arm around his shoulders. Sheol raises an eyebrow at me. I give him an equally confused look as I follow behind Clesandra.

Chapter 7

The commander stands at the center of the room, facing us. He's a tall, proud-looking man, probably in his late twenties to mid-thirties. He's got dark skin and short, military-cropped hair. A well-trimmed goatee makes him look rugged, yet sophisticated. His face bears no scars or imperfections that would suggest a commander with real-world experience.

"This is not how I planned for the two of you to meet." The man regards us coldly. I look at Clesandra, whose face is flushed. Her stare is intense and her hands are still balled into fists. By the look in her eyes, I wonder if she might decide to have a go at the commander.

"Planned?" I ask cautiously.

"Yes, I planned for you to meet Ms. Willows tomorrow. She's to get you caught up with agriculture training and see to it that you understand how the agriculture simulation room works. That plan has been…altered," he says with a smile. He motions for us to join him at the holographic table at the center of the room. I'm careful to keep a few arm lengths from Clesandra in case she decides to snap my neck.

The commander presses a button on the side of the table, and an image appears. My brother is happily building the tower that stood in the tavern moments ago. Jace has an impish grin on his face, as his fingers move effortlessly in construction.

"Your brother is a most clever individual for his age," the man remarks. "I was quite amused by the whole scheme he concocted with the knife. You should be more careful with your weapons, Willows," he scolds Clesandra. The color in her face grows a deeper shade of red. Her hands almost shake from controlling her anger.

"I'm sorry Jace took your weapon," I interject. Clesandra's nostrils flare and she nods in my direction.

"My fault," she grunts through gritted teeth. "Shouldn't have left it—"

"Regardless," the commander continues, "what I find interesting is not in the way the game was constructed, or your brother's ill-advised amusement at others' expense, but rather in the way the game was played. Particularly this part…" The images flicker in fast forward. He stops just at the point where I shoot the card Clesandra was bent on retrieving.

The commander folds his hands behind his back and smiles. "You're a good shot, just as good as Willows is with her knife. It makes me rethink my previous assumption that you would be best for an agriculture placement."

I shoot Clesandra a confused look, but she's focused on the commander. I imagine her rushing him and skillfully slitting his throat from ear to ear before anyone could stop her. I realize this might be a real possibility and slide a half step farther away from her.

The man's smile grows wider. "Follow me." He leads us out of the command room and down a long, narrow hallway of the ship. We stop at a room marked, "Simulation."

"I'd like to see how good your really are. How about we add a little pressure?" He gestures for us to walk toward the heavy metal door in front of us. "Now is as good a time as any to introduce you to this room. Willows can walk you through it."

Clesandra dips her head in compliance but her eyes never leave the commander.

The doors of the simulation room slide apart, and we step into a vast space that echoes with the sound of our footsteps. The walls, ceiling, and the floor are paneled like the command room. Yet, this room is empty. It's like walking into a vacant warehouse.

"This room," he continues, "is where the important training goes on. We have two rooms like this. One room is for agricultural training, and one for combat training and simulations that you will likely encounter on Panacea. It's often in this room that soldiers prove their true worth for our journey. Ms. Willows here," he indicates her with a tip of his head, "has quite the knack for knife throwing." A smile spreads across his lips and my stomach drops. I get the feeling that I might be here as target practice.

"I'd like to see what the son of one of the most prestigious generals on Earth is capable of. Panacea is field training level three!" the commander barks as he quickly backs through the door we came through.

"Level three? But we can't…that will…!" Clesandra is yelling but with no avail. The commander vanishes through the door as the dull, empty warehouse of a room transforms into a forest, alive with the sounds of unidentifiable insects and birds. Shafts of light filter through the canopy of trees, illuminating the soft leaf litter beneath our feet. I'm amazed at the sounds of rustling leaves as I shuffle my feet forward in the new environment. Panacea must be stunning if this simulation is accurate. The forest appears similar to pictures I've seen of trees in books and in geography class growing up. Never having the opportunity to leave the red desert sands of Asik, I can only imagine that this is exactly what a forest might have been like on Earth. The plants along the forest floor glisten with dewdrops, sparkling and dancing in the rays of light that reach them. There is an iridescent quality to the leaves and the small flowers that grow around us.

Mesmerized, I reach a hand out to touch a patch of turquoise blue moss growing on the side of a tree. My hand is immediately knocked away by something hard.

"Don't touch the blue!" Clesandra hisses.

I grasp my hand to my chest, yelping like a wounded puppy, as pain courses up my arm. Clesandra crouches with her back to me, hands outspread, knife at the ready in her right hand. A soft rustling in the underbrush to my left catches my attention. A deep, guttural growl, low and rumbling like an earthquake, interrupts the sounds of birds and insects. I feel the sound more than hear it. The hair on the back of my neck stands up as I strain to see what's lurking in the shadows beyond the trees.

Clesandra slowly angles her body to the left, just in front of me, as a pair of amber eyes peer through the shadows. My heart races and panic begins to take over. This is a simulation room, and nothing here should be able to hurt us, yet I get the feeling from the way Clesandra is poised for action that this is no ordinary simulation. The air around us goes quiet. No more sounds of happy birds chattering in the treetops. Not even the sounds of insects humming in the distance break the silence. The growling stops. It's as if everything, including myself, is holding its breath. Just as I think the beast is about to launch from where it is lurking and attack us, the glint of amber disappears from view.

Clesandra whispers something to me without moving from her spot.

"What?" I whisper back.

"—ee," she whispers again.

"Huh?"

"Goddammit! Get. Up. A. Tree," Clesandra whispers loudly, placing emphasis on each word.

I fumble around our little clearing in the woods,

looking for a tree that I can climb. There are hundreds of trees around, but not one of them will suit my needs since I've never climbed a tree in my life. About the only climbing I've ever done is on the rappel tower with cable lines attached to me. It didn't go well.

"This may be a bad time for a family history lesson, but I grew up in the desert! I don't know how to climb a tree!" I whisper back.

"Now's a good time to learn!" Clesandra screams. A gigantic creature, the size of a bear, launches itself out of the shadows and lands a few feet in front of me. I've never seen an animal like this before. It reminds me of a wolf on steroids. The creature is muscular like a Mack truck, yet light on its paws that are easily the size of my head. The animal rocks back on its haunches, three-inch long yellow teeth are bared in a vicious snarl. It's about to spring for my head when I catch a glint of blue and silver from the corner of my eye. Clesandra's knife finds a home in the left eye of the beast. It reels back in agony and falls to the ground dead. The stench of rotting flesh from the animal's teeth hits me, as it huffs its last breath into my face. Clesandra's knife magically flies from the creature's eye and returns to her outstretched hand.

She crouches low, scanning the shadows and gestures to a tree with low-hanging branches that should be easy to climb. I make a mad dash for the tree. Struggling my way up the thin branches, I hear the underbrush crash below me as two more beasts plow their way through to get Clesandra. I watch from above in horror, sure that Clesandra is going to meet certain death. As if by magic, her knife morphs from a six-inch blade into two identical three-inch daggers. The golden, thick-haired beasts, snarling and rabid with hunger, don't even make it two feet into the clearing before they're both on the ground dead. One has a dagger between the eyes, the other in the chest. The knives rip out of the beasts' flesh and return to Clesandra's hands, glistening red with blood. The forest is now alive with snarling and the sounds of saplings being smashed and crushed as another wave of beasts break into the clearing. A look of sheer terror has spread across Clesandra's face. She makes a mad dash for a tree close to mine. Despite her size and bulky muscular build, she's very agile, and she's up the tree in seconds and much higher than me.

Just in time, too. Four more enormous beasts enter the clearing, huffing and snarling. They bite at each other's necks and growl. Two of them tear around the clearing with their wolf-like snouts to the ground, picking up the scent of us.

"Climb!" Clesandra screams at me.

I struggle to go farther up the thin branches. As I climb, they continue to snap under my weight like hollow pixie sticks. "I can't! The branches keep breaking!" Looking down, I've got worse problems than the paralyzing vertigo I'm experiencing. The beasts have honed in on me being the weakest target. One of them bounds to the bottom of the tree I'm in and leaps straight into the air. It clings to the bark and begins to slowly maneuver its way up. The claws of the animal rake into the tree bark as it tries to maintain its hold. It gingerly climbs out onto a branch just below mine, snarling and spitting. Its amber eyes trained on my every move, and then, snap! The branch breaks, and the wolf-like creature tumbles to the ground with a sickening thud. It gets back up, snarling and shaking its shaggy head from side to side. Now two more creatures are at the bottom of the tree, biting at each other as they aggressively begin to climb the trunk.

"Here!" Clesandra's yells and I feel the wind from her knife as it narrowly misses the side of my head and buries itself in the soft wood of the tree trunk. I rip the knife, now slippery with animal blood, out of the tree. The weapon is light as a feather and hums gently as it vibrates in my hand.

I don't bother to tell her that I can't throw knives like she can. The beasts are inching closer up my tree. They're climbing slower now, being more careful not to break the branches.

I grip the knife between my teeth and make one last effort to climb higher into the thinning branches. The branch I'm holding snaps like a toothpick as I try to leverage my body upward. I'm left balancing on a thicker branch below, and the knife is hot in my mouth and slices into the corners of my lips. The next branch I reach for snaps in my hand. I'm about to throw the branch down at one of the beasts when I notice that the branch is completely hollow. I break a thicker branch, smiling to myself as I realize it's also hollow. The snarling below me gets louder and closer. I wedge myself against a thick branch and the trunk of the tree and slice a smaller hollow branch in half with the knife. It takes me seconds to whittle the end of the split branch into a point and feed it into the hollow tube of the other branch.

"What are you doing?" Clesandra yells.

Ignoring her screams, I plunge the knife into the tree trunk and take aim on the creature that's just inches from slashing me with its three-inch claws. I aim for the center of its eye, take a deep breath to stop the shaking in my hands, and force air through the hollow branch with as much strength as I can muster.

The dart sails out the end of the tube and finds its mark just where I intended. The beast howls in pain as it crashes down through the branches and lands on the ground. It paws furiously at its face, trying in vain to dislodge the dart, before running into the woods howling. I look below and see that three more of the beasts lie dead or dying on the ground beneath Clesandra's tree.

The remaining animals retreat into the shadows just as quickly as they arrived.

"Marvelous! Just marvelous!" a familiar voice announces as the world around us evaporates and I feel myself being slowly lowered to the ground. The commander approaches us in the empty warehouse environment. Nervously, I look around the room, certain that more beasts will materialize from the gray walls. Clesandra is heaving from exertion or possibly anger. Her face is red, and her hands grip both daggers in a defensive stance.

"Level three is fatal," she fumes.

"I knew *you* could handle it," he says to Clesandra, but he's looking at me. "I needed to see him in action." He smiles wickedly. "General Daniel Evericon once told me that his sons could handle themselves well under pressure. It's a shame he couldn't handle himself. He did also point out that he wasn't sure you'd have the drive, if you know what I mean. I don't know, though. After what I just saw, you may be more useful than I thought."

Rage whips through me at the insult to my father and the insinuation that I'm merely a tool for this man's use, but I say nothing.

He ignores my expression. "I was sure you would be best suited for agriculture. It would make sense to have you follow the path your grandfather and father established. Then again, your father left agriculture and found his calling in weapons. You may be more like him. If he could have seen you just now, inventing your own weapon, and using it…I think he would have been proud."

My stomach turns. Killing is not something I want

to be praised for.

"Yes, we can use a man like you." He ponders, not even looking at me now.

"Willows, you will get Evericon up-to-speed with agriculture and add him to the combat roster. We land in a week and I expect him to be ready. Evericon, you will meet me in the command room for a mandatory orientation in one hour. The commander spins on his heels and strides through the simulation room doors, leaving Clesandra and me behind in the vast, empty space.

Clesandra's face is the color of red-hot coals. Her hands and arms are shaking. The two daggers are so tightly clutched in each hand that I imagine the hilts have permanent handprints. When I least expect it, she lets loose the most aggressive scream I've ever heard and heaves both daggers at the doors the commander walked through moments ago. The tips bounce off the metal where his head would have been and clatter to the floor. The noise reverberates around us so loudly that I have to clamp my hands over my ears to block out the sound. Her weapons fly back to her hands like a boomerang, and she throws them again and again and again. Each throw has the same deadly accuracy as the first. I'm amazed there are no dents forming in the metal. I begin to wonder if I should take cover. The last thing I need is to become a target. Just as I'm thinking about backing away, Clesandra's shoulders hunch forward. She takes an enormous deep breath. The daggers fly back to her outstretched hands, and she calmly presses the tips of each knife together. The daggers hum and squeak as they morph back into one. As she exhales, the blade disappears into a tiny compact rectangle that she places in her back pocket.

Then she turns to me. Her shoulders hunched menacingly, her eyes narrowed.

I throw my hands up. "I ain't seen nothing."

Clesandra relaxes her stance slightly. "Good."

"He rubs you the wrong way too?" I ask.

"I see nothing good coming from this mission," Clesandra grunts. "I saw what happened to my home, Nacombe—riots, killing, bombing. People aren't people anymore. Kill or be killed. My whole family was killed. I had to fight to survive. Here's no better. Don't cross Smith. Level three is fatal. He kills here. Some survive. Become *special,* until you say the wrong thing, or do the wrong thing, or disagree and start trouble. Then you're dead. Watch your back, Sleeping Beauty. Ain't no one here watching it for you." She moves toward the exit and I'm involuntarily pulled in her wake. I want to ask her about the mission and what we will be doing on the new planet, but I'm worried that I might incite another episode of rage, so I bite my tongue. The commander is sure to tell me himself.

We slip through the doors of the simulation room and stand outside, not saying a word to each other for a moment.

Clesandra is the first to break the silence. "Find you in the morning," she grunts and disappears down the corridor. I have no idea where I'm going, but I walk in the opposite direction.

Chapter 8

It takes me the better part of an hour to locate the command room on my own. The entrance is plain with just the word "Command," in large, bold, official-looking font. I have no desire to be here. I don't want to walk through those doors to see a man who views me as a replica of my father. But I force myself to step through the archway as the doors slide open.

The room is poorly lit aside from a bright table at the center or the space, which is flickering and dancing with fluorescent light and color. The colors flash around the dark walls, illuminating the room like a disco ball spinning off-center. A man hovers over the table, seemingly immersed in the projection. He hears the sound of the doors slide shut behind me and looks up from his work. I can't make out his expression in the dark room.

"Light," his deep voice commands, and the room floods with fluorescent white light. All around the circular room are holographic boards. The kind you see in military command rooms, like the one my father spent more than half his life working in. I had only been in his command room a handful of times. The holographic maps in Dad's command room could project any place in the world. You could see the people moving on the streets in real time. Watch real security personnel catch criminals. See weapons testing in the desert from a safe distance and research the results. Negotiate face-to-face with other countries. I bet the walls here have the same capability to project Earth in real time. What's left of it from the bombings.

I think back to just before I was captured and drugged, as I watched what was left of my home get destroyed. I close my eyes for a brief second to shut the images out of my head, and then open them to see the commander quietly observing me from a distance.

I don't know what I should do. What's appropriate? Do I stand at attention? Do I say anything? What would I say? I choose a quiet and stoic appearance.

The commander walks calmly forward and extends his hand. Cautiously, I take it, careful to give his hand as strong a squeeze as I can.

"I apologize for my previous rudeness. I should have properly introduced myself earlier. Aeon Smith," he says. "I'm the commander of defense."

"Avery Evericon," I grunt in response, trying to sound tough.

"I know who you are." Commander Smith smiles. "I understand you have a brother on the ship with you."

"What about my brother?" I ask defensively.

Smith raises his eyebrows and smiles at my defensive tone. "You're lucky you have family left. After all, family is everything, isn't it?"

I'm not sure what Smith is trying to get at by bringing my brother into the conversation, but I don't like where this is going.

"It was a shame you had to live through the horrible things that happened on Earth. With your help and allegiance, that won't happen where we're going. I would hate for you or your brother…anyone…to have to go through that again."

I feel myself go rigid. "What do you mean?"

"Ms. Willows didn't tell you?" His eyebrows knit together thoughtfully. "Well, I'm not going to sugarcoat it and tell you we've left Earth for a better place. Things are complicated where we're going. Your brother may be too young to understand this, but you should know that there won't be a return voyage.

We've only permitted suitable candidates to make the journey to Panacea in the first place. We have no intent to go home."

"But if Jace hears there's no hope of going home—"

"Your brother has been told exactly what he needs to know to be successful in his new role," he says with a wave of his hand.

My teeth clench together as he dismisses my concern. *We're never going back to Earth. Not that there would be much to go back to…but it was home.*

"What exactly is his role?" I ask cautiously.

Smith ignores my question. "Join me." He gestures to the large, oval table in the center of the room where he was standing a few minutes ago. "Light," Smith barks. The lights blink off, and the table we're standing in front of is the only illuminated object in the room. Smith clicks a button on the side of the table and a three-dimensional, pale-purple sphere appears.

"This is Panacea," Smith says. "While Earth has been slowly devolving into chaos, scientists have been studying Panacea for over one hundred years. They've been sending their fastest probes into the planet's atmosphere and collecting data. Panacea is very much like Earth. There is a breathable atmosphere, water, plant life, animals, and even…a humanoid civilization."

I know he wants wonder, surprise, and fascination. But with my whole body feeling like it's made of putty, and the shock of losing two years of my life in minutes, I am going to need more information to get as excited to be here as Jace was this morning. I intentionally leave him hanging until he continues.

Frown lines form at the corners of Smith's mouth as he talks and I get the feeling he's sizing me up. No doubt, everyone on this ship has been glad to be here or easily swayed into feeling they need to be here…at least enough to please the commander.

"Panacea is going to provide our people with a way to survive," Smith continues. We've had a team of scientists and engineers deployed on the planet for nine years. They have created a safe haven where they can actively study everything from the plants and animals, soil, water, germs, and disease to the…culture." He pauses again and smiles, as if he's thinking about something that gives him great pleasure.

"So me, the other people on this ship, my brother…what are our roles in all of this?"

"There are a variety of roles that will be filled when we land. Some people will be trained in agriculture, others in medicine. You, now that I've seen what you can do, will be trained as a soldier for our main mission." He frowns at me. "Though you may need to put on a few pounds before going into the field."

Going into the field? I think back to Earth and the basic-training drills Jeremy and I had to endure. I hated it. I wanted to get through it as fast as possible. Of course, I would carry a gun to support Jeremy, make sure he was safe. But I never took pleasure in weapons drills like the others. Learning to shoot meant I would be taking a life sooner than later. I wasn't very good at picking up hand-to-hand combat, either. I've never been a very muscular person who could rely on brute strength to get through the drills like the others. I look down at my thin, gaunt arms. Even with fluid IVs and the muscular shock therapy that I'm sure was performed on my body while I was asleep, nothing could prevent some wasting. I've always been a little on the lean side anyway, but not like this. Not scrawny…more like a runner. *If only I could run away right now. But to where?*

"Main mission?" I ask.

Smith grips the sides of the holographic planet like a basketball and pulls it apart. The purple sphere expands to three times its size. A large, black area encompasses roughly one-third of the planet. "What is the black area?" I ask.

"Our probes haven't been able to explore those areas," he says with a tone of annoyance. "We have probes that fly out and insert access points for our holographic technology. It's like using security cameras that never run out of film."

I nod my head. "Just like Earth."

"Right," Smith agrees. "The probes that enter the atmosphere in the dark areas are lost forever. We have sent scientists on foot to those areas. Just like the probes, no one comes back."

Smith can see my concern and gives a little shrug. "We treat it like the Bermuda Triangle. As long as you stay away from it, you're good."

I know he's trying to lighten the mood and not scare me to death, but I can't force a smile to appease him.

Smith returns his attention to the sphere. He spends about thirty seconds of poking, prodding, and air expansions of the planetary holograph to find what he's looking for.

"This, Soldier Evericon, is our main mission." He indicates an area on the screen.

I come closer to examine the spot on the screen filled with beautiful stone buildings. The colors of the buildings and the natural landscape are extraordinary. An enormous mountain range forms a tight-knit ring around a lush, tropical countryside. The buildings are built into and around the edge of the mountain range.

Along the inside flows the most incredible-looking river, with water the color of opalescent lavender. It hugs and winds its way beside the base of the mountain to flow in an almost perfectly unbroken circle.

How is this possible? The water has to come from somewhere.

My mouth falls open at the intricate engineering of the buildings built into the mountain. An enormous set of stone steps leads from the base and winds up to the very top. Along the winding stone staircase are small, temple-like buildings. When examined more closely, I see intricate carvings of humans and ritual scenes. I'm reminded of my studies of ancient Greece and Egypt in high school. This is not an absolutely primitive community.

Far below are tiny moving dots of human-like forms too small to see clearly. They are moving this way and that, going about their lives. I want so badly to expand the image and observe it more closely.

"Light," Smith says. The holographic image pops like a balloon and fades like dust into a thousand brilliant colors. I want more time with the images.

"We are going to conquer that kingdom," Smith says with a grin. "Then we're going to establish an area where our people can rebuild." An evil glint dances across his eyes.

Conquer that kingdom? His words settle into numb ears. We're not here to find a cure for the people on Earth like Jace thought. We're here to take this planet for our own.

"If we already have an area built on the planet, why destroy them?"

"That's an excellent question."

Smith motions for me to observe the outer circle of holographic display boards surrounding the table. "Present water maps," Smith says. The entire circular room comes alive with color and light. "This, Soldier Evericon, is our extensive search for water on the planet. As you are aware, there is no longer enough drinkable water on Earth to support life. Panacea became a target for human relocation for the sole reason that there is a life-sustaining atmosphere and *water*," Smith says it slowly, careful to linger on the word, as he searches my face for acknowledgement.

I know very well the implications of the need for water. The government and media made certain to highlight that need early on, even before Earth went to war for the resource.

"Water is life," I breathe the slogan out sarcastically.

"Water *is* life," Smith repeats. "There's just one problem with Panacea. Water is a difficult resource to attain. Sure," he gestures to several points on the screens around him, "there are several shallow lakes, a few small streams, and a vast amount of water trapped deep below the surface. Unfortunately, there are only two sources of water that flow abundantly to the surface. One is in the dark spot that is uncharted by our probes. We can see a very large region from space that appears to be water, but once we pass into the atmosphere, we lose all ability to gather more information. The other, as you might have already guessed, is where the natives have established themselves." He pauses, waiting for me to catch up and acknowledge what he's saying.

Everything I've seen on the screens looks remarkably lush and green for a planet with little access to water.

"If there's so little water at the surface, how are the plants and animals that are not near those two places surviving?"

"They've adapted to survive. But like us, they're

living on small reserves and borrowed time. The plants have deep root systems that can tap the water below ground. The animals, aside from our *alien* friends," he says sarcastically, "have adapted to the constraints of living without much water. Our scientists are surviving by mining water out of the rocks and drilling below the surface. But drilling and mining are difficult and produce such limited amounts of water. Our camp produces just enough to meet our daily needs. Once our ship and the others land...well, it won't be long before we will need to relocate. There's really no other alternative. We need that water."

Our eyes lock. Smith searches for my surrender, my devotion and loyalty to participate in his war. *There has to be another alternative to annihilating a whole species to survive.*

"What about the disease on Earth? Isn't there a way to find a cure so we can go back? What about the other people we left behind—"

Smith shakes his head, annoyed. "Don't you think we tried to find a cure? There is no cure," he repeats. "Earth, June 21, 2050."

The boards surrounding the room hum to life. Pictures fill the holographic screens of different army installations around the world. The military bases must be the first things programmed to project. People on the screens are moving about, meeting in groups, working on projects and testing weapons.

"CBMA, Asik, time, 2331." Smith adds location and the military time.

"Chemical Biological Materials Agency?" I question.

"Just wait," Smith says.

My father appears in the frame of the video projection moments later. He looks frantic. Sweating profusely, he's carrying a small container with rows of fluid-filled test tubes. He places the container on a metal counter and begins transferring the tubes into a climate-controlled silver case.

"The camera, I'm not getting my face on the—"

"Shut up," Dad barks. He looks over his shoulder at the security camera and winces, clearly aware that he's being filmed. He clicks the case closed and resets the security access codes on the handle. Almost as an afterthought, he throws a black cloth over the camera. There's the sound of liquid splashing onto surfaces and rubber boots squeaking on wet floors. My father and the other man bicker in low muffled tones that make it hard to hear.

"You sure you want to do this? It has a high mutation rate. I don't think it's stable—"

"You don't get a say in this. Shut up and do your job."

"What about reversal...did you—"

"It's taken care of. It's in safe hands. No more questions. There isn't time," my father says.

Smith flicks a button and the screen goes blank.

"What's he doing? What's going on?" I ask defensively.

Smith doesn't answer. He simply states another time and place. "ROSCOSMOS, August 3, 2050."

August 3? That's the day after my brother was murdered. What the hell is Smith getting at?

This video surveillance tape shows the Russian Federal Space Agency launch hanger. A huge spacecraft is roaring to life. Black plumes of smoke and radiant sparks fly from huge rocket thrusters. Men in white-and-gray suits board the spacecraft. A team of soldiers in military uniforms runs frantically around the ship, detaching wires, closing doors, and shouting commands. Moments later, the hanger doors to the facility grind open, and the spacecraft soars out with a violent burst of fire and white smoke.

The spacecraft leaving means nothing to me at first. "Why are you showing me this?"

"I have reason to believe your father corrupted a team to steal that spacecraft," Smith says quietly.

"What? He couldn't…" Maybe it's the fact that I haven't used my brain to think, reason, and connect ideas in two years, but I can't seem to grasp what Smith is trying to make me see here.

"Those vials of blue liquid contained the deadly virus that infected your mother and sister. Your father was aboard that ship leaving the Russian Space Agency. He abandoned you and the rest of your family to save his own skin."

I feel dizzy trying to put all the facts Smith is telling me together.

"My father poisoned my family?" I breathe the words slowly, more anger and hatred toward him bubbling to the surface with each passing second.

"Not intentionally," Smith says, eyeing me cautiously.

"Did he or did he not kill my family?" I growl.

"He destroyed more families than you know. General Evericon destroyed my whole country." Smith's jaw clenches in anger as he speaks. "SomX1 virus infection map August 1, 2050," Smith says.

The board directly in front of us projects a basic world map. Enormous patches of red follow the coastline all the way from South Africa up to India and parts of China. I remember seeing similar maps pop up on my CARDD while my family was hiding out in our bunker. The only news we got of anything going on came in bits and pieces on our CARDDs and even then, I didn't think much of the information was reliable.

"SomX1 virus infection map August 21, 2050," Smith says after I've had a moment to take in the first map. The red patches extend the coastlines of almost all continents, absorb more than ninety percent of Africa, all of India and China, and well into most of what used to be the United States.

I feel myself shaking with anger. Asik is blanketed in red.

"We believe your father injected fish and planted them along the South African coast in June following a water export deal in Nacombe. The fish traveled the coastline in a matter of days. People fished them out to eat, only to help spread the virus," Smith says quietly. *The deal went south. This is the shit storm Jeremy was referring to.*

"Why would he do that?" I whisper.

"The *why* wasn't his worst crime. What's worse is he didn't immediately try to fix what he'd done when it was getting out of control."

"What do you mean…out of control?"

"The virus was never meant to kill people," Smith says. "Not directly, anyway."

"Wait, wait a minute. How do you know all this?" I interrupt. "How do you know this was done by my father?" Even as I ask the question, I'm well aware that my father was more than capable of something like this. Even so, I don't want to believe he'd actually do it.

The corners of Smith's mouth turn up slightly. "Your father and I worked together on this."

You son of a bitch! You helped my father kill my family.

"We met once before in L'eau," Smith continues, ignoring my look of anger. "We were negotiating privileges to the water in Canada. We discussed the idea of putting a virus into the ocean waterways that would sterilize the population. Your father was a brilliant man and he had a good idea how to do it. The idea of injecting the fish was genius. No water to feed cattle and poultry, fish from the ocean were pretty much a delicacy to coastal areas. Even with ocean populations running low from overfishing there were still plenty to inject with the virus.

"Of course, when I met your father, it was only an idea then. Something like that would be highly unethical. But when an unexpected super virus spread in my country after a water exportation negotiation went badly, I had a feeling it was him. No one else knew what we'd talked about. It wasn't supposed to happen like it did. With Earth's population growing unchecked, water use tripled in just five years. The virus was meant to sterilize a large enough group that there would be fewer people using resources within a generation or two. It was supposed to make the water last longer, so we could find a more permanent solution. When the virus was introduced, it mutated. It got out of hand so quickly. I told your father to manufacture the cure and send it out to reverse what he'd done. My whole country was dying. My wife, my children..." He spits out the last words.

"You want to know what he said when my country asked for help?"

He doesn't wait for me to answer. Instead, he points a small device at the screen. The map displaying the virus disappears, replaced by an official letter with Asik's military heading.

July 27, 2050

Commanding General

Dear Mr. Ambassador Smith:

The government of Asik and its

military forces will not offer assistance in your matter. Though the government of Asik is aware of the devastating events in your country, your situation lacks any sufficient threats to our country's national security. Therefore, it does not merit sending American forces to your nation for assistance. This decision will not be appealed, and any such action to coerce the government of Asik to send military forces to assist in your plight will be met with swift retaliation. May God have mercy on your country and its people that they may triumph through trying times.

Sincerely,
Daniel S. Evericon
Major General
Commanding

Smith gives me a minute to read the letter. My eyes linger loathingly on my father's signature at the bottom. He used to be a man I could look up to. Now he'll always be the man responsible for killing Mom, Caileen, Jeremy and who knows how many more.

From the corner of my eye, I catch Smith reading my reaction carefully. I know he wants me to blame my father for this. I do. But there's something about the way that Smith's been talking, the way he's looking at me now that makes the hair on the back of my neck stand on end. What if my father didn't use the tubes he took from the CBMA? What if someone else besides him created the virus? What if the virus was just an act of God? A way of nature culling a very destructive herd and Dad didn't have anything to do with it? *Stop kidding yourself. The man didn't have a soul. He did it. Probably didn't think twice. The heartless bastard wouldn't even send aide.* I think of Dad murdering my brother. He became such a different man when he became lead bio-chemical engineer for the weapons division. One devastating weapon design after another swept him up the chain of command, turning him into an obsessive nut case with an insatiable need for control. But as I'm standing in front of Smith, watching him study my reaction, I can't help but think that if my father hadn't been the first to plant the virus, Smith would have eventually done it himself.

"Why didn't he send a cure?" I ask cautiously. "Why didn't Jace and I get sick?"

"Those same questions keep me up at night, soldier. Why didn't he send a cure? Probably because he figured the only way to save Earth was to kill the people destroying it. Why didn't you or I or your brother get sick? Maybe we're just stronger. Who knows, a few more weeks and the virus could have mutated again and we'd all be dead. Those aren't the right questions to ask yourself."

"Why would my father steal a spaceship? Where did he think he was going with it?"

Smith shrugs. "It doesn't matter. There's only one habitable spot we know of well enough to take a risk settling and we're headed for it. The space agency logs from Russia show that the ship he stole wouldn't have enough food or water to reach Panacea anyway. I checked the logs myself. *If* that was where he was headed," Smith adds. "The man's as good as dead."

Dead. The word resonates in my head. *Good.* But something about Smith's frown rubs me the wrong way. His facial expression, his body language, the tone of his voice…from my brief encounter with this man, he seems so sure of himself, proud, confident. The deep frown lines by the sides of his mouth tell me the opposite. *He's not sure. He can't be certain that my father is dead. He wants to believe it. So do I.* I shake my head slightly. *It doesn't matter. If I ever see the man again, I'll kill him myself.*

Smith puts his arm around my shoulders and very quietly says, "Soldier, what happened on Earth isn't important anymore. Earth is gone. The real question you have to ask yourself now is what kind of legacy will you leave for mankind? What kind of future will you leave for your brother on Panacea?"

A future riddled with death and exploitation if I follow what you want.

"All we have left is the planet we're landing on. We're going to need people to fight for our cause. They'll have to fight to secure the resources that we need to survive. I'm going to need you to fight, soldier. Fight so that you and your brother have a bright future to look forward to, a future that doesn't involve more war." He pauses to let his words sink in. "Soldier 135, Jace Evericon, is to be trained in agriculture. He won't see a day of this war. That is, as long as strong, young men like you agree to help us."

"How can I refuse?" I say, trying to keep the sarcasm from my voice.

He turns to face me. "I guess you can't refuse." He smiles. "Unless, of course, there is no need for solider Jace Evericon on the new planet?"

He lets his words hang in the air.

Again, I'm reminded of my father. I think back to what Clesandra said in the simulation room, and I know that if I don't agree to join the war effort, I'll be killed. Those who did not fall in line behind my father were either killed, blackmailed, or threatened into submission. He never could look beyond being in control to see what devastation he was creating at home or elsewhere. But Jeremy could see.

At the start of the war, Jeremy was completely against fighting. He didn't want me anywhere near missions and insisted I join the space program. Dad kept telling him, me, and everyone, that the missions were diplomatic, strictly based on finding solutions, gathering intelligence, creating alliances and gaining importation rights. We should be proud to be a part of them. I also remember Dad executing thirty men in cold blood while Jeremy, I, and all other active duty soldiers in Asik watched. He told us the men were traitors. Had done something to compromise a mission and needed to be eliminated. If any other soldiers strayed or disobeyed, we might as well join the body count too. We learned firsthand just what our father was capable of and what he would do to anyone who stood in his way.

Maybe that was the real reason Jeremy enlisted in Dad's division. He wanted to be closer to the man because he made it his own personal mission to destroy everything Dad could engineer. He hated to see people suffer.

Smith interrupts my thoughts and very bluntly says, "I hope you understand what's at stake here. Panacea is an opportunity to save the human race. We must seize that opportunity at all costs." Somehow, he makes the statement a question, and his hand gripping my shoulder tells me the answer he wants to hear. He scans my face, as if he's trying to read my mind. I feel his grip tighten on my shoulder as I struggle to respond.

I have no idea what this man is capable of, but I know what my father was. More than once, I saw him publicly punish defiant soldiers, or look pleased when a rival went missing.

"Yes," I say carefully. I hope he can't read the anger and defiance boiling under my skin, as my arm muscles tense underneath the commander's grip.

Smith releases my shoulder and claps me hard across the back. "Excellent!" he exclaims. "Excellent. This is your chance to be better than your father was. To do what's right for what's left of humanity."

I force a smile to appease him. War in all regards is not what's best for humanity. Thankfully, the commander takes my smile as compliance and the rest of orientation is short. He instructs me that there will be a future briefing when we land, and that I should spend the remainder of my three days on the ship putting in some serious hours in the mess hall, completing agricultural training, and if I'm feeling up to it, hand-to-hand combat training.

I leave the command room with a heavy feeling. The message is simple—I'm a combat soldier now. I'll be forced to be a pawn in a war for a cause I don't have the urge to fight. No doubt, like the war that took the lives of so many innocent men, women, and children on Earth, I'll be the cause of many deaths. Or perhaps, just the death of Smith himself.

It takes me over an hour to find my room assignment. The ship, I've determined, is circular in design, with all rooms at the center of the ship. I picture a large flying saucer, the kind featured in B-flick movies about aliens and spaceships. Maybe if I'd listened to Jeremy and stayed with the space program, I would have an easier time navigating the spaceship.

The narrow hallways are deceiving. They appear straight and narrow but have a slight bend to them. Occasionally I'll pass people walking along the halls, but no one says anything. People avoid eye contact and interaction. Aside from the tavern, the ship is like a ghost town.

Along the way, I pass a multitude of doors. Some doorways have signs above them: Agricultural Simulation Room, Command Room, Tavern. Most others just have numbers. It takes me a few minutes to connect room numbers with soldier number. I remember Lupète told me that I'm soldier number 134 and take comfort when I find both Jace and Sheol's numbers underneath my number on our door.

I enter the small, narrow room. Two sets of bunks, one small nightstand, and a closed door between the beds, which I assume is a bathroom, are the only creature comforts I see.

Jace is asleep on a top bunk above Sheol, who's sitting cross-legged with a book propped open on his knees. The room is dark aside from a fingertip lamp Sheol's wearing on his index finger to illuminate the words on the pages. He pauses his reading when he sees me enter.

"Welcome to our jail cell. Like what we've done with the place?" Sheol whispers sarcastically as he snaps the book shut and gestures around him.

The room is empty, sterile, like the gray T-shirts with our soldier numbers printed on them. There's nothing decorative on the white walls.

"How's Jace?" I ask.

"He'll live," Sheol responds, his voice softening.

A nod is all I can muster as I slither into the open bottom bunk and fall asleep listening to the quiet, rhythmic sounds of Jace's breathing.

Chapter 9

The last remaining days in space are a blur. I spend a large portion of my time with Sheol and Jace in the tavern eating foods, some of which I've only read about in books. I can't help remembering that people on Earth are at war for a glass of water, but food and drinks appear here with a mere whisper.

When I'm not in the tavern, my time is filled with training with Clesandra. She has a knack for appearing out of thin air like she's constantly stalking my movements. She drops in at any time of the day and drags me to simulation rooms for training. Even though her demeanor is anything but friendly, I look forward to our time together most. When I'm with her I feel like I have a purpose on the ship, a reason to get up in the morning. I'd like to think I make her feel the same way, but she's not easy to read.

Clesandra forcefully guides me through combat-training drills and helps to build my muscle tone. We barely converse. When Clesandra does talk, it's mostly to angrily mumble something to herself about Smith, which makes no sense to me. She usually follows up with tantrums filled with knife throwing. The angrier she gets, the better her throwing accuracy becomes. Resisting the urge to coax information out of her, I follow her orders without question. The last thing I need right now is to wind up as a six-foot tall bull's eye. She gives orders. I follow. Life is simple.

Agricultural training is short-lived. Clesandra provides me with a list of plants that are poisonous and edible, and I use a planetary guidebook to find pictures of the plants on the lists. My body aches and my mind swims as Jace, Sheol and I prepare for our final briefing before entering Panacea's atmosphere. We're gathering with the entire ship's population in the combat simulation room this evening.

My breath catches in my throat at the sight of the digitized camouflage clothing folded neatly in my room. All the military personnel in Asik wore them, and I can't suppress the horrific images of pain and suffering attached to these uniforms. Gritting my teeth and tugging the gray, stiff clothing on, I join Sheol and Jace and head to the simulation room.

"This clothing makes me itch," Jace remarks as he tugs at the collar of his uniform.

I kneel down in front of him to loosen the button at the top of his collar. *He's not even going to war. Why should he have to wear one of these uniforms?* I think angrily as I tug the button loose and let the collar flop open.

"Ah, thanks!" He smiles and rakes his little hands across his neck. I return his smile with a fake, forced grin of my own. I don't like the idea of my brother looking like a miniature soldier. Thankfully, Jace doesn't take notice of my somber mood. He bounces along, chattering about poisonous plants, and how he's trying to build a leveled structure to save space while growing vegetables. I only half-listen and try to appear amused as we reach the simulation room and wait for the motion-activated doors to separate.

This room, which I know can be filled with dangerous, even fatal, holographic environments, now represents the sophisticated, intimate atmosphere of a banquet room. Rows of tables to seat six are angled on the left and the right of a narrow aisle, forming a V-shape toward the front of the room. A stage and an enormous holographic screen display an image of an idealistic home surrounded by lush, green plants. A man and woman dressed in matching combat uniforms in the foreground of the image are smiling and toasting full glasses of water, as a group of children in the background plays happily with a football.

"Can you believe this crap?" Clesandra growls, ambushing Sheol and me. Again, she appears as if from thin air. Bulldozing her way between us, she shoves me roughly in the shoulder and gestures to the screen. "Load of bull's more like it."

I nod, turning to look at her. The air snags in my throat when I see her in the digitized camouflage uniform. I try to cover the noise with a cough. Clesandra doesn't notice, but I catch Sheol rolling his eyes.

The women's uniforms are extremely form-fitting, with a solid, gray torso instead of the full camouflage that the men are wearing. Every curve of her body is perfectly accented. No other woman I've seen on the ship can compare.

"What's crap?" Jace pipes up from beside me before he notices Clesandra. He attempts to fade behind me and disappear into my camouflaged uniform when he recognizes her.

"Relax, kid." She glares at Jace, acknowledging his panic as he tries to vanish. "I'm over it."

"Sorry I took your knife," he squeaks. "I wasn't trying to start trouble."

"Like I said, I'm over it," Clesandra repeats. This time her face melts into what I imagine is her version of a grin, but it comes across as more of a grimace.

Sheol scowls at her. "Don't you have someone else you have to bludgeon?"

She gives him a dirty look and makes a move at fake punching him. He flinches backward and takes a defensive stance. They both shake their heads and glare at each other for a few seconds before Clesandra ignores Sheol.

I imagined more people to be on the ship, but there are no more than a hundred or two. Not much of a population to start a war or build a civilization with.

Clesandra punches me hard in the arm to get my attention, and motions for us to join the rest of the people who are now taking seats at tables around the room. Just as we're about to sit at a table near the back of the room, Lupète materializes next to us. Now dressed in combat attire with his long, curly hair pulled back in a ponytail at the base of his neck, he looks even more powerful. I avoid looking directly in his eyes.

"Soldier 135," he addresses Jace warmly.

The twelve-year-old cranes his head back to look up at Lupète. He seems to have no problem with Lupète's eyes. Jace smiles up at him like he's one of his best friends.

"You are wanted in agriculture." Lupète smiles back. He extends his hand out to my brother, and without question Jace waves good-bye to us and takes Lupète's hand like he would have with our mother. I start to protest as they turn and head out of the room, but Sheol puts his hand up to block me.

"He'll be fine with Lupète. Best buddies since he came out of cryo-sleep. It might be for the best depending on what this brief is about." Sheol frowns at me.

Warily, I watch Lupète and Jace as they walk away. When Lupète gets to the entrance, he turns back toward me and catches my gaze. I feel a zing of pressure shoot from the base of my spine to my head.

Watch her closely.

I hear the words in my mind. They aren't my own. Lupète points to Clesandra.

Her.

The pressure and pain evaporates when I stare at Clesandra. I look back at the door, but Jace and Lupète are gone. Left in their place is uncertainty and fear. *He just talked to me in my head.* I press my palm to my forehead to ease the sudden pounding. I feel like I should run after them. I feel like I should make sure Jace is okay. Just as I've made up my mind to run after them, the pressure in my head returns.

No harm will come to Jace. Stay with her.

"You all right?" Sheol asks, nudging my arm.

I massage my temples and look back at the door one more time.

"Yeah," I lie. "Who is that man again?"

Sheol shrugs. "He's one of the doctors. He's a bit of a strange dude, but I wouldn't worry. He seems pretty harmless."

A man who can somehow communicate in my head without speaking is anything but harmless. What else can this man do? The three of us take seats together. Clesandra is careful to wedge herself between the two of us at the table. She gives Sheol a look of pure hatred when he tries to sit next to me and doesn't readily move over to let her in the middle. His nostrils flare and for a minute I think they might try to kill each other. Commander Smith takes the stage in front of the holographic screen before they have a chance to.

"Good evening," he addresses the audience. Only a few people murmur a response.

"I know you must all have questions about our mission. Some of you I've had the pleasure of addressing individually." He pauses and looks at the crowd. His eyes meet mine for a split second, and then he moves on.

"For those whom I have not spoken with, welcome. Your service on this journey is invaluable. I realize this transition has not been an easy one. Most of you have lost loved ones. Some of you have lost whole families to the war, as I have." Smith paces back and forth across the stage in front of the projected image. He drops his head and pauses to allow the audience a moment to grieve.

The room is completely silent.

"Today is a new day. We have a chance to correct our path. That chance lies in a land that is no longer so distant." Smith smiles as the holographic image behind him fades to black and is replaced by an image of Panacea.

"We will rebuild our shattered lives. Each and every one of you matter more than you know. You are the collective heartbeat of the community. Without each of you, we are nothing. History has proven time and time again that when the opinions and basic needs of the community are ignored, chaos is an inevitable consequence." He pauses to let the words sink in.

"I'm going to lay it out for all of you. On Earth, we as a people, failed. We failed to see that even though the world was cut up into a jigsaw puzzle of countries with borders not to be crossed, we are all neighbors."

Images of Earth from space are projected around his head on the screen showing how the Earth's surface is divided.

"As neighbors, we failed to act with compassion and kindness in times of need and want. Instead, we followed our private ambitions, led by separate leaders with their own agendas. We spent our lives sucking up Earth's resources as if there was no tomorrow and spitting the polluted byproducts back into the rivers and streams we so desperately needed to survive. Pollution grew unchecked."

Images of children in the desert flash onto the screen. Covered with dust and huddling near the edge of a contaminated pool of water, they sift through with their fingers to remove plastic trash and brine to get the water. Uncomfortable murmurs create a low hum in the room.

"I know it's difficult to watch," Smith continues. "Worse yet, most of those children died of waterborne diseases. Instead of helping one another, countries diverted the natural flow of rivers for their own personal gain. When the resources began to run out, we turned a blind eye to our neighbors dying of starvation and dehydration. What's worse, we turned the remaining resources into private commodities that only the rich and powerful could afford."

Another video clip dominates the screen. The whole room watches in horror as filth-covered people beg at the feet of well-dressed patrons entering an immaculate building. The structure is smack dab in the middle of the desert landscape, yet fresh green palm trees adorn the entrance. Hanging baskets filled with lush flowers decorate the overhang. Through the front doors of the building, a glorious fountain at the center of a large, modern-looking room cascades clear, clean water. An S-shaped bar flows around the fountain, similar to the tavern. Exquisite bottles of every shape and size line the back wall of the bar. Some of the bottles are decorated and bejeweled to look more expensive and fancy. But liquor is not what is being poured for the guests from the great glass containers…it's water.

Wealthy people in the room are happily chattering as they lay down wads of cash, sampling the water as if they're on a wine-tasting tour. They completely ignore the cries of the people outside, some of whom are ramming their bodies against the doors in a futile attempt to gain entry.

I feel Clesandra go rigid in the chair next to me. Her hands grip the sides of her seat in a death lock. Sheol is observing her carefully from the corner of his eye. Every second of nonchalant laughter from the patrons in the water bar turns her face a deeper shade. I imagine her ripping her knife from wherever it's hidden in her uniform and slashing people to death in the water bar. Only it won't be people in the water bar tonight, it'll be everyone within striking distance in this room. I have to get her to stop seeing red.

Doing the only thing I can think of, I force myself to take her hand. Though we're nearly the same size, my hand engulfs hers completely. I hold it tight like a vise grip.

She whips her head around in my direction, nostrils flared in fury. The distraction works. Taken completely by surprise, she loses her focus on the screen. Oddly, she doesn't rip her hand away. For a moment, our eyes are locked. Electric energy shared between just the two of us. She's angry in a hauntingly beautiful way and her skin radiates heat up my arm. She lowers her gaze to our hands, and I'm thankful when I feel the tension in her arm and body fade away. I let out the breath I didn't realize I'd been holding and gently loosen my grip, allowing her to wiggle free. She plants both hands in her lap, and we return our attention to the screen.

The video fades to black and Smith steps to the center of the stage.

"That's just one example of a Water Bar established by the government of a country to let the people know their place in the world. You have to be rich to afford water. Those who can't afford it, go without."

People murmur with disgust.

"It's not hard to imagine how some of the injustices you just saw could lead to war," Smith continues. "Here's the problem as I see it. Governments, justice systems, and, of course, the media, are all influenced by self-interest groups bent on making a profit. And it's usually a short-term profit. They don't care who gets hurt in the process, or how many innocent lives are lost. At the end of the day it's how much money was made that matters. This whole idea is in conflict with the well-being of humankind. Without a doubt, there are a lot of good people in the world, but as a whole, we the people contribute to a system that is broken. Turning our backs and refusing to acknowledge global suffering. For what? Money? Economic domination?"

I steal a glance at Sheol, who's nodding slightly. Clesandra is muttering under her breath, but I can't make out what she's saying.

Smith sighs, collecting himself. "The good news is we have a second chance. We have a chance to get it right this time. We will become a close-knit community who lives together, works together, and shares each other's pain and happiness. It's only when people unite that they become powerful. It's my deepest hope that you will join me in rebuilding our lives on Panacea."

Smith ends his speech and the screen goes black. For a long moment the room falls silent. Then, as if by magic, we hear one person clapping. The sound is tentative and fearful until it's joined by others. Then the whole room is clapping.

Smith waits for the applause to fade. "At this time, I would like to dismiss the following soldiers to agriculture: one, five, eight…" Smith drones on, calling soldier numbers as people stand to exit the room. Many people are dismissed to agriculture, others to engineering, and a few to medical team briefings. In just a few short moments, the room that was filled with approximately two hundred or so people is cut in half. The vast majority of people left are men, though a few women, including Clesandra, remain.

"Ladies." Smith nods and acknowledges the five or six women who remain in the banquet hall. "Gentlemen." He gestures with his arm in a sweeping motion to the rest. "You are all here with me today because you have been chosen as elite soldiers. I have watched you closely during training. I have even placed some of you in exceptionally difficult situations to see how you would perform." He holds my gaze. "There are some of you in this room who performed better than expected."

The commander begins to pace back and forth along the stage. "You will need all the training and skills you have acquired in space on Panacea. Let's not get it twisted, folks. My welcome speech may have given some of you the 'warm and fuzzies' about our long-term goals on the planet but understand this— Panacea is anything but warm and fuzzy."

He looks out into the crowd. "Nine years ago, our first team of scientists and engineers numbered about three hundred. Panacea has since whittled them down to just over thirty. Natives and the environment killed many. Others requested immediate transfer from the planet back to Earth. They didn't sign up to be slaughtered. They weren't fully prepared for the harsh reality of what life on the planet would be like. Only the toughest, strongest, and smartest and…" he pauses to find my face in the crowd, "most creative will survive," he said.

"Our fantastic engineers have built us a safe zone on the planet. This zone will serve as our temporary home. Anything beyond the dome, whether it be plant or animal, should be considered *hazardous* to your health. Assume any living thing larger than a mosquito wants to kill and eat you. Hell, even the mosquitoes want to kill and eat you!"

Whispers and contemplations about the dangers of the planet spring up from all around us. Sheol leans his chair back and reaches behind Clesandra to slap my shoulder. She shoots him a look of pure annoyance.

"If we bunk together you're on bug-killing duty."

"Gee, thanks," I mutter sarcastically. Bug-killing duty or not, I cross my fingers that we do bunk together.

"We also have an indigenous population called the Mizuapa," Smith continues. He points a small device at the holographic screen and an image of the natives appears. People in the room don't hide their gasps of awe at the appearance of the locals. The natives closely resemble humans in body build and structure. However, unlike the humans on Earth, who are sun burnt and freckled brown from living in a desert wasteland, these creatures are gorgeous, sculpted, and healthy looking. Dark-ebony hair is contrasted by their light skin and aquamarine eyes. Their skin is so pale it is almost transparent. *Like Lupéte's.* Yet their skin has a subtle purple hue that shimmers slightly as if they are coated in fine mineral powder. The women have vibrant aqua, plum, emerald, gold, and silver tattoos on their faces and arms, making them look even more stunning.

"Beautiful," I whisper.

Clesandra turns her head just slightly to look at me. My cheeks flush. "Nothing compared to—"

She kicks the side of my leg and glares at Smith while I stifle a yelp.

Sheol leans forward. "Do I need to sit between you two?"

"Do not be fooled by their beauty," Smith is saying. "They are cunning, stealthy, and trained killers. They are not afraid of hand-to-hand combat.

"Both males and females have hollow bone

structures like birds, which makes them incredibly light. They move like wind through trees, yet they are strong enough to deliver a fatal blow with bare hands. Though they are a primitive society, they are avid learners. The Mizuapa captured several of our scientists for observation and study. None of them were returned alive...or intact. It is my understanding that the Mizuapa have learned what they want from us. Now they kill our people on sight. It's my duty as commanding officer of this crew to prevent you from being killed. I will not succeed with all of you," he says as he glances around the room.

"Many of you may be wondering what your job description will be on the new planet. I am going to make this simple. You are trained soldiers. Your only objectives are to provide safety and security and to make sure our people have what they need to survive comfortably on the new planet. On Earth, we needed three basic things to live—shelter, food, and water. We have already seen that when one of those basic needs is jeopardized, our lives and what make us decent human beings goes right out the window. Panacea is no different. We still need shelter, food, and water to meet our most basic needs."

Soldiers are nodding their heads in agreement. Smith can see the compliance and smiles. He's getting geared up to drop the "to do that we're all going to war" bomb. I steal a glance at Clesandra. She's not going to like what's coming next.

Smith pauses at the center of the stage. "There's just one little problem on our new planet. Just like Earth, there's a finite amount of resources available, particularly water. Our native friends have built their home on the largest spring of fresh water on the planet, and they are not willing to share."

Unsettled whispers rise up from the group.

"Now, I don't need to remind any of you just how precious water is. We all understand that we need it to survive. For nine years, our scientists and engineers have been studying the Mizuapa just as closely as they've been studying us. We've attempted to establish a diplomatic solution to our problem. For now, we've been able to get by with drilling immense well systems to tap into underground water. However, that water is running out. Each day that we drill deeper we waste time and manpower. We provide just barely enough water to satisfy the needs of our agricultural team. There is more than enough water on the planet for all of us to share and live peacefully. But like I said, the Mizuapa are not willing to share."

Clesandra has been doing a decent job remaining silent and keeping her ever-rising temper in check. I can see from the corner of my eye that she's ready to explode. I'm about to whisper something to her to try and calm her down when she shoots up out of her chair like a rocket.

"Lemme guess!" she yells out. "You're gonna make us take it from 'em? We all know how well that works!"

A few people mumble in agreement. Smith's relaxed expression turns cold. "If that becomes necessary, yes we will take it."

Clesandra deeply growls her disapproval at the commander's statement. Across the room, an enormous man, probably in his late twenties, stands up. The giant is built with so much muscle that his uniform looks like it's about to burst in places.

"Would you rather we suffer and die?" he snarls at Clesandra. The people seated around him agree loudly.

Sheol and I both pull Clesandra back down into her seat. "No! It's better that they suffer! We can sit back 'n watch 'em waste away while we take what ain't ours!" She spits.

"Enough!" Smith yells.

The crowd falls silent, though Clesandra is still mumbling angrily under her breath. I wish she would get her temper in check. Smith won't take kindly to her outburst.

"Calm yourselves. Calm," Smith speaks much more quietly. More soothingly. "Soldier Willows brings up an excellent point. It would not be prudent to just take what isn't ours and watch another species fall into extinction. However, Rustin," he indicates the massive soldier with a nod of his head, "is right. We will not sit back and allow ourselves to starve and die without a fight." The room erupts in applause.

Smith waits for the applause to die down. "I do think we are getting ahead of ourselves," Smith states calmly. "Our scientists have not abandoned hope of a diplomatic solution. There is still a team in the field working out details. We, for the moment, are on standby. For the next few weeks, we will train hard on Panacea. It will take your bodies some time getting used to the atmosphere. And it will be much easier for you to learn agriculture and safety training in a hands-on environment. I assure you, we are not going to rush into anything just yet."

He says this last statement with his eyes pinned on Clesandra. "Should anyone here feel that they would be unfit for their duties, I encourage you to come speak with me in private. I feel more than certain that a solution will be found." A devious sneer tugs the left side of his mouth and I get the impression that his solution is death.

Commander Smith spends a few more minutes talking about landing tomorrow morning, but most of the information is lost on me. I spend the remaining time watching Clesandra for any more signs of rebellion. When the commander releases us from the brief, Clesandra is the first one out of her seat and headed for the exit.

I smack Sheol in the arm. "I'll meet up with you later," I say, and take off, jogging after her.

Weaving in and out of people leaving the assembly, I catch up with Clesandra. Grabbing her arm, I pull her to a stop.

She wheels around, breaking my loose grip, and punches me square in the face. I hear my nose crunch and know it's broken. Blood spews down the front of my uniform and white-hot stars cloud my vision. Clesandra doesn't even pause to look back. She continues down the ship's corridor. I must be a glutton for punishment because I run after her. I catch up just in time to stop the door to her living quarters from cracking me in the face. Without thinking, I shove it open and slip inside before the door can lock.

Looking around the dark room, I don't see Clesandra. I know I watched her enter. Waiting for my eyes to adjust fully, I glance around and take a few steps forward.

"Clesan—" I don't even get the name out before I'm choked in a headlock with my hair pulled back and a familiar knife at my throat. The heat from the blade burns my neck, forcing me to crane back farther to ease the pain.

"You have a death wish, Sleeping Beauty?" Clesandra growls.

"It sure seems that way, doesn't it?" I choke out.

"What do you want?"

"You mean, right now? Breathing might be nice," I sputter. Colorful stars begin to pop and spin across my vision again. The blade evaporates as she throws me forward. I crumple to my knees on the ground, rubbing my neck.

"Now, what do you want?" she snaps.

Not bothering to get up from a kneeling position, I look up at her for a moment. Her eyes so luminescent—beautiful—yet filled with anger and pain.

"I just wanted to make sure you were all right," I say.

The anger in her face melts so slightly that if I wasn't watching I would have missed it entirely.

"I didn't think I would become a punching bag, though," I admit.

"I'm fine," she snaps and looks at the ground in front of her feet.

"Sh…yeah okay. And my nose isn't broken."

She winces and shakes her head. "You coulda blocked. You're a mess."

Taking the hand she extends, I let her pull me up from the ground. Clesandra gestures for me to sit, and I pick a spot on an open bottom bunk.

"Who's your roommate?"

"No one. I tried to kill the last one." She trudges off to the bathroom between the two bunks, leaving me to ponder if that statement is true or not. She returns with a wet towel and lobs it in my direction. The water is cool and soothing. Amazing, I think, looking at the towel in my hand. Water here is so readily available. And clean. Where is it coming from? In Asik, my mother or I would have to stand in line for hours waiting for the water truck to arrive. I hold the towel to my battered face, feeling the cool moisture dribble down my chin.

"You're right," I break the silence.

"About what?"

"Everything. We've already seen how this game plays out on Earth. I mean about the water and the war.

People will be killed. I don't think for a second that those scientists will find a diplomatic solution. There was no diplomacy shown on that video tonight."

Clesandra nods and takes a seat next to me. "Not many people can see the big picture. Even if they can, they're not gonna rock the boat. Just take orders like drones, killing without even thinking about it."

"I don't like to think of people that way."

"Yeah, well, that's the way it is," she says bluntly.

"Not everyone."

She shakes her head. "You know I'm right."

"You're not," I spit back. She goes quiet for a moment. "Look, you're right about the war. Fighting to control the water isn't going to help. But people…I still have to believe people are inherently good. Some people at least. We all start out good, anyway. Just make some seriously messed-up choices." I run a hand through my hair and sigh. "I don't expect you to understand."

"Try me," she grumbles.

"Well, for starters, I just found out my father was the one who started the virus."

"That was your father?" She pauses, soaking in the information before continuing sarcastically, "Nice guy. I guess you're gonna tell me he's inherently good too?"

"Maybe…maybe not. He wasn't always—" I fumble for the right phrase.

"A murderer?" She offers.

"Right." I grope through my memory banks, trying to grab onto any good parts of him but there aren't many memories. "When my brother and I were younger, seven or eight years old, we didn't see our father much. He worked a lot. Spent a lot of time in a science lab and took long trips overseas because of his work. Sometimes we wouldn't see him for months. It would kill my mother. But when he did come home it was usually the greatest reunion ever…usually…"

A gruesome memory tries to take the place of the one I'm telling her, but I squash it down.

"Mom would make a big fancy dinner. We'd eat more on his first day back than we would in three normal days. Dad would tell amazing stories about the places he'd been and the things he'd seen. Sometimes he would bring us exotic toys and trinkets. He talked about how he was developing diplomatic ties with other countries and experimenting with technology that was going to stop the water from disappearing and seed the clouds. It was exciting. I used to beg to go with him." I huff out a breath and look at the bloody towel in my hands. I actually wanted to go with him and not because I felt like I had to help protect Jeremy. "Anyway, he would hug us and promise we would soon. He was so confident and it sounded perfect. You don't know any better when you're little, I guess. A few years later the war started. I still don't really know which countries threw the first punch. I just know it got bad fast. Our military base went on full alert. Recruitment numbers rose. Dad helped create some radar systems and bio weapons to help deter other countries from attacking us. They worked so well that he was approached by the weapons department. That's really when he changed. He was suddenly less interested in finding a permanent solution and more interested in making sure our military base took full control of what was left of the water. He said it was diplomatic, but everyone on base speculated differently. Too many people weren't coming home. People on base were afraid of him. He became commander and started doing everything by force."

"By murder," Clesandra says.

I look at the bloody washcloth in my hands again.

"I'm not going to lie. I watched him force people to do things they didn't want to do. And I watched him kill— murder—too many people. He became a major general in command almost overnight. Said his new position would help end the war, but it only made it worse. It made him worse. But I can't help but wonder what he would have been like if there wasn't a war. Maybe he would have eventually found a solution." *Maybe Jeremy would still be alive.*

The image of Jeremy's bloody body hitting the sand after being shot swirls before me. I press the wet washcloth to my broken nose a little harder and wince at the pain. It does the trick and Jeremy disappears for a moment. "But my brothers, the rest of my family, we're not like him. We're not going to make the same choices or do the same things."

She scoffs. "You say that, but you soldiers are all the same in the end."

"Why is it so hard for you to believe that there can actually be good soldiers?"

"Because soldiers like you, like your father, killed my family," she says angrily and looks down at the palms of her hands. I take the wet cloth away from my face so I can see her better. Her wall of anger and sarcasm is faltering slightly. I want to know what memories, images she's trying to suppress right now.

It's a few moments before she continues. "The military, soldiers, they're supposed to be the good guys. They're supposed to protect us." Her voice wavers. "But they killed my family one by one. It was my fault too." She stares blankly at the wall across the room.

This is the first time I've seen an emotion other than anger or frustration. I don't know what to do. Anger I can deal with. Violence, I'm no stranger to it. But sadness is not something I do well. I try to think about what my mother would have done in this situation. What Caileen would do? I reach a hand over to touch her shoulder, but think better of it and drop it back into my lap. One broken bone is enough for the night.

"I'm sure it wasn't your fault."

"It was," she snaps.

"How?" I prod.

She looks up at the ceiling and then glares at me. "What do you care anyway?"

"Look, I cared enough to get a broken nose tonight."

She flinches and swallows hard. After several moments she takes a deep breath and says, "In Nacombe, my home country, people were divided. We were poor farmers. Our wells were the only thing that kept us alive. We grew enough food to feed just us. Then the government tapped into our well source. We'd dig and dig and dig. No water. They took it from us. Not just us, but everyone that had a well. They brought in their machines. They dug huge holes. Laid pipes and stole *our* water to feed *their* city. Then they built a wall. We lived so close we could hear the water running in their street fountains!" She's angry again now. Hot, angry tears flood the corners of her eyes. I've opened a painful vein in her life that I'm suddenly not sure I want to hear about. She pauses for a moment and wills the tears away.

"My father went to fight for our water. To get it back. 'Pay,' they told him. But we had no money. He refused to leave and they shot him! I had five brothers, all younger. My mother was useless after they killed my father. The babies were so hungry and thirsty they would cry and cry and cry. Then they wouldn't cry. They would just lie still. I knew they were close to death. So my oldest brother and I decided we were gonna get water. We heard from other farmers that some climbed the wall and were sneaking into homes to get water. We waited till night and climbed the wall. We were only gonna fill our jug from the fountain. We weren't even breaking into anyone's house." Her voice wavers again.

"We got our water and left, but they got our pictures on their cameras. Government soldiers came the next night and executed us one at a time, even the babies. I survived 'cause the soldier who shot me was young. I'll never forget the fear he had in his eyes. He wasn't dead inside like the other soldiers. Said I was too pretty to shoot in the head like the rest. So he shot me in the stomach." She lifts a corner of her shirt, revealing a massive, jagged scar that crosses her abdomen. He left me to bleed to death.

"The farmers down the street heard me cryin' and took me in. They fixed me up and taught me to fight. Night after night, I would join in their riots for water. So many people died. We started to plant bombs and blow up pieces of the city wall to get the water. Not soon after that I woke up in this place with no idea how I got here." She wipes her face with the back of her hand, not willing to look at me. "It's my fault my family was killed."

This time I do reach over to touch her. I find her hand again and squeeze it gently.

"Your family would have died without you. Anyone would have done the same thing."

"My family died anyway. I wish I would've died with 'em." She pulls her hand away. Her expression grows cold again, staring at nothing but the blackness of the room around her. We sit in silence for what seems like forever.

"You want to know what the worst part is?" she asks.

"No, but tell me anyway."

"There will always be a war. In the end, we'll all go to war. Ain't gonna matter who you are. When you're dying, or your family is dying, you'll do anything, even if that means killing someone. Sometimes I think it'd be better to be dead than participate. It's more humane at least." She finds my eyes in the darkness. "Smith's right. We're not goin' down without a fight."

I spend a long time thinking about her words before I respond.

"In Asik, there was a phrase people used to say all the time: Water is—"

"Life." Clesandra fills in the blank before I have a chance to finish.

"Yes," I say sarcastically. "Here's the thing…the handful of top government leaders don't actually have to *fight* the war. They just have to *sell* it. They sell it to people with catchy phrases and slogans. They post pictures like the one we saw tonight of what the ideal life should look like. And then they show videos of all the horrible things going on. Before you know it, civilians are bending over backward to join the military ranks because they've been brainwashed to think that war, oppression, and exploitation are in our best interests. My own father convinced himself that war was the only option. Before we even knew what was going on, he was designing bombs and buying other countries aid by giving them weapons that were ultimately used to destroy each other."

"What's your point?" Clesandra says.

"My point is that weapons are harmless without people willing to use them."

"Were you and I at the same brief? 'Cause I'm pretty sure I heard people cheering wildly for a fight." She scoffs.

"People are still divided. I heard just as many unsettled voices when you were yelling at that other guy."

"Rustin," she says through gritted teeth. "He's a trigger-happy, brain-dead, idiot."

I nod in agreement. "Look, the only person who can make you pick up a gun is you."

Clesandra shakes her head. "You ain't getting it," she says angrily, poking me in the side of the head. I swat her hand away.

"What *ain't* I getting?" I mock her angrily.

She scoots closer so her face is inches from mine. In a low voice, she whispers, "Look, Sleeping Beauty, you're a pretty boy with some real nice theories. But I'll tell you from experience that your little play-it-nice theory goes right out the window when you've got a gun pointed at your head. You should know. You were in the simulation room with me when Smith tried to kill us. I sure as hell didn't see you sitting in the grass saying, 'Here, kitty, kitty, I'm not gonna fight and letting those creatures eat you. No! You got your ass up a tree and helped me kill those bastards. How's it gonna be any different when Smith says he's gonna kill your brother if you don't fight?"

I know she's right. Jace is the only family I have left, and him dying is not an option. I say the only thing that comes to mind.

"I guess I'll think of something when the time comes. Maybe we should just kill Smith."

Her eyes grow huge, and in a flash, Clesandra tackles me flat on the bed. She throws her hands over my mouth, creating a sound-tight barrier and whispers in my ear, "Let me tell you something…you. Me. We're not the only ones who want him dea—"

She pauses, unable to finish the word. "But you don't say that crap out loud. I don't know how he knows or how he hears, but he does. Most conversations he keeps out of, but mark my words, if he heard you, you'd be in trouble. So keep your damn mouth shut!" With eyes of fury still burning holes into mine, she slowly lifts her weight off and takes her hands from my mouth.

"Keep *my* mouth shut?" I whisper angrily. "Keep *my* mouth shut! I'm not the one jumping out of chairs and yelling across a room full of people. You should learn to keep *your* mouth shut!"

"It needed to be said!" She gets up from the bed and starts to pace the dark room. "All the soldiers are gonna do is destroy lives. Take things. Kill people. I've seen it! I've lived it! I've played both sides of the coin, and none of 'em are nice, kind, humane, diplomatic…whatever ya want to call it." She's furious now. Her beautiful face contorted with pain. "Besides, unlike you, I can say whatever I want! And I'm not gonna pretend this situation is just peachy keen! Do it for me, you bastards, come kill me! Get it over with!" she screams at the ceiling and walls. "I know you can hear me!"

"Oh yeah?" I yell back. "How come you get to say whatever you want?"

She looks at me like I'm a complete idiot. "Because, unlike you, I'm alone. My family is dead. My home is gone. I don't got anything left to lose."

Stunned, and not sure what to say, I just look at her. This is the most conversation that I've had with Clesandra, even if it has devolved into a screaming match. I can't seem to sort through all of my emotions and thoughts fast enough. I want to tell her she's not alone. That there are still good people. That she can share her anger and frustration with me instead of bearing the burden on her own. But the words in my head don't make sense as I try to say them out loud. I slowly get up from the bed.

"Nothing to say now, huh?" she says. "Go on then, get out!" Her chest is heaving.

But I don't leave. I close the distance between the two of us and throw my arms around her in a hug. Her hands are still at her sides, and I feel her go rigid. She starts to struggle to get away, but I tighten my grip. I know that if she really fought me she could free herself. I also know enough about her now that she won't. Not tonight, at least. The tension never leaves her body. Her hands are clenched at her sides, but she lowers her face into my shoulder and stays there. I balance my chin on the top of her head.

Finally, I hear a muffled voice say, "Lemme go or I'll kick your ass."

I don't want to. I didn't realize how much I missed human contact. There's a hollow spot where my heart used to be that aches thinking of home, thinking about my mother and sister, my dead brother. Clesandra, for the briefest of moments, fills that void, gives me a reason to be here, to live. I don't want to lose that.

I have to force myself to lift my head from hers and slowly let go. I hold her arms tight at a distance and feel the muscles knotted beneath my fingertips. She lifts her head, and for a moment, we look at each other. I wonder if she feels the same electric energy that I do when I look at her. I've never experienced a feeling like this before. I don't know what to make of it. I want more but resist the urge to pull her back in. I let my hands fall to my sides. Embarrassed, I look at my feet.

"I should probably go." I make a move toward the door, and then spin back around. "Do me a favor though," I say. "Keep your mouth shut around Smith and the other soldiers. You may feel like you have nothing to lose, but now…" I pause to find her eyes in the dark room. "*I* have more than ever to lose." Then I turn on my heel and stride out of the room.

Chapter 10

"Wake up, Avery!" The voice seems unnatural and far away. There's an edge of urgency in it that makes my eyes snap open immediately. Jace is standing over me, shaking my shoulders. The shaking makes colorful spots pop and sizzle across my eyes. The pain from my broken nose almost takes my breath away.

"Stop, stop! I'm awake," I groan.

"What happened to you? Are you okay?" Jace's face is filled with concern.

"Would you stop all the shouting? It's not time to get up yet. The alarm hasn't even gone off," Sheol's muffled voice comes angrily from beneath his blankets on the bunk opposite mine.

"Get up, Sheol! Avery's hurt!" Jace's voice is piercingly high pitched and hurts my ears. Sheol groans and throws off his blankets to look at me.

"I'm okay," I tell them.

Sheol is unconvinced, which means my face probably looks about as bad as it feels. "I'm going to kill that girl." He thumps over to my bed to get a better look. "Jesus! I knew I should've gone looking for you last night," he curses.

"I'm fine. Really, it's no big deal. I didn't want to wake you guys last night when I came in." I push Jace away and trudge into the bathroom to get a look at my face. "Oh, wow," I groan. Hideous shades of black and purple cross the bridge of my nose and extend underneath my eyes. I touch my cheeks gently and wince at the pain.

"What did you guys do last night anyway?" Sheol asks.

I don't know why, but I feel myself get instantly defensive. "We talked mostly."

"Yeah? Just talking doesn't get you a broken nose," Sheol continues to grill me. "If I were you, I'd stay away from that crazy nut-job." He's standing next to me now while I examine my face in the mirror.

"She's not crazy," I say defensively.

"Well, she sure could be a little nicer," Jace pipes up from the other room. "She's mad a lot."

I roll my eyes even though I know Jace can't see me from where he's standing.

"Shouldn't we all be a little angry with this whole situation?" I whisper, as I poke the puffiness under my left eye.

"Why are you defending her?" Sheol is staring at my reflection with a mixture of confusion and annoyance.

I turn to look at him. "I'm not defending her. I'm just saying, maybe you should give her a chance. Get to know what's behind the anger before you judge."

A look of realization then repulsion crosses Sheol's face.

"Oh, Christ, don't tell me you actually *like* this girl?"

Maybe I do.

I feel my cheeks flush red with embarrassment. Trying to hide it, I go back to poking my face in the mirror. The pain that erupts beneath my fingertips does the trick. Unfortunately, Sheol has already reached his conclusion. He's about to say something else when the landing announcement blares over the intercom. Directions are blurted out too quickly for me to comprehend. Maybe Clesandra gave me a concussion too.

Sheol has disappeared from the bathroom. I trudge

out to see Jace and Sheol have nearly packaged what few belongings they have and are in the process of rolling their bedding into neat, little tubes.

"Did I miss something?"

"Apparently, falling in love with a crazy person has melted what's left of your brain," Sheol says through gritted teeth and ties his bed sheets extra tight into a poster-sized tube. "We're landing." Without saying anything else, he moves on to my sheets.

"I can get them!"

Sheol ignores me and keeps working. Jace has finished packing his belongings and is staring at me with a confused expression on his little face.

"Avery loves who?"

I force myself to smile at him. "Don't worry about it. It's not what you think." I spit the last few words in Sheol's direction. *But Sheol's right. I do like her. Not that this is even remotely a good time to be attracted to someone. Nothing says great first date like going to war. Clesandra's not the crazy one. I am.*

"You should probably get dressed," Jace says to me. His words take me by surprise. I feel like I'm looking at a tiny adult. When did Jace get to the point where he didn't have to be coaxed into his clothing in the morning? Where he makes his bed without question? He's dressed in his uniform with his bedding rolled up and tied. It's looser than Sheol's and a bit sloppy, but for a twelve-year-old, it's great. I look at him for a long moment. He looks like a little soldier. He looks like Jeremy…no, he looks like Dad. Shaking the image from my mind, I go back to the bathroom to get dressed. I don't want to think of my only remaining family member as a trained killer or a brainwashed drone.

When I emerge from the bathroom again, Sheol and Jace are ready to go.

"Come on." Sheol lobs my tightly wrapped bedding at my head. I catch it and we exit the room together.

The next place we stop is the hospital ward. Lupète is there with a room full of soldiers waiting in a line. The three of us join them. Trying not to be obvious about it, I scan the room for Clesandra. I don't see her. The only other face I recognize is Rustin's, the soldier from last night's briefing. He's five or six people in front of me. When he sees me enter, he pulls himself out of line and struts over to us. His back and shoulders are so muscular that his arms barely touch his sides.

"Nice face. Your girlfriend do that to you?" he sneers. Rustin is so tall I have to crane my neck back to see his face.

"Better be careful, thunder, or I'll do it to you too," Clesandra says. She appears out of nowhere and stands next to me.

Rustin's lips curl back in a hideous grin. He opens his arms, inviting her to try.

"Soldier 88, Rustin Glowerbak. You're next." Lupète's voice breaks the tension.

"Rain check, sweetheart?" Rustin raises his eyebrows at Clesandra. When she doesn't respond, he turns and slowly struts over to Lupète.

"I don't like him," Jace tells Sheol.

"No one likes that dumb oaf," Clesandra says sarcastically. Jace chuckles at her response and she smiles awkwardly at him. I wonder if Jace reminds her of one of her younger brothers. Sheol gives her an icy stare when Jace begins to rattle on about something he did last night while we were in the army brief. I elbow Sheol in the ribs to break his stare.

"Pay attention," I tell him more for myself than for him.

"Ow, jeez!" he grunts. "What the hell?"

"For God's sake, help *me* pay attention, would you?" I hiss.

He follows my gaze from Clesandra back to me. "Oh." He rolls his eyes. My eyes wander back to Clesandra. This time I feel the elbow jab in my ribs.

"Stop looking at her. You'll go blind if she decides to punch you again," he tells me.

"Avery Evericon," Lupète calls. I look at Sheol. Secretly I was hoping that he or Jace would be called first so I could pay closer attention to what was going on instead of being utterly distracted by Clesandra's presence.

I warily approach Lupète, careful not to look him in the eye. He takes my arm and inserts a small rod into a gap in my metal wristband. A blue holographic image pops up. Engrossed in the content and numbers that appear on the screen, Lupète expertly scrolls through and manipulates what I assume is necessary data.

His brow is knotted and furrowed in thought. He's frowning too. What the screen is telling him is a mystery to me, but I don't like the fact that the information is making him scowl. It takes him seconds to complete the task and he pulls out the rod. The screen evaporates like it was never there.

You are a curious creature.

I feel an uncomfortable pressure against my temples as he forces his words into my head.

"What?" I meet his gold eyes. His eyebrows are still furrowed in thought. "How are you doing that?" I can't keep the nervousness out of my tone. "What are you?"

He smiles. *Interesting...*

"Stop it," I growl, pulling my arm away, and rubbing my temples to stop the throbbing. We consider each other for a moment. Lupète narrows his eyes, regarding me thoughtfully.

"What…who are you?" I ask again.

You are different. Just what are your intentions? Lupète ponders in my head, ignoring my question.

I raise my eyebrows. "My intentions?"

Not so loud, Lupète warns. *It's not our goal to hurt you…anymore.*

"What? Anymore?" I whisper.

Do you think you would really be allergic to all the inoculations? You are very difficult to read. I had to make sure you won't endanger the commander and his mission.

"What the *hell* are you talking about?" I say very quietly and deliberately.

Lupète does a quick scan of the room. Some of the soldiers are becoming impatient. Others in line are watching our interaction curiously.

Lupète takes a lavender-colored pill from his coat pocket and holds it out to me. *Take the pill out of my hand. It's just a sugar pill, but it'll distract the others and make them think I'm doing medically relevant things to you. They look a little antsy,* he says in my head.

I cast sideways glances at some of the soldiers. Lupète is right. More than a few of them are eyeing us suspiciously. One man standing behind Sheol has his arms folded across his chest, tapping his foot impatiently.

"How do I know it's not poison?"

You don't. And we're wasting time.

"Take the damn medicine and let's get on with it," someone mutters from somewhere in the line.

Slowly I take the pill from his hand. He inserts another rod into my wristband and pretends to read information.

Look, I need to know what your true intentions

are, Lupète says in my mind. *I can't seem to get a good read on you. Everyone else here…they have pretty solid goals and devotions. You and Willows…a few others…are in constant flux. I need to know that you'll follow the commander's orders.*

"Or what?" I'm suddenly defensive.

Lupète cocks his head to one side and draws in a sharp breath while he glances quickly into my eyes, then back at the screen in front of him. I feel a sharp jolt of energy run the length of my spine up to my head.

"You're trying to read my mind, aren't you?" Startled, I start to get up.

Lupète's hand on my wrist suddenly becomes vice-like, holding me in place. There's so much strength in otherwise gentle hands.

You don't want to do that?

"Do what?"

Try and go for help? Who would believe you?

"You *are* reading my mind," I whisper in shocked awe.

"Everything all right?" Sheol asks, edging in a little closer.

"Perfectly fine," Lupète says with a smile. "It'll just be a few more minutes. Sometimes this technology can be a little tricky." Lupète squints at my wristband a little more thoughtfully and twists my arm around to get a different angle on the device.

I'm not reading your mind, only your future intent. I can see everyone's future…mostly, Lupète continues.

"And?" I ask even though I'm not sure I want to know what my future is. His expression and tone don't make the future sound promising.

I'm not sure. Smith wants a straight answer, but you are not as solid as the others. What you decide from minute to minute changes the large picture of what I see, not just for the commander and his mission, for the planet.

"There it is…" Lupète says for the benefit of the soldiers standing in line. He continues to pretend to be enthralled with what's on the screen. I glance around the room quickly. If my choices change Smith's mission that could be cause for concern. Good. Maybe he should be concerned. Who else's future might be in flux?

Most of the soldiers are making small talk with each other while they wait for Lupète to finish with me. Jace is still talking Clesandra's ear off. Sheol has his arms crossed and is scowling at the two of them.

Soldier Willows…her future is the same way. Annoyingly fickle. I do know that the two of you are somehow linked.

"Can you do the same thing…you know, speak in her head?"

Interestingly, no. You are the only one I can speak with. Not even your brother. I've tried. Now, his tone turns very serious, *I'd like you to tell me that you will do as Smith commands."*

"Why? What's Smith's future?"

Lupète stops reading the screen to look at me. He cocks his head slightly.

Perhaps it would interest you more to know what Jace's future is if you don't do as the commander insists?

I feel the skin on the back of my neck crawl. He doesn't have to say anymore. I already know what the commander's intentions are.

"Yes," I say through clenched teeth. "I will do as I'm told."

Lupète frowns, and I can't help but wonder if he meant to threaten my brother, or if his question was a serious one. He's been nothing but pleasant to Jace, and Sheol doesn't seem to see him as a threat.

Regardless, Lupète is clearly working for Smith. He can't be trusted.

"Good. That's what I needed to know." He's still frowning but continues, "You're all set." The holographic screen blinks off and I feel the pressure in my head dissipate, leaving me with an extremely dizzy feeling that's quickly replaced by throbbing.

He calls Sheol Culchanter before I have a chance to ask more questions. As if I could form words anyway. My brain feels like Swiss cheese. It's as if all the thoughts and memories I ever thought I knew were put into a blender on high speed.

In an attempt to reverse the process and mold all the blended bits of thoughts and memories back together, I find the closest wall to lean against and close my eyes. I press the side of my head to the cool hardness of the wall.

"You all right?" Sheol asks.

My eyes flutter open to find his face filled with concern.

"Yeah, yeah. I'm fine," I lie. Jace and Clesandra join us a few seconds later. "Guess I just didn't get enough sleep."

"Come on, Sleeping Beauty." Clesandra scowls. "If you get any more sleep, you'll be dead." Jace bounces after her as she leads the way out of the hospital wing and down the corridor the other soldiers were exiting.

"Where are we going?" I ask Sheol.

"Flight dock, where else would we be going?" He looks at me like I'm brain dead. I try to shrug it off. I know this is something I should be aware of. But, working with Clesandra to get caught up only covered the really important stuff like hand-to-hand combat and how to throw a fifty-pound weight. Even after her training, my face is proof that I still don't know how to block a punch properly.

We arrive at the flight dock a few minutes later and are greeted by a group of soldiers who usher us in six at a time. Jace, Sheol, Clesandra, I, and two other soldiers find ourselves in a small shuttle to take us directly into Panacea's atmosphere.

The pilot at the front smiles and gestures for us to take seats, except the seats aren't really seats. More like cushions that you stand against. We each take a cushion, and a flight attendant comes down the line and straps us in so tightly we can barely breathe. He pounds my harness in the chest, and my lungs practically collapse.

"Tight enough for you?" he asks.

"I can't breathe!" I tell him.

"If you're talkin', you're breathin'. Enjoy the ride, folks!" he yells, steps out of the shuttle and gives the pilot a thumbs-up. A door to the main ship slides in front of his face. My stomach and every bit of my skin practically plummet to my toes. Jace is screaming his head off next to me. It takes me a minute to realize that his screams are not of terror.

I try to turn my head to look at him, but it's stuck to the wall from the force, and it feels like my skin is melting. Liquid slides out of the corners of my eyes, pulled backward. Sheol is across from me. He has his eyes shut and is turning a putrid shade of green. Clesandra is strapped in next to him, and she's looking at Jace and smiling. For the first time I see a real smile from her. Pure joy painted across her face while she listens to Jace enjoying every minute of the ride. The other two soldiers look just as green as Sheol. One of them is even starting to wretch a little.

"Yee-haw!" the pilot screams from the front of the ship. "It ain't a real party till someone loses their lunch!"

He takes the shuttle into a straight-down nosedive and corkscrews left. That's enough for both Sheol and one of the other soldiers to hurl. Chunks of vomit spray out of their mouths and get sucked right back onto their faces and clothing. Clesandra's joyful look turns to one of horror at the sight of the vomit. Jace is laughing his head off next to me. I feel the contents of my own stomach catch in my throat as the acrid smells of vomit, sweat, and fear fill the small shuttle. All I can do is shut my eyes and hope we land soon.

Just when I'm sure we're plummeting to our deaths and the pilot has lost control of the ship, the aircraft levels out and starts to slow. Finally, I gain some mobility in my head and neck instead of having it stuck to the wall cushion.

"You boys ready for this?" the pilot asks.

"Yeah!" Jace yells excitedly.

One of the soldiers covered in vomit mutters, "Christ, kill me now." He continues to wretch violently though there's nothing in his stomach to bring up.

"Ready for what?" Clesandra asks.

The pilot swivels in his seat to face us.

"This." Smiling, he reaches above his head and pushes a large, yellow button that stands out from the rest of the gray metal buttons and switches. The sides and bottom of the shuttle melt away, and we're left suspended to our seats by only our harness straps. Fear grips my ribcage, and my hands automatically fly to the front of my harness, gripping the safety straps. But I don't fall.

The pilot slaps his knees with both hands, laughing his head off at our sheer terror. "Never gets old!" he shrieks.

It takes us all a few minutes of panic to realize we're not tumbling to our doom and that our feet are still solidly planted on the hard surface of the shuttle frame. Everything around us is transparent. It's like we're hovering above a vast expanse of trees in a huge clear bubble.

"Ooooooohhhh wow!" Jace exclaims.

"There's no sand," I hear Clesandra whisper to herself. The view is breathtaking. We soar over an undulating sea of green treetops that all have a slight tint of purple and blue from the planet's atmosphere. It's like Earth during sunset, except brighter.

"It's something, isn't it?" the pilot remarks.

"How come you made the shuttle disappear?" asks one of the young soldiers sitting next to Sheol. He's covered in his own vomit and still clutching the straps of his harness as if at any moment he might really plunge into the trees.

The pilot looks at him annoyed. "It didn't disappear. You're still in it. I made it invisible so that the natives won't get any ideas about following this one to Xinorsus."

"Xinorsus?" I ask.

"It's the name of our military base on Panacea. You'll see it in a few minutes. Roughly translated, it's supposed to mean, *New Beginning*. The damn natives like to kill us and take prisoners, though, so it might not be such a great new beginning for you guys. Let me know what the place is like if you're still alive next time we see each other."

The aircraft shudders and quakes as it bounces through clouds and air currents.

"So the natives can't see us at all?" I ask.

"Not unless you decide to jump out waving a flag to let them know you're here," the pilot yells over his shoulder. "But I wouldn't be surprised if they know we're here anyway. A group of them always hangs pretty close to the base. We send soldiers out periodically to run them off."

"Comforting," Sheol says sarcastically.

"Don't worry too much, though. Our team on the ground is armed and waiting for you. They won't let anything happen to you guys. Hey, look! There it is, folks!"

An enormous pyramid-shaped building emerges in a pocket of open valley surrounded by dense forest. If you weren't flying over the area, you would be hard-pressed to find it from the ground. The structure is incredibly impressive from the sky and far more complex than I imagined.

"Yep, she's a beauty all right," the pilot says, reading our looks of awe and amazement. He's right. The construction and engineering of this military base is profound even from the outside. It reminds me of pictures I've seen of Earth's Great Pyramid of Giza. The sloping sides of this structure converge into sizable columns of alternating green plateaus and transparent glass. A tall spire made of what I assume is some sort of metal reaches well above the pyramid. The ground is organized with a fleet of military-looking vehicles and aircrafts. Some of them are similar to ones we had in Asik. Others look completely foreign.

As we approach the end of the building, a long, glass-like tube stretches out from the base to an elongated strip of packed earth that must serve as a runway.

The pilot lets the shuttle hover in midair above the structure so we can get a good look at it.

"It's just like Lupète said it would be!" Jace exclaims.

"Really?" I ask. He didn't tell me anything about it at all. I guess he had more important things on his mind for me. I glance at Clesandra next to Sheol. How is it possible that one person can become the center of your universe in an instant? I quickly look back at Jace before she has a chance to notice me studying her.

"What did he tell you about it?" I ask Jace.

"Well, he told me…all about it. Everything we need to live is in there. Fields to grow crops—the fields are those green columns on the sides." He reaches out a hand to point. "And those spaces in-between are solar panels, but they're the cool kind you can see through if you're on the inside. And, oh…that spike-looking thing at the top—that's for water. Water comes up from the ground and shoots straight out of that thing and sprays all over the sides of the building to water the plants. You can't see it, but there's a water catcher thing that collects all the extra water and brings it back inside for drinking. We won't have to wait for trucks anymore. Isn't that great?"

"It sounds great," I lie. Jace obviously hasn't been told there's a water shortage.

"Hold onto your seats, folks. We're about to land," the pilot announces.

The pilot drops the plane into a vertical nosedive, heading right for the glass tube at the bottom of the pyramid. It's somehow even more nauseating to *see* the clouds and trees whiz by than to be surrounded by a gray wall of metal and not see anything. The pilot slams on the breaks, levels the shuttle, and glides gracefully into the tunnel effortlessly.

"Please keep your arms, hands, and feet inside until the ride has come to a complete stop." The pilot mocks. The ship shudders to a stop, and the high-pitched whir of the engines gradually fades. The shuttle returns to its previous metal shell, and I let out the breath I was holding. Jace has a goofy grin on his face.

"What?" I ask.

"Sheol puked." He laughs.

"Ha-ha. Very funny. Laugh it up, chuckles," Sheol grumbles.

"Maybe next time you won't eat three burgers and half a pie before bedtime on a flight day," Jace retorts.

"Thanks, Mom, I'll keep that in mind next time," Sheol says sarcastically, a lopsided grin tugging the left side of his face. His grin fades when he realizes he has to get through a layer of vomit to unlock himself from the harness. He wretches again as he smears vomit off the seat buckles to unstrap himself.

"Gross," Clesandra remarks. She expertly unlocks herself and takes a step away from Sheol. The other two vomit twins are still reeling from the experience and look like they'll be sick again.

The smell of vomit is starting to turn my stomach. I fumble with the buckles, trying to escape just as the door at the back of the shuttle falls open with a rush of fresh air. A swarm of people is standing outside, waiting for our arrival. Three medical support members board the vessel and immediately start examining our wrist bracelets, rattling off information, and punching numbers on holographic palm tablets. The two sick soldiers are swept away. They try to take Sheol too, but he refuses everything except a towel to wipe the vomit off himself. We're quickly processed and escorted out.

The glass tube surrounding the shuttle is both a runway and an entrance to and from the military base. A giant metal door is closed behind our shuttle, and we're ushered toward another door at the base of the pyramid.

I follow Sheol and Jace, led by a group of heavily armed soldiers toward the pyramid. Clesandra is the last to exit the shuttle. I pause to wait for her to catch up. Sheol shakes his head and rolls his eyes.

"She has legs, she'll catch up," he mutters, but I

ignore his comment.

She's standing at the base of the shuttle door, holding her arms out awkwardly and looking back and forth between them. One of the soldiers who greeted us upon entry impatiently tries to guide her toward the pyramid. He gets a rough elbow jab to the rib that doubles him over in pain for his efforts. He completely misses the vicious glare she shoots his way.

"What's the matter?" I ask, jogging over. She doesn't answer, but she doesn't have to. I see the tattoos on her arms—incredibly intricate swirls of faint gold and emerald traveling from the tips of her index fingers all the way up her arms. They disappear underneath her shirtsleeves and emerge again at the collar of her shirt. They move up the sides of her neck, along her cheekbones, and under each eye, accentuating her already stunning features.

"Wow."

"What the hell's going on here?" she says, continuing to examine her arms. She gently traces the designs with a finger.

"It's not really that impressive," the soldier who Clesandra elbowed in the ribs croaks, trying to catch the breath she knocked out of him. "All the women that come here get them."

"Are they dangerous?" she asks, looking at her arms like she's waiting for them to burst into flames or detonate.

"No. Your elbow is more lethal," he grunts, rubbing his ribcage. "We really have to get inside. Another shuttle will be landing soon." He forces us quickly to the base of the pyramid and through the door.

As soon as we pass through the doors we are greeted by a team of scientists dressed in red uniforms.

"Welcome to Xinorsus," one of them says, and

gestures to the huge room we're standing in. An enormous silver rod at the center of the room runs from floor to ceiling. A four-foot-high Plexiglas wall protects the rod. The high ceilings gradually step inward toward the rod creating an inverse pyramid. Structurally it seems impossible that the weight of the ceiling remains intact with no support beams. The floor and walls are made of ornate stone similar to what marble looks like on Earth.

Groups of soldiers, some that I recognize from our original ship, are being guided around the room by team members dressed in crimson uniforms. The people in red are acting as tour guides, pointing things out, and reading off information from their small hand-held screens that look like our CARDDs in Asik. Instinctively, my hand goes to my pants pocket, looking for mine, but it isn't there.

"I'll be taking...111 and 117. Mr. Oliver, you will be taking..." I'm vaguely aware of being split into small groups as I take in our surroundings.

Sheol whacks me in the arm. "We're in the same group." He smiles.

"Right." I smile absentmindedly and continue looking around. A man on my right clears his throat loudly, bringing my attention back to the group. A slim, beady-eyed man hovers around us impatiently.

"My name is Mr. Oliver, but you can call me Nico," he tells us. His beady, brown eyes dart back and forth between us and the rest of the people arriving. He sighs, pushes his dark-rimmed glasses higher on his nose, and runs a hand through his disheveled hair. He looks annoyed at the appearance of our small group. I can't really say that I blame him. Jace is only a child. Sheol reeks of half-digested hamburger and bile. I look like a scrawny concentration camp victim. And Clesandra...well, Clesandra is gorgeous, even if she's still wearing an uncomfortable sneer. She's moved on from glaring at her arms to trying to pick off the tattoos with her fingernails.

"They won't come off, gorgeous," Nico tells her with a smile.

"How come you guys don't have 'em too?"

Nico shrugs. "We think the women get them for mating ritual purposes. Even if you are able to tear them off, once your skin heals they'll come back." Clesandra glares at him defiantly and goes back to picking her arms.

"Don't pick them off. I like the tattoos," Jace says quietly. "They make your eyes look super green, like Mom's."

The statement freezes Clesandra, and she stops picking. She doesn't say anything or look at Jace, even though I'm sure she knows he's watching her reaction carefully. She just slowly folds her hands behind her back.

Jace looks at his feet. "I wish Mom were here to see this place. And Caileen. They would have liked all the trees."

I move next to Jace and put a hand on his shoulder. Sheol and I exchange a look, and he raises his eyebrows at me. I know he's expecting me to say something comforting or just to agree with Jace, anything to cut the tension in the room. But I can't think of anything meaningful.

Nico glances as us, expecting someone to say something. No one does. "Moving on then?" he says uncomfortably.

Nico leads us toward the Plexiglas surrounding the metal rod. The glass is the only thing separating us from the giant pit around the rod. Like a giant mineshaft, the rod extends far into the ground below until it gets too dark to see anything.

"How deep does it go?" Sheol whispers.

"It's still going," Nico answers. "Right now I think we're at sixty thousand meters. It's a good thing you guys got here when you did. We need a lot more manpower down there." We gaze down the shaft. The only thing we can see is tiny specs of light moving around the rod.

"So where's the water? I thought we'd be able to see the water, you know, up close?" Jace asks. I can see the disappointment on his face as he strains to see farther down the shaft.

"Oh, it's down there," Nico responds. "Waaaayyyyyy down there. Don't worry, though. You'll get to see it in action when the crops on the plateaus are watered. Come on, we have lots more to see."

For the next few hours, Nico escorts us around the military complex. The building is larger than it appears from the outside. The inner pyramid where we first entered was just the beginning. Branching off from the main room is a network of vertical rooms used as living quarters. Each living quarter is a triangular-shaped room. The sloped angular side of the room is made of three-inch thick solar glass. Nico is careful to explain that the glass doubles as an energy producer and an escape route in case of danger. He explains the pressure-release-locking mechanism on the inside of the panel, and has each of us take a turn lifting them to make sure we can get out if we have to.

Beyond the solar glass, the rooms are simple, furnished with just slightly more than the basics. There are beds, a small lamp, a sofa, and a small stone table. Each room has a tiny closet-like space that serves as the bathroom, with just one toilet. There is no sink or running water like on the ship.

"Where's the sink? We had a sink on the way

here," Jace says, noticing the lack of water.

"Water is very precious like it was on Earth. We use an antibacterial powder that serves all our cleaning needs. There will be no need to waste water on things like washing your hands or bathing," Nico explains.

Jace and I exchange a glance. "I hate that powdered stuff," he grumbles.

"Me too," I agree with disgust.

"Better hope Clesandra likes the smell of bathing powder on you," Sheol whispers behind me.

"Shut up, Sheol," I mumble.

Beyond our room assignments, we're taken below ground to a network of military training rooms, a mess hall, an enormous hospital, as well as agriculture and science wings.

"Now that you've seen just about everything there is to see on the base, there's only one last thing left to do," Nico explains, bringing us back to the main entrance.

"What's that? Do we get to see the water now?" Jace asks excitedly.

"No...you get to go to the welcome ceremony. You'll see what your daily schedules and job assignments are. Follow me."

Nico leads us through the main entryway with the irrigation rod and through a large, arched doorway. It's one of the only doorways that doesn't have metal sliding doors, pressure release hatches, or security thumbprint recognition scan devices. It's just a doorway, open and inviting. We pass underneath the arch and follow a long, dark tunnel that gradually winds its way downward. Dimly lit wall lights programmed to look like flickering candles guide our way.

I feel Jace glide up closer to me.

"It's kinda spooky in here, isn't it?" I look down

and give him a comforting smile.

"It's darker down here because we don't want to waste too much of our solar energy to light the tunnels. Most of the energy is used for keeping our security systems and drilling rigs running."

"So we're going to get job assignments?" Sheol asks. "I thought we were soldiers."

"Soldiers." Nico scoffs. "Don't get too comfortable with the idea of just being a soldier, boy. You'll have other jobs too. You have to be more than just a grunt to survive here. There are too many important roles that need filled," Nico says with an edge of disgust.

"All right, I was just asking," Sheol mutters, too quietly for Nico to catch.

The tunnel seems to go on forever. Eventually we come to a fork. The right fork continues downward deeper into the earth, while the other goes upward.

Nico lead us on the upward path. The farther upward we travel, the brighter the tunnel becomes. Soon we start hearing the sound of dozens of voices talking at once. The tunnel opens into a rectangular great hall. It's enormous, made entirely out of solar glass, and situated in a pocket of forest. The design reminds me of the greenhouses we had on the military base. We tried to grow plants in them so we would have fresh food. There wasn't enough water for the plants to grow. Even though our scientists tried to create vegetation that could grow without water, it was impossible. The greenhouses became giant glass containers filled with failed experiments—dead, dried-up plants.

The day's light is quickly fading outside. What little bit of the sky that pokes out from behind the canopy of trees has changed from purples and pinks to deep, saturated shades of crimson and yellow. Sunlight filtering through the branches above the glass walls paints radiant streaks on the stone floor. Tiny ridges between glass panels begin to flicker, adding a soft, yellow glow to the room.

People are milling around the banquet hall. Hardly anyone is sitting at the long tables laid with shimmering silver plates and crystal glasses filled with clear, sparkling liquid. Instead, people are making laps around the room, talking to each other and excitedly pointing out things on the other side of the glass.

I suddenly realize that the people, like me, have never seen trees up close. We're all so used to the desert sand. Here, beautiful trees and plants of many shapes and sizes twist and turn as they grow together. Indigo vines with exquisite-looking yellow flowers inch their way up the sides of the glass. I recognize some of the trees as the hollow type Clesandra and I climbed to get away from the beasts in the simulation room. I wonder how all of these plants are able to grow when there is supposedly a shortage of water. I must be thinking out loud because Nico answers me.

"Amazing, isn't it? The plants have a unique ability to draw water directly from the ground, farther down than you would ever imagine. If you cut down any of the trees you'll notice a hollow trunk. We designed our drilling methods from the trees. We're basically plunging an enormous hollow tube as far down into the planet's surface as possible and using pressure systems that the trees and plants naturally have to bring the water to the surface. As the water level drops, the tree's hollow core grows deeper. It's how we know there's still water down there. When the trees start to die, then we'll know we're in trouble."

"What happens when there's no more water?" Jace asks. I can hear the worry in his voice.

"Oh, don't worry," Nico tells Jace. "There's

plenty of water on this planet." He winks at Sheol, Clesandra, and I.

We'll be fighting for it. I think with disgust.

"We have a good system going on here," Nico continues in a carefree tone, trying to put Jace at ease. "We've re-vamped this place to be an ultra-protected, mean, green, living machine." He smiles at his impromptu rhyme scheme.

"But what if there isn't enough?" Jace asks.

"Look, we have a great well-drilling system. We're able to recycle our water several times before it's too degraded and unsafe to drink. Heck," he waves his hand carelessly, "we were able to get three hundred people to this planet on one ship. A journey that, let me remind you, took over two years. And we did it with only a few hundred thousand gallons of water on tap. I think we'll be okay here for a while…" he says, and then adds under his breath, "though others disagree."

Jace doesn't hear the last statement. He sees Lupète arrive with the next wave of soldiers and sprints off to greet him.

I watch Lupète wrap Jace in a huge hug. The tall man glances in my direction and gives me a wink. Electric energy zings through my body. He leads Jace over to the glass panel side to point something out to the boy. I feel like I should call Jace back but choose not to make a scene and just watch him carefully.

"This place was revamped?" Sheol asks.

"Yes," Nico says. "This pyramid was already here when we arrived. It's likely the natives abandoned it when the water shortage started. They've built a large colony in the mountains where there's another water source. When we found this place, it was like finding salvation, except for the natives. They've been killing and capturing us little bits at a time ever since we started living here. People just disappear into thin air.

Poof!" He draws an imaginary wand out of his pocket and waves it at us. With an unsettled laugh, he points it at me. "Poof!" He moves on to Sheol, then swings the imaginary wand in Clesandra's direction. She gives him a point-that-thing-in-my-face-and-I'll-kill-you look

"Po—" he doesn't finish the word. Instead, he awkwardly makes the motions of snapping the wand in half and stuffing the broken pieces back into his pocket.

"Anyway, the structure was a bit more primitive when we came to it, but we were able to use what materials we brought with us to start making this place an impenetrable fortress. We added the landing area, built solar panels into the open columns, re-planted crops, and updated the well system. But most of the building was already here, including the underground tunnels. We just added a few more additions. This area that we're standing in right now was an underground escape route. We just built a room on top of the exit. Neat, huh?"

He's looking at us for approval. Clesandra and Sheol don't seem inclined to give it to him. I toss him a bone.

"Neat," I agree. I suddenly feel the hair on the back of my neck prickle up. I turn to look for Jace and Lupète and see Smith enter.

Chapter 11

"Good evening, good evening!" Smith's voice echoes off the glass panels. "If you would all please take a seat, the ceremony will begin shortly."

Everyone quickly takes a seat at the long tables, and the chattering slowly dies down.

Sheol, Clesandra, and I take seats at the far end of the room closest to a solid wall of glass. Clesandra chooses her seat on the far side of Sheol this time. When she notices the hurt look I'm trying to hide, she shoots me a nasty sneer. Sheol raises his eyebrows at us.

"It's a little soon for a lover's spat, don't you think?" he whispers sarcastically.

I roll my eyes, but can't help wracking my brain to think of what I could have done.

All of the tour guides take seats at a large table at the front of the room. They sit on the right and left sides of Smith. Once everyone has settled into their seats, the commander addresses the group.

"Welcome! And thank you for being here. Your being here represents the hope that the human race will survive." He pauses as cheers and applause erupt from the head table of scientists. People from other tables join the applause enthusiastically.

"Our survival on this planet depends on the work of everyone here today. Your guides," he acknowledges the people at the table with him, "my family," he adds with a smile, "have shown you the inner workings of this military installation. We will be depending on all of you to help run and protect it. That said, you will all be receiving what I like to call, chore schedules."

The scientists nod to each other.

"It's hard work, but in the end, each one of you will know how to operate each system on this base. Why? Because those of you who are here today may be gone tomorrow. It is important that all of us know how to operate our core systems. I'm sure you've been told that our first group of scientists, engineers, and soldiers numbered in the hundreds. After nine years, the people that you see before you are all that's left." Smith gestures to the group of scientists who served as our tour guides this morning. "They have survived because they are smart and adaptable in the face of adversity. Every one of them can run any and all of the programs needed to protect this military base. And so shall each of you, in time. Your wrist monitors will display your daily schedule each morning. You can access the schedule by pressing the blue button on the left side of the device."

Everyone looks down at their wrists and presses the button. Tiny green holographic screens appear in front of us with tomorrow's daily schedule. Next to the schedule is a little blueprint map with a yellow flashing dot. I gently touch the dot and a map fills the holographic screen. The yellow dot is right under a small grouping of white letters marked "banquet hall." The map is showing my exact location in relation to other areas of the pyramid. *Pretty cool.* I tap the map again, and it disappears, taking me back to the main screen with the schedule. I scan over it and see I'm in agriculture awareness first, followed by an enormous block of time in combat training. I glance over Sheol's shoulder.

"What you got?" I ask.

Sheol has combat training first, then a large block of time in artesian geophysics.

"What's that supposed to be?" he asks.

"No idea, but it sounds scientific."

"Yeah, that's what I'm afraid of."

I want to know what Clesandra has. Hoping our schedules run together, I try to glance around Sheol and look at her screen. It's too late. She's already closed it and is watching the front of the room with her hands clenched in her lap.

"Are there any questions?" Smith waits for everyone to finish looking at their screens. "No questions? Well then, let the celebration begin!" He raises his glass out toward the group. We all raise our glasses in the air and toast to our first day here on the new planet.

Sheol and I clink glasses and take a gulp. The instant the cold liquid touches my tongue, my eyes roll back in my head, and a brilliant flash of white light fills my eyes. A sudden wave of searing pain slams the back of my head.

"Get out of here! Run!" a voice screams in my direction. My eyes start to focus, but everything is foggy, misty, off-color somehow and excessively bright. I try to cover my face with my hands, but they're stuck behind me for some reason.

"I'll kill you!" another voice says. This voice is deeper, hovering just over my head. I think I recognize it at first, but it has a harsh, metallic grinding to it that makes it sound unnatural. Panicking, I call Sheol's name.

Something hits me hard in the face. My hands ball into fists to fight back, even though I can't get them from behind my back. Something fragile in my right hand shatters as I close my fingers around it. In an instant, an unfathomable force sweeps my body away. I suddenly can't breathe. I scream but there's no air. I'm choking! Dying! I'm tumbling head over feet out of control. Sharp things scrape and gouge me, ripping my flesh open.

I think I hear screaming and try to aim for the sound.

There's another jolt of intense pain…

"Avery!"

Sheol. I recognize his voice. I flail my body around, trying to clear the blackness. Trying to get his attention. Trying to make sense of my surroundings.

"What the hell, man!" Sheol's voice is angry. It sounds far away, like it's under water. "What the hell's the matter with you?" His voice is getting louder now. The pain in my head is beginning to fade, and slowly I blink my eyes open.

The banquet hall is silent. Everyone is staring at me. The crystal glass I was holding is shattered in a million pieces. Shards of glass are everywhere on the table, on the floor, embedded in the palms of my hands. I look down at them in disbelief. Hiding my mangled hands in my lap, the blood oozes onto my pant legs. I look at Sheol confused. Clesandra has a shocked look on her face.

"Wh- what's going on?" I ask.

"You tell me!" Sheol's brows are knitted together in a look of anger and confusion. "Christ! Look at your hands!" He gets up from the table. Awkwardly, he looks at Smith, who's eyeing me suspiciously.

"I'm…permission to take him to the hospital wing…sir…Commander…"

Smith nods. Jace is coming toward me, but Lupète stops him. I shake my head at them.

"I'm okay. I'm okay. You stay," I mouth the words to Jace.

Sheol drapes my hands in a white linen napkin and leads me toward the exit. Just before I leave, I cast an anxious look around the room. Everyone is still staring at me. Some people look puzzled. Others look annoyed. Then I catch a glimpse of Lupète as he blocks Jace from joining us. He has a look of curiosity that baffles me. I start to feel a pressure in my head again. *What did you see?*

My eyes linger on his lips. They part a little more to show bright-white teeth. *Tell me.* I start to look up toward his eyes…

"Come on!" Sheol growls. He gently, but forcefully guides me forward and we step into the darkness of the tunnel.

"You mind telling me what your little stunt back there was all about?" Sheol asks when we're out of earshot.

"I-I'm not really sure."

My head is pounding. I press my arm to my forehead. "I think I had a flashback," I say uncertainly. "Or a flash forward? Hell, I don't really know." Shaking my head, I try to clear my foggy thoughts.

Sheol is studying me.

"I wasn't myself," I tell him.

"I'll say. You damn near scared me to death. Not to mention everyone else in the room. You just went off. Screaming and flinging your arms about. You were yelling something, but it was all gibberish to me. Couldn't understand a word. Then you started smashing the glass and rubbing your hands all over the broken shards! Are you on something right now?" he asks seriously.

"No, of course not. Why would you even think that?" I don't have many friends here, or even people that I can really talk to. The last thing I need is for Sheol to think that I'm a crazy person who might be on drugs.

"I'm just asking. I mean, I watched that Lupète guy try to give you some sort of pill earlier today. How should I know you're not on drugs?"

"Hmm…good point." I forgot all about Lupète and his *sugar pill*. "Well, I'm not." I cut in front of him to make my point. "I'm not!" I practically shake my bloodied hands in his face. "Okay?"

Sheol pushes me aside. "Okay. I just had to ask. Between the pill, what happened tonight, not to mention you hanging out with that nut-job girl, I'm really starting to think you *are* crazy."

We walk in silence for a few minutes. The tunnel stretches on forever.

"So what did you see…in this vision of yours?"

"Honestly, not much." I begin to tell Sheol everything that I can remember about what I saw. When I'm finished, neither one of us speaks for a long time.

Finally Sheol says, "I would blame it on the water if I didn't drink some of it myself. Hell, everyone in the room had some of that water. Best water I ever had." He lingers for a moment, thinking about it.

"Snap out of it, Sheol."

"Right, sorry. You were the only one that went off their rocker drinking it, though."

"Stop looking at me like that. I'm not crazy," I tell him. "Hey, don't you think we should be out of the tunnel by now?" I say, trying to change the subject.

Sheol nods and touches the side of his wrist monitor to bring up the map. He frowns at it.

"What?" I ask, looking over his shoulder. "Whoa, something must be wrong with that thing." The screen is popping and spinning and flickering in and out.

Sheol jabs at it a couple of times with his finger. "It figures I would get the defective one. Turn yours on."

I press the button with the side of my chin. "Nope, mine's doing the same thing." In-between the flickering, I can see we're way off.

"How did we go this far? We've been walking a straight line the whole time, right?"

"Yeah," Sheol agrees, peering at my screen. "I don't know, man. Maybe we should turn around? I don't remember the tunnel forking off at all."

"Me either," I agree. "But then again, I'm crazy," I say sarcastically. "You can't go by anything I say."

Sheol rolls his eyes at me. "Give it a rest. I don't think you're crazy. Let's just turn around and retrace our steps."

The moment we turn, we hear a low moaning sound coming from farther down the tunnel. Both of us freeze.

"Please tell me you're hearing that too?" I ask.

Sheol nods. "What do you think it is?"

"No idea." The map is still flickering in and out, making a vicious hissing sound. "If you look…when it comes into focus, it doesn't show any tunnels where we're standing."

The sound of moaning echoes off the stone walls again. It's one of the most mournful sounds I've ever heard.

"It sounds human," says Sheol.

"It sounds like someone is hurt."

"I don't know if I want to stick around and find out what hurt them. Let's go. This place gives me the creeps."

"We can't leave now," I tell him. "They could be hurt. Dying even."

"What if whatever is making that sound isn't human?"

"We won't know unless we look."

Sheol sighs. "Great time for you to go all noble. You couldn't help me fight off monsters even if you wanted to with your hands all sliced up like that."

"Shut up." I head off in the direction of the moaning. We don't get more than a few hundred feet from where we were standing when footsteps come our way.

"We should get out of here." Sheol puts a hand on my shoulder to slow me down.

Three figures come into view. All of them are men wearing crimson uniform shirts.

"Scientists," I breathe.

"Hey! You two aren't supposed to be down here. What are you doing?" the man in the middle asks. He's got a gun pointed at us. The other men draw their weapons too.

Sheol and I throw our hands up. The bloody napkin falls away, revealing deep, oozing wounds.

"We were…we were on the way to the hospital wing." Sheol tips his head in my direction. "Cut himself at the welcome ceremony."

"This isn't the way to the hospital." The man in the middle is unconvinced. "What are you really doing down here?"

"Look at his hands." One of the other men says. They see the blood dripping down my arms and lower their weapons. Sheol sighs with relief.

"Turn around, I'll take you there myself," says the man. "You two," he addresses the other men. "Report back to your stations and wait for my return."

Without a word, the two men turn around and fade back into the shadows as if they were never there.

The muscular man in the crimson uniform leads us back down the tunnel in the direction of the banquet hall.

"What's down there?" I ask.

The man's face is stern and serious. One hand remains on his gun, though it's tucked back into his belt.

"It doesn't concern you. Don't ask again," he says roughly.

Sheol and I exchange a worried glance. Eventually we come to a slight bend in the tunnel, and I see the fork we must have missed. It isn't long before we recognize where we are and see the hospital. The man walks us to the entrance, and without a word, turns and disappears back down the tunnel.

"What was that about?" I ask.

"You got m—"

Two people in white medical robes appear. One of them is a short older woman with strawberry-blonde hair. She enthusiastically takes my hands, which are still oozing blood.

"Lacerations! Abrasions! Deep wound tracks!" She holds them up for the other doctor to see. "They might even need stitches!" She's smiling with glee at my maimed hands. The other doctor seems annoyed. He's tall, lean, and looks to be in his late forties. His reddish, golden hair is curly and wild looking. He peers at my hands unimpressed.

"You know we don't use stitches anymore, Francine." He takes one of my palms and roughly twists it backward, opening up the wound tracks wider for inspection.

"Ow!" I scream. My knees buckle almost involuntarily as I try to wrench my hands loose. His grip tightens like a python around its prey. He frowns at me.

"Oh, I'm not hurting you."

"Please let me use the stitches, Davinic!" Francine pleads. "I haven't gotten to put stitches in someone since...well, since—"

"Exactly! You've never had to put stitches in someone because we don't use them anymore."

"You could just let me put a few in and then take

them out again? No one would have to know. You wouldn't tell anyone, would you dear?" she says, flashing me a smile.

I shoot Sheol a look that's meant for him to help get me out of here, but he's doing his best not to laugh at the two of them.

Davinic shakes his head and drags me across the room by my wrists. "No, no, we'll fill these in with…what shall we fill them in with?" He dumps me in front of a table and strides to a wall of cabinets. Opening the cabinet, I see hundreds of different-sized bottles and tools. Davinic rummages through, humming to himself. He can't seem to find what he's looking for. After a few minutes of poking around the shelves, he plants both hands on the sides of the open cabinet.

"Oh, for God's sake!" he grumbles. "I know it's here! Or it was here. Nobody ever puts anything away!"

"I guess we'll just have to use good, old stitches." Francine winks at me.

Davinic turns around and gives her a look of disdain. "Join me in this century, will you?"

She makes a face at Davinic, slides up beside him, and opens the cabinet right next to the one he's grappling around in. She pulls out a large, white tube-like container that has glowing green lettering.

"Is this what you were looking for, dear?" she says, holding the container in front of his face.

Davinic sighs. "Like I said, no one ever puts anything where it belongs." He snatches the tube from her.

"Stickapath. This will do just fine. You'll have to excuse her." He carries the tube to the table and leans in close to me. "She likes to do things the old-fashioned way."

"I heard that!" Francine pouts.

Davinic winks and unscrews the lid. "Also, we don't see many patients."

"Really?" Sheol says. "I would think you get plenty of patients with the way everyone talks about the natives attacking people."

The statement seems to take the two doctors by surprise. They exchange a glance.

"If a native attacks you, there's a good chance you won't make it back here before you're dead. We don't see too many patients," he repeats, turning his attention back to the container.

The gel inside is florescent green, and a soft, white mist drifts off the surface like steam. He scoops a big, wet glob of it out and spreads it on the wounds. The gel is cool and soothing. It starts to bubble and froth and the skin on my hands gets very tight and hard. In seconds, the gel starts to fizzle off. It fuses into all the nicks and scrapes to create a hard shell. Even the deep cuts fuse together.

I look at my hands in amazement. "This stuff is great! My hands don't even hurt anymore. What is it?"

Davinic smiles at Francine, who's still pouting about not being able to put in stitches.

"It's made from a combination of ground-up plants we found here and sterile mediums that we had on Earth. All that green stuff will peel off in a day or two, but you can feel free to use your hands just like you would normally." He turns my palms around, scrutinizing his work. "How'd this happen anyway?"

"I...well, I—"

Sheol jumps in. "He broke a glass at the banquet. Mr. Klutz over here tripped and fell. He slid into the broken glass."

I nod. Thank goodness for Sheol.

Francine frowns. "You better be more careful,

otherwise next time I'll have to put stitches in for good measure."

Davinic shakes his head. "Is there anything else we can help you with tonight? How about that nose?" he asks. "You fall and hit your head too?"

"Got punched by a girl," Sheol mutters loud enough for only me to hear.

I shoot him a dirty look. "I think I'm good," I tell them.

Davinic raises his eyebrows at me. "I could fix that in a jiffy. Really, isn't there anything else?" he coaxes.

"Oh, let him do it," Francine adds. "Like he said, we don't see many people down here and it gets…boring. I mean, look at the company I have here." She gestures toward Davinic, and a playful smile dances across her lips.

"I see how it is," he says.

"Besides, if Dale escorted you down here you had to be up to no good. So give us the dirt, just for entertainment purposes, of course."

"That's true. Dale doesn't like people. He didn't do that to your nose, did he?" Davinic asks.

"No…" I look at Sheol and he shakes his head.

"I don't know," I start carefully. I can't help remembering what Clesandra said about Smith hearing every conversation. That he has some way of knowing everything. What if something I say gets us or these people in trouble? But maybe the noise should be reported.

"Spill," Francine says a little more forcefully.

"He found us in the tunnel. Guess we were in the wrong one. We heard someone in pain, moaning. Have you heard anything like that?" I ask.

The color drains out of Francine's face. Looking very stoic, she turns to Davinic. I get an uneasy feeling in the pit of my stomach, and the hair on the back of my neck stands up on end.

He places a hand on her shoulder. "Did you *see* anything?" he asks calmly.

"No," I say suspiciously. "The man who brought us to the hospital wing stopped us from going any farther."

"Well, that's good!" Davinic is smiling again. "It's good he stopped you. There are tunnels that lead to huge ventilation machines. They use so much energy and force that they can suck a person right into the spinning blades. Slice them to bits in seconds. Good thing Dale stopped you before you went any farther. We'll have to let someone know that signs need to get posted. We can't have people just wandering down there. You were lucky!"

"So lucky," Francine agrees. The color is starting to come back to her face.

"But what about that noise?" I ask. I can tell they're hiding something.

"Sound of the machines." Davinic shrugs. "Well, you two better get going. Don't want to miss the whole banquet," he says, forcing us toward the door.

"Davinic," Francine says, "the banquet will be over by now, don't you think? Maybe they should just head to their sleeping quarters?"

"You're right." He nods. "You boys be careful now."

He leads us outside and points down the tunnel. "Go straight and then follow this tunnel to the right. It'll lead you right to the main hall. You'll know where you are from there."

He quickly backs into the hospital, and the doors close automatically behind us. I'm almost certain I can hear a sharp click as if a separate locking mechanism is engaged to keep us from coming back in.

"Strange," I whisper.

"Very," Sheol echoes. "First they can't get enough of us, and then they practically push us out the door. Did you see that woman's face when you mentioned the noise?"

"Yeah, machines my ass. They know something and they don't want to share."

"Maybe they can't share." Sheol points out.

"So much for getting to know and operate every part of this building," I whisper.

"You know what? I'm okay with that. I think I'll be okay with not knowing everything. I'm pretty sure that even if I know everything there is to know about this artesian geophysics thing tomorrow, I still won't be any good at it. I don't think people should be responsible for knowing, or doing everything."

I know he's trying to change the subject, but I press on anyway. "What if someone's in trouble?"

"If someone *is* in trouble, Smith can deal with it. Maybe it's none of our business. Hell, they've got armed guards in that area. I'm sure if there was a real problem it'd be taken care of," he says convincingly. "Come on, let's go."

I glance down the tunnel, not sure if I should follow Sheol or my curiosity. Eventually I give in and reluctantly follow him. The armed men would have stopped me again anyway.

A few minutes later we're back at our room. Jace is already inside, waiting for us.

"So? What happened with you?" he bombards me.

"Nothing. It was nothing. I'm fine." I hold up my hands for his inspection. "See? I didn't even need stitches."

Jace looks at me with a hurt expression. "You don't have to treat me like I'm a little kid. I was in the same room with you. You can tell me what's going on.

I can take it." He folds his little arms across his chest in annoyance.

I look at Sheol for help, but he just shrugs. "Look, Jace, I'm not even sure what happened myself. I haven't been able to wrap my head around it completely. So really, there's nothing to tell."

The expression on his face tells me he's not buying it, but I'm in no mood to try and explain what went on in the banquet hall. I lie and tell him I'm tired and maybe I'll try to explain more in the morning. He knows it's a cop-out, but it's the best I can do right now. I even flop myself down on the lower bunk of one of the beds for good measure.

Closing my eyes tight, I hope for the sleep that refuses to come. I can hear Sheol and Jace in the background talking quietly. I'm suddenly thankful that everything in this place runs on the solar glass. The sun has long since set, and the light in the room from our lamp has diminished to a soft, yellow glow. I know that Jace and Sheol won't stay awake much longer without light in the room.

Jace scrambles up to the top bunk above mine. It's not long before his breathing becomes slow and rhythmic. When I know he's asleep, I force myself to relax and try to drift off too. I press my side against the cold wall next to me and imagine Jeremy's beside me. When I wake up we'll be home and this will all have been nothing more than a bad dream.

Tink. Click. Screech. The sound of nails being dragged down glass fills our little room. My eyes pop open and stare at the wooden slats of Jace's bunk above me. The room is completely dark save the pale-yellow glow of the lamp. My eyes take a few moments to adjust.

Screech.

The sound is coming from the side of the room

with the solar glass.

Please be a dream. Slowly, unwillingly, I turn my head toward the glass wall.

Please be nothing. Please be nothing.

Sheol is standing in front of the glass, peering outside. His hands are spread out on the glass. He slowly drags them downward, forcing his nails across the surface. A hideous squealing sound fills my ears.

"Sheol," I whisper. "What the hell are you doing?"

"Shhh," he hisses. "Watch!"

He drags his nails down the glass again. My back teeth involuntarily grind with the sound. Sheol is scanning the darkness, but nothing is happening.

"What exactly are we watching?" I whisper, creeping over to him. I'm amazed that Jace is still sleeping.

"Shhh! Just wait." He blocks me from coming right up to the glass with his arm.

Suddenly, I see it. A pair of florescent orange dots appears and floats down closer to the glass until a furry face emerges in front of us.

It's a small animal, like a house cat, with enormous orange eyes, a slender, elongated snout, and large, oval ears. Webbing between its thin, angular legs allow it to glide gently forward. Suction-cup fingers tipped with razor-sharp talons make a clicking sound against the glass. It places its forehead to the surface, peering at us. A soft down of hair covering its body emits a pulsating red glow.

"What is it?" I ask, awestruck.

"No idea." Sheol taps the glass gently. The ears of the creature rotate to the sound, but its eyes remain on us. In the distance we hear a high-pitched screech much like that of Sheol's nails on the glass. The creature whips its head in the direction of the sound, opens its mouth to reveal rows of dagger-sharp teeth, and screeches three sharp ear-piercing bursts in response. It's so loud, Sheol and I clasp our hands over our ears. I turn to look at Jace's bunk. No movement.

"Don't worry about him. The boy can sleep through anything," Sheol remarks.

The creature returns its attention to us. Its glowing fur has slowly transitioned from red to a warm yellow, and we can hear a soft humming against the glass.

"Is it…purring?" I ask.

Sheol just shrugs and reaches up to tap the glass again. Just as he is about to make contact with the surface, she appears as if from thin air—a woman, graceful and beautiful. Her pale skin is almost translucent. Ebony-colored hair flows down to her midsection, which is clothed in elaborately designed garments.

Sliding down from above us, she hangs from the ridges that separate individual solar panels. The small animal scurries up her outstretched arm to her shoulder and nestles its head against her neck. She hands it something small, which it greedily snatches and mashes into its face. It leaps from its perch on her shoulder to the glass in front of Sheol. Squishing its face against the solar panel, dark liquid spills from its mouth as it chews.

Crunch!

The woman smacks her face against the glass. Both Sheol and I leap back. Adrenaline races through my veins, and my heart feels like it's about to crash out of my chest.

"Christ," Sheol hisses, clutching his chest.

The woman has her face pressed up against the glass, flattening her nose and lips. Striking pale-blue eyes infused with silver striations flick from side to side as she scans the inside of our room. It doesn't take her long to find the two of us standing right in front of her. Without thinking, I instinctively take cover behind the couch. All the stories in our briefings and on the shuttle ride over here about the natives capturing and killing humans and then sending their remains back in pieces fuel my muscles into flight mode.

I crouch hidden behind the sofa, waiting for the inevitable. I'm certain that at any moment the glass will shatter inward, allowing hundreds of natives lurking in the forest to swarm our room and take us. I look over at Jace who is still sleeping peacefully and shake my head in disbelief. If he only knew.

"Sheol!" I whisper. No answer. "Sheol!" I whisper louder. "Don't let her see you!" As if that's an option. There's still no response from Sheol, but no broken glass, either.

Pop! Like the sound of a person snapping their fingers, followed by light tapping and screeching of the furry creature's nails on the glass.

I curse under my breath and creep forward on my stomach to peer around the corner of the couch, just enough so I can see the solar panel wall.

Sheol is standing with his face just inches from the glass. The native woman has not moved an inch. She's staring at Sheol and grinning from ear to ear. I watch as Sheol tentatively puts a hand to the glass. The woman takes her finger and places it where Sheol's palm is, and the whole glass lights up with white rays of radiant energy. Seconds later there's a dull pop, like an electric jolt of energy. Sheol whips his hand away from the glass, shaking it vigorously. He's smiling, and the little, furry creature is scurrying wildly up and down the glass, making tapping and squeaking sounds. Sheol is about to place his hand on the glass again when I leap out from behind the couch to stop him.

"What are you doing?" I yell, this time loud enough for Jace to let out an annoyed moan of interrupted slumber.

Sheol jumps backward startled and the woman disappears with her furry creature in tow.

"What the hell, man?" Sheol wheels around.

"I could say the same thing to you! You heard what the natives are capable of. That thing could have come in here and killed all of us!"

"That *thing?*" Sheol snaps. Instantly, I regret my insensitive phrasing. "That thing? No. She wouldn't have killed us." He approaches me angrily, jabbing his index finger into my chest.

"Really? What makes you so sure?" I swat his hand away.

"I'm not sure, but we know nothing about these people."

"Exactly. What we do know is they're fond of capturing humans, cutting them up, and sending their body parts back in pieces." I point out.

With a disgusted expression on his face, Sheol shakes his head. "We haven't seen any proof of that. What *we* know is what Smith and everybody else here wants us to believe." He waves his arms in a circle. "All Smith wants is control of the resources. You, of all people, should know *that.* That woman? She looks just as human as any of us. She may be different, but what I just saw was…" He pauses to find the right words. "Well, she wasn't a killer. If she's the trained killer Smith says she is, she wouldn't interact like that. She was…curious." He throws up his hands in front of me. "Besides, trained killers certainly don't turn tail and run when a scrawny piece of meat like you comes running out from behind a couch!"

"Have you lost your mind? She did something to you, didn't she…the jolt, that electricity stuff." I reach out to touch his hand.

Sheol swats my hand away and rolls his eyes. "I'm

fine. You're the one who's acting like a whack-job," he says, stalking off to his bunk. He climbs in and faces the wall away from me.

Feeling defeated, I slink back to my bunk as well. Sleep never comes. I sit up all night staring at the wall of windows and thinking about what Sheol said. About not really knowing anything about the natives. About his implication that, with so many others here, I might be completely blind to the fact that what we were told might truly be made up. My head hurts from trying to work through everything that I know. Everything that I *think* I know.

I stare into the darkness, and my mind wanders, tiptoes around the comment Sheol made about the Mizuapa woman being just as human as we are. I'm reminded of a callous statement my father made about water refugees traveling great distances to survive.

"Those *things* are leeches, parasites. If we let them keep breeding and taking our water, there will be no more water left." He dehumanized them so easily that he had no problem allowing them to die or ordering them killed.

I shut my eyes tight to block out the memory. *I'm not like my father,* I tell myself. *That thing...*the tactless phrase loops repeatedly in my head. *Not like my father. That thing! That thing! That thing!*

Chapter 12

Dawn sneaks up on me. Even though I've been staring at the wall of glass all night, I barely realize the light in the room getting brighter. The solar lamp with its warm, yellow glow has fizzled out. The air in the room is crisp and alive with the sounds of birds and creatures just beyond the walls. My arm that was being used to carefully prop my head up has gone completely numb. It feels alien to me, like it's not my own. I shake it roughly, feeling the pain of pulsating pins.

Jace is cocooned in his blankets with just the top of his head visible along with a limp foot that pokes out and hangs off the edge of the bed.

Sheol is still facing the wall, his back to me, but I can tell by his breathing that he's awake. A dull beeping sound coming from Sheol's bunk catches my attention. The same quiet sound begins in Jace's bunk and then from the wristband on my arm. It's our alarms going off. The time on the band reads four in the morning.

"Dawn comes early here," I mutter under my breath.

Sheol groans loudly and smacks his wrist against the wooden bed frame to make the beeping stop. Jace sucks his foot into the cocoon and rolls over. He throws his pillow over his head to block out the sound. I can't help but smile watching him try to figure out why the sound won't stop. Eventually, he's awake enough to realize the sound is coming from him. Complaining loudly, he finally manages to make the obnoxious noise stop. Just as soon as it does, holographic screens pop up, revealing our schedules for the day. I have one hour to make it to agriculture awareness.

Though it's obvious Sheol is still annoyed with me from last night, he's pleasant and makes small talk with Jace and me as we dress and head to the mess hall for breakfast. He knows as well as I do that good friends are hard to come by, so for the time being he's willing to put our argument behind him.

The food in the mess hall is less than spectacular. On the ship, food and drinks appeared as if from thin air. Fresh meat, whole-cooked vegetables, even fried foods. It was more than a little easy to become spoiled in such a short time.

Here there's no meat. It's more like a serve yourself buffet of bizarre-looking plant products and an enormous pot of pinkish slime. I pass on the water at the beginning of the line, not wanting a repeat performance of last night. Instead, I go for a piece of fruit that resembles what an apple would be on Earth. Jace loads his plate with a little bit of everything.

"What? I'm hungry," he responds when he sees my surprised look.

Sheol's in the same boat as I am. It's hard to go from a juicy hamburger to pink slime, but my stomach growls viciously, so I scoop a large clump of the pink stuff onto my tray anyway. It's heavy and my stomach comes into my mouth at the sight of it spreading out onto my tray. I swallow hard. Trying not to think about the food, I scan the room. Sheol sighs and pushes past me. He knows I'm looking for Clesandra. I don't see her, though, so I follow Sheol to an empty row of standard-looking cafeteria tables. I plunk down across from Jace and Sheol. Starting with the piece of fruit, I'm happy to find that it has a slightly bittersweet taste. Tolerable. *At least I won't starve.* But I'm hungry from not eating dinner last night and it doesn't take me long to finish the fruit. Wincing, I pick up a spoon and stare down at the blob of pink goo. I'm in the process of psyching myself up to take a bite when Jace reaches across the table and loads up his spoon with pink goo from my tray. He stuffs it into his mouth and grins.

"It's no cherry pie, but it tastes good!" He smiles, pink slime lining his teeth and gums.

"Eh, gross."

Sheol scrunches up his face. "You're not really going to eat that crap, are you?" he asks me.

"It's not that bad," Jace assures me. "Do it, do it, do it," he chants.

I groan, knowing he won't stop chanting until I take a bite. I look away from the disgusting stuff, pinch my nose and take a huge bite. Surprisingly, it does taste good. It's sweet and goes down easy.

"Not bad," I tell them.

I find myself shoveling the goo in my face. Breakfast is finished quickly and people start moving away from the tables, checking their wrist bracelets, and leaving the room. I check mine too, and see that my hour has gone by quickly. The three of us leave the room together and head to our respective sessions. Jace goes to interactive environments, Sheol to combat training, and me to agricultural awareness.

The tunnel to agricultural awareness training is quiet and dark. Even though the tunnel is not completely empty I still feel alone. I wish I could be a little more upbeat like Jace. He always has the ability to see the good in everything. With all the pain and suffering that surrounded our family in Asik, the lack of food and water, Jeremy's death, Dad's disappearance, the virus that spread after the bombings, he's come out of it all right.

I tick off the events on my fingers, thinking about how he reacted to each. I'm not sure he truly understood Jeremy's death. There was sadness, but he quickly came to the conclusion that Jeremy was better off. Our father leaving…he hardly knew the man anyway. Dad disappearing was a relief to all of us, even Mother who loved and stayed with the man after he lost touch with reality. The bombings? Jace took that in stride too. I remember him ignoring the sounds of the bombs and Caileen's high-pitched screaming as she huddled against Mom. The screaming continued until she was too hoarse to make a sound. Jace would quietly build towers out of canned goods on the shelves, engineering masterpiece after masterpiece. He would invent rules for games with the buildings and convince me to play while we waited for the bombings to end.

Even now, while we're on a completely different planet surrounded by strangers, without the hope of ever seeing Earth again, Jace is still happy. Riding the colossal wave of life without thinking that it could come crashing down and obliterate everything in a heartbeat.

Lost in thought, I hardly notice the tunnel ending. There are people ahead, milling around in confusion. When I get closer, I realize the tunnel has, in fact, simply ended. Just a wall of dirt and stone stands in front of us. People are muttering in confused tones and checking holographic maps.

A man next to me elbows me in the ribs. "Who wants to look at a bunch of plants anyway, right?"

I shrug in response. The man is short and stocky, with disheveled brown hair and a full red beard. He's staring at me like he's trying to figure something out. "Hey? Aren't you the kid? Aren't you the general's kid from Asik?"

I shake my head, trying to pretend I don't know what he means. He squints and looks at me crooked.

"You are! You definitely are! Hey, Marty, where are you?" he calls loudly. "I found the kid! This is the kid, right?" He hops up and down on his tiptoes, peering through the throng of people.

The thirty or so people in the small area at the end of the tunnel fall silent, and all eyes on me. I try to look away, not wanting to be the center of attention. The crowd parts to let an enormous man through. He reminds me of Rustin the way he's built. He can probably crush my neck with one of his biceps.

He's bald, and his face has a slash mark running jaggedly from his forehead, across his right eye and down to his jaw. The scar is old and white, matching the faded color of his useless right eye. He looks me up and down with his good eye. His face is stoic and his hands are balled into fists like he's ready to fight. I take a tentative step backward, bumping into the tunnel wall behind me. There's no escape route with everyone suddenly crowding around to see what Marty will do to me.

"This is him, right? The one you were talking about?" The man with the red beard insists.

"You look just like him." Marty's voice is raspy and harsh like a fifty-year smoker.

I wince at the comparison to my father. "I know," I say, lowering my gaze. "But I'm nothing like my father."

Silence surrounds our tiny space at the end of the tunnel. When Marty doesn't respond, I slowly look up at him. He's considering me with a softer expression.

"I meant that you look a lot like Jeremy."

The statement takes me off guard and I don't know how to respond.

"Your brother is a good man. We weren't able to find him on the ship. You'll take us to him today," he commands rather than asks. A murmur of accent echoes off the dirt walls.

A solid lump forms in my throat, and I can't help

the images that flash in my head as I see Jeremy brutally murdered again.

"He *was* a good man," I say solemnly.

Understanding floods Marty's good eye. He purses his lips and nods. Then he turns around, and a few people dip their heads. Marty traces the scar on his face.

"I'm sorry for your loss. He will be missed," Marty says solemnly.

"He is missed," I agree.

Seeing these people makes me realize how wide a following Jeremy had. He was making an impact. "How did you know him?" I ask.

"He showed up with a small group of soldiers demanding to be allowed on base at Kinneret."

"Kinneret," I say the name softly. "Kinneret's the military base in Israel?"

Marty nods. "The last fresh water supply in Israel. Our people built a military installation to protect and distribute the water."

Sounds a lot like home. I wonder if they had outsiders that couldn't afford water.

"Your brother showed up ranting and raving that Kinneret was a target. How the desalination plants on the coast were going to be blown to bits and then the walls surrounding Kinneret. If we didn't let them in to upload a line of code in our computer database our weapons systems would be rendered inoperable. We took the group into custody. The minute we did, the desalination plants were destroyed. We had no choice but to believe him. Without your brother, Kinneret's infrastructure would have been the next to be crippled. Israel would have been at the mercy of another country. That man helped my country...survive." He extends his hand to me, and I take it without question. A few other people step forward to introduce themselves.

How many people knew my brother? How many cities did he provide aid? How did he do it without Dad's knowledge? Dad would've killed Jeremy immediately for betraying a mission like that.

"It was an honor to know your brother," someone else says as they shake my hand. "You'll do great things here. Just like him."

Just like him? I wish I could be just like him. Help all these people. Be a leader. What have I done so far? I'm a coward. I couldn't even stop Dad from killing Jeremy. Agreed to follow Smith's orders? Things are going to change. I may not have been able to help Jeremy, but I can protect Jace.

I'm just beginning to get a scope of what happened during the war beyond the military walls of Asik as people introduce themselves, when light from above us fills the dark end of the tunnel.

A plump man with white hair and beady eyes behind round, wire-rimmed glasses pokes his head down from a hole above us. He's got a pleasant but somewhat annoyed look to his face, like we've kept him waiting.

"Good gracious! Y'all waiting for an invitation? Well, let's go. Daylight's wasting!" he shrills, and throws down a rickety-looking rope ladder.

One by one, we climb through the hole. When I get to the top, I realize a wooden trap door was what allowed the tunnel to open at the top. The rope ladder is tied to an enormous tree out in the open forest. Our group is completely exposed. I do my best not to think about natives swooping down from the trees and picking us off one by one. There are no glass walls to protect us now. Just open air surrounded by plants shimmering in the glorious sunlight, and the sounds of small animals rustling around in the leaves.

Someone in our group echoes my fears.

"Y'all should be more worried about the plants killing you than our native friends." The plump man chuckles. His stomach jiggles in time with his laughter.

A few people exchange worried glances.

"Not to worry. Not to worry!" the man assures us. "If you follow all of my directions, you will leave here today with all of your body parts and, um…no scratches, blisters, sores…you get the idea!" He smiles and waves the group forward.

"First of all, I'm Dr. Albero. I will be teaching y'all how to…" He pauses to swoop over and smack the hand of a curious woman who is reaching up to pluck a yellow flower dangling from a tree vine.

"I will be teaching y'all how to survive out here." He shakes a finger disapprovingly in her confused face. "Didn't they teach you folks anything on the flight down here?" He scolds. "The number one rule out here is: If you don't know what the plant is, don't touch it. And it goes without saying that the prettier the plant, the more dangerous it is."

He waves the group back a few feet from the flowering vine. Stooping to grab a long stick, he pokes the base of the flower gently. Black barbs spray out from the center of the flower like it's coughing up machine gun pellets. He swings the stick in front of the flower. We watch dumbfounded as the barbs lodge deep into the soft wood.

"Keep this in mind, missy." He hands the stick to the woman for examination. "This is the very beautiful, but also very deadly, Nexmors flower. It would take hours to dig those things out of your pretty, little face. That's if you survive the potentially lethal dose of poison each one of those barbs contains. Nexmors flowers are rare, and lucky for you, this is a young one. Mature ones are stunningly beautiful. They can kill in seconds. And believe me, it wouldn't be the first time I've seen it happen."

Dr. Albero waves us forward, and we follow him wordlessly as he waddles into the forest.

"Now, for today we're just going to...walk. I will point out the plants that can hurt you, maim you, kill you, along with ones you can eat."

It takes about half an hour of trudging, tripping over vines, falling over roots, getting tangled in the underbrush, and being bitten alive by thousands of insects before the awe and wonder of the beautiful forest wears off. I find myself almost daydreaming about the red desert sands back home.

Dr. Albero, for his deceiving size and weight, seems to have no trouble navigating the woods. He points out more than fifty plants dangerous enough to put us in the hospital if handled incorrectly. Some spit poison acidic enough to melt skin. Others, like the yellow flower, shoot out thorns or barbs when disturbed. Some have oils on their leaves powerful enough to produce a rash that would make smallpox look mild.

After about an hour of carefully stepping over, crawling under, and generally avoiding many plants, we're all hot and sweaty. Dr. Albero decides to take pity on our group and allows us a brief rest in a small clearing. We might be resting, but the insects continue to mercilessly eat us. They leave oozing welts the size of quarters. The only one unaffected by the bugs is Dr. Albero. He's still in a jolly mood, yammering on about this plant or that. This one you can eat. This one will eat you, all without a single bug bite.

Finally, someone brave enough to echo the group's sentiment says, "Okay, what gives? You don't have a bite on you. We're all being eaten alive."

He smiles ruthlessly. "Why didn't you ask sooner? Rule number two: Ask and ye shall receive. All you have to do is mash up some of...the..." he mutters as he walks around, gathering materials. He gets a long branch and heads for a patch of blue moss on one of the nearby trees.

Someone in the group points out that he told us originally that the blue moss is poisonous to touch and will leave horrible welts. I distinctly remember being in the simulation room with Clesandra when she practically broke my hand to keep me from touching the stuff.

"Indeed, indeed...it is poisonous to touch directly. However..." He takes the long stick and twirls the end of it in some of the blue moss on the base of a nearby tree like he's twirling spaghetti.

"If you take the moss and you...um, mash it." He takes the stick with the wad of blue moss and *thunks* it down on a huge rock. "If you mash it...into a pulp," he grunts, taking the other end of his stick and grinding the moss into the rock. "You can, er...use the oil from the moss, as bug repellent!" He quickly scoops the lump of mangled moss off the rock with the end of his stick and throws it into the woods.

A goopy, slightly chunky, oily residue remains on the rock. Dr. Albero smiles at his work.

"Well, don't be shy!" He points to the rock. "Unless you like being bitten?"

A few people cast reluctant glances at each other before stepping up to smear themselves with the oil.

"Well, if it doesn't work, the welts this blue crap is supposed to cause can't be any worse than the bug bites, eh?" Marty shoves my shoulder and makes his way to the rock. I shrug and take some of the oil myself. It goes on blue, and then fades instantly to the colors of our skin. Almost immediately the insects disappear. It's like an invisible bubble around our bodies.

"Excellent!" Dr. Albero remarks. He looks like he's about to say something else when the smile from his pudgy lips fades. He scans the treetops above our heads. The chatter of animals and insects and the prattle we were making among ourselves fades away. A hush falls over the forest clearing as if everyone is holding their breath. Even the wind seems afraid to rattle the leaves on the trees. A few people in our group take stances like they're ready for battle. I scan the treetops, looking for what Dr. Albero is waiting for.

A few tense moments go by. Then the familiar sound of small animals begins again. It's almost like an orchestra conductor signaled a stop of all music and gradually reintroduced the instrumental parts. First the gentle wind in the treetops, then the annoying sounds of insect wings beating relentlessly around our heads, but thankfully no longer on our bodies. Next, there's the shuffling of leaves in the underbrush.

Dr. Albero's attention has not shifted from the treetops.

"What is it?" I ask.

My question breaks his concentration and brings him back to reality, as if I've snapped him out of a trance. He looks up to the treetops, then quickly to his wristband.

"Well, look at the time," he says in a spritely voice, trying to hide his obvious anxiety. "I've got to be getting you folks back! Follow me!" The pudgy man takes off at a brisk trot with the rest of us in tow. A few people in the group cast sideways glances at each other before jogging to keep up with him.

It doesn't take us nearly as long to get back to Xinorsus as I thought it would. I get the feeling that we were much closer to the military base than Dr. Albero led us to believe. He probably had us traipsing around in a close arch to the building. It's hard to tell how far we really ventured. Two hundred yards into the woods and you lose sight of the pyramid-shaped building through the dense forest. I'm completely out of my comfort zone. There were no trees in Asik.

Dr. Albero quickly leads us back to the tunnel we came through earlier in the day. He ushers us down the rickety rope ladder back into the dark, chilly confines of the tunnel system, but he doesn't join us. In fact, he doesn't say a word to us before he lets the trap door slam shut above our heads.

"Jeez, what's got his knickers in a knot?" the stocky man who pointed me out to Marty remarks.

Marty nudges the short man in the arm. "Let's go, we've got hospital duty next," he says.

Marty dips his head to me. "It's nice to meet another Evericon…on good terms."

"Avery," I offer.

Marty nods to me. "I'll remember that. Again, I'm sorry for the loss of your brother. He was a great man."

I nod in accord. The three of us follow the larger group down the tunnel and back out to the main entrance of the military base. People are milling around the large spire that runs down the center of the room. Some are leaning over the safety railing to peer deep into the ground. Others are lingering, making small talk with each other as they get ready to move to their next training courses.

I don't try to hide a sweeping glance as I scan the room for Clesandra, Sheol or Jace. Any familiar face will do. Finding no one and feeling more alone than ever, I flip open my holographic map screen and head in the direction of another tunnel. I linger at the entrance. This tunnel will lead me to combat training, but I'm in no rush to get there. Combat has never been my strong suit.

As I enter the tunnel, a tall man rushes by. He bumps me as he shoulders past and tosses a curt, "sorry!" over his shoulder. The back of his bald head is strikingly shiny and a strong, fresh scent of shaving cream fills my nostril. Instantly, I'm right back in Asik.

It's the first day of military orientation and the day is stinking hot. The pungent stench of sweaty, unbathed people mixed with the sweet, fresh smell of shaving cream was unbearable. Showering was one of the first luxuries to disappear just as fast as the lakes, rivers, and streams dried into pits of rock and sand. Shimmering, rippling heat waves blurred the air, mere feet in front of me.

"Next!" a man's gruff voice called.

It's only for training. Everyone goes through training. It's not like I'm being deployed yet. Calm down! Jeremy got through it, I can get through it, I told myself. I wasn't even being deployed. Then someone grabbed my shoulders roughly. I turned around to see Jeremy. He affectionately pounded my right shoulder.

"Relax!" His voice was joking and calm in my ears. His bright blue eyes were kind. He was always the one to take care of people. Nevertheless, he couldn't will away the panic I felt standing in line with the rest of the soldiers. Only two years older than me and yet I felt like a child standing in front of him, a sixteen-year-old child! I was ready to turn and run. Not that I would get very far on legs shaking as much as the heat waves rising from the ground around us.

"Chill! They're just going to shave your head. Then it's back to space training and staring at stars for you." He swiveled my shoulders around in his hands. "Oh, and you might have to do a few push-ups to prove that these chicken wings you call arms can support your body weight," Jeremy said sarcastically, rolling his eyes, mocking the whole process of orientation and basic training. I knew he could tell by the expression on my face that I was unconvinced and unwilling to joke about it. All soldiers had to get their heads shaved and go through orientation and basic, regardless of whether or not you were going on an overseas mission, like Jeremy, or staying on the base like me. It didn't stop the whole process from terrifying me, though. Thank God Jeremy showed up for moral support. He always had a way of being right where you needed him to be.

So there we were standing in line with the rest of the soldiers being herded like cattle toward a sweaty, beefy-looking man with an electric hair trimmer. We both hated it. We hated the idea of being forced to fight people who were just trying to survive. I hated not being able to find a way to fix the water crisis without fighting. I hated that our father was making us do this, or making Jeremy at least. I even hated Jeremy a little bit for not trying harder to get into space academy with me. I didn't want him to go away with Dad. The thought of someone else watching his back instead of me was terrifying. What if he didn't come home? Would he be the same person after being deployed? War changes a person. Killing someone definitely changes a person and I couldn't picture Jeremy killing someone in cold blood. I didn't want him to have to live with that. I didn't want *anyone* to have to live with that.

"I should be going with you," I told him.

"No, kid. You're right where you need to be. Plus, since you're in the space program, you get to see Mom, Jace, and Caileen almost every day. Even get to sleep at home and not in those crummy barracks."

"I wish you were staying too. You shouldn't have to go," I told him.

He shrugged. "Someone's got to. Besides, someone has to find you some water to bathe in. You're starting to stink! Good thing you're getting shaved down. All this…" He raked his hand roughly through my dark hair, making it stand straight up from the sweat and filth. "I'm tellin' ya. It ain't workin'."

"What're you grinnin' at, Sleeping Beauty?" Clesandra's harsh voice interrupts my memories. The slight tug of a grin creeping at the corner of my mouth remembering Jeremy's banter disappears as quickly as the memory. Clesandra is glowering at me with her hands on her hips. We're standing at the entryway of a huge arena-style gym, where mountains of complex-looking equipment and contraptions fill the space. I don't even remember walking all the way down the tunnel while I was thinking about Asik and Jeremy. My feet must have convinced the rest of my body where to go while my mind was preoccupied.

"Well?" she prods.

I run my fingers easily through my thick hair. Two years of cryo-sleep has allowed it to grow back thick and strong, like it was never shaved in the first place.

"Guess I'm just happy to see you." This isn't a lie. I'm grateful for company, and hers is always a welcome surprise.

She rolls her eyes and shakes her head. Sighing deeply, she grips my elbow with her vice-like hand and wheels me forward into the room. A group of about twenty or so people is already gathering to one side of the room by the corner of an enormous rock wall. I can hear wild laughter and a soft clunking sound coming from the crowd. We melt into the back of the group and slowly work our way closer to the front.

"Leave it alone!" a voice bursts out.

Clunk!

"Oww! I said leave it alone!" the voice yells again.

"Get out of the way, kid. It's just some dumb rat!" a voice jeers.

I recognize the voice instantly as Rustin's.

When we break through to the front, we get a clear view of Rustin. His massive arm swung back behind his head, ready to throw a large rock that's in his hand.

A gangly, pale, teenage boy with fiery-red hair is crouched, arms extended wide, in front of a limp lump of fur on the ground. The boy is no more than a few years older than Jace. The white, long-sleeved shirt under his camouflage uniform is spattered red, and a small smattering of blood coats the ground in front of his feet. The creature is making a soft-labored squeaking sound. I recognize the animal as the same type of creature that visited our window last night. However, this one has a deep reddish-brown fur with streaks of white and yellow.

"Get out of the way or you're gonna get hit!" Rustin warns. He cranks his arm back a little further.

The boy drops lower in his stance to defend the animal.

"Just throw it. He'll move," a man near Rustin says.

A wicked smile spreads across Rustin's face. "Last warning, kid. Move!"

The boy's lips curl back like an angry dog showing his teeth.

Rustin glances over his shoulder at the crowd of people gathered around him. It's shocking to me, but the mob is enthusiastic and encouraging, egging Rustin on even if throwing the rock means cracking the kid in the face to get at the helpless animal. One man in particular stands out. He's wearing a faded blue baseball hat, though I don't know what team. Sports were not a huge focus during the war.

"Curveball. Throw a tight curveball," the man

with the cap jeers.

"Shut up with that baseball crap, Pattison," Rustin snaps.

Pattison doesn't say anything else, but he rolls up his uniform sleeves, revealing tattoos of flaming baseballs and takes a slight step closer to Rustin.

Rustin reaches his arm back a little further, then whips it sideways, taking aim at the creature. The rock streaks out of Rustin's hand, and the enthusiastic mob holds its breath waiting for the impact that never comes. An almost invisible streak of blue intercepts the rock and knocks it out of the way. Before I can stop her, Clesandra is in front of the young boy, knife securely back in her hand, ready to attack.

"Came to play, did we?" Rustin growls at her.

The boy, taking advantage of Clesandra's distraction, scoops the wounded animal up in his arms and bolts out of the room and down the tunnel.

"If by play, ya mean kick your ass, then yes," Clesandra spits back.

"Bring it," Rustin snarls, taking a few steps closer to her. Pattison shadows Rustin's movements.

"You want me to take care of this?" Pattison asks.

Oh good, this jerk's got lackeys now too.

Rustin waves him away, not bothering to answer.

Without thinking, I step into the space between Rustin and Clesandra.

"Get out of the way," Rustin says. He towers easily a foot over me. I can feel his hot, smelly breath on my face as I glare up at him.

"No."

Rustin's face scrunches in anger. He looks at me like I'm crazy. *I am crazy.* But Clesandra is standing right behind me, so I force my hands into shaky fists and hope I seem intimidating.

"Better call off your scared, little puppy before I

have to give him a beating," Rustin tells Clesandra over my head.

"Get out of the way." She attempts to shove me out of the way from behind. Even though my legs feel like Jell-O, I hold my ground and will them not to shake.

I stare directly at Rustin. His lips curl back in an ugly grin. I know he'll enjoy crushing me. I feel his malicious energy hit me square in the chest as he reaches his hand, now a white-knuckled fist, back behind his head, ready to swing through me.

"It's so nice to see my boys so passionate about fighting." Smith's voice echoes off the stone walls surrounding the room. The clomping of his boots ring loud and clear as he approaches our group. "And...girls, of course," he adds as an afterthought to acknowledge Clesandra.

Rustin's grin turns into a grimace when he realizes he won't get the opportunity to kill me with Smith in the room. He settles for an overly forceful one-handed shove that sends me reeling backward into Clesandra. She dodges and gives me a disgusted look as I crumple to the ground trying the catch the wind Rustin stole from my lungs.

I hear Rustin's followers snickering while I gasp for breath. Smith's face is stoic as he approaches.

"Get up, soldier," he says with a tone of disdain.

I struggle to find my breath and my feet, but manage to stand up and face him. He turns his back to me and addresses the rest of the group. Men and women step into a straight line with feet together, hands at their sides, and heads held up, not looking at Smith. I know the lineup well. I quickly take my place at the end of the line next to Clesandra and stand at attention with the rest of the group.

"I asked for a collection of soldiers." Smith paces

back and forth in front of us.

"And yet it appears that some of us are not equipped to be soldiers."

He stops directly in front of me.

"Despite impeccable bloodlines," he whispers into my ear.

My face flushes with anger. I know he's purposefully insulting me to see what reaction he'll get.

"Some of us are not ready to be called soldiers!" Smith says loudly. "But rest assured, by the end of training here, you will be soldiers! You will be ready both physically and mentally. Ready to fight the enemy!" He continues to pace back and forth in front of us. His boots ring loudly with each footfall.

"You will defend our new land! And you will do so without question! Fail to do so?" He stops and stands right in front of me again. His eyes bore holes into me like hot laser beams, but I resist the urge to look away. Instead, I hold his gaze defiantly.

"You will be eliminated." He lets the last few words hang in the air before continuing to move on down the line.

"Training will be grueling! You will learn how to survive, and how to work as a team. You will handle a variety of weapons. Many will be new to you. There will be plenty of time to practice hand-to-hand combat skills on each other." Smith pauses in front of Rustin and smiles.

"But before we get to that, we learn how to climb!" Smith gestures to the complex-looking suspension course strung carefully from the ceiling and walls. A series of different-colored flags decorate the course at various intervals.

"The natives are extremely adept climbers. You do not want to find yourself alone with one and not have the ability to climb. The exercise is simple. First team to collect their colored flags gets to leave for dinner early. Teams that lose will run a ten-mile loop around the perimeter of the building. I'm sure runners will enjoy the one hundred and ten degree heat of the jungle," Smith says with a chuckle.

As he breaks us into groups of five, murmurs of angst fill the room.

I'm with Clesandra and two other beefy-looking men who obviously favor Rustin over me and Clesandra. Our fifth would have been the red-headed boy who disappeared with the animal.

"We're down a person. Ain't fair," Clesandra points out.

"It happens sometimes when you're at war. Deal with it," Smith responds matter-of-factly.

Clesandra snarls at him as he walks away. Elbowing me in the ribs, she whispers, "Down a person or not, least we'll have a leg up on these idiots."

Despite her confidence, I feel the color drain out of my face as I look up at the ropes course.

"One day of panicked tree climbing in a simulation room where creatures are trying to kill you isn't exactly an advantage," I whisper back.

She shrugs. "Panicked climbing is still climbing."

"There are four teams. Each will start with a vertical rope climb at the center of the room," Smith says, leading reluctant teams to gather around the four hanging ropes.

Clesandra stands poised under a rope that dangles two feet from the top of her head. Rustin faces off with her. The top of his forehead grazes the rope above him. Two other men just slightly smaller than Rustin take positions under the remaining ropes.

"From here, ladies and gentlemen…the room and the rules," he glances quickly at Clesandra, then nods to Rustin, "are yours."

Smith steps back and chuckles, which can only mean he wouldn't be opposed to seeing some bloodshed on the course today.

"Climb!" Smith yells.

Clesandra takes to her rope like sand to the desert. It's like she's been climbing all her life. I half-missed her leaping straight up to balance on the rope. Hand over hand she glides upward effortlessly. Rustin attempts to do the same, but he's built like a rhinoceros. It's much harder to leverage his massive body upward. The other two men are struggling also. One of them manages to get about three feet into the air before his arms give out, and he slides down the rope, yelping as his hands burn. Rustin takes a moment to study how Clesandra is climbing. She's easily ten feet in the air now and pauses halfway up to sneer down at him.

"Thought you wanted to play?" she taunts. I can see his blood boil under his skin. His face turns beet red, and purple veins begin to protrude from his neck. He abandons his rope to violently swing the one Clesandra is climbing.

Unprepared for the swinging, she almost loses her balance. Her grip on the rope begins to slip, and she slides down a few feet.

"Hang on!" I yell.

Taking a running leap, I grab the rope Rustin should've been climbing. I use the momentum of my running jump and the swinging rope to hurtle my feet into Rustin's stomach. It's enough force to knock him clean away from the rope and go fumbling backward. He's got so much mass that he stumbles backward for what seems like forever, trying to keep his balance. As luck would have it, force and gravity are on my side. He falls hard, but not hard enough to keep him down for long. He springs back to his feet, now purple with rage.

"What are you waiting for, Sleeping Beauty? Climb!" Clesandra yells from far above me. Looking up, she's already to the top of her rope and safely on a floating platform. I can almost feel the room shake as Rustin charges for the bottom on my rope. He's pissed off and coming for blood.

Climb, you dumbass, climb! I hear the words in my head willing my body to comply. Not fast enough. Rustin is on my rope and fueled with adrenaline. He doesn't take to swinging it like he did with Clesandra. Instead, he heaves himself onto the rope and begins to haul his massive weight upward. I flash back to the simulation room. Somehow, I feel myself almost floating up the rope, fueled by the fear of being eaten alive. I hear cheering from below as I climb, and screaming above from Clesandra.

"Let's go, Sleeping Beauty!" she yells. I look up and see her lying on her stomach, hanging off the floating platform. Her arm is extended, reaching for me. I want to grab for her hand, and I'm just close enough now, but Rustin's clumsy climbing a few feet below me is swinging the rope back and forth, near and far. I hear a yelp of pain and know Rustin is slipping, but I don't hear a thud. He's still coming for me. *For us!* I take a deep breath and let one hand go. Clesandra snatches it and swings me onto the platform.

"Let's go," she orders, grabbing my hand and pulling me toward the next obstacle in the ropes course.

"Wait." I pull my hand out of hers. Peering down from the platform, Rustin is still climbing. He's almost to the top. "Let's see how you like to swing."

Anchoring myself to the platform by straddling a beam, I grab the rope and haul it back and forth with all my might. Seconds later, we hear the sickening, yet satisfying thud of Rustin falling seven or eight feet to the hard ground below.

A wave of relief rushes over me and I wipe sweat from my forehead.

For the first time since I met her, Clesandra gives me a genuine, if not satisfied, smile. She extends her hand, and I let her pull me to my feet. Gripping the ropes of the floating platform as it sways under our weight, I take a second to glace down. I get a much clearer understanding of just how many people like me have little to no climbing experience. Not one person is able to get more than a few feet up the ropes before crashing down. A small crowd of people surrounds a motionless Rustin on the ground.

"Come on. Let's collect these damn flags and get outta here," Clesandra says.

"Don't we have to wait for our other teammates?"

"The objective is to collect the flags. He didn't say how many had to be collected by each person."

I tilt my head and follow her lead.

"Told ya. Panicked climbing is still climbing."

Chapter 13

We're sweaty, exhausted, and our hands are covered in raw, open blisters and rope burns. Clesandra and I, with our two tag-along teammates, are awarded the freedom of an early dinner. She links her arm in mine and leans on me as we drag our aching bodies into the mess hall.

The rest of the ropes course was challenging, but we could take our time balancing, navigating, and collecting the flags without the fear of Rustin or any of his followers trying to chase us down. Rustin was too injured to complete the rest of the course. Francine and Davinic were summoned to take him to the hospital wing. Several other soldiers, including our teammates, did eventually make it up the vertical rope climb, but by the time they did, we were so far ahead of them it didn't matter.

Even though we're early to dinner, we're still late by the standards of the rest of Xinorsus. Only a handful of people remain. I pick out Sheol's disheveled, sandy hair. He and Jace are sitting at a table with the red-haired boy from today's training and Nico Oliver who showed us around Xinorsus yesterday.

Sheol spots me and waves us over to the table.

"Finally, what took you so long?"

Jace and the red-headed boy are deep in conversation about something, but when Jace sees me, he leaps out of his seat and rushes to Clesandra and I. Wrapping us in a bone-crushing, little-boy hug, he proceeds to tell us all about the red-headed boy, Faysal, and the "animal" he has stowed away in his room.

"It's so cool!"

"It's alive?" Clesandra asks surprised.

"Yeah! Francine stitched her up real good! She even showed me how to put stitches in! But she only let me do one stitch." He pouts.

"Wait. How come you were in the hospital wing?" I ask. "Are you okay?" I grab his shoulders and look him up and down, searching for injuries.

Jace gives me a perplexed look. "That's where my job assignment was today." He pulls up his holographic screen and sticks it under my nose. "See?"

"Uh-huh." I push his arm away to where I can focus. "And you're there again tomorrow." I instantly feel bad about not even knowing where my brother was all day. He doesn't seem to mind, though. Grabbing my arm, he starts tugging me toward the exit. "You have to come see it!"

"Can't they eat dinner first?" Sheol butts in.

Jace looks embarrassed. "I guess so. Eat fast!" He scampers back to the table with Faysal.

"Thank you," I mouth the words to Sheol. I didn't realize how hungry I was until just now.

The dinner menu isn't much different from the breakfast menu with the same weird fruits and vegetables. This time I load my tray up. Food is food no matter what it looks like at this point. Clesandra does the same, and we head back to the table with Sheol and Nico.

"How's it going?" I ask.

Sheol extends his raw and blistered hands palm up. Clesandra and I show off our hands.

"We won, though." I can't help but gloat a little bit.

"You jerks! My team came in dead last and got stuck running the ten miles."

"Oh, shut up!" Nico bursts in. "You only ran about six before I saved all your rear ends."

Sheol can see the confusion on my face. He

glances at Jace and Faysal to make sure they aren't listening, and then leans across the table. With his voice just above a whisper, he says, "There was a disappearance."

"Disappearance?" I ask.

"Yeah, Smith made us run the perimeter of the building, and there was a lady on one of the other losing teams who was falling behind. Before we know it, Nico's screaming over an outdoor alarm system, directing us below ground into the nearest tunnel entrance."

"I keep telling Smith that training needs to happen only in the building right now, at least until we figure out why our field fencing isn't working properly. No one cares what I have to say, though," Nico says annoyed.

"I didn't see any fencing when we flew over the base," I say.

"There are lots of things you didn't see," Nico says.

"What's that supposed to mean?" Clesandra chimes in.

Nico raises a crooked eyebrow at her. "It means, darling, that, just like me, there's more to Xinorsus than meets the eye. You have no idea what this military installation or the people on it are capable of doing. In any event, you wouldn't see the fencing anyway," he says in a smug tone.

"Why's that?" I ask.

"It's invisible. I designed it to keep people and animals out. If you can see the fencing, then you can go over the fencing. Not that it matters now. The fencing hasn't been working very well. No matter how much defense I run, something keeps tripping the electrical units. Then people start going missing." Nico leans in close to Clesandra. "You might want to think about sticking close to me for, you know, protection."

Clesandra scrunches up her face in disgust.

"You mean like you protected that other person today?" I blurt out, my face red with anger. I don't like his smug tone. "Why are you telling us this anyway?"

My tone and the question seem to catch him off guard. His casual posture and smug demeanor falters.

"I…er…well, you should…know." He gestures to Clesandra. "She should know because she should be extra careful."

Clesandra and I are staring daggers into his soul. Sheol is watching us a little bit uncomfortably.

"Women are the main targets. I mean, men were targeted originally, and…well, they started to turn back up…in pieces. The women are never found." He's looking back and forth between the three of us. Clesandra has a narrow-eyed glare fixed on him.

I'm still trying to read him. Like Lupète, I don't know enough about Nico to trust what he's saying or his intentions.

"And it's not for lack of trying!" His voice goes up an octave. "The trackers in your—" He stops, as if he's said too much.

"What about trackers?" Sheol butts in.

The three of us watch the skin on Nico's neck flush red. Beads of sweat form on his brow. He waves our voices down with his hands.

"Shush! You trying to get me killed here? You didn't hear that," he says, and gets up to leave.

"Lift a cheek from that seat and see what happens to ya." Clesandra threatens, twirling her knife in her fingers.

Nico shifts nervously in his seat. "I knew I should've taken my dinner with the other scientists," he curses under his breath.

"What about trackers?" Clesandra presses.

He looks around the room cautiously before

motioning to his wristband. Trying to act like he's relaxed and having a great conversation with the three of us, he puts his right elbow on top of his wristband and rests his head on his fist. He indicates for us to do the same. We all take postures that are more casual with our arms folded carefully over our bands.

"This will only muffle the sounds of our voices," Nico whispers. "So keep it down."

He waits for us to show signs of acknowledgement before he continues.

"Let's just say that those things on your wrists do a lot more than wake you up in the morning. They take regular blood samples, they track your location, and they have a built-in wiretap so Smith and anyone else he wants can hear your conversations."

"That's how those bastards know everything!" Clesandra snarls. "How do we get rid of them?"

"Get rid of them?" Nico laughs. "You only get rid of them when you're dead. They aren't designed to come off, sweetheart," he says, shaking his head.

"So there's no area where these things won't work?" Sheol asks.

"I didn't say that. We know they don't work in areas that are uncharted—the dark spots on the planet. But anyone who goes in never comes back out, so you might as well assume them dead."

"What about the women who keep disappearing? You said they couldn't be tracked," I interject.

"I didn't say they couldn't be tracked. We *were* able to track them up to about a half-mile before the dark zones."

"What do you mean by *were able to?*" Sheol prods.

"Lately, with these new disappearances, the trackers seem to just stop working. As soon as they leave the compound, they don't work. They don't work even when you guys are out with Dr. Albero during agricultural studies. We can't always track everyone. It's like something out there is disrupting the signal. Within these walls we can track you just fine." He's looking at Clesandra now. "But beyond them is a different story altogether."

Clesandra is quietly puzzling the newfound information.

"You're sure there's no way to remove these things?" she asks again.

"If you find one, let me know. Look, in all seriousness, if you guys let it slip that I told you this, it's my head on the chopping block. As much as Smith says he wants people to know everything there is to know about this place and how to run it, there's still a chain of command. There are still rules and boundaries. If you break a rule or cross a boundary, be prepared for consequences." He looks at each of us to make sure we completely understand before he returns all of his attention to Clesandra.

"If I were you, I'd stay as close to the building as possible. Don't wander away from the group. We aren't sure why people are disappearing, or what is capturing them and taking them away. Be careful." Nico takes his arm slowly off his wristband. "If you'll excuse me now," he asks permission of only Clesandra. She nods. "This conversation?"

"Never happened," Sheol whispers.

"I'll catch you all later," he says over his shoulder in a much more relaxed and casual tone, even though the look on his face is anything but.

Sheol takes a deep breath and purses his lips in thought.

"I don't suppose you can pretend to be sick or something so you don't have to go outside the building during training?" I ask Clesandra.

She doesn't have a chance to answer or refute me before Sheol scoffs. "You're not really worried about her, are you? She's the coarsest person here. No one's going to try and capture her. She'd skin them alive just as soon as look at them!"

Clesandra looks hurt for a fraction of a second before her expression goes stone cold and heartless again.

"Real nice, Sheol," I say sarcastically. "Come on, you want to go see that animal thing with Jace?" I ask her.

"Sure," she says quietly.

"Oh, come on! I didn't mean anything by it!" Sheol says, trying to save face. "If anything it was meant as a compliment!"

I give him the cold shoulder and ignore him.

"You ready, Jace?"

He pops out of his chair like a jack-in-the-box. Grinning from ear-to-ear and practically dragging Faysal toward us, we head out of the room. Sheol follows us, not wanting to be left behind in the mess hall, but neither Clesandra nor I acknowledge him.

Faysal leads us to his room. Like Clesandra, he doesn't have a roommate assignment, which is probably a good thing now that he's harboring a strange creature. When he opens the door, we're hit with a sweet aroma of fruit. The walls and ceiling are covered with elaborate and colorful abstract designs and drawings. I realize in a second that the smell is coming from the walls. Faysal must have literally ground up different plants to make the various colors needed for his artwork.

"Whoa," Sheol says in awe.

Fayal stares down at his feet embarrassed and awkwardly pulls the long sleeves of his shirt closer to his fingertips. His face flushes the same fiery color of his hair.

"You're not hot in those long sleeves?" Clesandra asks.

"I...uh, have to protect my skin from the sun. I...burn easily." Faysal tries to come up with a quick response, but it feels fabricated. He sees me looking at him suspiciously and awkwardly pulls on his sleeves again.

"Unlucky," Clesandra says. "Red-haired, fair-skinned, and from a desert...very unlucky."

Her statement eases my suspicions. Redheads do tend to burn more easily, but he's inside now. Why wear the extra layer if you don't have to?

"So you're an artist," Sheol states the obvious.

"Not really. I just like the colors."

"No, you're definitely an artist," Sheol exclaims. "This is incredible! How'd you get the ceiling?"

"Bunk bed moves." He points to it without looking up. Faysal moves toward the bed where the small creature is comfortably sleeping cocooned in his pillowcase. He sits down and gently strokes the animal's head. It lets out a high-pitched squeak and yawns, showing rows of dagger-sharp teeth.

Jace plunks down on the other side of bed. "Can I pet her?"

Faysal hesitates, and then says, "I guess so. But be gentle. She's had a rough day."

With fingers like feathers on the wind, Jace strokes the fur on the top of the animal's head. Its eyes pop open wide, like luminescent emerald orbs fixed on Jace's fingers. Startled, Jace freezes his hand, hovering it an inch above the animal's head. I ready myself to jump between the creature and Jace if it decides to attack, but it does just the opposite. It shuts its enormous eyes and brushes its head against Jace's hand before settling back into the pillowcase.

Jace looks up at me in awe. "Cool."

I nod my head. "Good thing you stopped Rustin from killing her," I tell Faysal.

"No, it's a good thing you guys showed up when you did. That guy would have killed her and probably me, too, so thank you."

"What are you gonna do with her?" Clesandra asks.

Faysal shrugs. "Nothing, I guess. I arrived here a few weeks before your ship showed up and she's been here ever since. Left my escape hatch open for some fresh air one night and woke up with her in my pillowcase. She's as friendly as can be. I leave the hatch open a crack each night. She comes and goes as she pleases. Never thought she'd follow me to training, though. I didn't even notice she was following me until that jerk was throwing rocks up at the ceiling. He was aiming for her."

"I'll give him something to aim at," Clesandra growls.

"I think we'd all like to," I add.

"Don't worry, I'll bet he'll be the first to die in the war," Jace pipes up.

The room falls silent. No one expected that phrase to pop out of Jace's mouth, least of all me.

"What are you talking about? There's no war here." I smile at him, and try to downplay what he just said.

"Don't take this the wrong way, but you're a horrible liar. I told you before. You don't have to treat me like a little kid. I know what's going on. I knew what was going on at home too. And I know what's about to happen here."

Looking at the twelve-year-old boy standing before me, I feel like we've switched places. That he's me. Older. Supposed to be wiser. And I'm him. But instead of being strong and adaptable like Jace, I'm a twelve-year-old boy who's scared to death to be here. I'm away from home and facing combat training with people who would like no more than to kill me. And I'm terrified of what Jace is about to say next. I'm petrified that by acknowledging that he's aware of the impending war, it will rob him of any semblance of a normal childhood.

Normal childhood? What's normal anymore?

The words come slowing out of my mouth as I try to squelch my fears and resume my role as older brother. "What's about to happen here?"

Jace glances up at the ceiling, as if searching for the best way to explain what his mind wants to say.

"It's not really that it's about to happen, more like it *is* happening. At least, it's happening how it happened on the old, black boxes."

"Boxes? What are you talking about?"

"You know, the big black, rectangle boxes that fit in that old machine in the cellar? Caileen and I watched them when Mom went to wait for the water trucks."

It's like being sucker-punched in the stomach remembering the videotapes Jace is talking about. Caileen, Jeremy, and I discovered the videos and the old television set that could play them years ago. We were hiding from Dad, who'd gone off the deep end after an overseas trip fighting for water importation and exportation rights.

I was only nine at the time. The day was oppressively hot. The air conditioner was running full blast, but it was still close to ninety degrees inside the house. Mom didn't seem to care about the heat that day. This was the day Dad was coming home. We hadn't seen him in almost six months. Mom was flitting around the house cleaning, preparing this and that. Ordering us to make our beds and brush our hair.

She hummed to herself as she tried to turn mashed-up preserved canned goods into culinary masterpieces. There was a joyous energy in the home despite the oppressive dry heat beyond its walls. Mom looked so vibrant, so full of life. An emerald green scarf wrapped around her head to keep her long, dark hair off her neck. Her rosy cheeks flushed red from the heat of the day and from scampering around the house. Every now and then she would pause, leaning on the kitchen counter, or on a door frame to catch her breath and gently caress her plump stomach before moving on to her next task.

"Hurry now. Brush your teeth. Comb your hair. For goodness sake, tuck in your shirt, Jeremy! Your father will be home any minute, and I want this to be perfect," Mom would say, herding us around the house, getting ready for his arrival.

There was a nervous excitement to her tone.

"Do you think Dad will be excited when he finds out Mom's pregnant?" I asked Jeremy.

"Sure. He should be very happy to know he'll have another son." His tone was reassuring, but the smile on his face seemed forced for my benefit.

"Come on." He gripped my shoulder tightly, and steered me into the bedroom we shared. "If *I* have to clean this room, *you* have to clean this room."

A few minutes later we heard the front door open and close quickly with a loud bang. Dad was home. He never closed a door quietly. He always wanted to announce his presence with as much noise as possible.

"I'm home! Where's my family?" he yelled. His voice from far away seemed friendly and inviting, beckoning us to join him at the front door. Caileen was already wrapped in his bear hug when Jeremy and I trotted around the corner to greet him. He spun her out of his arms lightly and welcomed us to join him. We did without hesitation. Dad was always happiest on his first day home from a long trip. Or at least it seemed that way when we were young.

Dad smiled down at us. "I missed my boys," he said, holding us at arm's length and looking down at us proudly.

"You both got taller," he remarked. "Keep growing like this and it won't be long before the two of you will be joining me on my trips."

I can't forget that overwhelming, happy feeling of hearing him talk about how we would get to go with him to countries overseas. He made it seem exotic and exciting instead of filled with death and suffering.

"Now," he said, looking over our shoulders. "Where's my wife?" he called loudly for her to hear.

That happy feeling I felt moments before faded instantly when Mom appeared from the kitchen. She came forward slowly. Hand on her swollen belly and eyes on the floor like she was ashamed of something. I looked from her to Dad, confused. The stroke of irrational anger on my father's face registered at the same time that his burly hands closed around our necks. I felt my feet leaving the ground as Dad started screaming.

"Again? You're pregnant again?" His fingers dug deeper into my neck with each word and I started to lose consciousness. I heard Caileen and Mom wailing to let us go. I sensed Jeremy struggling from the way Dad's grip changed and shifted.

"Do you realize this whole world's in crisis right now?" he screamed. "There's next to no safe drinking water left on the planet! No water to drink! No water to grow crops! And people like you, Julia," he screamed, hoisting us farther off the ground, "can't seem to stop having babies! How are we going to take care of all of them?"

I couldn't see what was going on anymore, my vision nearly gone from suffocation. But I heard Mom begging him to put us down, pleading for his forgiveness. That she was sorry. That she didn't mean for it to happen.

"Didn't mean for it to happen? Who meant for this to happen? Meant it or not, I'm going to fix this!" His tone was cynical, violent. Different from the man who's voice I knew and loved. I struggled to take one last breath as blackness filled the space where thoughts used to be.

"Please let them go! Our children are everything!"

And then there was a loud bellow and suddenly I could breathe again. I was on the ground gasping. I felt a set of arms dragging me. Then two sets of arms. Vision came and went. I heard screaming and slamming. Knew something bad was happening. But I also knew I had to get up. *Run.* That voice in my head kept telling me. *Get up and run!*

"Jeremy, take them! Go! Keep them safe!" Mom screamed. More slamming. Screaming. Pounding feet.

So I ran. We ran. Out of the house into the blazing-hot midday heat and down into the cellar. Jeremy slammed the door shut and locked it from the inside. Even though there was a code on the outside of the door to get in, he knew if it was locked from the inside, we would be safe. The three of us sat huddled together, listening to the screaming. The slamming. Then finally the deadly quiet, which was somehow worse than the screaming.

For a long time we sat and stared at the door, waiting for something to happen. Sure that Dad had killed our mother and that we would be next. Wondering how it would be possible for someone who seemed so loving, so proud of his family, to snap and turn violent in an instant.

Andrea Perno

"I'm hungry. Do you think it's safe to go out yet?" Caileen asked.

"We aren't going out," Jeremy told us. But he got up and started searching the shelves in the cellar for something we could eat without having to heat it.

"Help me look for cans with labels that say 'fruit,'" Jeremy commanded. "We can eat those without cooking."

We started rummaging through the cans on the shelves and that's when we discovered the old television set. It was covered with a white sheet in a corner and packed in with larger cans around it. Next to the TV was a huge cardboard box filled to the top with black, rectangular videotapes.

"Hey, look at this!" Caileen exclaimed.

We gathered around the machine. Jeremy was fascinated.

"I know what this is. Our teacher has one of these in the classroom," Jeremy told us. "These are movies! And that's an old movie player," he said, pointing to the TV. He pushed a button on the front of the machine and it clicked loudly to life, buzzing obnoxiously with gray-and-white fuzzy dots.

"Looks like it still works!" he yelled over the noisy buzzing. Taking one of the videotapes from my hand, he shoved it into the slot at the bottom of the television.

Nothing happened at first. It took several minutes of button mashing to figure out how to work the old device. Eventually, the screen crackled to life. A continuous white line moved from the bottom of the screen to the top as the tape played.

We were astonished with what we saw. It's our home. But the area wasn't desert. Standing in front of our house was a small boy. He looked just like Jeremy, but it wasn't Jeremy.

198

"I think that's Dad," Caileen said. The resemblance was striking. It had to be him. He was so little, probably no more than two or three years old.

"Can't be Dad," Jeremy said. "These things are too old. Look, the date on this one is 1980. Dad wasn't even born yet," he said, holding up a handful of the videotapes.

"I bet it's Granddad then," Caileen said.

The boy on the video thumped down on the ground in front of the house. He ran his pudgy, little hands over the dry earth, pulling up clumps of crunchy dead, brown grass. He held them up in front of the camera, smiling.

"Grass?" he asked.

"Not anymore," said the voice behind the camera.

The little boy looked up, confused. "Grass?" he asked again.

"Nope. It's dead."

The little boy's happy smile faded. "Not grass?"

"Nope, no more grass," the voice answered. The camera panned around the house. Our house looked almost the same from the outside. Same rusty red-colored bricks accented by a brilliant blue, cloudless sky. Only here on the video there were small, scrubby-looking plants around the exterior. They looked as burnt and dried out as the dead grass under them. Way in the distance, the other houses and hills rippled with heat waves.

"Thirsty," the little boy announced.

The camera panned back down to the boy who was now standing and trying to smack the dried grass and dust off himself.

"You just had a drink." The cameraman's voice was annoyed.

"Thirsty," he said again. This time a little bit more persistently.

"In a little bit we'll go get something to drink."

The child's face wrinkled up in anguish.

"Daddy! Thirsty now!" he wailed.

"Okay, okay, come on." The cameraman led the crying child into the house. He went to the kitchen sink and turned the knobs. Brown, filthy water spilled from the faucet. He shut it off, cursing under his breath about the government not providing clean water and went toward the refrigerator. In it there was a large opaque pitcher sitting on the shelf. He went to pick it up and cursed under his breath again.

"I just filled it this morning," he grumbled, panning the camera down to the little boy again. "It's empty. See? You have to wait until later when I go get some more."

The little boy's lower lip quivered and tears formed at the corners of his eyes. "Thirsty!" he sobbed.

"Stop your crying! We're all thirsty!" the man snapped.

This only incited an obnoxious high-pitched wailing from the child.

"Okay! Okay. You want water?"

"Y-y-yes," the little boy sobbed.

"We have to go for a long walk. Can you do that with me?"

Sniffing a trail of snot back into his nose the little boy nodded his head furiously.

Immediately, the scene on the camera screen changed. This time the little boy was standing at the edge of a large body of water. The camera panned left and right, taking in the whole scene.

"Hey, I know that place!" Jeremy said. "That used to be Lake Superior."

"Oh wow, when it actually had water," I added.

"Shhh." Caileen hushed us.

The camera panned the lake, and out on the still

surface, hundreds of commercial boats were pumping water into large holding tanks. Groups of people gathered at the water's edge with huge, white signs, yelling and protesting.

The lake's water was receding at an alarming rate. The ground about a hundred yards up to the water's edge was littered with reddish-brown sand and pebbles worn smooth from hundreds of years of gentle crashing waves. What used to be dense forest growth surrounding the lake was now dead and dried. Trees were withered. Dead leaves, slowly turning to dust, formed a crunchy carpet under barren branches. Families gathered at the water's edge, filling huge jugs to take back to their homes.

"At this rate, the lake will be gone by the end of the summer," the cameraman whispered to himself. He panned the camera back to his son. The little boy was squatting on the ground, dipping his hands into the water and drinking right out of his little fists.

"Do you feel better?"

Turning to the camera, he smiled a bright, innocent, pudgy-cheeked smile.

"Good. Let's fill our jugs and get back home. It's time to get out of the hot sun."

The video snapped to black, and the television set rumbled to life again with hundreds of gray-and-white fuzzy dots.

And so began our night of watching tape after tape on the television set. Each video filmed Asik as the lake drained, as the crops in surrounding farms disappeared and were replaced by desert sands. The videos also followed our grandfather's growth as he joined the military to fund college, as he transitioned from college as a biochemical engineer. We watched him film his own work trying to help grow drought-resistant crops and find a way to seed the clouds to bring rain back to our area. We watched our Earth fall into ruin through our great grandfather's eyes, then the eyes of our grandfather. Watched hope turn into frustration, pain, and desperation. Watched the Earth slowly wither away into what we came to know as home growing up.

And the last video in the box was the filming of our own father's birth. It was filled with just as much emotion and desperation as the videos showing Asik slowly devolving. Our father's birth was not a happy video. No smiling faces, no celebratory pats on the back and congratulations. Only hushed whispers of, "How are we going to take care of *it*?"

I shake my head to clear the memories. Looking down at Jace, I realize how lucky he is to be alive. Dad beat our mother within an inch of her life the night we discovered the television set and the videotapes. She spent three weeks in intensive care. While there, she gave birth to a very premature baby boy. Dad spent months apologizing for what he'd done. But his relationship with us, with Mom, was never the same again.

Even so, Mom never left him. Made excuses for him. Blamed what was going on in the world and his job for his behavior. But deep down I think his reaction to Mom being pregnant with Jace was simply a reincarnation of what life was probably like for him when he was born. Birth being seen not as a gift, but as a burden. Mom always treated us just the opposite. She treated us like we were precious. She always told us we were special and that there was a reason we were born. Otherwise, it wouldn't have happened. Thinking back to all the orphans delivered to the military gates, I wonder if their parents thought of them as gifts.

"What do you mean it's happening here?" I ask, coming back to reality.

"It's pretty obvious, Avery," Jace says annoyed. "The plants growing on the sides of the building aren't as healthy as they look. The well being drilled doesn't have enough water to grow the crops we need. Even the ground around the outside is starting to dry up like—"

"How do you know all this?" Sheol interrupts.

"Agriculture training," Jace says. "People are trying to hide what's going on, but—" "If you're observant, you see things," Faysal cuts in. "Come on. It's better if they look for themselves," he says, going to the escape window. He pushes the window out and starts to climb through it.

"Are you crazy? We're not going outside. People are disappearing!" I say.

Faysal raises his eyebrows.

"Disappearing? Maybe they're simply choosing to leave."

He slips out the window with Jace running to catch up.

"Hey, wait! Jace, get back here!" I yell after him.

"Come on, fraidy-cat!" Jace yells over his shoulder as he swings himself out the window after Faysal. I shake my head angrily and Clesandra, Sheol, and I hurry after them.

Outside the building, the light is just starting to disappear behind the trees. The faded pinks and purples of the sky are turning into brilliant shades of crimson and violet. The air is dry but no longer has the vicious burning heat that I'm used to in Asik. Instead, the night air is still and cool. Faysal's room is higher up on the pyramid-shaped building. Looking down to the base far below, I feel a rush of adrenaline push me backward.

"Ain't used to heights yet?" Clesandra scoffs. "After all that climbing?"

"The height's never been an issue…fear of falling on the other hand…"

"Now you are being a fraidy-cat," Sheol grunts, mocking Jace. "The building's just one giant staircase if you ask me."

"Shhh," Faysal scolds. "Use your eyes, not your mouth." He points into the distance.

I strain, trying to see what Faysal is indicating, but all I see is a never-ending vista of forest. Trees so close together they seem planted on top of each other.

"What am I looking at again?" I ask.

Faysal and Jace exchange a look. Not being able to see what they see, I feel my face flush with frustration. I've never had the detail-oriented nature Jace possesses naturally, and I can only imagine how acutely Faysal interprets the world around him being the artist he is.

Jace points to the trees in the distance. "The tops, they're all starting to turn brown."

I squint and can barely tell the difference in color that Jace is pointing out.

"And here." He bends down and ruffles the leaves of the plants growing on the surface of the pyramid. The leaves are a faded greenish-purple with just the tips starting to turn a grayish brown. They crumble in his fingers and crackle off their branches too easily.

"These plants won't last long without water," Jace remarks.

The image of the little boy on the videotape plucking dead grass out of the ground flashes before me again. Jace is right, even if I don't want to believe it.

"These plants are supposed to be crops that will feed us in the next few months," Faysal adds, plucking one out of the ground. He turns the plant upside down to show us the hollow root system.

A single drop of water drips out of the hollow stem.

"This plant should be filled with water. It shouldn't be brittle and dry like it is," Faysal says, frowning. "We're not far from seeing the last drop out here. When we do, it's going to come down to…"

"Who's gonna fight for it," Clesandra finishes his sentence.

Chapter 14

Now that Jace and Faysal have pointed out the dying plants, it's all I see everywhere. The tops of the trees are turning more distinctly brown with each passing day. When I'm outside the building for trainings with Dr. Albero, the ground looks drier, grainier like sand beneath my feet. The dirt cloud that rises around us and settles onto our clothing and in our lungs is suffocating. Those aren't the only changes starting to show up as the days drag into weeks.

Food is scarcer. What used to be an all-you-can-eat buffet-style mess hall has changed dramatically. Workers now divide food portions systematically, careful to make sure each person gets an equal amount. Smith and the scientists talk about the change as necessary to ensure every person receives a proper amount of calories for the day, but we know different.

Standing in line behind Sheol and Jace in the mess hall, the tension between the workers and those being fed is palpable. Today the portion of what looks like mashed-up fruit and vegetable pieces is almost twice as small as yesterday. But I'm not that interested in the food. Farther down the line there's a table with small cups of pre-measured rations of water. I used to walk right past it, worried I'd have more hallucinations like I had at the welcome ceremony. Avoiding water didn't last long and thankfully I've had no more visions. All I can think about is how dry my mouth feels. Water is all I really want. A full day of sweating through intense combat training drills with no water makes me desperate to drink about twelve cups on the table. But I know I'll only get one. I can't look away from the cups as the line inches closer and closer. I don't even notice the small ration of food dumped on my plate, just the cups of water. I can't get there fast enough. Finally, I'm in front of the table, waiting patiently for the woman to hand me my ration.

I take the cup slowly, careful not to spill a drop. The liquid inside isn't even clear anymore. A few weeks ago, we drank the most amazing, clear, delicious water that had ever passed my lips. Looking inside the dingy, fragile paper cup in my hand, the water is a muddy-colored, grayish brown. Less than appetizing, but I don't care. I tilt the cup and let the grainy texture slide across my tongue and down my throat. It's gross, but I'm so thirsty I hardly notice the metallic aftertaste that's probably the result of some unnatural by-product from excessive drilling.

The liquid is half gone in one gulp. I drink the rest more slowly, trying to make it last. Lowering the cup from my lips with a shaky hand, I notice Jace and Sheol studying me with worried expressions.

"What? I'm fine," I say to appease them and lead the way to an empty table. I allow my body to sink slowly down on the hard metal bench, trying to keep a straight face and not wince. Every muscle aches from training. I'm sore, exhausted, and thirsty. Even just the effort to lift a fork full of plant goo to my lips is a task. The only comfort I take is noticing how carefully Sheol lowers himself down into his seat. He doesn't hide his wince of pain.

"Think they'll give us a day off or something soon?" he asks.

"Or something," I grunt.

"What do you mean I only get one?" An unmistakable bellow comes from behind us. It's Rustin, back to his normal self and making everyone's life around him miserable. He's towering over the water table and the small woman behind it. Nostrils flared, skin flushed red, delusional rage contorting his face. He snatches the water cup from the woman's hand, gulps it down, crumples the paper cup in his fist, and viciously throws it into her face as he helps himself to another cup.

"You can't do that!" the little woman squeaks.

He smiles cruelly and continues to drink cup after cup. People behind him in the line rush the table to make sure they get water before it's gone. Rustin slaps them out of the way like flies, hurling their bodies backward. Security guards appear and swarm the mob, trying to diffuse the situation.

Rustin hurtles several of them across the room too before a medical correspondent shoots him with some sort of tranquilizer. The sedative works right away. Rustin staggers around the room, snarling like a rabid beast, and swinging his massive arms around as he tries to maintain balance. He staggers toward me, arms outstretched and grasping at the air in front of him.

"You did all of this!" His arms hit nothing but air. "I'm going to kill you!" he growls. Seconds later, his knees buckle and he hits the floor with a sickening thud. The security guards quickly restore order in the mess hall and leave, struggling to carry a passed-out Rustin from the room.

A few minutes later it's like nothing happened. I can't get the scene out of my head. It's just a matter of time before all hell breaks loose on this planet.

Chapter 15

Staring at the wooden slats holding the military issue bunk beds together, I trace the grainy texture with my eyes and let my mind wander. Sleep has eluded me yet again. Sheol's sad sighing is the only thing that breaks up the silence. He sits up every night, waiting for his native visitor. For the first couple of weeks she was a regular, visiting him every night. I used to watch them and pretend to be asleep. At first, it was just to make sure Sheol wasn't going to be an idiot and let her in so she could kill us. Then it was to study their behavior. Sheol was always mesmerized, and she acted like a curious child. Very different from how Smith portrayed the natives.

Now she no longer visits. Sheol waits for her, night after night, like we used to wait for the water trucks. Everything I know, *or think* I know about this place, the people, feels wrong.

It's been a few weeks since Rustin's episode in the mess hall. We all thought, or hoped, that his would be an isolated incident. It's not the case, though. Unrest is spreading like a disease. Fighting is an everyday occurrence. No one is permitted in the mess hall anymore. Water and food rations are brought right to our door in the evenings after training. *We're being fed like caged animals*. Whispers of war are a part of every conversation. Combat training is more intense. Smith reminds us daily that for certain individuals, a special test is coming. As if training without water isn't test enough.

In an effort to combat the dozens of people collapsing from dehydration, Davinic and Francine have engineered a synthetic hydration saline from organisms on the planet, which is injected daily right into our bloodstreams. The injections help. They're meant to stabilize us. To decrease our thirst and the need to drink, but they don't last long. Only three days. And they come with horrible side effects. I'm no longer as thirsty during the day. Instead, I have horrible headaches, all my joints absolutely ache, and Sheol and I have developed an awful, painful, blistered rash inside our mouths.

The rash is nothing compared to the side effects Clesandra suffered.

Her body reacted so negatively to the injections that her kidneys shut down. She spent two days in the hospital ward, hooked up to machines cleansing her blood. Jace and I visited her every day, but she was so out of it I hardly think she noticed.

Clesandra doesn't get the injections anymore. Instead, she continues to get daily rations of water while we get a ration of water every three days.

Jace and Faysal have become best friends. The two of them are assigned agriculture roles and spend almost every waking moment together. When they're not at agriculture training, Jace spends the rest of his time with Faysal and Lucky. Lucky, the cat-like, squirrel-like thing that Rustin almost killed is doing well. I miss my brother now more than anything. I hardly get to see him since combat training takes the majority of the day. But I'm happy he doesn't have to train for war. As Smith promised, Jace has been able to avoid a role as soldier. I pray he sees as little of this mess as possible.

Yawning, I glance at the wall of windows. A rosy dawn light is just starting to filter through the treetops and warm the room. Sheol is asleep on the floor in front of the windows, and Jace is snoring loudly. I don't even have to look at my wristband to know that the morning alarm will be going off any second now. I shut my eyes tight in one last vain attempt to claim five minutes of sleep. Seconds later, the annoying alarm pierces the silence.

Rubbing my bloodshot eyes, I peel myself out of bed and slip on a standard issue pair of steel-toed boots. They feel heavy on my feet.

"Ugh, is it morning already?" Sheol groans.

"You wouldn't be so tired if you went to sleep and stopped trying to flirt with the natives."

Sheol's face flushes crimson. "Hard to flirt with someone who isn't there," he says with a sheepish, lopsided grin. "Wish I knew where she went."

I shake my head and extend an arm. As I'm pulling him up from the ground, my wristband lights up with today's schedule.

"Oh goodie," I grumble, not even bothering to look at the screen, "more combat training drills."

"Nope, not today, we don't. Look, you and I have the same schedule. A briefing in the hospital ward."

"Hospital ward?" I turn my attention to the screen.

"Looks like it. Have to be there in twenty minutes. So much for breakfast, huh?"

"Wonder why we're in the hospital ward today?"

"Don't question it. Any day we're not in combat training is a good day in my book," Sheol remarks.

"Guess so," I say. I can't help the uneasy feeling starting to creep into my stomach. Jace's wristband tells him he's in agriculture today, so we wish him a good day and head out of our room.

The uneasy feeling that settled in my stomach is confirmed the moment the doors click shut behind us. A security detail is waiting. They roughly take us by the arms and escort us to the hospital like criminals.

Sheol attempts to ask questions and crack a few jokes to lighten the mood, but the guards don't look amused.

When we arrive, about a half-dozen other soldiers are present, Clesandra included. Off to one side of the room, two armed guards have Nico restrained. He's not struggling. His face is as pale as a ghost and emotionless. Beads of sweat speckle his brow. When he sees us he mouths the word, "Sorry."

My stomach twists into a nervous knot.

Commander Smith is standing at the center of the room, looking alert and aloof. Hands clasped behind him, head and shoulders back, he's standing tall and smiling as soldiers file in. His smile gets wider when he sees me enter, but it's not a friendly smile. More like a maniacal, just wait-and-see-what's-going-to-happen-to-you kind of smile. My stomach twists tighter. Instinctively, I gravitate toward Clesandra as a few more soldiers fall in behind us.

"What do you suppose this is all about?" I whisper to her.

She doesn't say anything at first. "Remember the simulation room?"

My stomach does a belly flop. "Why?"

"They know Nico told us," Sheol interjects. "Why else would they have him in custody too?"

"So what if we know what the wristbands do? It's not like we can get rid of them. What about the rest of the people? You don't think Nico told them too?"

"Probably said something they shouldn't have," Clesandra remarks.

"Maybe we're—"

"You," Smith starts out in his deep, booming voice. The expression on his face and his tone are cold and heartless. "We're brought here today because you can't be trusted."

Murmurs of confusion and dissonance erupt around us.

"Some of you," he looks at Sheol, Clesandra, and me, "are aware of how we know you can't be trusted. Others of you have shown through actions and words that you are…opposed to our mission. What good is a soldier who refuses to fight?" He pauses and looks directly at me. "There's only one thing worse than a soldier who won't fight. That's a rebel soldier who decides he's going to fight back, and to betray his people. Betray his species. Deny the survival of the human race. To be sure that you can all be trusted, I propose a test."

Soldiers exchange uneasy glances. Clesandra presses her shoulder into mine. "Simulation room," she snarls.

"This test will allow us to see just where your loyalties lie," Smith says.

My stomach tightens. I can almost feel the pulsating anger radiating off Clesandra. I cast a glance at her from the corner of my eye. Her face is beet red, and her jaw is clenched tight.

Smith nods to the security detail in the room and they descend, forcing us into handcuffs. Like a few other soldiers, Clesandra doesn't go quietly. It takes three men to restrain her and take her knife.

"Not yours! You have no right…give it back," she bellows.

One of the men is badly slashed in the process.

They forcefully guide us one by one past Davinic and Francine.

I'm dragged after Clesandra, who is taken to Davinic first. He takes her wrist and starts to force something into her wristband. She resists, swinging away from the men holding her in place.

"No!" She breaks from one of the men's grip and wheels around, trying to throw her handcuffed wrists around the neck of the other man. She almost has him before a third grabs her arms and slams his knee into her stomach. The air in her lungs bursts out of her like a popped balloon.

"Leave her alone!" I scream. I feel a rush of adrenaline flood my arms and try to free myself. The two men hold me back and threaten to use their Tasers. I force myself to relax only slightly, remembering how it felt to be jolted with electricity in Asik. All I can do is watch in agony as Clesandra gasps for breath and is dragged toward Francine.

Keeping my eyes on the guards holding Clesandra, I hardly notice being passed to Davinic. He takes my arm roughly and inserts a chip into the front of the wristband.

"This is a self-destruct chip," he whispers as he manipulates the screen. "It can be used at any time to kill you. Play by the rules wherever you're going," he says with a grimace. One of the officers grunts disapprovingly at Davinic for talking to me.

Davinic lowers his eyes submissively and passes me down the line to Francine.

Self-destruct? The knot in my stomach does a back flip, and I feel like I might throw up.

Francine takes my arm. She's gentler with me. Her face is filled with sadness and her hands are shaking. She cradles my right arm against her chest and fills a syringe with the familiar solution meant to keep us alive for the next three days without water. She pulls me in closer, her face just inches from mine, as she lines up the tip of the needle with the blue vein in the crook of my arm.

"Just do what he wants," she begs. I wince as the needle slides under my skin. "You have your brother to think of. Family is precious, and you're one of so few who have any family left."

Her words are spoken so quietly and with such

sadness that a massive lump forms at the back of my throat. I'll do anything for Jace.

Francine removes the needle from my arm and sits back. Her eyes are red from the tears she's holding back. She must know where we're going and it isn't good.

"What's Smith going to do to us?" I ask nervously.

She shakes her head sadly.

"Move, soldier," a security officer commands. He grabs my arm and shoves me forward. Clesandra is a few feet ahead of me being led toward a group of men who are holding a dark cloth. She's still struggling to catch her breath, but when she sees the men and the cloth, she finds another surge of energy to fight back.

"Don't let them take you!" she cries over her shoulder at Sheol and me. Her voice is shrill and high-pitched in her panic. "They're going to kill us!" Her last few words are muffled as the two security guards throw the dark cloth over her head. They drag her away kicking and screaming.

"Clesandra!" I scream after her, and try to struggle away from the men holding me. Their grips start to falter. I struggle more, and then all of my muscles contract at once in a horrible, violent, involuntary spasm. The darts of their Tasers bore deep into my ribcage. From somewhere far away Sheol's unintelligible screams of pain fill my ears.

Chapter 16

Soothing. Warm. Too warm. Hot. Too hot! Why is it so hot? Burning! Pain!

My eyes pop open and brightness, like staring into the white-hot part of a flame, blinds me.

"Hot!" I hear myself yell, as I struggle to make sense of what's around me. *Are they burning us? My hands!* I wrench them away from the heat. They slide through a grainy substance. Blinking violently, I try to force myself to adjust to the brightness.

There's a blurry figure lying to my right. To my left there are more blurry bodies. There's so many of them, at least five that I see immediately. I count another three as my eyes continue to adjust. They're motionless. There's a vastness around them. It's so hot. My tongue feels like a piece of leather in my mouth. Holding my hands in front of my face, I wiggle my fingers and try to make sense of my surroundings and force my eyes to finish adjusting.

It's so hot, but there are no flames. I realize I'm kneeling on the ground. *But it's not ground.* It's sand, miles of it, shimmering, and white-hot beneath me. A moment of panic crushes my chest. We were dumped in a desert to die. What a cruel, ironic way for that son of a bitch, Smith, to kill us.

A blood-curdling scream pierces the silence. One of the other soldiers who was in the hospital ward with us is kneeling in the sand and screaming. He holds his hands to his blistered-red face.

"They left me!" he screams in disbelief. It's like he doesn't know I'm a few feet away. Here with him. The shock on his face is terrifying.

Clesandra. Where is Clesandra? Sheol.

Panicking, I bolt to my feet and trudge through the deep, white sands to the bodies lying near me. I roll one over. *It's not Clesandra.* The man looks dead. His face burnt to a crisp on one side. I touch his neck to find a pulse. None.

No. This can't be happening. Where's Clesandra?

"Sheol! Clesandra!" I get no response. I start searching the sands, looking at each body. *Red hair. Too big. Too short. Damn it. Where are they?*

Then I see a dark braid poking out from beneath a black cloth hood. Face-down in the sand.

"Clesandra!"

Rushing over, I flip her body and rip the dark hood from her face. Her eyes are closed, mouth open.

"No, you can't be dead." My heart is racing as I check the pulse at her neck. There's a steady thumping under my fingertips and I gasp with relief. Cradling her head in my lap, I smooth sweat-soaked hair from her forehead and pan my surroundings, still looking for Sheol and useful items.

Weapons? Around the motionless bodies in the sand are guns, a variety of them. There are many weapons I'm familiar with practicing in combat training. *Why are there weapons?* I see a canteen on the ground a few feet away.

Gently lying Clesandra's head on the black cloth, I dash for the canteen. Grateful to feel it heavy with liquid I rush back to Clesandra. Tearing it open, I tip it to her lips.

She comes to life like a jack-in-the-box. Her eyes snap open, wild but blind and unseeing in the sun reflecting the white sands. She screams and goes instantly into attack mode. Grabs me by the shoulders of my camouflage uniform shirt and flips me onto my back. On top of me in a flash, cutting off my airway as she jams her forearm to my throat.

I try to get her name out. A phrase, anything so she knows it's me. She's got me pinned with one hand and is searching for her knife in her pockets. It's not there. She can't find it and uses her free hand to swipe at her eyes, trying to force them to adjust faster. I can feel myself starting to lose consciousness and use my last ounces of strength to try to push her off.

There's a scream and she's thrown off me. I glimpse a flash of sandy-colored hair.

"Get off him!" Sheol yells.

"Sheol," I choke out, trying to catch my breath. He's got her pinned to the ground, a handgun to her temple.

"Sheol. Let her go!"

"Avery?" she calls.

Sheol's still got her pinned. She's not moving a muscle under threat of being blown to pieces.

"Goddamn it, Sheol! Get off her!"

"Sheol?" she says in surprise. I can see the realization reach him a moment later. She's blinking wildly, trying to force her eyes to see.

"What the hell's going on?" she yells.

Slowly, Sheol lowers the gun and gets to his feet.

"They left us," another soldier says. "They fucking left us here to die."

His face is wild and filled with terror. A few moments later, we hear groans from other people starting to wake up in the hot sands.

Sheol helps Clesandra to her feet. She shields her face with a hand, searching.

"Avery?"

"I'm right here," I say, waving my hand near her.

She squints at me and reaches out to touch my face. "What happened to you?"

"What? Nothing. I'm right here. I'm okay."

"But your face?" She gently touches my cheek.

I wince at the pain that erupts under her light touch. I gingerly touch my face and feel the unsightly blisters bubbling on the surface. I look at Sheol more closely. He, too, has similar blisters starting to form. *Sunburn.* Sun exposure is one of the quickest ways to die in a desert. I run back to the soldier who was dead when I found him.

"Sorry, man, but we need this more than you."

I rip his clothing from his body and tear it in chunks.

"Here." I throw strips of cloth to Clesandra, Sheol, and the other soldier. I don't even need to tell them what it's for. We've spent our lives in the desert. We quickly construct our best makeshift head coverings to keep the sun from continuing to scorch us.

"Why would they drop us here?" Sheol whispers.

"Why else? Punishment, we won't fight for the war. They're making a statement," Clesandra growls.

"Why are you doing this to me? You said you wouldn't do this to me. I know you can hear me, you bastards! You said you wouldn't do this to me if I helped you!"

In the distance, Nico is on his knees, bellowing at the sky. He's pleading.

"Take me back. Please take me back! I helped you!"

Clesandra, growling under her breath, makes a beeline toward Nico. She reaches him in seconds and hauls him up by the collar of his shirt.

"Look, you little worm. What did you do?"

Nico's eyes are glassy and only half-focus on Clesandra. "They said they wouldn't do this to me," he whimpers.

"Do what?" I ask, joining Clesandra.

Nico looks at me and smiles. "I built this place for them…for you…as a testing ground."

His smile goes lopsided, and he laughs hysterically like a madman. He looks at Clesandra, and his body begins to shake.

"This arena was built mainly for him." He points at me. "But it's also meant to kill you," he tells her, bursting into a fit of laughter again.

Clesandra's face contorts in anger and she drives a knee into his crotch. "What do you mean?"

Nico crumples in pain, but Clesandra holds him upright while he coughs and groans in agony. She makes another move to strike him.

"No, no," he croaks. "I'll tell you. Smith had this place built to test Evericon," he squeaks, glancing in my direction. "Make sure he's fit for war. That he won't be a traitor. And you." He smiles at Clesandra. "You were supposed to die months ago in the simulation room. But you won't survive this one. Won't be able to secure your fate—"

"Fate? What do you mean about securing her fate?" I ask.

The other soldiers are starting to realize what's going on. They, too, are drawn to Nico.

"There's no such thing as fate. Not really. But that doesn't stop Lupète from getting the commander and everyone he comes into contact with to believe something they have no business believing. They think, or rather, *he* thinks, that everyone here will be the only thing that prevents the mission from being a success."

I realize Nico must be talking about Lupète's ability to see the future. Lupète must have seen something he didn't like or couldn't figure out.

"So we're being tested?" I ask.

"Yes. The commander has to be sure he can trust all of his crew. Personally, I think we should have just eliminated all of you. But the commander seems to think he *needs* you." He laughs. "Lupète's got the commander twisted around his little pinky finger with all his so-called visions. But Lupète can't fool me." Nico's beady eyes dart between the two of us.

"No one needs you." He glares at Clesandra. "No one needs you either," he says to me, then bursts into another fit of laughter. "And you know what? They don't need me either. Not really. People are disposable. There's nothing *special* about any of us. If Smith wasn't sure about you, he should have just killed you both. Then maybe we wouldn't be here. It wouldn't have gone this far." He gestures to the empty, vast expanse of desert.

"But you weren't supposed to leave me here! You ugly bastards!" he yells up at the sky again. "I helped you! I built this for you! This is how you repay me?"

He stares at the sky for a long time, like he's waiting for something, but nothing happens.

"They think they've won," he whispers. "But come." He gestures frantically to all of us. No one moves to come closer to him. His eyes are dilated like he's high.

"Come here." He waves us in more emphatically. Sheol and I close a little distance. "I-I know how to get you out of here." He smiles at the sky. "They think they're so clever leaving me here to die, but they forget I created this place."

Other soldiers start to come in closer to hear what Nico has to say.

"This place is nothing more than a—" His voice is cut off by a high-pitched squealing whistle coming from somewhere on his body. Nico's eyes grow wide with terror.

"No!" he yells. "You promised!" He leaps to his feet, sprints a few feet away, frantically rummaging through the sand. The whistle turns into a rapid three-beat beep.

"You won't euthanize me like some freaking animal!" he screams.

He finds what he's looking for—a pistol—and places the barrel of it in his mouth. Hands shaking, he looks at us.

Clesandra makes a move to run over and stop him from eating the bullet, but I instinctively grab her arm and swing her away from going near him. I yank her head into my chest, blocking her view so she won't see the explosion of gray brain matter I know will come when he pulls the trigger. We wait for the bang and the sickening sound of his body hitting the sand.

Click.

I look back, shocked that the gun didn't go off. Nico is distraught. His eyes are as wide as saucers, and his hands shake violently. The beeping becomes a four-beat staccato. High-pitched and menacing. In a panic, Nico uses both hands on the handle of the gun to rapidly pull the trigger again and again.

Click, click, click, click, click.

No bang.

Nico takes the gun out of his mouth and crumples to his knees in despair. The pistol falls out of his hand. The rise and fall of his chest is quick and erratic. He's not ready to accept death. Moments later, his body goes rigid, his muscles contract and spasm. The veins in his neck and arms stand up stiff, as if filled with liquid, and then…*pop.* The sound is just a dull thump. All the veins and arteries in his body explode, spattering the sand red.

The soldier who was lamenting about being left behind renews his screams of anguish. Sheol turns and throws up. Other soldiers stand nearby in disbelief.

Clesandra pries herself out of my grasp to look.

"It's the self-detonation chip. They're going to kill

us!" she yells, trying to tear the wristband off her body.

"Greetings, soldiers," Smith's voice and projected image appears in front of us.

"You left us all here to die!" the hysterical soldier screams at the holographic image.

"Soldier 198, I have not left you. You don't have to stay here." The soldier's face contorts with what I think is a mixture of confusion and relief. "You have a choice to make. If you complete the task I'm about to give you, you can return to Xinorsus with me today," Smith says calmly.

"Oh, please," the man pleads. "I'll do anything. Don't leave me here."

I glance at the eight other soldiers. Most of them look just as confused as Soldier 198. Sheol and Clesandra look disgusted.

"What do you want, Smith?" Clesandra sneers.

"It's quite simple, really. I want to make sure none of you will compromise our mission with your *feelings* for the natives on this planet. I need to know that you will kill on sight and take orders without question. As you can see around you, there are several weapons provided. By the way, Ms. Willows, yours is just…there." His projected self-image points to a small, rectangular shape in the sand. "Hope you don't mind, but I had our scientists examine the weaponry a second time. They have a unique design. Our weapons' team has the proper samples now. They will serve us well against the natives." Smith smiles viciously.

"You have no right!" Clesandra snarls. She strides over and scoops her knife out of the sand. The blade sprouts out of the handle the instant she touches it. She hurls it at the commander's image. The knife sails through his forehead without so much as distorting the image.

Smith laughs wickedly. "That anger should come

in handy in a few minutes." He glances upward and points at the sky. An enormous aircraft appears hovering above us and starts to descend. Popping and zapping sounds crackle like heat lightning as the aircraft passes through some unseen electrical field far above us. Our small group scatters when the wind from the ship kicks waves of sand into our eyes. The ship never lands. It just hovers in midair, three to four feet above the ground, and dumps eight unidentifiable objects out of the bottom of the aircraft. Once the load is dropped, the aircraft soars into the air, remaining a few hundred feet above us within the fabricated electrical field.

Only after the blowing sands start to die down do I realize that the objects aren't just objects. They're people dropped onto the hot sands. They aren't humans from Earth either. They're natives. Their hands and feet are bound behind their backs. Dark hoods, like the ones thrown over our faces in the hospital ward, block their sight and disorient them. A single word and number in bright, white lettering is printed on the hoods. Soldier 134, *my number.*

The natives are communicating with each other, yelling, but their dialect sounds like gibberish to me. The tone of their voices is nervous and frantic.

"What are you playing at here?" one of the other soldiers asks.

Smith's expression is cold and serious.

"There's one for each of you. I command you to kill them. That is the only way you may return home with us today." His tone is emotionless.

"If we refuse?" Clesandra snarls.

"Die here." Smith shrugs. "It's what your life will be like without going to war for our water in a few short weeks anyway. But of course," the commander pauses to look right at me, "no one can force you to pick up a gun and pull the trigger." He glances at the soldier who was begging to leave the desert. "It's your choice. Oh, and soldier Evericon? You should know that we need every able-bodied man and woman to join in the revolution. I'm thinking that if some of you *choose* not to come back with us, a mandatory draft of men and women ages twelve and over is in order to ensure we have enough people."

"You mean enough people to sacrifice?" Sheol spits.

"We will all have to make sacrifices to survive," Smith says.

"Not like this." Sheol shakes his head.

I can feel myself go rigid at the thought of my brother forced to go to war. I can't let that happen. *But kill an innocent person? One who can't even fight back?* I look at the poor souls bound with their faces covered. Disoriented by the heat and their situation. Some are starting to cry out. Most of their skin is exposed to the burning sands beneath them and the scorching sun above. They aren't used to the heat and the pain. They don't even have shoes or boots on their feet. Thin, raggedy garments no doubt put on them by soldiers at Xinorsus are the only things covering their exposed skin. Only in the hot desert sun for mere moments, and their skin is already starting to turn red and blister.

"I won't do it!" I yell at the commander.

"Are you sure?" He pulls a holographic palm reader out of his pocket and runs his fingers across the screen. A secondary projection of Jace appears next to him.

"Jace!" I yell at the image, but he can't hear me. He's in the hospital ward with Francine and Davinic. Francine is showing him how to mix some sort of chemical concoction from a battery of plants and liquids laid out on a table. The two of them are chatting like best friends. Jace is smiling and happy. Seconds later, a holographic image on his wristband lights up. Happy conversations between Francine and Jace cease.

Jace reads the words aloud. "Combat training?" he says bewildered. "Lupète said I wouldn't have combat training until I turned thirteen." Francine's forehead wrinkles with concern. Her eyebrows expand upward as she brings a pair of red reading glasses to her eyes and squints at the screen.

"Davinic, come here." She waves him over. "Am I reading this right?"

The image of Jace in the hospital ward evaporates.

"You wouldn't," I snarl.

"Could be a simple mistake," Smith says casually. "Or maybe it's not? It's your choice. I'll be watching." His projected image disappears, leaving the eight of us and our corresponding victims alone in the desert to ponder what we're going to do next.

Chapter 17

Our small circle of eight soldiers is quiet, looking at the group of natives in front of us. Barely able to move, they're wiggling, trying to escape the hot sand beneath them.

"This is madness!" Sheol is the first to break the silence.

The soldier who was pleading with Smith is frantically searching the sand.

"What are you doing, Zayden?" another soldier asks.

"I'm getting out of here." His voice has an edge of panic. "And you should too. I can't be left here. Not here. No more sand. No more of this life." He's muttering to himself now as he digs through the sand. "I don't care what it takes. I'm not being left here," he whispers and finds a gun. With shaky hands he fires a test round into the sand a few feet in front of him.

"You aren't really going to do this, Zayden. This isn't right. You know this isn't right."

"I'm not being left here. I have to." Zayden looks at the other soldier, who must be a friend either from Earth or from the journey to Panacea. Zayden's eyes plead with the other soldier to understand, for all of us to understand. "I have to," he whispers more to himself than to us.

Zayden raises the gun. Both hands are on the handle. His arms shake violently, trying to steady the weapon.

"Don't do it," Clesandra says. "If you do, you let Smith win." Zayden pauses to look at her, and then turns his attention back to the hooded victim in front of him. For a second I think he's going to lower the gun.

Bang!

The native's body convulses in the sand.

Zayden's legs give out and he lets the gun tumble out of his hands. The hovering ship above us swoops down, creating a swirling, stinging cyclone of sand, and Zayden is scooped up. It's that easy. He's gone.

"Damn it," his friend curses under his breath. He starts searching the sand for a weapon too.

"What'd ya think you're doing?" Clesandra screams at him. The tall man finds the weapon he's looking for, an M16 rifle. He marches a few feet from the victims.

"Don't do this, soldier!" Clesandra begs.

"You don't have to do this," Sheol adds.

"Doesn't look like there's another choice," he snarls back. "Look, this isn't something I want to do. Killing people, it's not fun for me, but the commander's right. We have to be ready to kill people. The natives aren't going to just let us take their water. We're going to have to kill them, or let them kill us. I can't continue to be squeamish about it." He raises the gun to his shoulder and presses his cheek to the metal.

"This is not a battleground. We aren't even at war yet. These people aren't trying to fight us!" Sheol yells at him. "How can you justify doing this?"

"Don't need to justify it. It has to be done. And these prisoners are bound. If they were set loose and trying to kill us, you wouldn't try to stop me."

"Has to be done?" Clesandra says, getting between the soldier and his soon-to-be murdered native. "This doesn't have to be done."

"They haven't done anything to us." Sheol backs her up.

"Get out of the way," the soldier barks. "Unless you plan on getting shot too." He turns the gun on Clesandra. She steps sideways but continues to follow him as he approaches the seven other victims lying on the ground. The natives have gone quiet now. They aren't trying to get away from the hot sands. They've stopped communicating with each other. They just lay there lifelessly as if they're already dead.

Bang!

We were all so preoccupied with the soldier with the M16 that we don't realize another soldier...

Bang! Bang!

Two other soldiers shoot natives. The aircraft whirls down and sucks them up. Only four of us are left and four natives still alive. One of them is whimpering.

"You're really going to kill these innocent people?" Sheol asks.

"People? They aren't even human," the soldier says. Even as he's trying to justify what he's about to do, there's a glint of doubt in his eyes. Regret even.

Their voices seem so far away. Muted and dull to my ears, which are ringing from the gunshots. The handgun that I barely remember picking up feels heavy in my hands. The smooth metal feels somehow cold, though I know it should be burning my palms after lying in the hot sun. *I've shot before. At targets. Not at people. But how hard can it be?*

I look at the gun in my hands, and then back at Sheol and Clesandra. They're still trying to convince the other soldier to lower his weapon. Something in me knows he won't. *I have to do this. I have to kill my prisoner for Jace. Will they understand I have to do this? Will they forgive me? Will they join me? Clesandra is too proud. Strong. She won't. Sheol might.*

I look over at the hooded victims with my soldier number. *It'll be like shooting something that isn't even alive. Except it'll bleed, you moron! Look at all the blood on the sand! Are you really going to add to that?* The natives bleed so much. The sand under the dead bodies is turning a rusty red, just like the sand at home. My stomach turns. *God forgive me.*

I pop the revolver open and spin the cylinder. There's a bullet in every chamber. I feel myself click the cylinder shut, hardly aware of what I'm doing.

"General Evericon once told me that his sons could handle themselves well under pressure." Smith's words echo hollowly in the back of my head. *I'm just like my father after all.* Then another thought creeps in. *Why not kill yourself?* But that would leave Jace alone with Smith. *I can't do that either.* My attention drifts away from my victim distracted by Sheol and Clesandra's yelling.

"You don't have to do this," Sheol says again.

The soldier raises the gun and takes aim at the still body on the ground. He's about to fire, index finger on the trigger. Sheol's got his hands on the top of his head, gripping his hair like he can't believe what he's about to see.

"Wait!" Clesandra screams, jumping in front of the native on the ground. She whips out her knife. It glows a magnificent florescent blue against the white desert sands.

"You gonna try and kill me?" the soldier spits sarcastically. "I'll bet you that native's life you can't throw the knife and kill me before I shoot you dead between the eyes." He raises the gun and takes aim at Clesandra's forehead.

Make her move! Make her get out of the way! Tackle the solider! Do something. Say something! Anything! Just don't stand there! There's a part of me that's screaming internally. Willing me to stop this madness and find a way out of this indescribable hell. But I'm locked to my place. Feet and mouth frozen, but my head bobbles back and forth between each person like a rubbernecker at the scene of a horrible car crash.

"I'm not gonna kill you," Clesandra snarls, slipping behind the native. She holds her knife at the prisoner's throat.

"What are you doing?" Sheol barks.

"Gonna do the dirty deed for me then?" the soldier scoffs, lowering the rifle slightly.

"No," Clesandra says as she whips off the native's hood. "I just thought if ya were man enough to kill someone, ya might as well look 'em in the eyes when ya do it."

My stomach hits my feet the instant the hood is removed. It's the native who came each night to visit Sheol. She looks terrible, like she's been beaten and starved. Her eyes are shut tight, trying to block out the blinding sunlight.

"Zap," Sheol whispers in disbelief. "Not this one," he says, stepping in front of the soldier's rifle. "You'll have to kill me first."

"Get out of the way," the soldier snarls, flipping his gun around, and striking Sheol's jaw with the butt of the rifle. Sheol falls to the ground. He lingers on his knees for just a second before quickly climbing back to his feet. The side of Sheol's face turns black and blue instantly. He spits a wad of blood at the soldier in front of him. Hands clenched at his sides.

"Like I said, you'll have to shoot me first," he says.

"Have it your way." He raises the gun so it's square with Sheol's chest.

"You wouldn't dare," Clesandra hisses. She raises her knife, ready to throw it at the soldier.

His finger flexes on the trigger.

Bang!

Chapter 18

I barely feel the gun roll off my fingertips. Afraid to take a breath, I look at Clesandra. She's staring at me with a look of shock. My ears ring. I feel like I'm underwater. I can't surface. My lungs are going to pop.

What have I done?

It wasn't a clean shot. The soldier is lying on the ground, writhing in agony.

"You shot him," Sheol says in disbelief.

I can't answer. *What have I done?*

"Not good enough, though," Clesandra mutters.

A shudder runs up my spine. *I just shot a man in cold blood. He's a soldier from Earth. What have I done?*

Clesandra slowly gets to her feet and stalks over to the soldier lying in the sand. He's choking and making a gurgling sound. Blood seeps from the corner of his mouth. His eyes are wide, seeing nothing.

She bends over him and tilts his face up so he can look at her. "By the way, I would've taken that bet." She skillfully slits his throat ear to ear and lets his head roll back in the sand.

"Well, Sleeping Beauty, I'm guessing you just bought yourself an extended stay in the desert."

And I've also signed a death warrant for my brother. "What have I done?" I finally voice the words so that my own ears can hear them.

"What now?" Sheol asks.

Beep.

My eyes fly wide open in panic and swoop down to my wristband. *I'm going to die.* I look over at Nico's bloody body a few yards away. *I'm going to die a horrible death. Smith will probably show a video feed of my death to Jace and all the other soldiers as an example of being a traitor. My brother will watch me die and know I'm a murderer.*

Beep.

Sheol and Clesandra are by my side in a second.

Beep.

"You're going to kill him?" Sheol yells at the ship hovering above us.

Clesandra is desperately trying to find a way to get the band off my arm. I know she won't be able to.

"Get off!" I push her away from me hard. "Sheol, listen to me!" I can hear the panic in my own voice, and it scares me to death.

Beep.

I know I don't have very long.

Sheol's panicking, too, and I need him to listen. Clesandra grabs my arm, and I shove her into the sand. Grabbing the collar of Sheol's shirt and dragging him with me away from her, I force him to focus on only me.

"You have to shoot your prisoner," I say very seriously.

Sheol's eyes are darting away from mine, trying not to focus on me and what I'm saying.

I force him to look at me. "You have to! Someone has to go back to Xinorsus and protect Jace," I whisper. "She won't do it. I know she won't." I indicate Clesandra, who's back on her feet and coming at me like a bulldozer. "You have to do it!" I yell at him.

Clesandra practically runs me over. Sweeping my feet out from under me, she tackles me to the ground.

"Now you listen to me," she says, "you're not gonna die. You can't, not after I—"

Beep, beep, beep. The noise floods my ears in rapid three-beat successions.

"Sheol, do it!" I yell. I'm not even paying attention

to Clesandra. I'm only focused on the uncertainty in Sheol's eyes. I know he can see the pleading expression on my face. *He's not going to do it.* I watch, terrified, as his eyes dart back and forth between the prisoners and me. Debating. *Oh God, he's not going to be able to do it.* After what seems like an eternity, I finally see a shift in him. He picks up the gun I dropped and looks at me.

"I'll take care of him," he says solemnly, and turns toward the prisoners.

Realization crosses Clesandra's face. She looks at me, then back at Sheol.

Beep, beep, beep.

The sound is getting louder and more high pitched, drowning out some of the words she barks at him.

Sheol raises the gun to take aim at his hooded victim. He pauses for a moment, unsure.

"Sheol, do it!" I yell.

"Shut up!" Clesandra hisses. She takes her knife and it sizzles into two daggers. I realize what she's doing, and start to struggle against her. She backhands me across the face, sending an eruption of stars to blind my vision. I hear Sheol yelp, and then feel an incredible blinding pain in my arm.

"No!" I yell, fighting against the pain. *I think it's happening. I'm really dying. This is it.* The pain is unbearable. I can hardly think. It's like a sawing, ripping pain. I hear Sheol's voice in the distance.

"What are you doing?" he yells. I know he's not dead, and I'm grateful.

"Help me, Sheol!" she hollers back.

Beep, beep, beep! The sound is getting faster, louder, shriller. The pain is more intense. I force my eyes open, desperate to see my friends one last time before I die.

Clesandra is slashing my arm off.

"You can't do this!" I wrestle what's left of my arm free from her grasp. The band is still attached and beeping wildly. So much blood is spraying everywhere. I look away from the blood and my mangled arm and throw up in the sand. I start to feel myself losing consciousness. Sheol is next to me, shaking my shoulders. *How did he get here so fast?*

"Smith will kill you if you help me," I hear myself say.

"Stop fighting me," she grunts. "Not gonna lose you too."

"Avery, stay awake!" Sheol shakes my shoulders harder. The pain is too much.

I'm beginning to slip in and out of consciousness. I can hear Sheol and Clesandra yelling at me, but I don't care. I'm so very tired all of the sudden. Tired of fighting. My eyelids are heavy, and I struggle to prevent them from closing. As they flutter open and shut, two golden orbs appear. Far away at first, but then they start moving, coming closer. I should be afraid, but I'm not. Moments later, I see them as eyes. Lupète's eyes. I recognize them at the same time as a forceful pressure encircles my brain.

Do not give up. His voice pervades my thoughts. *I was wrong about you. This is not the end. If this is the end for you, it is also the end for Jace, for Sheol, for Clesandra, and for the rest of Panacea.*

A sudden vision of everyone I love amassed in a giant grave rocks me to my core. I scream and cry out, listening to the horrific sound reverberate off my eardrums. But I'm dying and there's nothing I can do for them.

My vision becomes more disjointed. I resist the blackness creeping in. Clesandra and Sheol's faces blur and shimmer in front of me. It's quiet. There's no more screaming. I can feel hands on my body, but there's no more pain. *Yep, this is it. I'm dead.* Dread envelopes my body, knowing that everyone and everything I cared about will soon be lost. I struggle to sit up. Clesandra is holding my hand. The wristband is on it. Something flies away from her. *My hand. She threw it?* I squint. The light is so bright. I can see Clesandra's beautiful lips moving, yelling something at Sheol, but I can't hear anything. Just a dull buzz in my ears. I try to focus on her face and it multiplies. Sheol is doing something to my arm. The pressure is intense. My head lolls to the side in his direction. He's tying his belt around my arm. *Sheol, buddy, I'm dead, that's not going to work.*

Clesandra jabs her fingers into my neck. They feel oddly slippery against my skin. I try to bring all three of her faces together in front of me. I do for a fraction of a second, and I see the pain and agony in her eyes. See her lips moving, screaming something that I can't hear. I know she can't find a pulse. My eyes flutter closed, and this time I can't seem to force them open. It doesn't matter. I want to tell them that I'm okay right now. Dying isn't so bad. When they join me, they'll see. This is better.

Something is compressing my chest rhythmically. Softness presses against my lips, and then there's an intense pressure in my lungs. I don't know what's happening to me. The blackness that crept in pops and sizzles. It's replaced by an undulating wall of bright colors.

"Avery?" The voice sounds far away, but I know that voice. I would know that voice anywhere. Out of the wall of colors comes my older brother. He looks just as I remembered him. Tall and slender, dressed in a white T-shirt over camouflage pants.

"Jeremy." A smile comes to my lips when I say his name. Blackness seeps in and starts to take him away from me. There's a pressure in my lungs again. The blackness fades into colors, and Jeremy's face becomes clearer. This time the pressure in my chest feels strangely like happiness. I feel like I'm about to burst.

"I missed you," I tell him. My body becomes fluid and light. I'm able to climb to my feet and look around. Sheol and Clesandra are gone. I must be dead.

Jeremy closes the distance between us. His smile is wide and inviting. He throws his arms around me and pounds my back hard.

"I missed you, too, kid." He pushes me out of the hug but keeps his grip on my upper arms. "It's been too long."

This time I throw my arms around him. He pats my back and lets me cling to him a while longer.

"I thought I would never see you again," I whisper.

"I know," Jeremy says. "But, Avery, you have to leave."

My heart sinks, loneliness and fear take the place of happiness. I push myself away so I can see his face. "Leave?"

"You have to be strong and complete your mission."

"Mission?" I shake my head in disbelief. "You can't be serious. I can't complete Smith's mission. It's not right. I don't want to go. I want to stay here with you."

Jeremy frowns, disappointed. "There are people who still need you. Jace still needs you."

I feel a pang of guilt that's quickly replaced by a flash of anger.

"What am I supposed to do, Jeremy? Follow Smith's orders? Kill the natives?"

"Tough decisions have to be made."

My chest feels like it's about to explode. Jeremy's face fractures and crackles with bursts of color.

"What's happening to you?" I reach out to touch his face. He's out of reach and fading fast.

"They need you." Jeremy's voice is a whisper.

"I don't want to be responsible for killing people."

"Relax, kid. You'll do what's right."

"Wait! Please!" Jeremy disappears, and I run toward him. My eyes flutter open again as Clesandra pounds her fists into my chest. She collapses forward onto my body, burying her face in my neck.

"Clesandra, look! He's back!"

She sucks back a sob and balls her hands in my shirt. Using my chest to push herself up, she scans my face.

I am back, and so is the pain. I can't stop myself from screaming out in agony. Sheol and Clesandra look terrified. Clesandra heaves me into a seated position against her and forces me to hold what's left of my arm in the air. I glance at it briefly and almost lose consciousness again. Clesandra amputated the limb mid-forearm. Even though her blade is incredibly sharp, my pulling away from her created deep, jagged, uneven slashes of shredded skin well above the amputation site. Sheol tied his belt around the stump to help stop the bleeding, but blood is still dribbling out and flowing down my body at an alarming rate.

"My knife, hand me my knife," she says to Sheol. He fumbles around in the sand for it and hands it to her quickly.

"What are you going to do?" I ask, fearing she might try to cut more of my arm off.

"Have to stop the bleeding," she grunts. "This is gonna hurt." She takes my arm and pinches it between her knees. "You ready?"

"No."

My answer doesn't stop her from holding the burning blade of her knife to the exposed arteries and veins. The pain is excruciating, and I black out instantly.

***

"Avery, wake up." Sheol is slapping my face and calling my name repeatedly. "Christ, man. You have to stop disappearing like that. You're scaring me to death. Stay awake."

"My arm," I whimper. The pain is an intense throbbing, burning sensation.

"I know, buddy, I know. We're trying to fix that for you."

I glance at my arm out of the corner of my eye, afraid I won't be able to handle seeing it fully. Clesandra is bent over, wrapping the stump with strips of fabric. The bleeding seems to have mostly stopped, but searing pain radiates up to my shoulder as she ties the strips. I squint against the pain and look up. The sun, lighting the purple-hued planet, is high in the sky. The intense light and heat beaming down on our bodies is cooking us from the outside in. Smith's aircraft is gone. The other soldiers are gone too. I look away from the frightening pools of blood seeping from beneath the murdered natives.

"Where's Smith? Where's the ship?" I ask.

"Gone," Clesandra answers, as she tears another strip of cloth from the bottom of her pant leg.

"Smith left us here to die. That's our punishment for saving you." Sheol fills in the blanks.

"You didn't kill your prisoners."

"Even if we decided to kill our prisoners, we're too much of a risk to the mission now," Sheol tells me.

"You shouldn't have helped me." I grit my teeth

against the pain as Clesandra yanks the strips tighter on my severed arm.

"You'd rather die?" she asks.

"We are dead. How do you think we're going to get out of here?"

Clesandra yanks the last strip as tightly as she can, probably in anger at my words. I cry out in pain. Tears flood the corners of my eyes.

"Please stop!" I beg her.

She looks at me, and her angry expression softens slightly. "They have to be tight," she whispers.

"We'll find a way out." Sheol tries to console me.

"What about them?" I ask, looking in the direction of the four natives still bound on the ground. The one Sheol's fond of is watching us. Her luminescent-blue eyes, darting, take in the whole scene.

"Leave 'em," Clesandra says. Seeing that I'm not going to pass out again, she's busy gathering a small arsenal and the water canteen.

Sheol and I exchange a glance. I know he's thinking about the woman who visited our bedroom each night.

"We can't leave them here to die," he whispers to me.

I look over at the four of them. Their skin is now scarlet in the hot sun. I think about how Smith made them out to be vicious killers. Then I think about the young native watching us. She never once tried to kill Sheol, Jace, or I. Conflicted, I nod.

"Cut them loose. They should have as much of a fighting chance as we do."

Sheol picks up a Bowie knife and cautiously approaches the woman he calls Zap.

"Sure ya want to do that?" Clesandra looks at Sheol suspiciously. He ignores her. Watching the native's face as Sheol advances, I half-expect her to become violent, threatening, or maybe do the opposite and cower at the sight of the knife. I can only imagine what she must be thinking about us, about our species. In the last few days, she's been captured, perhaps tortured, and dumped here with us to be burnt to a crisp in the sun. She's watched and heard unthinkable violence occur in the last hour. She can clearly see dead bodies of her own people in the sand. I've shot a man. I cringe again at the thought. Clesandra and Sheol have cut off my arm. Now he's approaching her wielding a knife. She should be terrified, yet her expression is stoic.

Sheol slips behind her, quickly slashes through the binding, and jumps back. He holds the knife in front of himself ready for an attack. The two of them look at each other carefully. Very slowly, almost painfully, the woman draws her hands from behind her back. Her facial expression never changes, and her eyes never leave Sheol's, but I can tell by her careful movements that she was bound for quite some time and is fighting the pain of moving cramped, sore muscles. Despite the pain, she gracefully glides up from the ground to stand in front of him. The two of them are so close in size that they stand nearly eye to eye. She extends a hand for the knife.

All of the color drains out of Sheol's face, and I can almost feel the fear he's projecting.

Don't give her the knife.

"Not a chance," Clesandra says.

The woman turns her head to look at her. Clesandra is standing with her own knife at the ready.

The native looks back at Sheol and points to the rest of the prisoners. She extends her other arm further, palm up for the knife in Sheol's hand.

To my surprise, he turns the blade around in his fingers and gently presses the handle of the knife into her palm.

"Idiot," Clesandra hisses. "Get up," she says to me. "Lover boy over there's going to get us killed, and we ain't gonna be around here for it." She's trying to tug me to my feet. I cry out in pain as she reaches under my armpits and hauls with all her might.

I try to help her, but my feet won't hold my weight. The desert spins violently. I struggle to stay conscious. Suddenly, I'm truly aware of how desperate our situation is. *I'm too weak to even stand up. I'm not going to make it.*

"Help me out here," she scolds.

I can't even make words form sentences. Blackness drifts in from the corners of my eyes.

"Stop, stop," I moan. "Me…leave." I'm not even sure what I'm saying. My whole vision grays, but I can still hear things happening around me.

Clesandra yells something. My body drops back into the sand.

"Come any closer and I'll—"

"Clesandra, no!" The voice sounds like Sheol, but I can't be sure.

"Mine! Give it back! I'll kill you. Don't touch him!" Clesandra yells. I can feel the panic in her angry words. I want to help her. I try to stand, move, do something. It's like the wiring in my brain and body has been completely disconnected. I can't do anything to help her even if I wanted to. I try to will away the dense fog and bright, prickly spots obscuring my vision, but they won't go away. I strain my ears to hear what else is going on, but it's like a horde of angry bees are building a hive against my eardrums. I feel a hand press to my forehead. It's cold and soothing. Vibrant colors splash across my vision. The colors come together and form a brilliant body of clear, purple-hued water. It's so calm and serene, like a pond at sunset.

Not a single ripple disturbs the pristine surface. I'm mesmerized by the perfection I'm witnessing.

Calm. Be still. Rest. I feel the words rather than hear them. As if I've been drugged, my body relaxes, and the pain in my arm fades to a dull throb.

For a moment I allow myself to focus on only the pond in front of me. I take a deep breath and absorb the calm serenity. The feeling is short-lived. I think of Clesandra and Sheol. What are the natives doing to them? I can't bear the thought of them being murdered while I'm…*where the hell am I right now?*

I turn around away from the body of water and all I see are trees. *Oh, God. I have to get out of here. Where is here?* Starting to panic, I turn back to the water. It's not water anymore. It's now a pit of fire. Flames wash in on the bank and lick up the sides of trees. I back away from the fire and trip over a rock or branch and tumble down. The back of my head smacks the ground, and white-hot stars dance in front of me.

The white dots dissipate. I'm on my back looking up a rich canopy of treetops. I scream and scoot backward on my rear-end, half-expecting the burning branches to drop down on top of me.

"Avery!" Clesandra yells.

"Avery, stop!" Sheol shouts and grabs my shoulders.

It takes me a minute to register what's going on. The burning pond is gone. I'm no longer alone. Clesandra and Sheol are here and so are a group of natives.

"Where are we? How did we get here? How did we get out? Where's Smith? I have to get Jace." My pulse is racing and the pain in my left arm is throbbing out of control.

"Relax. Shhhhh," Sheol says soothingly. "You're going to be okay. The desert was just a simulation bubble. We got out."

"What? How?" My brain is a jumbled mess of questions. Pain from my amputated arm is racing up and down my body, making it hard to focus.

"Easy. Calm down. Look," Sheol says, picking up a rock and throwing it to his right. I watch the rock explode into a firework of sparks as it bounces off an invisible wall in the distance. "Nico created an electrified dome. Like the simulation room on the ship. The desert is there. Zap got us out. She disrupts the electric field or something," Sheol tells me.

I try to connect everything in my head but I can't make sense of the details. Even though the forests on Panacea are tropical and hot, I'm suddenly very cold. My body shivers involuntarily, making the pain in my arm unbearable.

Seeing my discomfort, one of the natives, a tall, muscular man with wild looking dark hair approaches me with his hand outstretched in front of him. He reaches for me.

"No! Don't touch me! Don't hurt them!" I'm still confused by the whole situation and incredibly dizzy. How did we get here? Where is the desert? I push off Sheol, trying to stand. I scream out in pain, remembering that I no longer have a hand to leverage my body up.

Clesandra drops down in front of me defensively. The native continues his approach.

"He was pretty damn clear. He doesn't want to be touched," she snarls.

"Niteg," Zap addresses the man calmly. She says something else in her language that stops the man. Niteg's startling yellow eyes regard Zap with confusion before he backs away.

When Clesandra is convinced the native will leave me alone, she scoots behind me and holds my arm above my head. "Still losing blood," she says, cursing.

I try to ignore her words and the pain radiating all over my body. I scan our group instead. Nothing at all about where we are makes sense. We aren't in the desert anymore, but all the natives are sporting gruesome desert sunburns. Looking distraught, they mutter to each other in their own language. I don't understand. Zap's anxiety is starting to rise listening to them. She glances nervously from her friends to Sheol, Clesandra, and me.

Zap joins the three other natives in a tense huddle. They touch each other's arms.

"What are they doing?" I whisper.

"Sharing information," Sheol answers.

"What?"

"It's hard to explain. They can talk faster that way...I think," Sheol says.

I shake my head, not really understanding, and take a huge swallow of air. As I gulp it down, I realize how thirsty I am. My vision swirls again. Clesandra pushes sweat-soaked hair away from my forehead.

"What now?" I ask.

Sheol and Clesandra exchange a look. Zap disconnects herself from the group and approaches us. My muscles tense involuntarily and I try to stand again. It doesn't work, and Clesandra scolds me for trying to move.

"It's okay," Sheol says. He stands to meet Zap and takes her hand.

Their palms glow together for a moment, then Zap lets go and turns back to her group.

"We're screwed," Sheol whispers.

"What do you mean?" Clesandra asks cautiously. "How do you know that?"

"What's going on?" I ask nervously.

The two of them ignore me. "She just showed

me," Sheol tells Clesandra.

"What?"

"She just showed me," Sheol says again, as if repeating what he said would make it any clearer. "There's no water between here and where we need to go for at least a week's walk."

"We're not gonna make it three days without water," Clesandra breathes.

"Exactly," Sheol says defeated.

"Can we dig for it? Like on the base?" Clesandra asks.

Sheol shrugs. "It might be worth a try." He scans the area for something to dig with and chooses a fallen branch nearby. He scoops it up and jams it as hard as he can into the ground. He starts to rake it through the dry ground, moving small mounds of earth. Zap looks at him confused and goes to him immediately.

"Digging the water up," he tells her without stopping.

"Too deep," she says.

"They know English?" I say surprised.

Sheol ignores me but stops digging for a second to look at her. "How deep is too deep?"

"Too deep," she says again, and then touches his shoulder. Sheol looks at the tiny hole he was digging, and with a frustrated yell he hurls the branch into the forest. His shoulders slump down.

"Water is miles below the ground," he says to Clesandra. "We'd kill ourselves trying to get it up."

"The plants here all look healthy," Clesandra points out. She's right. Though the surface of the ground is dry and dusty, all the plants look well watered.

Zap pulls a small weed out of the ground. It doesn't come willingly, but when it does, Zap holds it out in front Clesandra and points to the roots.

"Big," she tells Clesandra.

"Huh?"

"I think she's trying to tell you that the roots can grow and reach the water, but it would be too far for us."

"Thanks, I didn't get that," Clesandra says sarcastically.

Sheol glares. "I'm just trying to help."

"I'm not an idiot," she snarls, her face beginning to turn red.

Sheol, choosing to avoid a fight, gets up and stalks to the edge of the tree line. He leans against the rough bark, avoiding eye contact with anyone in the group. Zap looks from Sheol to Clesandra and back to her three other friends. The uneasiness she's feeling is palpable.

A week of traveling without water is impossible. We're all going to die. Just thinking about water makes me desperate for it. I press my tongue to my front teeth and try to conjure a mouthful of saliva. I'd take anything at this point. My body feels like it's on fire. I squirm, trying to ease the discomfort, but moving only causes more pain.

"Stop moving. Relax," Clesandra says.

"So hot. Thirsty." My head, almost involuntarily, tosses from side to side.

"Easy. You've lost a ton of blood. It makes you thirstier. Stop talking. Save your energy."

"I'm going to die. Oh, Jace. I'm never going to see him again. I have to—" Clesandra slaps my cheeks. "You stop it right now," she commands. "No one is dying. You hear me?"

I stop struggling and gulp air. "You're gonna be fine," she whispers. Her words offer little comfort. Her beautiful features are contorted with worry and she's staring off into the woods. She must be terrified because I feel her pinching my waist.

"Oww! Stop pinching me."

"I'm not pinching you," she says.

There's another sharp pinch in the same spot. "Oww! Yes, you are!"

"Oh, God…what the…?" she curses.

Zap and Sheol hear our yelping and spin around. To my horror, enormous beetle-like creatures are slowly spiraling up out of the ground. Each one looks like a gray stone with muddy-brown spots and beady-red eyes. They're just a little bigger than a golf ball and beginning to surround my body. Clesandra drops my arm and swats at them as they use long, talon-like pinchers to gnaw into my clothing.

I try to swat at them or scurry out of the way, but my muscles won't comply, and all I get is excruciating pain.

"Ah! No!" she yells, leaping to her feet, and dragging me away from the swirling pit of insects that continue to surface. Sheol runs forward and begins to smash them viciously with the heel of his boot. They pop and ooze a yellowish foul liquid. Sheol covers his nose and mouth with his arm to avoid the stench and continues to squash them.

"No kill!" Zap yells, running toward Sheol and shoving him away from the bugs. Zap looks frantically around the clearing, muttering something in her own language. The other three natives rush into the forest and disappear from sight. They don't go far. We can hear them crashing through the underbrush, yelling things to each other. Moments later, the youngest dives back into the clearing. He trips and fumbles what he's carrying. Sheol catches what appears to be a rotting chunk of a tree stump before it hits the ground.

Zap waves her arms in front of Sheol, anxiously beckoning him to give her the piece of wood. He hands it over, and she rips the piece of cloth from her shirt and ties it to the bottom of the hollow stump.

The other two male natives come crashing through the forest back into the clearing, carrying their own logs. They tie pieces of their clothing across the base of logs, load them up with thin branches, and begin grabbing handfuls of the beetles and shoving them into the hollow logs. The men yelp in pain as the insects repeatedly bite them.

When the beetles surface from the ground, they make a beeline toward me. Clesandra heads them off waving her knife and occasionally stomping a bug or two into oblivion. Zap continues to yell, "No kill," at Sheol and Clesandra, who ultimately refuse to listen to that order. If the insects get close enough to my body, she crushes them violently or slashes them with her knife. Sheol kicks them back toward the pit they were coming from, and Zap and the others scoop them up.

"They're everywhere!" I scream, and swat at the bugs with my one good arm.

"Get Avery out of here!" Sheol yells.

Clesandra looks at me and realizes the beetles are coming up from the ground beneath me again.

"What the hell are these things?" she screams, swatting more from my clothing. She tries to hoist my body onto her back. Strong as she is, she's too weak to do it.

"And *where* exactly do you want me to put him?" she spits at Sheol.

He looks around the clearing. "There!" He points to a tree with low-hanging branches.

"You're kidding, right?" I yell.

"You climb and I'll hand him up to you," Sheol offers.

"This is ridiculous!" Clesandra screams, smashing a few more bugs coming up from the ground.

"You got a better idea?" Sheol barks.

Clesandra curses, but heads for the tree.

"Okay," she says, straddling the lowest branch.

"All right, buddy. Up you go!" I do my best to assist Sheol. He lifts me up to Clesandra, who grabs underneath my armpits and yanks me into the tree with her. She pins me up against the trunk and tucks me into the crook of two branches that intersect. We're only two to three feet off the ground, but it's just enough to confuse the insects.

They crawl around the spot where my body used to be, creating a frenzied pile where a puddle of my blood has collected on the ground.

"Look," Clesandra says. "They want his blood."

Zap and the other natives barely hear her. They're still trying to shove as many of the creatures into the logs as possible. When they can no longer fit any more in, they throw a covering of dirt on the bugs and tear another strip of clothing to seal the top of the logs.

The remaining beetles clamor over any drop of blood they can find. It's not long before the creatures disappear back into the ground as quickly as they came. Any trace of blood from my severed arm, gone.

It's like everyone in the clearing draws in a collective breath of calm. Zap looks at Niteg and the other two natives and smiles. There's a tiny glimmer of hope in her, but I'm not sure why.

"What the hell was that all about?" Clesandra shouts from her branch in the tree.

Sheol shakes his head and scrapes bug guts off his boots in the dirt. "Damn things stink," he mutters.

"Terracalx," the youngest native says, holding up a log filled with the insects toward Sheol's face.

He takes a step back. "Terra-what?"

"Drink," Zap says excitedly to Sheol and Clesandra. "Here."

Clesandra and Sheol shoot each other a nervous glance. Zap sets the log down and slowly lifts a corner of the cloth. One of the insects scampers out, and Zap grabs it by the back of its rock-like shell. The creature tries to flip itself around and grab her fingers with its pinchers, but Zap is too quick. Grabbing a stick on the ground, she mashes the insect's head off. Yellowish guts ooze out. Sheol and Clesandra look disgusted when Zap brings the body of the insect to her mouth and squeezes the juices out. The smell is overpowering. She smiles at Sheol, who has a foul look on his face.

"Has she smelled those things?" Sheol whispers to Clesandra.

Clesandra grins. "Makes you wanna give her a great, big, wet kiss. Right, lover boy?"

"You're a piece of work, you know that?" Sheol grumbles.

"We go," Zap informs the group more confidently. "Niteg," she says to the largest male native. Zap points to the tree where Clesandra and I are, and he steps forward to help retrieve me. I start to resist, but every movement causes excruciating pain. I can't climb down on my own.

Once on the ground, it takes two people to steady me so I can stand on my feet. The trees swirl and tilt. Everyone's faces start to multiply again. Two of the male natives attempt to pick me up to carry me.

"I can do it…on my own." My teeth grind against the pain.

"Let us help you," Sheol says, annoyed.

Clesandra climbs under my good arm to help balance me. I twist away from her and scream in pain as the other native grabs my bad arm to keep me from falling. Darkness obscures my ability to see for a few seconds.

"Damn it, Avery," Clesandra curses.

"You have to work with us," Sheol says calmly.

"Strong…I have to be…"

The ground suddenly looks far away under my feet.

"You're going to pass out," Sheol warns. He turns to Clesandra and says, "He's going to…" The same cool hand from before is on my forehead again. The searing pain in my arm fades, and an image of a fast-flowing waterfall emptying into a shimmering pool of translucent water distracts me. For a moment, I fight back. I try to escape again and get back to Clesandra and Sheol. But I'm also aware of how thirsty I am. The feeling is overpowering. I'm drawn toward the water. The farther I walk forward, the less thirsty I am. My mind calms and I stare at the water pouring down from the sky, mesmerized.

Chapter 19

"Wake up, Avery." The voice is soft and sounds far away. I turn my head and look away from the beautiful waterfall in front of me. Everything in the distance is a blur of beautiful colors.

What is this place? How did I get here? How long have I been here? The concept of time up until now has been meaningless. I look back at the beautiful water and calm serenity of this place, conflicted about whether or not I really want to try to find the voice. It's so peaceful here. There isn't any pain, any danger or threat of war, and yet…it's also very lonely.

"You can't sleep forever. Please wake up," the voice whispers. I recognize it at once. The sadness and desperation in the tone makes my decision for me. I climb to my feet, walking away from the pond in the direction of the sound. The colors of the landscape blur, swirl, and fizzle away.

It takes a while for my eyes to adjust. I'm lying on my back on a raised bed of some sort of soft plant material. There's a low-hanging intricately woven ceiling of branches above me. The ceiling is tied directly into walls of woven vines. The shelter is tiny and stiflingly warm. A fine film of sweat covers my body. I tilt my head down and see a blanket of dark hair across my chest. Clesandra's head against my skin is warm and comforting. She's still muttering to herself.

"Please wake up."

I slowly reach my good arm up to stroke her long mane of hair with my hand. I can't feel any pain in my left arm, but I'm not ready to even think about looking at it.

The instant my hand touches her hair, her head

springs up from my chest. Her eyes are wide with surprise.

"Hey there," is the only thing I can think to say.

"Hey there?" She scowls. "You've been asleep for five days, and the best ya got is hey there?"

"Sorry?" I'm not sure why she's angry with me.

"You know what, Sleeping Beauty…" She lets her sentence trail off as she gets up.

I grab for her arm as she's starting to move away from me. "Please, don't leave." My fingers close around her wrist, and I'm amazed at the sudden strength I have to hold her. I look at my arm and it doesn't just feel different—it looks different too. It's not scrawny and weak anymore. *I should sleep for five days more often.*

Clesandra looks stunned too.

"Sorry," I say, loosening my grip. "What I meant to say was, good morning?" I ask more than tell her.

She narrows her eyes and shakes her head, but comes back to sit next to me again.

"It's the middle of the day."

"I've been asleep for five days?"

"Five days solid."

I wrack my brain for the last thing I remember before passing out. *Clesandra is cutting my arm off. Sheol gave a knife to the native, Zap. Passed out. Zap got us out of the simulation arena somehow. Strange bugs eating me. Passed out again. Then…*

I put a hand to my forehead. "I can't remember how I got here. Where's Sheol? Where are we? I have to get Jace." *Jace.* Adrenaline fills my bloodstream. I bolt upright and the room spins violently.

"Not so fast. Lay down, stupid." Clesandra pushes me back down. "Lover boy and his native toys are fine." She hovers directly over me and gently slaps my cheeks. "Oh, no you don't, no more passing out now."

She searches my face for any sign that I might become unconscious again.

For a moment I forget about Sheol and Jace, forget about my missing arm, forget that I'll have to come up with a way to find Smith and kill him. All I can think about is how gorgeous Clesandra's green eyes are, and how close her face is to mine. I reach up and run the back of my hand down her cheek. She pulls away from me, scowling.

"Don't worry," I tell her, "as long as you're here, I think I can manage to stay awake."

She rolls her eyes, feigning annoyance. "Think ya can also manage to eat something?"

My stomach growls loudly at the mention of food. "First tell me what happened. What I've missed."

"You're awake! I knew I heard voices!" Sheol bursts through a flap of vines next to me that I didn't realize was there.

Both of my arms fly up instinctively, ready to protect myself. That's when I notice for the first time that I have two arms. Sort of.

"What the…?" I say, holding them up in front of my face. The right arm is normal and the left one…I know that the left one was cut off below the elbow. Just thinking about it, I can still feel the phantom pain of Clesandra's knife. And yet, before my eyes is an arm, or at least most of one. The end of it comes to two rounded knobs covered over by fresh pink skin. Just above the knobs is a layer of sinuous-looking tissue that dangles. Some pieces are fibrous and look like they're starting to grow together.

"Don't worry." Sheol pushes Clesandra out of the way so he can wrap me in a huge hug. "A couple more days you'll have your hand back good as new."

"Say what now?" I ask, still looking at my arm nervously.

"Come on." Sheol looks at Clesandra annoyed. "You haven't told him anything?"

"He just woke up," she growls.

"Nice to see the two of you getting along so well." I try to break the tension between them.

"Sheol?" a quiet voice almost whistles the name.

"In here," he calls.

"Great." Clesandra rolls her eyes.

"She is great. Thanks for noticing." Sheol winks at me. "You're going to love Zap. She saved your life."

"Really?" Clesandra snarls. "She cut off his arm to keep him from blowing up?"

"He would have died without her blood." Sheol glares at her.

"We all could've died—"

"Guys!" I burst out. "Blood? Someone mind giving me just a few answers before you rip each other to shreds?"

"It'll make more sense if Zap just shows you. Unless you have a problem with that too?" he says to Clesandra.

She glares at him but doesn't respond.

A thin slot in the vines opens and a tall woman slips in. Zap, as Sheol has affectionately named her, is radiant. Her long, dark hair is twisted and braided as elegantly as the woven branches and vines that make the room. She glides over to Sheol and slips her hand in his. The palms of their hands and the tattoos on her arms emit a low, pulsating light. She cocks her head to look at him quizzically.

He smiles fondly at her.

"No, more like…an annoying sister," he says.

"Annoying sister?" Clesandra fumes.

I lean my head closer to Clesandra. "What am I seeing here?"

She sighs, annoyed. "They do this a lot. It pisses

me off."

"What exactly are they doing?"

"Talking."

"But she isn't saying anything," I say, confused.

"Annoying, isn't it? They don't have to say anything. It's like talking in code. She knows enough English to understand most of what he's saying out loud, and she speaks it well enough too. She prefers to use pictures and feelings to communicate."

"Oh, right," I say, pressing a hand to my forehead and remembering small bits and pieces from Zap communicating with the other natives.

"They do it all the time," Clesandra says. Then she shoots me a devious little grin, "Makes me want to skin him alive."

At her last phrase, Zap looks shocked. She glares at Clesandra and angrily mutters something in her own language that sounds like beautiful mumbo-jumbo.

"Christ, Clesandra," Sheol says, gently pulling his hand out of Zap's grasp. "You didn't need to show her that image."

"I didn't show her anything," she says in a smug tone. "You did."

"You planted the phrase on purpose."

"And you filled the image. Next time talk to all of us, not just your little girlfriend."

"Fair enough," he grumbles. "Zap will fill in the blanks for you, Avery," Sheol says leading her toward me. "You should show him what happened in the desert...and the blood transfer thing you did. You know, stuff he wouldn't remember."

Zap nods, and kneels next to me. My heart races with fear even though I know from watching her interact with Sheol that she won't hurt me. She bends over so her face is inches from mine. I glance at Clesandra, who has her arms crossed across her chest, wearing an expression of what I think might be close to jealously. *As if she should have anything to worry about.* My eyes flit back to Zap's. I flinch when she reaches a hand up next to my face. She pauses for a second with a puzzled expression. Her eyebrows drawn together like she's thinking hard about something.

"Safe?" She says it more as a question, not sure if she picked the right word. I don't respond right away, so she looks to Sheol for confirmation.

He nods encouragingly. "She's trying to tell you it's okay."

"Will it hurt, what she's going to do to me?"

"She's not going to hurt you. It'll feel weird…at least it was for me. You get to see what she saw. Feel what she felt." He furrows his eyebrows. "I'm not explaining it well. Just…don't worry. You'll be fine."

I swallow hard and look back at Zap.

She reaches her arm up next to my face again, and then gently places her hand on my forehead.

My eyes forcefully roll back in my head. When they come into focus, I'm standing in the desert again. It's hot. Much hotter than any day I've experienced in Asik. The sand is so bright and reflective my eyes feel like they're burning. It takes much more time for them to adjust than it should. When they do adjust, I'm standing in front of a blurry figure. It's Sheol. He's in a defensive stance with something raised in his hand. It's a knife. I suddenly realize I'm not me, I'm Zap. This is what she sees…saw.

"Not a chance."

My head—Zap's head—turns toward the voice. Clesandra is crouched in front of Avery's body—my body— with her knife raised. She's terrified. Clesandra is covered in blood, and Avery looks pitiful. Blood is oozing from the bandages she tied on his arm.

His skin is sweaty and pale. The only visible signs that he's still alive are staggered breaths through moans of pain and unintelligible words. It's such a disorienting sensation knowing I'm seeing this through Zap's eyes.

Turning back to Sheol, Zap points to the bodies of her people lying in the sand. A rolling feeling of sadness and desperation washes over me. My heart is hammering in my chest and adrenaline pulsing in my veins. Zap holds out her hand for Sheol's knife.

He spins the knife around and places the handle into Zap's palm. The metal is so hot it burns my hand—Zap's hand—she almost drops it in the sand. So fueled by adrenaline, she practically flies to the bodies of her people and begins to cut them loose and remove their hoods, praying they're still alive.

All three remaining natives are male of different builds. One is slender and strong with dark, spiked hair. Ihi. Zap's memory fills in the name even though she doesn't speak it. Another native is younger with angular features yet to be grown into. Zeekir. The third, Niteg. He's a large muscular male with long, wavy hair. They, now scarlet from the sun and starting to blister, embrace each other.

Blurred images that don't immediately make any sense flicker within me. They flash so quickly that they seem mostly like blasts of color. Then there are clearer images of brutality and torture. A terrifying close-up of Smith's sneering face before a black hood blocks the light. I see needles and blood. I see chains and a dark room that stinks of urine and feces. Next there's a stinging pain of emotions—pain, suffering, anguish, horror, disbelief, mixed with gratitude and love. Each native, through this embrace, is sharing their experience over the last few hours or perhaps days, with each other.

I feel like I'm trespassing, getting to feel and see

what they see. It should be private.

The next image that comes through Zap is from Niteg. He touches Zap's arm and transfers a vision of taking the knife in Zap's hand and brutally killing Sheol, Clesandra and I. The murder is so vicious and skillful I wonder how he was captured in the first place. Ihi and Zeekir feed on his vision and submit their own murderous ideas.

"Calm," Zap says to the men. The word coming from her mouth sounds like gibberish but the translation in her head to the English language is as fluid as me learning the native's names without hearing them spoken. Zap sends the three men the image of Clesandra removing the hood from her face, me shooting the soldier who was about to kill her, and Sheol cutting the bonds that set her free. She also sends images of Sheol from our room in Xinorsus. Attached to the images of Sheol comes mixed emotions of curiosity and interest.

Again, I feel out of place, like I shouldn't be seeing or feeling any of this.

Suddenly the visions burst. The connection with the others is broken. Zap points to Clesandra and gives a command. Her spoken words make no sense but the meaning in her head is crystal clear. "Disarm and immobilize the female. We will help the males only."

Niteg and Ihi spring into action. Zeekir, the youngest, is the only one to hesitate. "Why the female?" he asks.

"She inflicts too much pain."

I want to jump and scream and try to convince Zap myself that she's wrong. That Clesandra is a good person. That she had good reason to cut off my arm. But I'm powerless in Zap's head. This is her story. Not mine.

Zap watches Ihi and Niteg complete her

command. They move like the wind. Clesandra is crouched over my body, poised for action.

"Come any closer and I'll—" She doesn't finish the threat.

"Clesandra, no!" Sheol yells.

Clesandra splits her knife and throws. Despite her deadly accuracy, the natives are much too fast. They anticipate her actions. Her two targets side-step the blades aimed at their hearts and catch each dagger by the hilt without so much as blinking their eyes.

Niteg takes Clesandra from behind. She struggles in vain.

"Those are mine!" she yells at the slender native, who now holds both her daggers. "Give it back! I'll kill you. Don't touch him! No, please!" Ihi is bent over my body, pressing his hand to my forehead.

Niteg wraps his arms beneath Clesandra's armpits and grips the sides of her head. The tattoos along the backs of his hands and arms glow a bright yellow. Clesandra goes limp.

Zap returns her attention to Sheol. He's backing away from her quickly as she approaches.

"What'd they do to them?"

Zap drops the knife and holds both arms outstretched to show she means no harm. Sheol trips over himself as he's going backward and falls into the sand. With no weapons to protect him, he puts his arms up defensively to block what he thinks will be a forthcoming blow.

"Not hurt," Zap says. The voice coming out of her mouth sounds like bird song, light and airy.

Sheol doesn't hide his confusion. "You know English?"

She nods and struggles to speak another word in my language. The words she chooses in her head are so clear and yet she struggles to put them into spoken form. "Small."

"What did he do to him?" Sheol points to my body.

Zap's inner confusion as she tries to find words that her lips can form best is overwhelming.

"Sleep...not feel pain."

"And Clesandra?"

"Niteg." Zap points to the muscular native holding Clesandra's head. "He makes...not hurt us." She points to her friends. "Not hurt." She points to Sheol's chest, also indicating him.

"Clesandra won't hurt me."

"Hurt." She points to Avery's arm.

"She had to," Sheol says quietly. He lowers his fists slightly.

She shakes her head.

"Is she dead?" Sheol asks.

Zap shakes her head vigorously. "Niteg makes her...still...so listens...not hurt."

"She can hear us?"

Zap ignores Sheol's last question. Her heart is hammering again with an intense welling of strange emotions as she holds out her hand, offering to help him from the sand. He searches her face for deceit. Reluctantly, he takes her hand and she pulls him to his feet with ease. The strength in her movements is shocking, just as it was to hold Clesandra in place a moment ago.

As Sheol's hand makes contact with her skin, there's a surge of energy shared between the two of them, a charge, like being shocked when you touch an electric fence. The energy is pulsating and powerful. Another surge of adrenaline makes Zap's heart race. She grips Sheol's hand tighter, and she transfers an image of touching an electric fence and then walking through it.

Sheol smiles in understanding. "Nico said something about building this place. I bet he built it with an electric fence. That's exactly how we're going to get out of here," he tells her.

Zap's body swells with happiness at the thought of escaping alive. She turns to her friends, and gives them a command in their language. "Leave her." The translation fills my head. Niteg drops Clesandra's body in the sand and joins Zeekir and Ihi next to Zap. Clesandra doesn't move. Ihi and Niteg carefully leverage my body up to carry me. Zap starts to head out in a direction away from the carnage of fallen bodies and blood. She only pauses when she realizes Sheol isn't following.

She turns back to look at him and holds out her hand, inviting him to join her.

Sheol has a distraught look on his face. He runs a nervous hand through his sweaty blond hair and looks back at Clesandra's body. "We aren't going to leave her here, are we?"

"She hurts," Zap says, pointing to my stump of an arm. The bandages are now completely saturated with blood. "She hurts you." Zap points to a purple swollen mark on Sheol's arm where the back of her knife struck.

Sheol covers the mark with his palm. "She stopped me from killing one of you."

"Kill? You like she?" Zap says confused.

"No, no, God no, it's not like that…but she saved me from…killing," he points to one of the dead natives to hopefully make his point, "you guys."

Zap tilts her head in confusion. There's an edge of frustration at not being able to understand Sheol's point. She walks over to him and slips her hand in his. Then she does something incredible. She begins to walk through his memories, carefully extracting all the memories and emotions involving Clesandra. Like fast-forwarding a movie, I get a glimpse of all the times Sheol ever interacted with Clesandra, but I get it from his perspective. I get to see the first time they met. Feel his anger and protectiveness for me and for Jace after Clesandra choked Jace in a headlock when he took her knife. Witness his sadness at being ditched after the briefing when I chased after Clesandra. Feel his angry jealousy when I breezed over his comment about Clesandra being bad news after she broke my nose. See how envious he was of her that the two of us had combat training together without him. Worse yet, that we were growing closer, that he realized how much she meant to me, how much we meant to each other.

His projected emotions are greatly mixed. He doesn't particularly care for Clesandra. He'd be happier if she was never a part of the journey here. But there's also the heartbreaking hesitation for leaving her behind because he knows how much she means to me.

What Zap is showing me makes me feel awful. I shrink inside for ignoring Sheol's feelings, for not seeing how he felt, for not being a better friend. It would've been so easy for him to leave Clesandra and disappear with Zap and the others. To make up some sob story about how she died trying to save my life. I probably would've believed it.

Zap finishes sifting through Sheol's memories and let's go of his hand.

"I won't leave her," he tells Zap quietly.

Zap nods and then guides Sheol toward Clesandra's body. Kneeling next to her, Zap places a hand on Clesandra's head. An electric current runs through Zap into Clesandra. Her eyes crawl their way from the back of her skull and regain focus. Zap steps back, allowing Sheol space next to Clesandra.

"I thought you were going to leave. I could...hear.

People were…talking." Her voice is staggered and filled with emotion.

Sheol extends his arm for Clesandra and pulls her gently to her feet and then into his arms.

"I would never do that." He hugs her for a moment, and I feel a pang of jealousy that is not solely my own when she hugs him back.

"Go now?" Zap says impatiently. Clesandra swipes at her face and Sheol joins Zap to begin walking.

Sheol and Zap head in one direction and keep on walking…and walking...and walking. They walk for what seems like miles, baking in the hot sun.

Zap's strength and energy is starting to falter in the heat. She looks down at her arms at the unsightly blisters forming. Sheol takes notice of it, too, and removes his head covering. Carefully, he places it on her head and they continue on. Zap looks back at her friends, who are also starting to struggle in the oppressive heat and from the strain of having to carry a lifeless body. A trail of slowly dripping blood marks our path in the sand.

Soon we hear a low hum of electricity. Nico did build this place with an electric fence. Zap confidently reaches a hand up. A strong, painful jolt of electricity flows into her body. The field doesn't falter. A feeling of immediate panic washes over her. She replays for herself the image and memory of slipping through the electric field surrounding Xinorsus. It seems so easy.

She reaches her hand up again to touch the field. The electricity jolts painfully through her body, causing her to stagger backward. *She's too weak to do this now.* I think.

Zap looks at Sheol and shakes her head. She looks down at her hands and crumples to her knees in the sand. There are a few tense moments as realization reaches the other natives.

Sheol puts a hand on her shoulder to comfort her. The contact between the two of them radiates a sharp electric charge. She has a moment of clarity and hope. Zap gets to her feet quickly and holds her hand up in front of Sheol. He doesn't understand immediately, so she grabs his hand and forces his palm to hers. The two palms glow and sizzle with electric energy. Her eyes meet his. She's sending him an image of touching the fence together. He doesn't hesitate. Hand in hand, they touch the air in front of them. It fizzles and crackles in a staggering array of sparks.

The images in Zap's memory flash forward to evening. The group looks weary and tired. Sheol and Clesandra's burns from the desert are deepening in color as night sets in. Clesandra gently presses a finger to her arm and winces as she pulls her hand away, leaving a white fingerprint. Curiously, the native's burns are beginning to look less intense. In fact, they appear to be fading and healing while Sheol and Clesandra's are just beginning to hit the peak of pain and ugliness.

Clesandra and Sheol spend the next hour making a basic shelter. They argue about the best way to create a bed in case bugs try to eat me again. Zap shows them how to make a raised bed. When the task is complete, Zap examines my body carefully. She projects an overwhelming feeling of dread.

Sheol and Clesandra are having a low conversation nearby.

"There's nothing else we can do," Sheol tells her.

"Look at him. He's getting worse." Clesandra sounds worried.

I do look worse. My bandages don't appear to be leaking any more blood, but my skin has taken on a yellowish hue. Zap watches me shiver involuntarily.

The youngest native, Zeekir, takes one of the beetles, cracks its head off, and attempts to squeeze some of the liquid into my mouth, but it simply dribbles out the side. Frustrated, he starts to get another one of the insects.

"Zeekir," Zap says forcefully. She gestures for him to leave me alone. He glances at Sheol and Clesandra before joining Niteg and Ihi who are curled up against a nearby tree just under the protection of the shelter.

Sheol, obviously distraught by the whole thing, steps outside. Zap watches him go. Her energy shifts in a desire to follow him. She tunes her ears toward Sheol, listening carefully to the sound of his footsteps in the leaf litter surrounding the shelter. When she seems satisfied that he's not going far, she chooses to join Niteg and the other natives. Zap divides her attention between listening for Sheol and watching Clesandra pace.

Left standing by herself, Clesandra awkwardly approaches the edge of the raised bed. She puts her back to the group of natives watching her vigilantly, trying to ignore their presence. Looking my body up and down, not sure what to do, she takes her hands and vigorously rubs them together to create heat. She places them on my arms and rubs them up and down, trying to generate enough warmth to stop my body from shivering. It works only for a moment. Seeing some sort of hope, she does the next best thing and climbs up next to me. Curling up against my side, she tries to transfer as much heat from her body to me as possible. She lays her head against my chest and closes her eyes tight. The moment she does, the tattoos on her arms glow a vibrant greenish yellow. She's stunning. I find myself wishing I could have remembered at least some of this in real time.

Zap is fascinated and refuses to take her eyes off the two of us for a long time.

Eventually, the images in Zap's control flash forward again. Night and day, day and night, Clesandra never leaves. I expect to see images of camp being torn down and us moving on, but it never happens. Maybe they're too afraid to move me. Maybe they're simply waiting for me to die.

Zap spends most of the day watching Clesandra hover over me and weaving walls to add to the lean-to structure. I get bits and pieces of broken conversation, hushed words. Sheol and Zeekir try to force liquid from the insects into my mouth without success. Night falls again, and I continue to worsen. The bandages on my arm are turning black with dried blood, and a foul, yellow slime is beginning to form along the upper edges of the cloth. What's left of the good skin is becoming a deep, burnt shade of red with speckles of black. Reddish-blue streaks radiate from beneath the bandages up almost to my neck. My arm is clearly infected and getting worse by the minute.

Night transitions into day, then back to night two more times. Niteg and Ihi become restless. Zap tries to calm and console them, convincing them that being here is where they need to be. But by nightfall on the third day, Niteg and Ihi take their stumps full of insects and never return. Zap and Zeekir are the only ones who remain with Sheol, Clesandra, and me.

The images jumble together again, and the next clear vision Zap shows me is that it's morning, or perhaps midday, since the light seems overwhelmingly bright. Her body surges with adrenaline as she hovers over me. I look worse than ever. My skin is pale white and hangs loose on my boney frame. My severed arm is covered in postulant blisters. The reddish-blue streaks have turned blackish-blue and now engulf half my face and parts of my chest. Zap is watching me gasp for air. She looks over at Sheol and Zeekir, who are roughly dragging a sobbing and fighting Clesandra out of the lean-to.

Zap is holding something in her hand that looks like a small tube. Not a tube, a slender hollow branch from some sort of plant. All the bark and green has been stripped away. She looks at the branch, takes a deep breath, and shoves it deep into a vein in her left arm. Blood instantly begins to flow from the end of the tube. She holds pressure on the top of the tube with a finger, then takes the mangled stump of my arm. The bandages are gone, showing the ragged, torn tissue beneath. Pinching off the tip of one of my clotted arteries, she shoves the other end of the tube directly into it. An immense and immediate pain transfers from Zap to me. It's unbearable. All the images she's showing me jumble together and form nothing but a rippling white wall of agony. It feels like her entire life force is leaving her body. Like it's being ripped away. I want to scream for her to stop, but the pain keeps coming.

Suddenly, everything does stop. The pain stops. The images stop coming. I expect to see Zap show me something else, but instead she peels her connection away from me. It's as if someone is gripping my brain in their hands and slowly releasing the pressure. My eyes roll forward and come back into focus. Zap is standing over me, her hand hovering above my forehead.

"You gave me your blood," I say quietly.

She tilts her head to the side. "So you live."

"Why?"

Zap doesn't say anything, just simply points to Clesandra.

"I don't understand."

"Her half. Your half," Zap says matter-of-factly.

I look at Clesandra for meaning, but she's staring at a spot on the ground in front of her feet with her arms folded across her chest.

I look at Sheol instead. He shrugs. "Girl's got a thing for you."

Clesandra sucks in a sharp breath and rolls her eyes.

I look from person to person, trying to comprehend all the information I've just been given.

"Sorry to bombard you, man," Sheol says, reading my look. "It has to be a lot to process." He gives Zap a guilty look. "We should've waited..."

"I needed to know," I tell them.

Sheol nods. "Come on," he says to Zap. "Let's give him a minute. We can go see if Zeekir managed to catch anything for lunch. You must be starving."

The most I can muster is a nod.

Zap and Sheol step through the curtain of woven vines. Clesandra shuffles her feet uncomfortably and looks after them. I can tell she wishes she could be anywhere else in the world than right here with me. She has to know that Zap showed me more than Clesandra would ever want me to see. Showing any sign of vulnerability or kindness that might make her appear weak isn't an option.

Carefully, I prop myself up on my elbows. "So, I'm your half, huh?" I say with a smug grin.

Clesandra glowers at the ground in front of her feet, not looking at me. "What does she know," she mutters.

"She knows enough. So do I. Well...?" I let the question trail off.

"Well, what?" she snaps.

"Would you come over here already?"

Her stunning green eyes meet mine, and I can't

quite read the emotion behind her gaze.

"Please?" I add.

She kicks a rock by her feet, trying to decide what to do.

Not waiting for her to figure it out, I do my best to leverage my body into a seated position and drop my feet to the ground. The woven walls tilt violently, and I clamp my eyes shut to stop the spinning. Before I can open them again a pair of warm hands, one on my chest and one on my back, are stabilizing me.

"You really are crazy, ya know that?" Clesandra's voice is still harsh, but it has an edge of what I think might be fondness.

"Crazy about you," I say, looking at her.

She shakes her head. Her long, dark hair, no longer plaited in a braid, cascades forward across her shoulders.

"Stop talking like that. Smith will use it against you when he finds out you're still alive," she whispers, raising her wristband in front of my face.

"You think he can still hear you?"

"Not taking chances. Not sure why he hasn't activated the self-detonate on Sheol or me."

"If he can't hear you or track you, maybe he thinks you're already dead."

"If that were the case he'd stop sending search planes," she whispers.

"What?"

"Planes have been coming and going every few days. Trackers probably don't work on these things, but if I know Smith, he wants proof we're dead."

"He's got all that high-tech software that's supposed to be able to see all parts of the planet at the click of a button. I've seen it for myself. Why can't he see here?"

"Zap," Clesandra answers.

I nod in understanding. "She disrupts the signal. That explains why the trackers won't work around here. If that's the case, why hasn't Smith sent ground troops?"

"He did."

"Zap didn't show me any of that?"

"She shows what she wants. Takes information she wants too," Clesandra mumbles. "Ground troops ain't comin' around again anytime soon. The two bigger guys, Niteg and Ihi, took care of the first group. They gave Smith a whole new perspective on combat training."

No doubt. I think to myself. After seeing how the natives dodged Clesandra's knife throws in the desert, I can't even imagine what they did to Smith's troops. I shake my head, not wanting to think about the carnage these people are capable of.

Looking down at Clesandra's hand against my chest, I say, "Now wait a second, since when do you care what Smith hears? I thought you had nothing to lose." I look up, searching her face.

She scowls.

"Come on. When are you going to stop playing the tough-girl routine with me? I know you better than that." I reach my good hand up to her face to tuck a stray strand of her hair behind her ear. She goes rigid as my fingers graze her cheek and her eyes lock onto mine. I let my hand slide through her hair and gently down the back of her arm to rest at her elbow. The intricate tattoos on her arms glimmer the same vibrant yellow-green from the memory Zap showed me. Clesandra's breath catches in her throat and her eyes widen.

Neither one of us can seem to breathe right. I choke down a nervous lump in my throat, afraid to move a muscle and spoil the moment. I let the corner of my mouth tilt up in a sheepish grin.

"You feel it, too, don't you?" I say softly.

"Feel what?" she whispers.

"This."

I gently run the tips of my fingers back up her arm, illuminating the tattoos even more. When I reach her face, I let my hand slip behind her head and pull her forward until our lips meet. She doesn't resist.

Chapter 20

I've never kissed a girl before, so I have nothing to compare the experience with, but what I feel is extraordinary. The world melts away. I'm able to forget the death of my family. Forget the war on Earth and all the poor souls who lost their lives. I forget being abducted by Smith to be a pawn in his own war. Forget that days prior I would have died without our newfound friends and the quick thinking of the woman I'm with right now. Forget, for at least, a moment.

A curious warmth spreads the length of my body, and my skin tingles with an unexplainable energy. My stomach does back flips, and my chest feels like it's about to explode, but I pull back, fighting against the force inside me that yearns for more. Our lips separate, but I maintain a gentle grip on the back of her head. I lean my forehead against hers, hoping it might ease the spinning room. We're silent for a moment before she whispers, "I felt that."

I smile and gently brush my lips against hers again before letting my hand slip down to her waist. She leans her weight into me, guiding me down so I'm flat on my back, then lifts her head so our faces are far enough away that she can look at me.

"This wasn't supposed to happen," she tells me, starting to get up. When she lifts her hand from my chest, I catch it and intertwine my fingers with hers, holding her in place.

"Supposed to or not...it did."

"Did what?" Sheol's voice is like nails on a chalkboard. We're both so caught up in our own moment that we jump at the sound of his voice. I drop Clesandra's hand like it's molten lava, and she pops up off the edge of the bed and shoves her way past Sheol through the vine doorway like her life depends on it.

"Sorry," he says when he sees my distraught face. "Didn't mean to...um...uh...interrupt?"

"It's okay. She might need some time to process."

"She hasn't left your bedside except maybe to pee. What'd you say to her?"

"It's probably not so much what I said to her...never mind. She'll be okay."

I can tell Sheol wants to ask more questions, so I divert his attention.

"Hey, if I was asleep for five days...I mean, I know I got Zap's blood and all, but how am I..." I hold up my arms in front of my face. "I don't look scrawny. And aside from some dizziness, I feel like a million bucks."

Sheol chuckles. "The dizziness will pass. You've been lying down for a few days. Plus, Zap showed you a lot, and when that happens you get lightheaded. She makes me lightheaded just by..." his voice trails off.

"Sheol," I snap.

"Right, right." He clears his throat. "You're not scrawny anymore because she gave you a transfusion of her blood. It nearly killed both of you in the process. I had to run in and disconnect the tube thing. You were both screaming bloody murder."

"I don't remember any of it."

"Probably better that way. Anyway, after she gave you her blood, you improved dramatically. The natives' blood has natural healing properties. It's probably why they look so perfect." He smiles again, letting his mind wander off. "We thought you would be up and about in no time, but you just wouldn't wake up. It's no wonder Clesandra nicknamed you Sleeping Beauty."

"Blood doesn't keep you alive for five days. How did I eat? How did I...use the bathroom?"

"You had no problem eating after you started to improve. We would just mash stuff up and put it in your mouth. You made it disappear." He smiles. "The bathroom stuff...you probably don't want to know. All I have to say about that is, well, that she-devil you like so much might as well be a saint. With you anyway," he adds sarcastically.

"Oh, no," I groan, thinking about Clesandra having to take care of me like that.

Sheol shrugs. "She never complained. I'm telling you, she's got some sort of weird thing for you. Maybe she's not a robot after all."

I glare at him before I realize he's messing with me.

"All right, kid." Sheol comes to the edge of the bed. "We can play twenty questions later. I know Clesandra wants you to stay in bed forever just so she can stare at your pretty angel face," he jokes, "but seriously, man, get up."

I feel like I'm more than ready to, spinning room and all, so I let Sheol help me sit up and I carefully swing my legs to the floor.

"Now, before you go any farther," Sheol starts, "put these on. Sorry there's not much left. We made fresh bandages from them."

He hands me a tattered pair of what used to be military-issued camouflage pants and looks away. Glancing down I realize that I'm practically naked. Just a raggedy pair of undershorts separates my body from the rest of the world.

"Please tell me you were the one who stripped me?"

He shakes his head. "Sorry. I like you and all, but I'm not much for stripping guys."

"Very funny," I grumble, tugging the pants on over my undershorts.

"Come on," he says, lending me a shoulder to balance. The room tilts again, but I'm able to remain focused and balance with Sheol's help.

"Hey, look at that! You're standing," Sheol says proudly. I grin and let go of his shoulder to take a few tentative steps. My legs hold my weight easily, and aside from a little stiffness and a throbbing headache, it's like I've just woken up from a nap...*a very long nap.*

The more I'm up and moving, the more the dizziness starts to fade away. My muscles feel strong, much stronger than I'm used to feeling. I stretch my arms and legs, happy when my body complies with all my requests. The only other pain I feel is a slight throbbing in my severed arm.

"So this is supposed to grow back?" I say, looking at my arm more closely.

"Yep. It started to grow back as soon as Zap gave you her blood. I don't think she even thought that would happen."

"Cool," I say, while manipulating the stump. Stringy fibrous bits of skin and muscle twist and swing. Even though I don't have a full hand or fingers yet, I try to tell my brain to move them anyway. The stringy pieces of muscle and tendon contract and expand at my request. "Way cool."

"Oh, gross." Sheol scrunches up his face and looks in the opposite direction. "Knock that crap off before I throw up."

"Anything else I should know from being asleep? How come you guys stayed here instead of hiking on?"

"We didn't think you were going to make it. Clesandra insisted that it would be more dangerous to move you. Zap agreed with her, I guess. 'Bout the only thing they do agree on. Plus, we're over a perfect, little pocket of Terracalx. All you have to do is put out a little blood and you've got water for a week."

"You're talking about those bug things, right? What exactly are they?"

"I call them camel bugs. They live underground and collect water in their bodies. I guess they save it for when they need it, like camels. Zap thinks they're only in certain parts of the planet because she hasn't seen any of them where she lives. Zeekir and I take your dirty bandages and lay them out on the ground for a few minutes, and they appear, like magic. We've got loads of them hanging up in trees outside. Come see," he says.

It's the first time in weeks I've been outside in the forest. I have to shield my eyes so they can adjust to the brightness. The forest is more beautiful than I remembered. The enormous trees tower above the ground, creating an intricate woven canopy above our heads. Light cascades through the leaves, dappling the ground at our feet. Insects and birds create a chaotic, yet hauntingly striking chorus of sound.

Zap and Zeekir are hunched over something on the ground, mashing it with stones, and Clesandra is pacing back and forth, occasionally throwing her knife at a nearby tree. I watch her. Her form seems off, like she's distracted. More than once she misses the tree trunk entirely and curses at the dagger when it returns to her hand. I smile, hoping her inability to focus has something to do with my kissing her a moment ago.

"Out of practice?" Sheol sneers.

Clesandra whips around, daggers in hand. "Damn it, Avery. You're not supposed to be up yet." Then she wheels on Sheol, daggers raised. "He's not been awake for more than an hour and you're dragging him out of bed."

Zap materializes next to Sheol, ready to get between them.

"Oh, relax," Clesandra snarls at Zap. "If I was gonna hurt him, I would've done it already." To make her point, she lets the knife disappear.

Zap doesn't seem convinced, so she steps in closer to Sheol.

"Call off your creepy mind reader, will ya?"

"Why don't you calm down?" Sheol tells her. "I was just kidding, jeez."

"Creepy?" Zap says the word aloud.

When neither Sheol nor Clesandra elaborate, Zap reaches her hand forward to touch Clesandra, but Clesandra backs away, hands up defensively.

"Oh no ya don't. We're not going there again. Call her off," she says to Sheol.

Sheol catches Zap's arm before she makes another move toward Clesandra. "I'll tell you later," he says to her.

"You," Clesandra says to me. "Let's go. Back inside with you."

"I'm fine, really," I protest.

"You should rest." She points to the shelter.

"I've been resting for five days," I argue. Then a thought comes to mind. "All right, I'll rest a while longer, but you have to come with me."

She glares at me and purses her lips in frustration. It's not the ultimatum she hoped for. Conflicted between wanting me to rest and not wanting to be left alone with me, she looks at Sheol for support. He's not going to offer it. Throwing her hands up in defeat, she says, "Fine, you need to eat something anyway."

I wink at her. "I'll be okay, I promise."

We spend the next few minutes eating an unappetizing meal of mashed-up plants and insect parts, and finish it off with a few camel bugs. I find myself wishing I was still unconscious for the meal. It tastes disgusting, and the liquid from the camel bugs smells foul and has a thick texture that makes me wretch. Sheol and Zeekir laugh with amusement.

"You'll get used to the taste," Sheol says.

"Right," I gag. My appetite is completely gone, but my stomach grinds viciously, telling me to keep eating. In between bites and gagging fits, I steal a glance at Clesandra. When she notices me looking at her, she looks at the ground.

"So," I start, "when can we get moving? You know, back to Xinorsus?"

Sheol exchanges a nervous glance with Zap.

"What is it?" I ask cautiously, afraid of what the answer will be.

"We aren't going back to Xinorsus," Sheol says bluntly.

"What are you talking about? We have to go back. I have to get Jace." A little welling of adrenaline makes the food in my stomach toss like I might be sick.

"For all we know, Smith could have already killed him," Sheol says.

"Sheol," Clesandra scolds. "Do you really think now's the time for—"

"Time for what?" I cut in defensively.

"Look, buddy," Sheol says, matching my tone. "Xinorsus isn't exactly safe."

"Nowhere on this planet is ever going to be safe with Smith in charge," I spit back. "My brother needs me. How can you, even for a minute, consider that he's not still alive? I thought you cared about him too."

He looks hurt. "I do care about him. You know I do. I just think the best option for us—"

"The best option for us is to go back and get him," I growl.

"Zap and I—"

"Oh no, don't you go bringing her into this." I put my hand on my head because it's starting to throb wildly, and little black spots are dancing across my vision, making me dizzy again.

Clesandra grabs at my arm to steady me. I try to smack her away, but miss.

"Shut up, Sheol! Stop upsetting him!" she hisses.

Taking a deep breath, I allow Clesandra to balance me. "I'm going back for him," I say matter-of-factly.

"Told ya." Clesandra raises her eyebrows toward Sheol and Zap.

"Have to tell home," Zap states.

"Wouldn't your two grunts have done that already?" Clesandra asks.

"Niteg and Ihi. And only if they made it back alive," Sheol says. "We can't be sure."

"Just like you can't be sure about Jace. I'm going back, with or without you guys."

"Look," Sheol tries again, "why don't we let Smith come to us with Jace? We know that he's going to be attacking the natives' village."

"He may have already," Clesandra cuts in.

"Jace and the other soldiers would be with Smith, and we could just intercept him," Sheol says.

Sheol's logic makes sense, and I'm quiet for a moment, mulling it all over in my head. There's a nagging fear in the back of my mind. It's been five days since Smith dropped us in the desert bubble to test our loyalty. It's a test that I clearly failed and with dire consequences for my brother and my friends. My guess is that the test was a swift precursor to getting into battle formation to make the first attack on the natives' homeland. What if Smith has already begun to put Jace through combat-training drills? What if Smith puts Jace at the front lines when they attack? I've already seen that the natives are more than capable of swift and vicious deaths. Why would they spare Jace? Every soldier, no matter how old, would be considered a threat. My mind races with a million ways Jace could be killed. I can't bear the thought of that happening. Maybe they haven't left Xinorsus yet. If they are still sending search planes out looking for us, then maybe Smith is focusing on that first.

"No," I tell them. "Even if we all were able to get to the village before Smith and the others attack, there's still a chance that the natives might accidentally kill Jace in the fighting." I shake my head. "I have to try to get to Xinorsus before they leave for battle."

"And what if Smith has already left? What if he's already at the village and taken control?" Sheol asks.

Then God help us all. "I can't afford to think that way," I tell him.

The five of us are quiet for a few minutes. "Maybe we should split up," I add.

"No, no way. We stick together," Sheol argues. "Safety in numbers, it's just basic math."

"Basic?" Clesandra growls. "Ain't nothing basic here. But you're right, we should stick together."

"We can't be in two places at once. We have to split up," I tell them.

"Split is best," Zap interrupts. Sheol looks at her as if she's crazy, like maybe she misunderstood.

"Split," he says the word again, and then draws a picture in the dirt with a stick, showing our group of five splitting up.

"Yes. Split," Zap says confidently. Her forehead wrinkles. "It's better. They go." She points to Clesandra and me. "We go." She points at Zeekir, Sheol, and herself.

I look at her suspiciously. It's interesting that she wants Sheol and Zeekir, but not Clesandra. I try to put the notion that Zap might try to kill or capture Sheol for her own purposes out of my mind.

"I can go by myself," I say.

"No, you're not going alone. You're too accident prone." Clesandra points out.

"Then it's settled. We split the group. You can come with me." I wink at Clesandra.

Sheol and Clesandra both glare at me.

"I don't like it." Sheol shakes his head.

"I don't like it either, but it's the best plan I can think of. Clesandra and I will go back to Xinorsus to see if Jace is there. If he is, we'll get him out and meet you guys at the village. If Smith is already at the village, then you and Zap can get Jace and we'll...figure out a place to meet later."

"We meet here." Zap offers.

Sheol looks at Zap reluctantly. "Avery, you make it sound so easy. There's a lot that can go wrong with that plan."

"Hate to point out another problem," Clesandra butts in. "When she leaves," she points at Zap, "we...I become visible again." She holds up her wristband. "Smith will know where I am, which means he'll know where you are."

Our group falls silent.

"Then it'll just have to be me who goes. I'm the only one without a tracker." I give Clesandra a small smile. "Thanks, by the way. I never did thank you...all of you...for saving my life."

Zap dips her head, acknowledging the gratitude.

"Yeah, yeah, I saved your life. That's all nice. You aren't going alone. Who's going to watch your ass so you don't get killed?"

"Girl's got a point," Sheol says.

"I'm not going to let you risk your life for me. You will go with the others," I command her.

"You don't get to tell me what to do," Clesandra snaps.

The two of us glare at each other in tense silence.

"We go together most of the way," Zap breaks the silence. "Together," she repeats, as if that statement changes everything.

"How far is Xinorsus from the natives' village?" Sheol asks. Zap touches his arm, transferring the information. "About a three-day hike to Kaitsjauji," he relays.

"Kaitsjauji?" I ask.

"I'm probably pronouncing it wrong. But that's the name of her home."

"Three days? That gives Smith a huge window of time to find us. Plus, you and I don't know how to get back to Xinorsus," Clesandra says.

"Or the village," I add.

"I help." Zap bends down and picks up a stick from the ground.

For the next few hours, she draws us an intricate map in the dirt. She's careful to point out treacherous parts of the forest where plants and animals are hostile. She shows us edible fungus and vegetation that we can use for insect bites and minor injuries. I secretly find myself wishing that I had less combat-training sessions and more on planetary awareness and agriculture. I'm bound to forget something crucial. I also notice that Clesandra hates everything to do with Zap sharing her memories and images, even if they're being used to benefit us. I make a mental note to coax information out of her later.

When Zap finishes, Clesandra, Sheol, and I spend the next hour using crushed-up insect bodies to make ink in an attempt to re-draw Zap's map on scraps of clothing to carry with us. It's not a perfect science, and I'm not the artist that Faysal was in Xinorsus, but I'm pleased with my crude recreation. Hopefully, the maps will be enough to get us where we need to go when our group separates.

By the time we're finished, the light is fading out of the sky. The forest air takes on a harsh chill, making me wish most of my clothing wasn't used to make bandages. The five of us make a small and unsatisfying meal of crushed-up insects and a few more camel bugs before Clesandra forces me back into the lean-to. She can't stand to watch me shiver.

I start to resist until I realize she's coming with me.

"You aren't getting sick too," she growls, pushing me through the woven vines.

Zeekir joins us and curls up on a small nest of dried branches and leaves tucked into a corner of the shelter. Zap and Sheol remain outside, and I can hear them talking in low voices. Sheol correcting her speech every now and again and answering questions she has.

The temperature inside the shelter is only slightly warmer, but I'm grateful for the small creature comforts of having walls and a ceiling. Though I'm exhausted, I reluctantly climb back into the bed of leaves made for me five days ago. I know I'm better, but something about having to close my eyes and go to sleep makes me worry that I might drift off and not want to wake up. Clesandra echoes my fears by threatening to beat me wildly if I decide not to wake up in the morning.

"You sure know how to tuck someone in," I say sarcastically.

She winces at my words, and I take them back immediately.

"Just kidding. If I don't wake up, I'll beat myself senseless...from the dream world no less."

She sits down next to the bed, careful to keep just out of arm's reach. "Did you dream anything?" she asks.

I don't know why, but the question takes me off guard.

"It's not really so much that I dreamed," I start to tell her. "It didn't feel like a dream anyway. It felt real."

In as much detail as I can, I tell her about the waterfall. I tell her about how the passage of time didn't matter. How there was no pain or fear, only relaxation. As I'm telling her, I find myself wondering what it would be like to truly forget about the trials of life, the pain and suffering, to ignore the time of day and just...*be*. I wonder if the Great Lakes on Earth had that kind of power over a person. Maybe my father got to see a little piece of nature's perfection. Maybe then I could understand why he fought so hard to control it—to have it for himself.

"It sounds perfect, why wake up?" she asks.

"Because you weren't...I heard your voice," I say quietly. "So I had to."

"Why? You didn't have to wake up for me. Not when you were in such a perfect place."

"It wasn't entirely perfect," I tell her honestly.

"Sounds perfect," she mutters, looking away and twirling a stick between her fingers.

"Well, it wasn't," I say again.

"What wasn't perfect about it?" she snaps.

"There you go again with that tough-girl routine," I say frustrated. She snaps the stick she was twirling in her fingers and hits me with a vicious glare. "Look, it wasn't perfect because..." The words get caught in my throat and I'm suddenly not sure if I should say them.

"Because why?" she presses forcefully.

I purse my lips together and swallow down my frustration and annoyance. I think about how badly I wish I could have shared the experience with

Clesandra. With Jace, my mother, and Caileen. I would give anything for them to feel just one second of peace and be able to forget the war. My heart aches.

"I was alone. I couldn't share it with the people I love." I choke the words out. "I was there without you."

Her face contorts with a mixture of emotions—pain, frustration, sadness, and then a flush of red along her jaw line that makes me think she might scream at me. But she just turns her head in avoidance.

I slip off the edge of the bed and drop down next to her. My sudden movement startles her, and she starts to get up to move away, but I catch one of her arms and she freezes. Her tattoos flare to life and I feel that same inexplicable energy in the pit of my stomach.

"Let go," she whispers.

"Not a chance." I keep my hand tightly around her wrist but stand up with her so she doesn't have to hunch over.

We stand eye-to-eye, and I match her icy stare. Neither one of us says anything for a long time. I wait impatiently for the tension to leave her body, but it never does.

"I said, let go," she says again, but the threatening edge has faded.

"I will never let you go," I whisper, and pull her against my chest. She doesn't say anything, but the tension in her body starts to lessen, and as I look down, I see the glow of her tattoos radiating up to her neck. A dead giveaway that this is what she wanted. I smile to myself and kiss the top of her head.

"You better wake up tomorrow," her voice is muffled against my chest.

"I promise." I interlace my fingers with hers, and guide her toward the raised pile of branches and leaves. When she realizes where we're going, she starts to resist again.

I raise my eyebrows. "You didn't have a problem lying with me while I was sick."

"That was before..."

I grin. "I'll keep my hands—*hand*—to myself."

"It's not your hands I'm afraid of," she mutters.

My cheeks flood with heat.

"Come on," I coax. Reluctantly, she climbs up next to me, and I pull her head down to rest on my chest. Wrapping my good arm around her, I wait for the rest of the tension to slowly melt out of her body. When it does, I reach up to smooth her hair with the palm of my hand. She nestles deeper against my side, and a wave of contentment sweeps over me. It doesn't take long for her to fall asleep. I listen to the rhythmic sounds of her breathing, the drone of insects outside, and the quiet muttering of Sheol and Zap. Not wanting to fall asleep, I strain my ears to hear what they are talking about, but eventually exhaustion takes over and my eyes drift closed.

Leave now. Get up and go. A far-off voice from somewhere behind me orders. I spin around. Where am I? There's nothing but pitch-black darkness. My stomach flip-flops in fear. This has to be a dream. I spin around several more times, hoping the darkness will lighten.

You have to leave, the voice says again, this time from somewhere to the right of me. I turn and peer into the blackness, straining to see. Out of the darkness, two faint sparks of yellow appear. The sparks are coming closer and moving quickly. Adrenaline fills my blood, and I get ready to run from whatever is approaching. By the time I realize what it is, it's too late to look away. I'm trapped.

A pair of golden eyes locks me in place.

"Lupète," I breathe. "Where am I?"

Dreaming, he says. The rest of his body materializes in front of me, but I'm unable to look away.

"How are you here?"

You have to go. Leave now before they wake, he says, not answering my question.

"What are you talking about?"

She cannot go with you.

I know he must be talking about Clesandra and the others.

"I don't understand."

His eyes turn to angry slits, and he grabs my face in his hand. I had forgotten how enormous the man was. His palm engulfs my whole face, and his fingers brutally dig into my skull. Similar to how Zap presents memories and images, my eyes are forced to the back of my skull. I cry out in pain as images begin to crystallize.

Clesandra and I are standing near a hole in the ground. She's holding something in her hand. I try to ask her about it, but she can't hear me. A noise in the distance catches her attention. There's the metallic rumble of something coming closer. She looks at me anxiously, takes out her knife, and motions for me to get my gun ready. We're standing tensely, weapons ready, hardly breathing, when I hear the whipping and crunching of branches and leaves. The sound is coming right toward us. All I can think about is the two of us in the simulation room when we had to survive against the wild wolf-like beasts. But I know it's not a beast. A second later, there's a sharp pop. Something hot slices the side of my face and blasts a hole in a nearby tree. The gun I was holding flies out of my hand and lands somewhere in the underbrush.

"Get down!" Clesandra screams, tackling me flat onto my stomach in the dirt. We start to scramble, trying to take cover, but they're already there, crashing through the underbrush on some sort of open, one-man aircraft that resembles a flying motorcycle. Soldiers, at least four of them, blurred camouflage whips past us. I catch a glimpse of what looks to be a modified M16A2 rifle.

"Drop your weapons!" one of the men yells.

Clesandra drops her knife, and we throw up our hands in surrender. Our weapons are no match for rifles.

"Tie his hands," the cold, hard voice of Rustin pounds my eardrums.

"What about her?" one of the other soldiers asks.

"I'll take care of her," Rustin sneers. "It's only Evericon he wants. On second thought, tie her hands too."

The soldiers descend on us, binding our hands behind our backs. I kick and struggle against them.

"Let her go," I snarl.

Rustin chuckles. He drops down on one knee so his face is inches from mine. "Let her go?" He laughs. "I haven't had any play time with her yet."

Struggling against the ropes and the two soldiers restraining me, I lean my head back and spit in Rustin's face.

"Untie my hands and I'll show ya what play time is," Clesandra snarls.

Rustin's neck and cheeks flush purple with fury. Swiping his face with the palm of his hand, he kicks me as hard as he can in the stomach. The air pops from my lungs like a punctured balloon.

"Avery!" Clesandra yells. "I'll kill you!" she screams at Rustin. He turns an ugly grin in her direction before kicking me two more times.

"Don't worry, sweetheart, you and I are about to get properly acquainted." He kicks me again for good measure, knocking the fight right out of me.

"I bet you'd like to watch what I'm going to do." He pulls my head back by my hair so I can see Clesandra.

"Coward! Fucking coward! I'll kill you. Won't take much if you let me go," she hisses and struggles against the two soldiers holding her.

"I'd like to see you try, sweetheart." He drops my head. The two soldiers let go of her, and the only thing preventing her from charging Rustin is the fact that her hands are bound. She throws herself to the ground and tries to maneuver her hands behind her feet so her arms are in front of her. Rustin realizes what she's doing and tackles her.

"No you don't." He throws all of his body weight on top of her while she kicks wildly. "I always did like a little fight."

"Let her go!" I choke out, still trying to catch my breath. I struggle harder, and one of the men smashes the side of my head with something hard. Probably a rifle. I struggle to remain conscious as they lift me by my arms and drag me through the underbrush away from Clesandra.

"No! Let her go!" I scream. I make another futile attempt to fight back, but the men drag me deeper into the forest. I hear muffled screams from Clesandra. A painful emptiness coupled with panic when I realize there's nothing I can do for her grips my body.

Pop! The screaming stops and Lupète comes into focus. I fall to my knees, released from his grip on me. I clutch my chest and try to stop hyperventilating.

They will find you if she goes with you. And he will kill her, Lupète says very seriously. *She must be protected.*

"How do you know that will happen? You can't know that will happen."

I see more than you are even aware of. Just as I know in moments, you will be awoken sharply. You won't want to remember what I showed you. You'll try to convince yourself that it was all a bad dream. Maybe it was. Are you willing to risk it?

"Avery...Avery!"

Suddenly awake, I gasp a huge lungful of air.

"Avery, you're okay, you're okay." Clesandra's head hovers above mine, her face filled with concern. I look around the small room. Sheol and Zap are curled up near Zeekir, snoring loudly.

"I'm fine," I tell her.

"You were dreaming," Clesandra says quietly, smoothing the sweat from my forehead. I smile to put her at ease.

Should I tell her it was more than a dream?

Chapter 21

"Do ya want to tell me about it?" She yawns, tucking her head under my chin and settling back down.

"It was nothing," I lie. "Go back to sleep." I kiss the top of her head and pull her in closer while I wait for her to drift off again.

I stare at the woven ceiling, trying to trace a single vine's origin with my eyes, not wanting to think about what Lupète just showed me, and trying to decide if I should believe it happened at all. Then I curse under my breath because that's exactly what he said I would do. *What should I do? Who is that guy anyway?* I try to put him out of my mind. I barely know anything about him, except that he can somehow see the future.

"This is crazy," I whisper, trying to clear my thoughts. *What's real anymore? Maybe this ...all of this...is just some long, intense nightmare. Maybe I'm still dreaming. Maybe I'm still in this pseudo coma, and this is just a part of it. No, it can't be.* I pinch my arm with my hand. *You're a dumbass. This isn't some TV show. You can't just pinch yourself to wake up. Even if you could, do you really think you would wake up in a nice, big house with everything you could have ever wanted and the perfect family?*

I take a deep breath. Real or not, I can't live knowing that my brother isn't safe, and I couldn't possibly live if I knew I caused Clesandra's death by letting her come with me.

Glancing down at the gorgeous woman sleeping against me, a hollow emptiness opens in my chest for what I'm about to do. I know when she wakes to find that I've left her, she'll never trust me again. She won't understand. Whatever we have now—or are starting to have together...I can't bear to finish the thought. If I'm lucky and leave now, I'll get enough of a head start that Clesandra won't be able to track me down. She'll travel with the rest of the group under Zap's signal-blocking protection. Smith will never know she's alive or where she is.

It's one of the most painful decisions I've ever had to make. I carefully slide myself out from under Clesandra and tuck her neatly into the bed of leaves and branches. A lump catches in my throat as I spend one more precious moment looking at her. Will this be the last time I see her? Bending down, as softly as I can, I kiss the corner of her mouth. I glance around the small shelter, taking everything in one last time. Zeekir is still curled up in his little nest, his face buried against the woven vine walls. Zap and Sheol are sprawled on the ground near the entrance of the lean-to. Zap's head tucked into the crook of Sheol's arm, his other arm wrapped protectively across her shoulder. Zap's tattoos glow faintly under his touch, just the way Clesandra's do for me. I find myself wondering about the statement Zap made earlier.

Her half. Your half. Is Sheol Zap's half? It would explain a lot about why she was at Xinorsus each night.

Sheol's mouth is slightly open, head tipped back snoring loudly. I'm going to miss him terribly. I've only just gotten to know him, yet I feel like we're best friends, brothers almost. I wish I would've known him better on Earth.

"Keep them safe," I whisper as I gingerly step over his legs. As I'm about to leave, I notice a thin, black handle protruding from Sheol's pocket. *A gun. What luck! He must have taken it from the desert Smith planted us in.* I'm usually not one for stealing, but I feel like Sheol would be okay with letting me have this since I'm going alone. He has Zap's skills for protection and Clesandra's ability to throw knives.

I carefully twist the weapon out of his pocket and tuck it into the back of my pants. Ducking through the vine opening as noiselessly as possible, I slip into the shadows of the forest. Using the map provided by Zap, I alter the directions only slightly to run a mostly parallel path.

A ruby dawn light is rising above the planet, making the leaves on the trees glisten and dance with magnificent shades of red, orange, and yellow. The sudden early light makes me nervous, so I quicken my pace. It's not easy-going—dense tangles of underbrush force me to climb, crawl, and in some cases go completely around the plants. I desperately try to remember hiking with Dr. Albero. Which plants are dangerous? Which will give me a vicious rash or infection? I try my best not to touch any of the plant life, but that's next to impossible. I silently curse Sheol and Clesandra for cutting away so much of my clothing to make bandages. My tattered shirt is grimy and my long pants are so short that my undershorts peek from beneath the cut edge.

After hiking for maybe an hour, my arms and legs are torn up from climbing through weeds and vines with brutal thorns and burrs. More than once I trip over myself and nearly fall to the ground. What's worse is I don't have two hands to catch myself. Several times, as I'm tripping, I try to grab onto a tree to steady myself with my bad arm only to realize that there's no hand to latch onto what I'm grabbing for. My brain, or body, doesn't quite know what to make of the situation—a hand is supposed to be there. But it's not. Not yet at least.

Even over the last few hours of sleep, my stump has grown dramatically. There's a rounded, bulbous spot starting to sprout where my hand will be. The skin is pink and itchy, at least it was in the morning. Now it's as raw and scraped-up as my legs from trying to steady myself from tripping over logs, roots, and vines.

Eventually I have to rest. My head is pounding as if someone is squeezing my brain, and my arm is throbbing in time with the pounding in my head. I sit down and lean my back against a tall tree. The sun is well up in the sky now, and the ruby-red dawn has transitioned to the pale-purple-and-yellow light I'm used to.

I press my head back into the bark of the tree and shut my eyes for a brief moment. My stomach growls loudly. It reminds me of a grievous error I made when I left camp this morning. Wiping the sweat from my brow, I curse under my breath. All those logs hanging in the trees with camel bugs, and I've left without a single bit of food or water. *Idiot. How stupid are you?*

"Very," I answer myself aloud.

I'm suddenly aware of just how thirsty I am. Almost desperate enough to drink the smelly liquid from the camel bugs. I groan out loud, acknowledging my utter stupidity, and punch the ground. Pulling out the map, I look at the length of travel I'll have to endure. It's at least a week of hiking, maybe slightly more if I go out of my way to run a parallel course.

"Well, you smelly things like blood, right?" I mutter, picking up a branch and

stomping it with my boot to fragment the hollow end. Taking a sharp point at the end of the branch, I dig it into one of the more severe scrapes on my leg. Just enough to draw a few drops of blood. I squeeze them out onto the ground in front of me and wait. Maybe I'm not too far from camp that the bugs will still come. I wait for what seems like an eternity, and I'm just about to give up hope when a little spiral of dirt below the blood starts to form.

"Yes! That's right. Come and get it!" I hiss, crouching over the ground with my branch raised. Only five show up. One of them doesn't come fully out of the ground. It sees me and scurries back into its hole. I make a meal of the four I'm able to catch, sucking the liquid out of them first, and then chewing up their foul abdomens. It's disgusting, but it gives me hope and a little bit of fuel to continue. I'll just have to hope that I can find more bugs to eat on the way, or perhaps a small pocket of water in the forest to drink from. I've already spent too much time here. The others should be awake now and realizing I've disappeared. I cringe, thinking about what Sheol and Clesandra's reaction to my desertion will be.

Climbing to my feet, I groan at the unwelcome stiffness in my muscles from sitting too long. I try to ignore the pounding in my head that I'm sure is from dehydration and take off at a brisk walk.

The farther I press on, the easier travel becomes. The tall trees shroud the ground, choking out some of the dense underbrush and brambles that held me up in the beginning. The leaf litter crackles and pops under my feet, making me wince at the amount of noise I'm making as I trudge on. It sounds so loud that I stop frequently and listen to see if I can hear footfalls from Sheol, Clesandra, and the others.

When I stop to listen, all I hear is the constant chattering of bird-like creatures in the trees and the annoying drone of insect wings beating around my head. Occasionally, a larger animal rustles the bushes and leaves, making me jump and pull my weapon. Nothing ever charges from the shadows, but I'm on constant alert anyway. The last thing I need is to be eaten by the type of animal Clesandra and I dealt with in the simulation room. I know there are larger animals lurking in the woods because the farther I progress, the more trails I see crisscrossing the forest floor. The trails are narrow and go in every direction imaginable.

After some time I find a path that seems to be following my parallel route exactly. I gratefully step onto it. The leaves and dirt are beaten and compacted to make a sturdy trail that is much quieter to travel.

I pick up the pace and find myself flowing in an easy rhythmic jog, my footfalls echoing the pounding in my head. Unexpectedly, my mind drifts back to the first few weeks of basic training in Asik, before Jeremy left with my father's unit overseas.

Men between the ages of thirteen and forty-two were recruited to basic training. *Recruited.* The thought still disgusts me. By 2048, Asik and the surrounding areas were getting desperate. The world population had reached billions, and the usable freshwater on the planet was nearly gone. The Everglades in the South were gone. The Ogallala aquifer in the Midwest had run dry, as many others had or were about to. Statistics about water pollution, expansion of the deserts, output rates of desalination plants, agricultural downfall, and riots dominated the nightly news. My mother would become so distraught that Caileen or I would eventually break down and shut the TV off. Jace would try to distract her with games and mental puzzles, but it wasn't enough to block out the reality of the situation. Countries were creating strongholds around the remaining water sources. Importation and exportation was coming to a standstill. No countries were willing to share resources with each other except at an enormous price. My father and his team were working toward diplomatic negotiations. *At least that's what he claimed.* But it was becoming more and more difficult. Eventually, a draft of soldiers to fight for water rights was imposed. But it wasn't called a draft. It was called *recruitment.*

It might as well have been mandatory. If you didn't join you were shunned. Whole families were shut out of the military compound without hope of receiving aid or water rations. It was as bad as a death sentence to be beyond the military walls.

Those who agreed to enlist faced the horrors of basic training. Up at dawn every single day, eat a measly breakfast that barely filled our stomachs, get screamed at by drill sergeants, then out into the sweltering heat of the desert with fully loaded packs and rifles. We marched, and we ran...and ran...and ran. We were forced to run to the point where exhaustion, dehydration, heatstroke blur, and death seem like a pleasant escape.

One man was driven so blind by thirst and exhaustion that momentary hallucinations caused him to open fire on the rest of the squad, killing fourteen and wounding thirty before the sergeant gunned him down. We were given the rest of the day off after the incident. The next day we were back to the same old drills as if nothing had happened.

I'm not sure how anyone survives basic training. As I jog along the forest path, I can literally hear the deeply enthusiastic voice of our drill sergeant belting out his favorite cadence.

> *Up in the morning in the hot desert dunes,*
> *Gonna run all day till way past noon.*

> *We'll cross the deserts fighting for the war,*
> *Can't stop movin', I want some more.*

*In the heat of the summer, in the
dark of the night,
There's an Asik soldier, itchin' for
a fight.*

*For water now, my body wails,
Ain't gonna get it if we fail.*

*If I fall and lose my life
Pray my death will end the strife.*

*Marching into the red sunset
We're off to war to pay our debt.*

I remember each and every line, and they replay in a loop over and over in my head. My feet automatically fall into step with the rhythmic beat as quickly as if the drill sergeant was here screaming in my ear.

Then I think about Jeremy. I picture him jogging along beside me, mocking the sergeant's cadence with his own. A small grin tugs the corner of my mouth, thinking Jeremy and what his chant would be.

Each time the sergeant's lines repeat in my head I make up a line that Jeremy would say instead.

*Holy shit, it's hot out here.
Would someone please toss me a
beer?*

*I joined the army overnight,
Who the hell do we have to fight?*

*Sweating my balls off with no cash.
All I have is an itchin' rash.*

All I want is a damn drink,
I'll take it all but the kitchen sink.

If I die out on the field,
Please make sure my lips are
sealed.

Now I'm through the hornet's nest,
Tell the Sarge that I passed the test.

As I run now, I let Jeremy's chant fill my ears and help drive me forward to keep a quick pace.

It seems like hours of marching and jogging following the narrow animal trail in the forest before I can go no more. I'm tired and hungry, beyond thirsty, and daylight is starting to fade fast. I don't quite have the weaving skills Zap has to construct perfect walls, but I'm able to find a grouping of boulders with a tiny overhang to lean some branches against. I do my best to create a three-sided shelter and hope that no large animal smells me and decides to make me a late-night snack. Shelter is not far from the animal trail, and I have a bad feeling in the pit of my stomach that whatever made the path might come looking for me, so I plant my back to the rock wall and balance the handgun in my lap, ready to fight at a moment's notice.

Despite my best attempt to draw some more blood from a small cut on my leg and flush out a camel bug or two, nothing comes. My tongue feels like a hard piece of leather in my mouth, and my stomach is grinding angrily for the food that won't be coming tonight. I fear that tonight may be the first of many without a meal in my stomach or enough water to drink. This is what it must feel like to be an outsider in Asik. Survive or die. Tomorrow I must make it my mission to catch something, even if it is a few bugs to eat. Eating any insect will provide at least a small amount of liquid.

I lean my head against the cold, hard stone of the boulders behind me as the light disappears and the choir of insects and nocturnal creatures begins to sing. Tonight the forest is a much more lonesome place. Each beat of insect wings and whistles of creatures nearby sound hauntingly eerie like the unnerving musical foreshadowing in a horror movie. My mind wanders back to the others. I miss Sheol and Zap terribly. I miss Clesandra most of all. A painful void in my chest cracks open when I think about how angry and distraught she must be. The pain is so much that my whole body aches. I suddenly have an indescribable urge to go back. The pain of being apart is almost more than my desire to go back to Xinorsus for my brother. *Are you actually thinking this right now? What about Jace?*

Distraught, I curse at myself for being so love struck. I don't understand the overwhelming feelings or the pain that threatens to steal the very breath from my lungs. What is it about this girl? *Stop it. Stop thinking about her! Jace, he's your only concern.* And I do hope against hope that Jace is okay at Xinorsus without me. That Smith hasn't begun to put him through combat training. He's too young for that. The other soldiers would crush him. I have a moment of panic thinking about Rustin and what he might do to Jace simply because he's my brother. My hand reflexively curls into a white-knuckled fist. I'll kill him if he so much as thinks about touching Jace. Trying desperately to think of something else, I tune my attention to the sounds of the creatures nearby.

I'm not sure when I fall asleep, but when I wake daylight is just starting to creep through the branches.

I give silent thanks for an uneventful evening and zero visits to my dreams by Lupète. I stretch lightly and tuck Sheol's handgun into the back of my pants. As I tuck it back, I realize with a start that my severed arm has re-grown the palm of my hand and five little finger digits are beginning to sprout.

"Incredible," I whisper, turning my hand over and wiggling the little, pink stumps. All of the cuts and scrapes from yesterday's travel have also started to heal and turn an itchy pink. *Now if only I could produce my own water*.

Creeping out of my shelter, I peer around to make sure the coast is clear before stepping back onto the animal trail. My muscles are still sore, and the pounding headache from yesterday persists. I know the headache is most certainly from lack of water. If I want to survive this and make it to Xinorsus to find Jace, I'll have to find something to drink.

As I'm trekking along, I turn over any small logs or rocks, looking for signs of insect life that might help me. Not that I have a clue what bugs would be safe to eat. My stomach groans thinking about the camel bugs. Even their foul smell and bitter taste would be a feast. The best I can come up with is some moss growing on a nearby log that I remember Dr. Albero saying was safe to eat. I wad up as much of it as I can and cram it into my pants pocket. I stuff the rest into my mouth and chew on it. It tastes like dirt and iron, but I choke it down anyway and pick up my rhythmic jog, hoping the trail I'm on is staying true to the parallel route back to Xinorsus.

Chapter 22

I'm not able to keep up the jog for long today. I've been at it for maybe an hour or so, and already I'm feeling weak and fatigued. *There has to be water here somewhere. Where would it be?* My brain feels a little bit like mush, and I try to shake off the dizziness that's creeping over me. Then I remember Jace and Faysal at Xinorsus. Faysal yanked a plant out of the ground by the roots and a little drop of water popped out of the bottom. I keep my eyes peeled for small, scrubby-looking weeds and plants that would be easy to pluck out of the ground. Eventually, I find a few and set to ripping them out by their roots. It's not easy. All of the plants here seem to have really deep root systems, and most of them break off at ground level rather than allowing me to pull them all the way out of the ground. I try cutting the plants apart with sharp stones, tearing them out of the ground in a rage, then resort to carefully digging them up.

Digging proves to be most effective. After I carefully dig them from the ground, I'm able to pinch off the bottom of the root stalks. Sure enough, a few drops squeeze out onto my tongue. I gobble them up greedily, desperate for more. It isn't enough, not by a long shot, and it takes more effort to dig up the plants than it's worth.

I resort to slashing my leg, much deeper than I really need to, with a sharp rock. I spill my blood on the ground, hoping to attract a horde of camel bugs. I put out more than a few small drops to entice the creatures, but after an hour of waiting, I give up. Nothing comes. I limp back onto the trail with not only a pounding headache, but a throbbing leg wound.

Great, just great.

By midday, I'm beginning to worry that I won't make enough progress today. Clesandra and the others will have full stomachs and logs full of camel bugs to work from. I can't let them catch up to me. Even on my parallel path, I can't be too far from where they'll be traveling. I pull out the map and give my best estimate of where I am. It'll be at least another full-day's hike before we would split up and go on our separate paths to Xinorsus or the village. I need to keep well ahead of them so they don't catch up and Clesandra is forced to stay with the group.

I eat another mouthful of moss for staying power and keep moving. Up until now, the forest has been very flat, relatively easy to travel aside from brambles and vines. As the light begins to fade, the path gets narrower and starts to slope sharply down into a valley. Patches of darkness obscure my sight. I feel like I need to keep making progress, but with evening approaching I'm not sure I should risk traveling down into a valley I can't see well in. I'm still trying to decide what I want to do when a large shape moves past me in the bushes and makes the decision for me. I pull my gun from my pants, aiming into the shadows with a shaky hand. Holding my breath, I wait for whatever creature it was to hunt me down. Nothing happens. Weapon still drawn, I glance around the area for anything that would serve as shelter. There are no rocky outcroppings to tuck myself into tonight, only an endless sea of trees. I find a tree with low branches and decide to make it suit my needs for the night.

It's harder than I thought it would be to climb with only one good hand, but I make it up the tree far enough to feel sure that nothing will get me. I cram myself into a sturdy spot in the branches and strain my eyes, searching the ground and the bushes nearby. The light is all but gone from the sky now, and I can hardly see anything.

The darkness tonight feels somehow more oppressive. A wave of fear and loneliness crashes over me. In moments, all of the light is completely gone. Like it was sucked out of the planet by a giant hose. No moon like on Earth to give even the faintest glow. No streetlights or vehicle high beams, no houselights or flashlights, not even the small, indigo light on a wristwatch to gain comfort from the oppressive, crushing blackness. I shut my eyes to calm the momentary panic creeping over me. Somehow the darkness behind my eyelids is less frightening. But then there's the rustling and rooting, the shifting of leaves and the grunting of creatures. The sound is coming from everywhere and nowhere. I'm suddenly terrified that something *will* climb right up into the tree with me and I won't even see it coming. No one would know I was eaten. Jace would be without a brother. I force my eyes open, straining to see. What I see terrifies me. Far down in the valley below, a city of tiny amber eyes blink back at me, and the symphony of nocturnal animals pick up where they left off last night.

Whatever you are, stay down there. I grip the handgun tightly with both fists and take the safety off.

Chapter 23

I stay awake until I see the far-off glimmer of light starting to rise over the planet and the amber eyes down in the valley disappear. None of the creatures came to eat me and I feel foolish for staying awake all night. Now I'm completely exhausted. *Twenty minutes, just close your eyes for twenty minutes. You have to sleep.* I don't want to listen to the voice of reason in my head, but I desperately need sleep, and I'm sure I can afford a twenty-minute nap. So, I put the safety back on the gun, lean my head against the rough tree bark, shut my eyes, and allow myself to relax enough to drift off.

"Get up, ya son of a bitch!" The voice is angry and close to me. I jolt awake so violently that I nearly fall right out of the nest of branches I'm cradled in. My hands fly instinctively to my lap where the gun is, but it's gone. Panicked, my eyes dart around, looking for the voice.

"Looking for this?" The voice comes from above me. There she is, perfectly balanced on a branch above my head like a bird of prey ready to attack. I'm overjoyed at seeing Clesandra, and then terrified the next instant. Sheol and Zap are nowhere around. No Zap, no blocked signal. Smith's troops could be hunting her down as we speak. Clesandra twirls the handgun casually on her index finger, then flips it around and points it right at my head. The fleeting moment of indescribable joy at seeing her here now mixes with panic as I scramble to get out of the line of fire. There isn't really anywhere to go but crashing down through the branches to my death.

"Christ, put the gun down!" I put one hand up to block my face from a potential bullet. "You can't be

317

here. You have to leave. Now!"

She drops gracefully down onto the branch I'm sitting on. The gun still pointed at my forehead. She pulls the hammer back, and the safety clicks off.

I try to melt into the tree bark behind me, my heart hammering wildly.

"Okay." I put my arms up above my head slowly. "Okay, I know you're mad," I say quietly. "Just put the gun down. You don't need to do this."

"How dare you?" she growls. I can see every ripple of muscle on her body tense. Like a vicious predator about to devour her prey, her lips peel back in an ugly snarl. "Just leave in the middle of the night?" There's a hint of pain behind the anger that crushes me.

"I had to," I say quietly. "I didn't have a choice. You're not supposed to be here," I tell her more urgently. "You have to go back with Sheol and Zap. It's the only way you're going to be safe."

"Had to?" She thrusts the tip of the gun at me. "Had to? What're ya playing at here?" She huffs and blows a stray strand of her dark hair away from her face.

I hesitate, not sure what I should tell her. If I tell her about the dream, would she believe me? Who would believe something like that? Stuttering, I try to come up with a believable excuse.

"You and Smith workin' some kinda sick, twisted angle here?" she accuses. "'Cause if ya are, so help me—"

"No." I shake my head, offended. "You know I wouldn't." I say the words calmly and deliberately as I look from her to the barrel of the gun and back again. "I had to leave, you wer—"

"Then why!" she yells. The creatures and insects in the area fall silent.

"I don't want you to die."

"What?" She lowers the tip of the gun slightly.

Wincing, I decide to tell her, to try to explain the best way I can. The story sounds preposterous to me when I hear it out loud. Even so, she doesn't interrupt, just listens the whole way through. When I finish she stares at me like I'm a crazy person.

"Avery, it was a damn dream," she says, finally lowering the gun. I hear the safety click back into place, and I'm free to exhale the huge lungful of air I was holding.

"Maybe so, but here in this place, on this planet, with these people...and Lupète is...well, I'm not willing to risk it. You have to go back to Sheol and Zap now."

"No. I'm not leaving. You probably wouldn't have made it anyway. What kind of idiot doesn't take food and water with them? Your planning is pitiful." She scowls.

"You aren't listening to me! You have to leave right now. Zap is the only one who can block the tracking signal on your wristband. Smith could be sending out troops as we speak. He probably already has." I turn myself around and start to maneuver down from the tree. "Come on, we have to get you back to Sheol and Zap."

Clesandra climbs down with me. The second my feet hit the dirt she slams me up against the trunk of the tree.

"Now you listen to me—" she starts, but I don't let her finish. A sudden surge of adrenaline and anger makes me spin her around so her back is against the tree. Shocked again at the strength I have from Zap's transfusion, my reaction takes us both by surprise. Immediately I begin to apologize. Clesandra doesn't hear a word I'm saying. Her face flushes crimson. She shoves me backward, grabs my good arm, and twists me around by my thumb. My body involuntarily follows the motion, and she sweeps my feet from under me, letting me crash to the ground. I land flat on my back, and my head smacks the ground hard. Stars momentarily cloud my vision. When they clear, I see her standing defiantly above me.

"You *can't* come with me." I can't seem to stress the words enough.

"Try to stop me and see what happens to ya."

"It's not me I'm worried about."

"You should stop worrying about things that ain't gonna happen."

I know it's no use arguing with her. Even though I'm terrified Smith will find her, find us, or worse yet, use her self-destruct chip, I'm selfishly glad she's here. I only hope I'll be able to protect her now that I know what's coming in the future.

"I hope you're right." I rub the back of my head with my good hand. "You aren't going to go back even if I tell you to?"

"Nope."

"Even if it means your stubbornness will get you killed?"

"I died in your stupid, little dream. Dreams ain't real life." She extends her hand to pull me up from the ground. "Believe me, I know it's safer with the group. But I just can't seem to stay away." She adds the last part under her breath.

"What do you mean you can't seem to stay away?"

"Don't worry about it. Let's go." She turns away from me.

I grab her wrist. "No, wait a minute. What'd you mean by that?"

She glares at my hand around her wrist.

"Ya outta know I'm not afraid of cutting off arms," she threatens, twisting out of my grip and walking to a nearby tree.

"Yeah, I like my chances."

"Catch," she says, pulling a hollow log out of a patch of bushes and chucking it at me. "Bet ya haven't had much to drink in two days."

I almost cry when I see the log filled with camel bugs. I help myself to two of them. I'm about to start in on a third before Clesandra cuts me off.

"We ought to ration them, don't ya think?"

"Right. Sorry," I say guiltily. I follow her back onto the animal trail and head down a steep hill in the direction of the low valley. "Seriously, though, why can't you seem to stay away?" I ask again.

"You're not gonna drop it, are ya?"

"About as much as you're going to go back to Sheol and Zap."

She sighs heavily in annoyance and walks a little faster ahead of me without answering.

"How come you can't admit that you might actually...I don't know...like me?" I ask. I can literally feel the scowl she's giving me without seeing her face.

"It's more complicated than that," she mutters.

I'm about to argue with her when a small flash of brown catches my eye in the trees. "Hey, did you see that?"

"What?"

I stop and scan the treetops but can't seem to see anything.

"Come on. We're wasting time." Clesandra sighs, annoyed.

"There's something...here. Last night when it got dark I saw hundreds of eyes. You know, maybe we shouldn't use this path anymore."

"Come on, I was tracking you all yesterday and I didn't see anything."

"I saw them at night," I remind her. "Just when it

got dark. I'm telling you there were a lot of them. Whatever they were."

Another flash of fur in the treetops ruffles the leaves over our heads.

"I saw that," Clesandra says cautiously, taking her knife out and handing me the gun.

I cradle the log of camel bugs under one arm and hold the gun outstretched in my good hand. The insects and birds have gone quiet. The only sound is our own tense breathing and the occasional rustle from far above our heads.

"Yeah, okay. Maybe we should leave this trail," Clesandra concedes, and we quickly retrace our steps back up the steep hill.

We don't get more than a few feet when a shrill, high-pitched screech stops us in our tracks.

"I know that sound," I tell her.

"Is it a big animal?"

"Not exactly. It's the kind of animal that Faysal has."

"Okay, they're friendly then."

The forest around us comes alive with high-pitched screeching. Only now, it's more like squealing, and it's coming from all directions.

"That doesn't sound friendly."

Small furry heads with open mouths showing rows of dagger-sharp teeth emerge from between the leaves of the trees. Each creature has its own unique-colored fur. Some are brown with bits of white and black. Others are orange and tan with stripes and spots. Their enormous orange eyes follow our every movement.

"They're everywhere," Clesandra whispers in awe. She throws her hands up, waving her knife and screaming at them, "Ah! Get outta here!" Not a single one of the creatures moves or runs away. They pin their large, oval ears behind their heads, hissing and snarling at her with open mouths.

"I don't think they're afraid of you."

"Thanks for the update," she says sarcastically. "What do they want?"

"How should I know?"

There are literally dozens of the furry animals, their gangly legs clutching the branches or hanging by their tails. Some are starting to get bold and inch their way out of the trees toward us.

I slide closer to Clesandra so that we're back to back. One of the animals above us abruptly drops off its perch and lands on my shoulder. Screaming, I smack at it with the barrel of my gun. It howls in pain and rakes its sharp talons into my arm, slicing deep, jagged gashes. Clesandra stabs it with her knife and flings it to the ground dead. The trees and bushes rattle and shake with more angry creatures ready to attack. None of them are looking at Clesandra or me anymore. They have their enormous un-blinking eyes on the log tucked under my arm.

"They want the bugs," I tell her.

Clesandra splits her knife into two daggers. "That's our only source of water. They can't have it!" she screams, as the woods erupt and hundreds of the animals bear down on me in a swirling ball of frenzied fur. I have no choice but to throw the log into the air. I grab Clesandra's arm and run off the path, dragging her with me. She screams all imaginable obscenities at me and tries to fight me off to go back for the log, but we both know it's a lost cause. We take cover behind a nearby tree and watch our water supply be devoured in seconds by the throng of angry creatures. They scream and tear at each other, fighting for every last drop just as viciously as outsiders in Asik fought to flip over water trucks delivering to the military base.

As quickly as they came, they disappear back into the trees, screeching and howling. Their fighting over the camel bugs didn't come without casualties. A half-dozen furry creatures lay bleeding and dead around the log.

"Come on," I say quietly. "Might as well keep moving."

Clesandra's face is purple with anger as she fumes over the loss. She stalks over to the log.

"There's not going to be anything left," I call after her.

"I'm not leaving empty-handed," she says, gathering up the dead animals by their long, furry tails. "If we have to be thirsty, we sure as hell aren't going hungry too. Here." She thrusts three of them at me.

"Right. Good thinking."

She doesn't say anything, just slings the remaining carcasses over her shoulder by their tails and cuts off the animal trail into the woods. I follow her wordlessly, not sure if I should ask whether or not she knows where she's going.

Her path is not nearly as easy to follow as the animal trail. In her anger, she seems to be picking the most difficult, dense, overgrown parts of the forest to travel through. She blazes a trail ahead of her by slashing at vines and branches with her knife, not caring that I'm behind her being slapped by all the branches she pushes through.

It's not long before I have to beg for a break. Her frustration and anger seems to have mostly burnt off, so she agrees and finds an open spot among the tall trees to sit. I plunk down next to her, leaning my head back against the tree behind me. Shutting my eyes for just a few minutes, I try to relax and catch my breath. I thought I was traveling fast the last two days. It's nothing compared to the pace Clesandra sets.

"Do you think you might be able to go one day without getting hurt?" Clesandra mutters. A dull ripping sound next to me makes me crack my right eye open. She's torn a thin strip of cloth from the bottom of her own pant leg. She reaches over and grabs my arm that was slashed by the creature.

I can't help but chuckle.

"What?" she grumbles.

"Admit it. You like me."

She rolls her eyes. "Shut up or ya can bandage yourself."

"Okay, okay." I let her wrap my wounded arm.

"Your hand, it's almost grown back," Clesandra remarks while tying the cloth tightly around my arm. Peering down, I'm amazed at the progress. My fingers have grown to their full length and no longer look like knobby sausage blobs. Even my fingernails are starting to come back. Clesandra pokes at my palm with her fingernail, and I take the open opportunity to try and lace my new fingers with hers. She pulls her hand away.

"All right. Break's over." She gets to her feet quickly, picks up the animal carcasses, and trudges back into the dense underbrush.

Should have kept my hands to myself. Sighing heavily, I climb to my feet and jog after her. We jog and hike for what seems like hours without a break. More than once, I try to engage her in conversation, but it's impossible. The more I try to talk to her, the faster Clesandra moves. Eventually, I learn that silence means we get to hike at a pace that's reasonable for human beings.

By midafternoon, traveling at Clesandra's blistering pace is starting to have its consequences. We're sweating profusely, breathing heavily, and starting to stumble over ourselves from exhaustion.

The next clearing in the forest we start to pass through I boycott walking altogether and collapse against a tall tree. Clesandra pretends not to notice and keeps walking straight through the clearing into the forest. She probably thinks I'll suck it up and keep following, but I'm done for the day. There's no drill sergeant out here to scream in my ear or threaten to shoot me if I don't comply. With probably only two or three hours of daylight left, I claim this spot as camp for the night.

Closing my eyes, I listen to the sounds of her footsteps fade into the forest until I can't hear them anymore. For a split second, I have a sinking feeling that I was wrong and she's not going to come back. That I'll have to tear ass after her to catch up. Then I hear the satisfying sound of annoyed muttering and shuffling footsteps coming back in my direction.

Clasping my hands together behind my head, I lean back and smile to myself.

"What's a matter with you? Get up, we're burning daylight."

"No."

I don't have to open my eyes. I can feel her frustration.

"No?" she growls.

"No," I say matter-of-factly.

"I thought ya wanted to find your brother."

Her sarcasm touches a nerve, and I open my eyes to make sure she sees my offended reaction. "I do," I snap. "But killing ourselves getting there isn't going to do anyone any good."

We're silent for a few moments. She scans my face for any sign that I might change my mind and decide to keep traveling. I've made up my mind, though. The more I sit against the tree, the more exhausted I realize I am. My muscles are sore, my mouth has become its own mini-desert, and the sweat on my body is starting to dry and chill me. I practically have to drag myself up by the tree bark to stand up. I start to move around the clearing, collecting large branches.

"What are ya doing?" she grumbles.

"Making us a shelter."

She doesn't respond, just helps me drag branches. Together we create a makeshift lean-to between two tall trees. It's not perfect, but it will help keep some of the heat in as the planet cools off for the night. The more I'm here, the more this planet reminds me of the weather in Asik—perpetually dry, little to no rain ever, insanely hot during the day, and surprisingly cold at night.

With shelter constructed, Clesandra sets to gathering more branches, smaller ones this time. She creates an upright cone shape and stuffs dried leaves at the center. When I realize she's planning on starting a fire I get suddenly nervous.

"I don't think that's a good idea. Smith or his men might see the smoke from the fire and come looking for us."

"Relax, we've got enough daylight left that a little white smoke won't even make it through the treetops. Besides, ya never know what kind of disease these things are carrying. Best to cook them first."

"How are you even going to get it started? We don't have matches."

Clesandra gives me a devious smile. "Ain't got matches." She chuckles. "I've got the best match of all." She pulls out her knife and hovers the blade just inside the cone of branches. The heat causes the dried leaves to smoke and flare into fire. She smiles an I-told-you-so smile, then splits the knife into two daggers and throws one to me.

The dagger sticks in the ground a few inches from

where I'm standing. "Make yourself useful and start skinning," she says, pointing the tip of her dagger to one of the animal carcasses.

Yanking the knife out of the ground, I sit against a tree and carefully start cutting the fur off one of the dead animals. I've never skinned an animal before, so I'm grateful when I see Clesandra skin one and do my best to follow her lead. She starts at the back feet and expertly slices around the ankles of the animal, carefully peeling away the fur, and leaving behind the fatty tissue, muscle, and skin.

I do my best to imitate her, but my cuts seem amateurish and hesitant. I look up to see how she's continuing, but she's finished skinning hers before I've got the slices around the ankles made.

Seeing me struggle, she shakes her head, huffs a little, and sits down across from me. Then she shows me how to carefully peel the fur away from the skin.

"How'd you learn how to do this?" I ask, trying desperately to match her skill with peeling the fur.

"Ya never caught a rat or a stray cat to eat?"

"No," I admit. "Most of my food came from cans."

"Humph, military brat. Where I come from ya either grow your own food, or live off the rats and rodents that try to eat the food ya grow."

"I'm sorry," I say.

"Sorry for what?" She looks up from peeling.

"I don't know. It's not right, you having to live by eating rats. The military bases should have supplied you with real food." The thought of people having to survive that way disgusts me, though I know the military bases in Asik stopped supplying outsiders with real food and water early on.

"The military never cared about making sure we had food," she grunts. "Only cared where their food was coming from. Besides, eating rats isn't so bad."

I crinkle my face in disgust.

She shrugs and takes the animal out of my hands to finish peeling the fur away herself. "Kept my family alive. And these little tree rat things are gonna do the same thing." She lays both of the animal pelts on the ground, takes the head in her hands, and carefully plucks out the eyeballs. Clesandra holds one of the amber-eyed globs out to me.

I look at her like she's crazy.

"Take it," she commands.

I reluctantly take one of the squishy blobs.

"Cheers," she says, holding hers up, and then pops it into her mouth. Even though it's squishy, I can hear her teeth crunching on it. She spends way too much time chewing it, and every second I watch her eat it I feel like I might be sick.

"Eat it," she says, still crunching hers.

"No thanks. I'll wait for the cooked meat if you don't mind."

She swallows hard. "Actually, I do mind. Eat it," she commands again, this time with more force behind her words.

Looking at the sticky blob between my fingers, I feel my stomach flip over. I look at her pleadingly.

"You'll eat those stinking camel bugs and not this? Animal eyes are made of mostly water. It'll help. Eat it now before I stuff it down your throat myself."

The mere mention of water makes me aware of how dry my mouth and throat are. I also know we've lost a ton of fluid sweating while we hiked. Despite being absolutely repulsed by the idea of eating raw eyeballs, I throw it into my mouth and mash it between my back teeth. The eye explodes with a liquid-filled center the minute my teeth crunch down on it. It's chewy and fibrous, but I'm pleased to discover it doesn't taste like much of anything.

She smiles when I finally swallow. "Not bad, right?"

I nod.

"Bring over the others. The eyes will go bad soon in the heat, so we might as well eat them all."

I don't object. The small mouthful of liquid makes me desperate for more. We spend the next few minutes plucking out eyeballs and eating them.

"You're amazing, you know that?" I say when we finish.

"Like I said, ya wouldn't have survived if I didn't come along."

"You're probably right. I'm glad you just can't seem to stay away," I quote her from earlier. Her cheeks flush red, and she looks at the ground. Avoiding the topic, she takes a nearby branch and whittles all the bark away with one of the daggers before running it through the two skinned carcasses and leaning them into the fire. Watching her, I'm amazed at the skill she has with her weapon. The heat from the blade melts the bark away from the branch, hardly touching it.

"Remarkable." I regard the other dagger in my hand. For once I can afford a little more time to actually look at it.

I turn the dagger over, examining it. It's such a unique weapon, unlike anything I've ever seen before. The blade itself has a shiny metal luster illuminated by a low, pulsating blue field of energy around the edges. The handle is lightweight and fits perfectly to my hand. I find myself wondering why Smith allowed her to have it.

Seeing me examine the blade, she holds out her hand for the dagger. As I hand it to her, I see what I think might be the tiniest flicker of nervousness in her eyes. But it fades so quickly as the knife passes into her palm that I think I imagined it.

She presses the tips of the two daggers together, allowing them to morph back into one. There are two small buttons on the side of the handle. When the upper button is pressed, the blade disappears and leaves behind the small metal tube.

"How'd you come by a weapon like that?" I ask.

"It was given to me for safekeeping," she says quickly, tucking it into her pocket.

"Who does it belong to?"

Her face contorts with emotion. There's anger, which is always her first defense, but behind that, I notice a twinge of pain and sadness, which she quickly masks with anger.

"It doesn't concern you." She turns away from me to occupy herself with cooking.

I look at her back, confused. There's obviously far more importance and value to the possession than I imagined. Perhaps it was passed down from one of her family members, though I can't see a poor farming family having any such weapon.

"You can tell me. I won't—"

"Ain't none of your business," she snaps. "Doesn't matter who it belongs to anymore. Smith has what he wants from it. I failed." Clesandra turns toward me, her face red with resentment. "I don't want to talk about it."

Her statement only makes me want to ask questions, but I bite my tongue. "All right, I was just curious." I assure her. She doesn't fully relax, but goes back to cooking and soon the animals are turning a crispy black. Satisfied, she leans them against a nearby rock and kicks dirt on the flames, suffocating the fire until it goes out.

Sitting side by side in silence, we each eat one of the animals. It's the best meal I've had since arriving on the planet. The meat is lean and gamey, but it has a delicious burst of flavor that reminds me of the burgers Sheol and I ate in the tavern. Despite being blackened on the outside by the fire, the inside is juicy. For a moment, the leather-hard feeling of my tongue and the dry burning sensation in the back of my throat is quenched.

"Thank you. I needed that," I tell her.

Clearly not used to receiving any gratitude or praise, she dips her head, and then climbs into one of the trees on the far side of the clearing to tie the rest of the uneaten animals. When she returns, she picks a spot close to me to sit and leans her head back against the rough tree bark.

The light in the sky is starting to fade, and the ground temperature beneath the trees is dropping rapidly. Like last night, I get the same crushing feeling the darkness brings with it. I glance around our little clearing for any sign of animals that might threaten us tonight and wonder if building a shelter on the ground is safe. I don't see any eyes watching us in the darkness. In fact, I hardly hear the sound of insects in the area. The forest is quiet. I glance at Clesandra, who for the moment has her eyes closed. She looks like an angel and seems unaffected by the silence in the forest. Her hands are tucked under her thighs for warmth. Raised bumps ripple on her exposed skin and I slide closer to her, wrapping an arm around her shoulder.

She flinches at my touch and her eyes pop open, one hand going for her knife.

"What're you doing?" she says suspiciously.

"You're cold."

"I'm fine." She scoots herself a little farther away.

"Why do you keep doing this?" I can't keep the annoyance from my tone.

"Doing what?" she snaps.

"Pushing yourself away? You have to know how

I feel about you. And you can try to hide behind this wall you've created," I wave my hand up and down in front of her face, "but I know how you feel about me too."

"You seem to think ya got it all figured out," she spits back sarcastically. The tattoos on her arms and neck flare, making her glow a luminescent green in the encroaching darkness. "Why can't you understand that some things aren't that simple?"

"If you don't care about me, then why come find me? Huh? Answer me that."

Her face twists and her hands ball into fists.

"I can't control it!" she hisses. "I already told ya, I *couldn't* stay away."

"Why?"

"I literally can't stay away." Her face scrunches up as if she's trying to come up with a way of explaining. "It hurts to stay away from you." She bangs her fists against the tree behind her, and then squints at the sky. "It just hurts."

I sit there in shocked silence, trying to comprehend what she means.

She grips her head and she drops her chin to her chest.

I'm not sure what to do or say or how to take her words. I stare at her, watching her go through an array of emotions. Ones that I know she's not good at dealing with. Unfortunately, that makes two of us. I can't find words to form sentences to the questions racing through my head. Not bearing to see the tortured state of mind she's going through anymore, I do the only thing I can think of and move closer to her again. I drape my arm around her shoulder. This time she doesn't flinch or pull away or fight my touch. I pull her closer. Even though she doesn't relax and still keeps her hands clenched in fists at her sides, she tips sideways into me, leaning her head on my shoulder.

Gulping down the uncomfortable lump in my throat, I whisper, "I don't want you to stay away."

"Fooled me," she mumbles at the ground. "You're the one who left."

I wince. "Well, I'm not going anywhere now." Even as I'm saying the words, Lupète's voice burns in the back of my head, his mental presence gripping my brain, letting me know what a fool I am. How weak I am for not pushing her away. For not truly protecting her by distancing myself and leaving her behind, or making her go back to Sheol, Zap, and Zeekir. *I will protect her. She's safer with me.* I think the words fervently, convincing myself that it's true and pull her tighter to me.

"Come on, it's getting colder," I say, pulling her to her feet, and leading her to our makeshift shelter. We built it much smaller than I thought, and our two bodies next to each other literally fill the entire space. Lying on our sides within the wooden frame, I drape one arm protectively over her shoulder and pull her close. Even though her back is against my chest and I can't see her face, I can tell she's still awake. Her breathing is irregular and tense, fighting back emotions I can't even begin to understand. Feeling guilty that I'm the cause of her internal torment, the best I can come up with to do is run my fingers gently up and down her arm and kiss the back of her neck. Her tattoos glow brightly under my embrace, and I lie awake, tracing the outline of the designs with my fingertips.

It's a long time before I feel Clesandra truly relax and her breathing become neutral and rhythmic. Even as it does, I continue tracing the tattoos. Her words keep me awake through my own desperate exhaustion. What did she mean by not being able to stay away from me? Did she mean that she wishes she could stay away? What's forcing her to stay? Exactly what kind of pain is keeping her with me? Is it a physical pain? Is it emotional anguish? Her words confuse me, and I hate the doubt that creeps into the back of my mind that she may not feel the same way I do about her. Then a flame of anger at the whole situation begins to burn a hole in the pit of my stomach. How wrapped up I've become with this woman, when I should be more concerned with finding Jace and making sure he's okay. He's the one last scrap of home and family I carry with me, and here I am concerning myself with whether or not Clesandra is as much in love with me as I am with her. *Stupid.* Yet, without her, I wouldn't be alive. Whether she cares for me or not, I will always be in her debt. Despite her feelings for me, I'm falling more helplessly in love with her. *Get a hold of yourself!*

With her tattoos still glowing, I can look on her easily despite the darkness. My eyes trace the outline of her body, from the sculpted muscles in her arms to the perfect curve of her hips. My eyes fall on the metal rectangular tube of her knife protruding from a pocket in her pants, and I can't help wondering where it came from and why it means so much to her. Where could she have possibly come across a weapon like this? I wonder if I might learn its origin printed somewhere on the handle. I know it's wrong, and I know she might wake if I try to ease it out of her pocket to have a look, but my curiosity gets the better of me. I run my fingertips the length of her arm a few more times to make certain she's asleep before slowly extracting the metal device.

Turning it over several times in my hand, and leaning it close to Clesandra's glowing arms to see, I look for any identification. There are no words or script anywhere on the metal handle, just two small buttons on the side. I know if I press the top one the blade will appear, so instead I press the second button. To my surprise, a chamber at the very bottom of the handle releases and a tiny square of carefully folded paper falls out and lands on Clesandra's hip. Picking up the paper, I painstakingly unfold it, doing my best not to tear it. The paper is coated with a fine, red dust that puffs out as I unfurl it. It's a five by seven photograph. Worn and faded from the dust and over-handling. I lean the photograph as close to Clesandra's glowing tattoos as possible to get a good look. I can't stifle the gasp fast enough the second I register the photo.

The sudden sound startles Clesandra from her sleep. She struggles in the close confines of our shelter. She reaches for her knife which isn't there, and winds up tearing the whole shelter down on top of us in her panic to find it.

I drop the photo and grab her arms. "Stop, Clesandra, stop!" She struggles against my grip until she realizes it's me.

"What...what's going on?" She pushes me away. "Where's my..." Her eyes dart around the fallen branches in the darkness. I bend down to pick up the paper and the little metal tube of her knife from beneath a branch at my feet. She knows.

"Avery, I...it wasn't me...I..." Her voice is pleading, not like her angry, in-charge nature, and it conflicts me for the briefest of seconds.

"This is none of my business?" I shake the paper and the knife at her in disbelief. "None of my business?" My voice quivers with an unexpected wave of emotions. "Where? How?" The words don't form real sentences, but they don't need to. I hold the paper up to my face again in the darkness even though I can't see a thing without holding it right up to Clesandra's tattoos.

She makes a strange sound in the back of her throat, trying to come up with words. Her sudden inability to speak makes me angrier.

"How'd you get this?" I yell, not caring if anyone nearby might hear me. "How?"

"He gave it to me!" she chokes out.

"When?" My voice falters, fighting back hot, angry tears.

"A few months before I woke up on the ship, but I swear it wasn't..."

"Shut up!" I spit, trying to figure out why he would've given it to her. Why he would have had it himself. I drag in a huge lungful of air before asking the next question. "How did you know him?"

"Avery, please...it's not like—"

"How?" I shout, feeling a bit like a child having a tantrum.

Her fists ball up, and she looks away from me, regaining her strength and composure.

"You had no right to—"

"Tell me," I press.

She looks at me with her lips pursed. Her nostrils flare as she inhales, and I'm suddenly not sure if I want to hear what she's going to say.

"During a night raid," she starts. "The people I worked with, the ones who saved me when the soldiers executed my family. They were gonna raid an overseas crew that had just arrived in Nacombe. We were low on weapons and explosives to help get us into the city walls where water was being kept. We knew the people on the ship had what we wanted, because the only ships that ever came anymore, traded weapons. The city near us had the water, and they needed weapons to keep us," she points to herself, "out. We waited until the ship docked, and the captain and some of the crew went into the city for negotiations."

She shakes her head, remembering the night. "It was a bloodbath as soon as we boarded the ship. Alarms and sirens. We thought the ship had a small crew and most of 'em were in the city. That's what other ships did. There were a lot more people than we thought. It was like they knew we were comin'. We couldn't get away fast enough. I tried shooting at people but ran out of bullets. I tried to go overboard and make a swim for shore, but people were shooting at me, so I took cover and snuck down into the belly of the ship. There was so much shooting and screaming. Each bullet hitting someone was like watching my family being executed all over again. So I hid. I ducked into a dark room. Thought it was empty. Bolted the door behind me and sat in the dark, listening to the screaming on the deck like a coward. A *coward*," she says with tears in her eyes. "But I wasn't alone..."

"He was there."

"Yes." She nods. "Don't remember exactly what he said to me right then. I was tryin' to get out. I remember his hands, though. Like yours. Exactly like yours. Strong. I fought him. I tried to kill him in the dark. He pinned me against the door with that very knife." She points to the tube in my hand. "He asked me if I was ready to die. I told him I got nothing left to live for, so he should go ahead and do it. The war and the city took everything. It didn't matter if I lived or died." She pauses and looks at the palms of her hands before continuing.

"He turned on the light beside me. I figured it was so he could see my face when he killed me. Then he...let me go. I shoulda ran. But I couldn't. There was something about the way he looked at me, like he wasn't just looking at me. He wanted to know what I lost. He wanted to know...everything." She pauses and looks out into the dark forest for a minute.

I know the look she's talking about. He had a way with people, a subtle ability to open a person up whether they wanted to or not. Whether it was through his touch, the way he looked at you that made you feel completely safe, or how he was able to crack a joke at just the right moment that could, for the briefest second, erase all the pain and anguish that absorbed your thoughts. He did it with me often.

"So you told him," I say quietly, my immediate anger fading.

"Yes. I told him everything. I talked about my family, about the soldiers who killed them, about what I was there to do that night. He didn't say anything for a long time. When he did speak, his words weren't what I expected. He asked me if I thought what I was doing was right."

Our eyes meet for a moment and we try to read each other's thoughts.

"It's hard to know what's right anymore," I tell her quietly.

"Is it?" she asks. We look at each other without speaking, those two little words and the implication behind them, bouncing around inside my head. *Is it? Is it really that difficult to know what's right and wrong?*

"What did you tell him?" I ask finally.

"I didn't. I didn't tell him anything. I just waited for him to kill me. But he didn't." She puts a hand to her forehead still in disbelief. "You wanna know what he did?" she says, suddenly overwhelmed. "He put the knife in my hand. Told me that this is what I came for. That I was holding the prototype of a weapon that would change military offense and defense during any war. I can't remember what he said it's made from. Some type of special mineral or bacteria. His team was in Nacombe to work with scientists to replicate it. Make more weapons, even worse weapons. They were going to give some of the material to the military in Nacombe in return for water. That knife was gonna buy a month's worth of water to take back home."

She throws up her hands in disgust. "One month of life! For years, decades of future destruction." She shakes her head. "And here he was, just handin' it over to me." She leans in, her face inches from mine. "You know what I coulda done with this?" She snatches the knife from my fist, flings the blade open, and holds it close enough to my face that I can feel the heat. "I coulda bought myself a nice, comfy spot inside the city with this weapon. Hell, I coulda bought my whole damn family a spot in the city. If they weren't already dead. They wouldn't have to worry about being thirsty again. But what good would that do?" I can see the agony in her expression. "There'd still be hundreds, thousands of people without water. Where's their spot, huh?"

I know deep down she's right. Even if she used the knife to buy herself or her family a spot in the city, there would be so many more that would still go without. Even knowing this, I have a nagging feeling in the back of my head that I wouldn't have been strong enough to resist that temptation. What do you do when you're at death's door? When your family desperately needs something to survive? I wouldn't have done what Jeremy did. I would've sided with my father on this one and traded the weapon.

I hope she can't read my thoughts. Her breath is hot on my lips as she continues. "I told him I didn't want it. He could keep it and if he let me go, I would leave and tell my people that I was lucky to have survived and that I didn't find what we were looking for." She takes a step back from me and looks at her feet.

"What did he say?" I ask.

"That is was okay, if that was my choice. He muttered something about how his choice was going to be harder."

I start to ask her what he meant by that, but she raises her hand and continues.

"I don't think it was ever his intention to trade the knife, even if that's what he was told to do by his commanding officer. He wasn't gonna give it to the people in the city."

The missing puzzle pieces up until and surrounding Jeremy's murder are all starting to fit together in my head. The surveillance tapes Smith showed me involving my father. The negotiations my father was doing in Nacombe. Clesandra's knife was the bargaining chip in that deal. Of course, Jeremy wouldn't let that deal happen. It would mean thousands of people would die. It also meant he was signing his own death warrant if Dad ever found out he sabotaged the mission. That has to be why he murdered Jeremy. He was looking for the weapon and thought Jeremy still had it.

"It didn't really make sense to me at first," Clesandra continues. "I just wanted to get the hell outta there, but I couldn't leave. There was still screaming and yelling going on above deck. He told me he would help me leave, but that I had to wait till things calmed down. So he shut the light off so people wouldn't think we were there, and we sat with our backs to a wall and listened to the people above for a long time. I woulda been happy to sit in silence and wait, but that wasn't his way. He apologized for what the war did to my family, that it wasn't fair, and he wished he coulda done something about it. He talked like he really could do something about it. And ya know what? I think he mighta."

She searches my face for a second before looking

away. "Maybe I don't know him like you do, but I don't think he woulda stolen water like so many of us in Nacombe did to survive. I don't think he woulda traded for it either. Lookin' at him, he, he had a bigger plan. He said he would do everything he could to make sure what happened to my family wasn't gonna happen to other families. I couldn't respond. Didn't know what to say. But he kept on talkin', whispering things about his own family and his life. About his brothers." She looks at me. "I think he missed you more than you know." Her last words and pained expression fill me with grief. My eyes ache to conjure up the tears my dehydrated body doesn't allow. All I'm left with is a dry, choking sound deep in my throat that turns into a solitary sob when Clesandra reaches out to touch my arm.

"Avery..." she starts, but I shake her off, not able to control the turmoil inside. Turning away, I grip the family photo of my brothers and sister tightly, feeling the paper begin to crumple in my fists. I never knew Jeremy took this from the house when he was deployed. I wonder how often he looked at it. It was just a simple candid photo Mom snapped of the four of us a few weeks before recruitment. We were standing around one of Jace's brilliant creations. He had built an elaborate tower with suspension bridges made from yarn, silverware, and Q-tips. I don't even remember exactly what the premise of the game was, but Jeremy was standing with a pebble in the fingers of one hand. The other is showing Caileen and me his crossed fingers. He was getting ready to play and Jace was standing off to the side with his arms folded across his chest, a smug grin on his young, chubby-cheeked face.

I want to smile because the moment was such a happy one for us, but I can't. I miss them all too much. I hope the photo brought Jeremy some small slice of happiness where he went.

"Avery," she says again more insistently, breaking my thoughts. "Ya have to know...I didn't." She pauses, and I turn back to look at her through bloodshot eyes. "I didn't kill him. I swear I didn't kill him, you have to believe me." Her voice is pleading. "I didn't kill him. I loved him."

Chapter 24

I look at her shocked. She covers her mouth as soon as the crushing words escape her lips. She's looking at me like she can't believe what she just said and tries to take it back.

"That's not what I meant...it's not like how I...and you..." Her eyes beg me to allow her to take back her words. "Avery..."

"Don't."

The blow is devastating. It's not enough to know my brother is dead, that he's never coming back. Clesandra was the last person to have any real connection with him before he was murdered and she kept it from me. On top of that comes the realization that the one person left, besides Jace, who makes me feel like life is actually worth living, is in love with Jeremy. My brother. My *dead* brother.

"Why didn't you tell me?" I croak.

"I had the knife. I figured it'd only be a matter of time before you discovered the photo. I didn't want you to think I killed him. I didn't." She insists again. "I swear—"

"I know. My dad killed him. I watched him do it," I tell her bluntly. "But how did you know he was dead?"

"I didn't. Not at first. When I woke up on the ship in space, I asked for him. That Lupète guy told me there were two Evericons on the ship, but Jeremy wasn't one of them." I can see the grief in her expression as she says the words.

"When I saw you, I thought he'd lied to me. You look just like him even in sleep. Your pal, Sheol, was quick to set me straight, though. He made sure I stayed away. You weren't him, but I couldn't—"

"No," I cut her off, "I'm not Jeremy." A twinge of envy rises up in me. If I were in his shoes, I wouldn't have been able to do what he did. I would've traded every last thing in the world to make sure my family had that water, even if it was only a month's ration. It would mean another month I would get to be with them. Thinking about it harder now, I probably wouldn't have shown mercy to Clesandra. I might have even killed her. The realization is crushing. *I'm a heartless killer just like my father.*

"I guess I'm nothing like Jeremy."

I suddenly wish things were different. Jeremy was a good man with better intentions...*better than me.* He saw the bigger picture and somehow always knew how to get to it, how to defend what was right. Things would be different if Jeremy lived and I died in his place. It should've been that way. Jace and Clesandra would've been better off.

"I'm sorry," I hear myself say.

Clesandra shakes her head.

"Sorry I'm not him. That I'm not the man you love."

"Stop it. You know that's not what I meant," she says, taking a step closer to me.

"No, seriously, you don't need a person like me here. You need him. If he were here, Smith would never have tested us. We wouldn't be out here in the woods right now. Jace would still have someone nearby to protect him. Jace needs him, not me."

"Stop it."

"No, I'm serious, think about it. What have I done but get us into trouble? You're going to die because of me."

Because you're too weak and selfish to force her away, Lupète says in my head, and it makes me even more furious.

"You would've been better off never meeting me." The bitterness puddles behind my eyes, too weak to force its way out of my dried-up tear ducts.

"I'd have been dead already if I never met you," she whispers, taking another step closer.

"You and Jeremy saved my life." She's now standing inches from my face. "Jeremy made me realize that what I was fighting for ain't right. I was merely surviving. But the way I was doing it was wrong. When he finally helped me get off the boat after things settled down, he insisted that I let him make sure I got back to my village safely. He wasn't gonna let me go alone. Nobody cared about me like that since my family was killed. It was...nice." She looks down at the ground and tucks a stray strand of her dark hair behind her ear.

"When we got close, a gang of my people captured him. I tried to help him and convince 'em he was only helping me, but they wouldn't listen. They took the knife, bound him in one of the slum huts, and beat him. I couldn't help him, and he wouldn't tell them anything. They tortured him until he couldn't tell them anything even if he wanted to."

She takes a deep breath. "After they finished, they worked with the weapon themselves and discovered some of its uses. They were sure the knife could be altered to create other weapons. Horrible things they came up with. Weapons like guns with bullets that always returned to the weapon after a kill. They planned to take it into the city in the morning to see what they could get for it. It was exactly what Jeremy was trying to avoid. No more blood and suffering." She shakes her head with revulsion. "When the men were asleep, I killed the guards, stole the knife back, and helped him hide in empty slum huts deep in the village." She pauses, looking at my pained expression.

Thinking about Clesandra taking care of Jeremy, cleaning his wounds, watching over him like she did for me, opens a strange and selfish pain in my heart.

"It wasn't more than a day, maybe two," she continues, "before soldiers came looking for him. They left with him, thinking he'd been kidnapped and lost their precious weapon. I left with the knife so it wouldn't be turned into something worse. It's what he wanted me to do in the first place.

"Your brother helped me see past the war. And I got to do something right for a change. I'm sorry he died. I wish he hadn't. But you," she thrusts an angry finger into my chest, "don't get to wish he's here instead of you."

I start to argue with her again, but she holds a finger up to my lips, stopping my words. "Shut up and listen," she hisses. "You remember that night after the briefing? Before we landed on this planet?"

I don't answer, but she knows I wouldn't forget it.

"Bet you didn't know I was gonna kill myself."

The air freezes in my lungs. She says it so easily.

"Yeah. Didn't know that, huh?"

"Why?" I choke out.

"Why?" she asks incredulously. "I wasn't gonna be like Smith. Kill innocent people just to survive. I did that already on Earth, and there ain't nothing good or right about it. I didn't have anything to live for. No family. No friends. The only person I cared about after my family died was him, and he was dead too. But then you just had to come after me that night," she says in an annoyed tone. "I gave you no reason to care about me. Jeremy either. Yet, there you were. You seemed so...genuine, making sure I was all right. It was like you really did care."

"Do," I correct her immediately.

The tattoos on her arms flare with a sudden burst of light at the word. She searches my face as if she's looking for an untruth. "If you hadn't followed me that night—"

"Don't say it again," I beg, not wanting to think about her taking her own life. I look down at the crumpled picture in my fist. In the glow of Clesandra's tattoos I look at Jeremy's happy face, but somehow all I see is him being murdered. The gun is going off again and again with no one to stop it. I should've done something that night. I should've run out and stopped it. Shutting my eyes tight against the vision, I thrust the paper at her, not bearing to relive the moment of his death.

She doesn't take it from me. I look up at her, pleading.

"You loved him too. You should have it. He probably would've wanted it that way." I look away from her and hold the paper out in front of me. When she still doesn't take it I ask, "Don't you want it?"

She looks at me with a hurt expression. "You're a real idiot sometimes. He's gone, Avery. What I said...it's not like that. Look, the only reason I even kept the damn picture was because I need to remind myself sometimes of what's really important. When I look at him, when I'm with you, there's still hope that we're not gonna just repeat the mistakes we made on Earth. I don't need a picture to remember *him* by. Not with you here. I know you think he's somehow better than you, or would somehow do more than you, but you don't give yourself enough credit. You're a lot alike. Despite what you may think or feel, I have what I want and what I need right here. It's just hard to admit..." Her voice trails off.

"Why?" I press, suddenly fully focused on her eyes, her expression, how very close her face is to mine. "What's hard to admit?"

She sucks in a breath. "I think the reason it's so hard to stay away from you, to admit I care, is because..." She pauses. "It means...now *I* have something to lose."

She closes the last few inches, takes my head in her hands, and presses her lips tightly to mine.

I want to reciprocate her kiss so badly, but I force myself to push her back and hold her at arm's length. Her hurt and confused expression kills me inside.

"Look, I'm not the person you think I am. I'm not like Jeremy. I wouldn't have done what he did. I would've taken your knife and traded it if it meant my family would have water to survive for another month. I would've killed you! I'm as bad as everyone else."

"You know that's not true."

"What makes you so sure?" I say, dropping her arms.

"If that was true, you wouldn't have refused to do what Smith asked in the desert. You're not like Smith. Weren't you the one who convinced me that a weapon is only dangerous if you have people to use it? If you were like Smith, you would've killed a native and be back at Xinorsus safe in your little bed, watching over your brother. But you're not. You're here with me because you believe in something bigger."

Her faith in me is powerful. It's nice to know she thinks of me like this, but I don't know if I can live up to her expectations. There's a part of me that wants to believe she's right. I desperately want her to be right. Can I force myself to believe she's right enough for it to be true? If her life or Jace's life or Sheol's life hangs in the balance, will I be able to make the right choice? Will I be able to handle the ultimate sacrifice of death if it comes down to it, or will I choose self-preservation? Doesn't she realize that I'm the direct product of a killer? A cold-blooded murderer. I could become just like him if I haven't already begun to. After all, I know her death is merely days away, perhaps sooner if Lupète's vision is true. Not forcing her away is as bad as pulling the trigger of a gun. What if I can't protect her?

A million questions and scenarios are playing through my head when she puts her lips to my ear and whispers, "I know what you're doing right now. No use trying to guess who you are or what you'll do. You're never gonna know until that very moment. What you do will depend on who you are inside." She presses her hand to my chest, feeling my heart hammer away like a freight train about to come off its tracks.

What I am inside is the genetic copy of a heartless executioner quickly approaching his breaking point.

"Why are you telling me this?" I ask.

"You need to hear it," she whispers. "We aren't like Smith and the others. Jeremy is proof that people can still think for themselves. There's still time to fix this and fight back."

"What if you're wrong?"

"I'm not," she says with a confidence that startles me again.

I push her back so I can look in her eyes, searching for meaning, and wishing desperately that I could read her mind or see her thoughts and emotions like Zap can.

She sighs. "Look, with you, I just know...maybe Sheol's right and I *do* have some weird thing for you." Her eyes shift back and forth between mine, waiting for a response. Anticipating my loss for words, she says, "And I'm done trying to ignore it because..."

She doesn't have to finish. I can see the assurance that I'll be able to do what's right in her eyes. Like Jeremy, maybe her faith in me is enough. We were both born into a world tearing itself apart by greed and self-indulgence, until there is nothing to take but life itself. The least we can do is try to change it. We can't be the only two people who yearn for lives better than we had on Earth. Those soldiers who were with us in Smith's man-made desert could've been rebel allies.

Looking at her now, I know she's thinking the same thing. Fueled by a renewed desire to get my brother back and defeat Smith, I take Clesandra's hand.

"All right," I tell her.

I feel the electric energy between us crackle to life again like heat lightning in a dust storm. This time we close the gap between each other simultaneously. My lips crush hers, and she tangles her fingers in the hair at the base of my neck. A rush of ecstatic agony floods my body as her lips part slightly, allowing my tongue to taste her. Her mouth, her body pressed against mine, everything is suddenly so warm despite the cold nighttime air. Clesandra opens her mouth a little wider and drops her hands to my waist, grappling to undo my belt. I know I should stop her, but I'm consumed with an insatiable need to do just the opposite. I have to have her like I need air to breathe and water to drink...to survive. The need is undeniably primitive. We tear at each other, staggering around the pitch-black clearing, bouncing off trees and tripping over the fallen branches of our makeshift shelter.

At the same time, I feel a tug of pressure in the back of my head. Not now! I think angrily, willing Lupète not to interrupt.

Stop this before you...

Get out! I scream the words in my mind.

My right foot snags on a branch that doesn't give, and I tumble backward, dragging her down on top of me. Lupète is gone from my mind. Our lips separate, allowing a fleeting moment of clarity.

"Wait, wait."

Taking a breath, I hold her at bay with one hand and rip branches out from under us, then hurl them sideways into the woods. I can't see anything else in the darkness besides the glowing green light radiating all over Clesandra's body. Her rich, green eyes blaze into mine, making her look almost dangerous and feral with hunger. I was going to try and stop her again, but the moment of clarity I had seconds ago falters. I yank her to me and cover her mouth with mine.

Twisting her under me, I can no longer think clearly. My mind goes blank, and she takes away my doubt, fear, and self-loathing, and replaces it with hope and a future, however uncertain it may be.

Chapter 25

Moaning, I wake from the tapping sunlight filtering through the canopy leaves on my face. My mind is fuzzy. The remnants of what I did—what *we* did—last night begins to come into full focus. Wild and passionate images flash behind my closed eyelids, making my blood stir and my heart race. I open my eyes and the sun is high in the sky. Leaves on the trees drift lazily in the breeze. Clesandra's head is nestled in the crook of my arm, one hand tucked under her cheek as she sleeps, the other draped across my bare chest. I tilt my head down to look at her and suck in a startled breath when I notice she's completely naked. The morning sun is causing her olive skin to pink. She stirs at my movements and yawns. Suddenly, her eyes pop open, nervous and frantic.

"What is it?" I ask, squeezing her shoulder. She calms immediately.

"You're still here."

A wave of guilt smashes my chest. "You thought I would leave again?"

She doesn't answer. I turn over so that I'm hovering above her, my face inches from hers. "I'm not going to do that. You hear me? I won't."

"You better not." Her eyes are wide. Holding her breath, she glances sideways, and I realize I have both of her wrists pinned to the dirt. Her hands are turning white from my tight grip. I flatten my palms.

"What exactly are you going to do?" She grins, glancing down. I follow her gaze, lingering on every curve of her body, seeing them for the first time in the daylight. My cheeks flush red. I roll off her before I lose control of myself and stand to gather my clothes.

"We should get moving." I cough, and without looking, pass her clothes to her.

"You weren't so shy last night," she mumbles.

We dress quickly, gather the remaining animal carcasses from the trees, and Clesandra leads the way out of the clearing and back into the woods.

As we cross into a thick strand of trees, I glance back to take a mental picture of this area and this moment. There are the animal bones of a good meal, and the toppled branches of our shelter strewn around. The impression of Clesandra's naked body still visible in the dirt makes my pulse race. Then a glint of white paper catches my eye beneath a branch. I walk back and carefully pick up the photo. Brushing off the dirt from the image, I look at Jeremy's smiling face.

"I'm sorry I didn't do anything to help you," I whisper, "but I promise things will be different here."

Clesandra appears next to me and touches my elbow. I quickly fold the picture up and hand it to her to put back inside the hilt of her knife.

"It's the only picture I have left of him. I still need a reminder too," I tell her quietly. She nods and tucks it safely away.

For hours we travel in the hot sun as it climbs higher into the sky and begins to bake us. The heat and lack of water makes us weary and irritable.

"Do you even know where we're going?" I question her. "You haven't looked at the map Zap made us draw. Not once."

She glances at her wristband. "We ain't lost." She swings the band near my face and pushes through a thick clump of underbrush. A nervous knot forms in my stomach. How long has she been following directions on her wristband? It's just another reminder that Zap's protection has long since disappeared and that Smith's men are tracking her signal.

As if echoing my thoughts, we hear a mechanical rumble in the distance. Clesandra freezes, listening.

"Plane," she hisses, grabbing my arm and dragging me down to the ground in a thick clump of scrubby bushes.

"They're tracking you." I scan the sky through open pockets in the canopy. "You never should've come after me."

"Are we really going to have this argument again?" she snarls.

We huddle, fuming in silence, as an aircraft passes overhead once, twice, three times before disappearing.

"See? Gone," she says, climbing out of the bushes like nothing happened.

"For now," I grumble. "Ground troops could've been dropped off anywhere near here."

They are tracking you right now. Lupète's deep voice bounces off my brainstem with a wave of fractured images. Rustin is leading a gang of soldiers through the forest. A man is kicking over Clesandra's tripod of branches from last night's fire. Rustin is pointing to the imprint of our bodies in the dirt, sneering and saying something offensive to his men. Their laughter makes my ears ring.

"How could we have been so stupid?"

"What now?" Clesandra wipes her brow even though her body isn't producing any sweat.

"Lupète...Rustin's men are leaving our camp..."

"Huh?"

"Or have already left, it's hard to tell time with his visions. We didn't even try to cover our tracks."

"What're you talking about?"

"They're coming after you. What aren't you getting about this? They're in the forest, tracking us down right now! Lupète just showed me."

I pace back and forth nervously, not sure what to

do. It's too late to try and go back to Sheol and Zap. It's probably a two-day hike to Xinorsus. We have no idea how close they are—maybe a few hours or only a few minutes separate us from Rustin's gang. We might as well have laid down a neon strip that leads straight to us.

Clesandra stands directly in front of me now, peering at me.

"We need to get you some water," she says, reaching her hand up to touch my forehead.

"Christ," I snap, "I'm not sick!"

"You're not healthy if you're seeing things."

"This isn't a hallucination. This is real."

"Have any of these...visions," she says carefully, "actually happened?"

I glare at her and purse my lips.

She thrusts her hands up at me. "My point," she says. "Come on, you're just thirsty. The heat's messing with your head. It's messing with mine too."

I want to argue with her, but we're wasting time. The longer we stand here, the closer Rustin's group could be getting.

"We're not far from Xinorsus. Hope they still have water there," she adds.

"Right," I say, not wanting to state the obvious. Even if they have water it's not as if they're going to let us stroll right in and ask for a drink. We might as well be seeing "wanted" posters plastered with our faces on every one of these trees. But I keep my thoughts to myself.

"How far is not far?" I ask.

"According to this," she looks at her wristband again, "if we stop yakking and taking breaks every five seconds we could be there by nightfall."

Nightfall? I could see my brother by nightfall?

"How is that possible? Zap made it seem like the

journey would take a week."

"This way's more direct. I don't know. Maybe she didn't want us to get back at all. A week is a good, long time to die of exposure. Come on. I'm dying of thirst here and we still have a long way to go."

So we head deeper into the woods, following the guidance of Clesandra's wristband. I try to ignore the annoying frequency of Lupète's words and visions. The farther we travel, the denser the woods become. Trees grow thick and heavy with trunks so large that if Clesandra and I joined hands around them we wouldn't be able to touch. Even though it's early afternoon, it's dark in the forest. Almost no light escapes from the tree's reaching canopy. The thick, thorny, scrubby-looking underbrush thins, is choked out by the tall trees. What remains is a carpet full of crunchy leaf litter and an array of vibrant-colored fungus decorating the trunks of nearly all the trees. Blue moss dappled with yellow flowers dangle from upper branches.

"Beautiful," I whisper in awe.

"Yeah, well, don't touch any of that crap. The prettier it is, the more deadly."

"Right," I say, remembering Dr. Albero's training. We tread carefully so as not to brush against any of the fungus. The farther we go, the darker it gets. Trees practically grow on top of each other with rich, dense canopies. The sound of animals rustling and chattering in the treetops returns, as does the unwanted buzz of insects.

"Great," Clesandra growls, slapping at a fat orange-and-yellow creature to stop it from flying inside her ear. She backhands it right into the side of my neck, where it sinks its stringer mercilessly. I smash my hand into my neck and the insect's fluid-filled insides pop.

"Sorry," she says gently, poking the massive welt

forming on my neck.

"Gross," I mutter, wiping the guts on my pants. Then it hits me. "Wait a minute," I say excitedly.

"What?"

"Water." I hold my hand out for her to see the bug guts.

"I don't know if we can eat these bugs," she says warily. "I don't recognize most of them."

"No, no, not the bugs. Well, yes, the bugs, but not to eat. They have to have water to survive, right? So do the animals in the trees. Yesterday we hardly saw anything. No animals, no bugs. Now they're everywhere. We have to be close to some form of water." I swat at the insects hovering around my face.

Her eyes get a little wider with excitement.

"Wait here," she says.

"Where are you going?" Nervously, I follow her movements around the trees. She's searching up and down, looking at all of the trees carefully.

"Yes," she says to herself. "You'll do." She takes out her knife and starts slicing the fungus away from the bark. The tree she's chosen has far less of the colored stuff than any of the others.

"What are you doing?" I ask again a little more nervously.

"Gonna take a look." She scurries eagerly up the thick branches, slashing fungus out of her path as she goes. I watch her from below and dodge falling fungus as it rains down. Not being able to help the anxiety building from wasting more precious time, I yell for her to hurry up. Rustin's group could show up at any second whether she believes they will or not.

The tree is so tall that she quickly climbs out of sight. Left alone, I spin around nervously and peer as far into the shadows as I can, listening for any sign of Smith's soldiers coming after us. All I hear is the obnoxious buzzing of bugs around my head as they try to fly into my ears and eyes.

"Come on, Clesandra," I whisper to myself, and snort out an insect that's managed to get partway up my nose.

There's a rustling above, then a dull thump from the other side of the tree that startles me.

"You're right," Clesandra says, poking her head from around the side. "It looks like there's a small pond that way." She points into the trees. I can see her desperate look of thirst and feel the parched pain at the back of my own throat at the mention of water that seems so close.

"Only one problem, we're not the only ones that want a drink."

"What's there?"

"Animals, lots of 'em."

"What kind of animals?" I ask, thinking of the simulation room and the wolf-like creatures that tried to kill us.

"Don't really know. It's hard to tell from far away. There are lots of different types, I can tell you that."

I get an uneasy feeling in my stomach. "Too dangerous," I tell her.

"We need water," she insists. "We haven't had anything to drink in almost two full days. Animal eyes are great, but we're not gonna last much longer." She pleads, "I'm so thirsty."

I know she's right. The pounding headache I have is persistent, I'm absolutely exhausted, and neither one of us is sweating despite it being over one hundred degrees out here. I purse my chapped, cracked lips together and shake my head.

"Let's at least check it out," she begs. "If it's too dangerous, we'll leave."

There's a look of pure desperation on her face.

I've seen it before on men in the desert during basic training. I've seen people run away from the group blindly into the sand because they think they've spotted a pool of water. I've watched grown men, friends, and family members nearly kill each other, fighting to get to the front of the line during a water-delivery day. Thirst can drive a person absolutely mad. Clesandra is starting to get that wild look of distress, especially since she's laid eyes on a source.

"Okay. We'll look. But if it's too dangerous, we're leaving. Got it?"

She doesn't respond, so I grab her arm and spin her to face me. "Got it?"

"Got it." She shrugs me off. Reluctantly, I follow her through the trees. The farther we go, the louder the sound gets. Yelping and yipping, squealing and chattering. Then I see it. My half hope of getting water evaporates. The body of water is like a large puddle bubbling to the surface. No stream or creek feeding it. Animals large and small surround the puddle, gnashing their teeth and claws at each other, forcing their way in for a turn at the water. We watch for a minute. As violent as it seems, it's also orderly. Larger animals first, then they back away and wait for the smaller animals, and then the larger animals move in again. It's like watching a beautiful choreographed dance. As long as all participants know their place in the routine they don't get hurt. We, however, have no place in their dance.

We're a few hundred yards away from the scene. I pull Clesandra up by her shoulder. "No way." I spin her to face me.

"We haven't even tried to scare them off." She twists out of my grip.

Stop her, Lupète's angry voice commands with fragmented images of wild creatures tearing her limb from limb.

"I'm trying to," I growl under my breath. "Clesandra, no," I tell her again more forcefully. "They'll kill you!"

She's blind with thirst and doesn't hear what I'm saying. Whipping out her knife, she approaches the group of animals, waving the weapon above her head and shouting.

The sound around the pool goes deathly quiet as the animals register her presence. She continues to approach with confidence.

"Come back! Are you crazy?" I hiss. She acts like she doesn't hear me. Some of the creatures turn and bear their teeth, snarling viciously. Two wolf-like creatures pin their ears back and make a threatening half-rush on Clesandra, warning her not to come any closer. Other animals snort and shake their necks, or stomp the ground with their paws and hooves.

Their warning gestures are enough to break through Clesandra's blind desperation to get the water and stop her in her tracks. I catch up to her, grab her arm, and pull her backward. She twists out of my grip and makes another attempt at waving her arms and screaming to get the animals to leave.

"Stop it!" I yell.

One of the larger wolf-like animals approaches with its head low, teeth bared. It rushes straight at Clesandra and slams on the brakes one hundred feet or so from her. Instinctively, I take the gun that's tucked in my belt and chamber a round. The animal spins furiously toward the water, then back to Clesandra.

"Let's go," I hiss.

She takes another step forward.

The animal rushes in another few feet, spitting and snarling.

Bang!

The animal flinches and runs a few steps back. Startled, Clesandra turns to me.

The gun is still in my hand and pointed at the sky. A faint, white mist of smoke drifts from the barrel. "We need to leave now." I grab Clesandra's arm. "Now," I command more insistently, as she tears loose from my grip again. "We tried. This isn't safe." Her whole body is shaking.

I reach my hand out to her. "Come on. We'll find another way to get water."

She looks at the water, then back at me. Shaking her head, she reluctantly reaches to take my hand.

"Thank you," I breathe.

The moment our hands connect, Clesandra's body flares with light. The tattoos radiate a piercing-green aura.

No! Stop her! He'll know what she can do! Lupète's voice screams, making my head feel as though it's going to explode. My knees feel like they won't hold my weight, and I nearly collapse from the pain reverberating in my head. I try to tell Clesandra to stop, but no words form.

Clesandra doesn't make another attempt at the water, but she doesn't back away either. All of her muscles are tense, her hands ball into white-knuckled fists gripping the hilt of her knife, shaking violently. The animals have their full attention on her, but she's looking past them into the water. The puddle is bubbling and frothing, welling up from the ground, and spilling out over the edges of the hole. Looking at Clesandra, I notice a startling change. Her eyes have shifted from a rich green to a vibrant, piercing blue. The animals stop their approach, quiet their growling and snarling, and drop to the ground, averting their eyes from her.

"What's happening?"

She doesn't answer. Her sole focus is on the water, which continues to rise out of the ground and pool at the feet of the animals, as it rushes toward where we're standing. When the water reaches our feet it stops, as if an invisible force is holding it right in front of us. Clesandra turns to look at me. A chill runs down my spine. It's like she's looking through me. When she speaks, I know it's still her.

"Ain't ya gonna drink?" she asks, taking a step forward into the water. It comes just up to her ankles. Kneeling down, she cups her hands in the water and brings it to her mouth. I do the same. As the cool, refreshing liquid passes my lips and flows into my belly, a jolt knocks the air from my lungs.

"Water is life." The words scroll behind my eyeballs in blood-red font. Lakes recede until they disappear; pollution-filled swamps where children bathe; a teenager kicks a stray dog away from a muddy pothole in the road and kneels to drink; a home ablaze with four empty fire trucks idling nearby; miles of endless sand; hundreds of people waiting for water deliveries; outsiders riot and loot; orphans abandoned in front of military compounds; sick children who are skin and bones; my mother's agonized weeping face as she cradles my dead brother's head against her chest; the rat-tat-tat of machine gunfire and distant explosions, air raid sirens, and terrified crying.

Then blackness until the banner of soldiers who are toasting glasses of water while children play happily in the background spins across my vision. Terror and pain, screaming fills my ears. There are flashes of light, bodies falling, pools of blood, stone buildings on fire, a terrified child wails as she stands over the body of a dead parent. Jace, in combat gear, is pulling the trigger of a rifle and falling backward from the recoil, congratulatory high-fives between soldiers covered in the blood of their victims. Sheol, Zap, and dozens of other natives are lined up, blindfolded, and shot execution-style. Their bodies hitting the ground make a sickening thud.

Choking and sputtering, sick to my stomach, I try to will the visions away. I don't want to see this, don't want to believe it will happen here as it did on Earth.

A hand touches my cheek like a mother soothing a sick child. The visions stop and my eyes refocus. Clesandra is standing in front of me, her warm palm against my cheek. She has a shocked look on her face.

"It won't happen," she says. "We won't let it."

"You saw too?"

She nods. "I know how we're going to stop it." She opens her palm. There in her hand is a single, tiny crystal teardrop. I look at it in disbelief, and then notice that we aren't standing in water anymore. The animals have gone. The water is gone. All that remains is a dried-up hole in the ground where the pond used to be.

"How?"

"I don't know. I just...I wanted the water. You needed it. I needed it. In my mind I made a decision to not leave without it. The water...it..." She looks at the tiny crystal in her hand and shakes her head, bewildered.

Stunned, I walk to the edge of where the pond would've been. Not an ounce of moisture remains. A gust of wind kicks swirls of dust and dirt into the air.

"And this is what's left?" I ask, looking down into the pit.

"It's all...it's in here." She's still looking at the crystal. "I don't know how, but I...the animals weren't going to let us have it. So I took it."

"Impossible," I say in disbelief.

"Yeah. Can't be impossible if I'm holding it in my hand."

"Oh God." I look at the pit again. "This is the future of this planet. This is why Lupète wanted me to stop you. Smith will do the same thing, you know. Take the water. It'll be just like Earth. Everyone who gets in the way will be killed," I say, still reeling from the vision of seeing Sheol executed and Jace firing a loaded gun. *Smith.* The name stirs anger in me. *He'll know what she can do.* He'll use her as a weapon. He'll stop at nothing to have her now.

Staring into the dried mud cracks that create an abstract pattern in the ground, I can't help the overwhelming feeling of dread from creeping in. If Clesandra can absorb all of the water from this small pond into a tiny crystal, what might she do with the rest of the water on the planet? What will Smith force her to do?

"I can take it from him." She holds the crystallized droplet up to the sunlight and watches the spectrum of light shimmer off the surface. "People will fight to control the very last drop. Smith thinks he has control, but I can take it."

Her words startle me. Looking at Clesandra, her stunned demeanor has shifted to one of fascination mingled with what I think might be greedy desire.

Kill her. You have to kill her. Lupète forces his voice into my head again more strongly than before. I put a hand to my forehead to stop the pounding.

Kill her? I love her. I try to project back to him.

I look back at Clesandra and I see my father in her. I see his mental break with sanity and his insatiable need to be in charge of Earth's waterways. My heart pounds in my chest as her beautiful face is replaced by his.

Kill her! Kill her now! Lupète's voice screams so loudly that I do have a sudden urge to kill her. It takes everything in my power to force him out of my head and remind myself that she isn't my father. He would do anything to gain control, even if it meant killing and poisoning his own family. Clesandra wouldn't—she can never be allowed to get to that point. No one person should ever have the ability to control something this important. I want to rip the crystal right out of her hands, to somehow take away the ability she has to suck all the water out of the ground, to reverse what just happened. Even if I don't understand it at all.

"Avery? What's wrong with you?" My father's face morphs quickly back into the woman I love. She's looking at me like I've got three heads, and I realize I must be staring at her ferociously. I try to project a less-threatening expression, but she sees right through it.

"What?" She presses again.

"I've seen that look before," I mutter.

"What's that supposed to mean?"

"Nothing. Nevermind."

"No." She scowls. "Spit it out, Sleeping Beauty."

My jaw clenches. "My father used to get that same look when he—"

"I ain't him," she snarls defensively.

"No, you aren't. But this isn't the way, either." I point to the desiccated land at my feet. "We can't just take it."

"So we're just gonna let Smith take it then?"

"You're not getting it!" I'm almost yelling at her now. "It's not yours to take. It's not anyone's to take. That's how the whole mess got started. Take, take, take! You're as bad as the men who re-routed your family's well if you take this water."

My words strike a nerve. She closes her hand around the tiny crystal and refuses to look at me. The skin in her cheeks flushes. She knows I'm right. I can see the pained expression on her face. Deep down I know it's not her intention to steal water from the natives or the animals on the planet. She knows it won't solve the problem, but even the best of intentions can change when you suddenly realize you have a position of power.

"Put it back," I tell her.

Her fist is still clenched around the droplet. Her lips move as she says something, but her words are drowned out by a deep metallic rumble. I feel the color drain out of my face and my pulse quicken. I remember that sound.

"They're here," I say even though I know she can't hear me.

She holds her knife at the ready. Her eyes drop to the gun I'm holding. We stand tensely, ready for a fight. She looks at me, and I read the question on her lips.

"The vision?"

I nod.

She takes a deep breath, smashes her lips into mine, and presses the crystal droplet into my left hand.

No! I hear a scream in my head that isn't my own.

As our lips separate, there's a sharp pop, and a bullet slices open a shallow gash in the side of my face and ricochets off a nearby tree. My gun is flung out of my hand as I fall backward into the dirt. By some miracle I manage to hold onto the crystal.

"Get down!" Clesandra screams, throwing herself on top of me. The aircraft squeals as it flies over us. I glimpse the rifles I saw from Lupète's vision. A thump and rustling in the leaves lets me know the men are now on foot. A bellowing voice orders us to drop our weapons. Clesandra flings her knife in the direction of his voice and it sticks in the man's thigh. He yelps in pain but has the sense to grab the knife before Clesandra can call it back.

"She fucking stabbed me!" he screams.

"Shut up and tie his hands," Rustin's voice commands.

"Her too?" one of the other soldiers asks.

"I'll take care of her," Rustin sneers. "It's Evericon he wants. On second thought, tie her hands too."

Clesandra and I both fight the men who descend upon us, but there are too many of them.

"Leave her alone!"

Rustin snickers. He drops down on one knee so his face is inches from mine.

"Leave her alone? I haven't had any play time with her yet."

I scream and hurl my body in Rustin's direction. I almost tear away from the two men restraining me. Everything is happening just like in Lupète's vision. Adrenaline floods my muscles.

"I won't let you kill her!" I spit in his face. A hot wad of saliva lands on the bridge of his nose. He swipes at his face and kicks me as hard as he can in

the stomach. My lungs burst and I fall forward, gasping for air. The two men hold me up as Rustin continues to beat me mercilessly.

Clesandra screams something, but I can't make out what she's saying. The only thing I can focus on is trying to breathe and making sure the crystal stays clenched in my fist.

Rustin pulls my head up by my hair so I can see Clesandra. "I bet you'd like to watch, wouldn't you?"

The men let me fall forward into the dirt, and Rustin casually strolls toward Clesandra. She has a look of pure hatred on her face as he waves the two men holding her away.

"I can handle her, boys."

She tries in vain to slip the ropes binding her hands

from the back of her body to the front.

"Oh no you don't, sweetheart." Rustin tackles her. "Hold him up so he can watch."

The two men haul me up by my elbows, making sure my head is fully up while I still gasp for air.

"Let her go!" I choke, feeling my fists clench so tightly that my fingernails dig half-moon gashes into my palms. The tiny crystal in my left hand begins to crunch.

Drop it. Throw it into the woods. Get rid of it. Lupète's voice resounds in my head.

"I think I'll have a little fun before I kill you," Rustin whispers into her ear and kisses her temple. She yanks her head away and slams it back into his. The collision of their skulls slamming together makes an appalling crunch. It's not enough to even stun Rustin, though. It only makes him angrier. He wraps his hands around Clesandra's neck. I watch in horror as he chokes her.

"No! Let her go!" I make another futile attempt to fight against the men holding me. My fists clench a little tighter and the fragile crystal in my hand shatters.

Chapter 26

All the water trapped inside bursts, creating a mini-tidal wave that crushes us. The force of the water is unfathomable. It lifts my body, tosses me, and smashes me against rocks and trees. I open my eyes to try and see, but can't. Everything is a blurry jumble of lights and shadow. *Up! Which way is up?* Twisting my arms around, I struggle to break the ropes binding my wrists. My lungs burn from lack of oxygen, forcing me to take a breath. Immediately I regret it. My lungs flood with water, choking me more. *Where is Clesandra? I have to get to her.* My body scrapes the ground and the ropes around my wrists snag on something hard. There's a pop and immediate pain. My arms flail uselessly, smacking into trees, until I finally come to rest against a log and the tidal wave withdraws.

I lie on the ground for a second, gagging and sputtering, trying to call Clesandra's name.

"Avery!"

There's the sound of shuffling and violent splashing. I bolt to my feet, dizzy and still coughing out gallons of water. Rustin's group is scattered. One is unconscious against a rock. I can't tell if he's dead. Another man is impaled through the ribs on a branch. He's moaning, and blood is dribbling from the right side of his mouth. There were others, but I don't see them. I turn my head in the direction of the splashing and find Rustin struggling with Clesandra. She's thrashing and kicking. Her arms are still bound, and he's trying to hold her head under the few inches of water that remain.

Somehow I find the strength to sprint at Rustin. In my head I envision plowing into him like a freight train with him toppling end over end. He knows I'm coming, and with one fluid motion of his massive arm, he sweeps me away like I'm a bothersome fly. I'm the one who goes tumbling end over end. By the time I get back up to face him, he's dragged Clesandra to her feet, has her choked in a headlock with a handgun—my handgun—against her temple.

"One way or the other you're going to watch her die," he says through gritted teeth. Blood oozes from a deep gash above his left eye, making him look even more sinister.

"Let her go," I order.

Rustin smiles. A haze of blood coats his teeth.

"I'll come with you willingly. Just let her go." I'm nearly begging now even though my hands are balled into fists.

There's a crackle of radio contact that resonates from Rustin's wristband.

"Glowerbak, orders have changed. Both subjects are to be brought in alive."

Rustin's smile turns into an ugly grimace. My heart sinks. Smith knows about Clesandra and what she can do. That's the only reason orders would change.

"Not...gonna...get to...kill me...huh?" Clesandra chokes out. "To bad...gives me more time...to kill you."

"Just you wait, sweetheart," Rustin snarls. "Before long I'll kill you both." He smashes the butt of the gun into the side of Clesandra's head. Blacking out, she goes limp in his grasp. I make an angry rush on Rustin, but he points the gun at my head, halting me in my tracks.

"Careful, Evericon. Didn't say what condition I had to bring you back in." He pulls back the hammer of the gun.

"Stop messing around, Glowerbak." One of Rustin's team members approaches.

Rustin narrows his eyes at the man. "Tie his hands," he orders, pulling a length of cord from a pouch on the side of his uniform and throwing it to him. The man catches it mid-air and approaches me.

"I said I'll go willingly. Just don't hurt her." I side-step out of his grasp.

The man, who can't be much older than I am, gives Rustin an unsure look.

"That was an order, soldier," Rustin bellows, making both of us jump and cementing his authority.

There's loud splashing in the distance and two more men approach. Both are soaked and frantically moving toward Rustin. I recognize one of them. He's a tall man with dark, short-cropped hair and a flaming baseball tattoo poking out from a ripped sleeve. Pattison. He looks injured from the wave. Several deep gashes from tree branches or rocks decorate his face and arms, and he drags his left leg painfully.

"Tidal wave took out two of the Z1S9s, sir," he says. "The other three appear operational."

Rustin curses under his breath. "Where's Culbert? Maybe he can fix 'em."

"Dead, sir," says Pattison. "Head smashed on a rock."

The announcement of a dead soldier makes the impaled man moan more loudly.

"What should we do with Braxton?" the man tying my hands asks.

Rustin grumbles under his breath, rubbing the side of the gun against his temple as he thinks. I glance at his men, sizing them up. All of them look terrible. Thin and gaunt, their skin is a sickly pallor as if they haven't eaten or had anything to drink in days. I wonder how bad it's gotten at Xinorsus. Even Rustin doesn't look like himself. He's lost muscle mass, and a gigantic vein on the side of his head is pulsing wildly in time with the never-ending headache of dehydration. Everyone is soaked and weary, sporting injuries that are just beginning to purple while waiting for Rustin's orders.

"Keegan," he addresses the young man who tied my arms. "You stay with Braxton. Pattison and Sirval, you'll help me bring the prisoners back to base and send a medical team out here."

Keegan looks concerned by those orders. "What if natives find us? Or an animal comes to eat him?"

"That's why you have a gun. Shoot," Rustin says, annoyed.

This is not the answer Keegan was looking for. "But, sir, he can't have more than a few more minutes left to—"

"Are you arguing with me, soldier?" Rustin turns the gun on Keegan, whose face blanches.

"No, sir," he says slowly.

"Good." He waves his gun at Braxton. "Go see if you can help him."

Rustin turns the handgun on me again. "You had something to do with this. It came from you," he accuses.

I raise my eyebrows in response.

"I don't know how you did it, but so help me if you pull something like that again I'll shoot you dead. Orders or no orders, got that?"

I glare at him, wishing I had another crystal filled with water that I could smash on the top of his head.

"You hear me?" Rustin bellows, his angry tone bordering on rage.

"You'd already be dead if I could pull something like that," I tell him.

Rustin's upper lip twists in an ugly snarl as he approaches. Clesandra is still gripped up in one of his massive arms, making her look like a tiny ragdoll. The handgun he holds is pointed at my chest. Rustin thrusts a lifeless Clesandra at Pattison and comes to stand in front of me. He's terrifyingly large. I have to crane my head back to meet his vicious gaze. Lost muscle mass or not, he could still crush me if he chose to. Feet planted square, I muster my best scowl, taunting him to try.

"You're mine after Smith is done with you. Your girlfriend too." His breath on my face is hot and smells of rotting teeth. In my mind, my hands are free, and I'm able to rip the gun from Rustin's grip and put three bullets into his skull before he knows what hit him. My wrists involuntarily strain against the cord wrapped around them.

Rustin spins me around by my shoulder, gouges the tip of the pistol between my shoulder blades, and steers me deeper into the woods, away from Keegan and Braxton. I steal a sideways glance at the two of them. Braxton looks like he's knocking on death's door, sputtering nonsense words and coughing up blood. Keegan is terrified to be left alone with a dying man who might as well be chum bait for any nearby animal that wants a free meal. Even so, he's trying his best to console the man.

Less than one hundred yards into the woods, we find the vehicles that Rustin and his group used to come after us. We wouldn't have had a chance in hell of outrunning his group. They rode after us on hover capable, lightweight, turbine engine aircrafts. They look like giant two-seater bullets decked out with weaponry I'm not familiar with. The machines have an open-air design, with swiveling hand console mounts and metal stirrups for the rider's feet.

When Sirval slides his finger along a touch screen on one of the small center consoles, the machine roars to life with a heavy metallic grinding.

"How are we going to secure the prisoners for transport?" Pattison asks Rustin.

There's nowhere they could tie us to prevent us from causing problems if we wanted to. My mind swirls with ways of trying to escape. There's no way we can ride with the men if our hands are bound. We would most certainly slip off.

Rustin mulls it over in his head for a second.

"Switch prisoners," he tells Pattison. "Give me the girl."

Rustin smiles viciously when he sees the vengeful look I send his way.

"You wouldn't want to do anything that would get this pretty, little thing killed, now would you?" He stokes her limp head with the side of the pistol. Clesandra is beginning to come to with a painful moan that tears at my insides. Rustin smashes her in the side of the head again, stilling her movement.

Enraged, I make a rush on Rustin. He grunts and presses the barrel of the gun against her bleeding temple.

"Uh, uh," he grunts with a malicious grin.

"I'll kill you," I tell him. Rustin just laughs.

"I don't know," Pattison says to Rustin. He looks at me warily. "I don't think this is the right play to—"

"Trust me. He won't try anything stupid. Nothing that will get her hurt. You know I'll throw her right off the back," Rustin taunts.

"Do it and you're a dead man," I threaten.

Rustin laughs a deep throaty laugh and carries Clesandra's body to the vehicle Sirval started. He shoulders the man out of the way and mounts the machine. Throwing Clesandra across his lap, and manning the controls one-handed, he kicks a bar near the foot grip and the motor revs.

"Well?" he addresses his men, annoyed. "Let's go, you idiots."

I glare at Rustin, making sure he isn't hurting Clesandra, before I turn my attention to his other two men. Surprised, I notice that Pattison is also glaring at Rustin. However, he quickly turns his disgust into timid insecurity when Rustin looks at him. Pattison and Sirval exchange a quick glance before Pattison reluctantly unties my hands. I watch both men carefully, sizing them up like an animal surveying prey as they move toward the aircrafts.

Sirval moves quickly with long, purposeful strides. He doesn't appear to have any serious or life-threatening injuries. He still looks strong and determined. Pattison, on the other hand, doesn't seem to agree with what Rustin has to say. Like Keegan, he's quick to ask questions rather than flatly take orders. I study his indecision and watch his labored movements as he tries his best to hide a painful limp. Injured, more easily overcome, that's a plus.

Looking at Pattison's leg, I find the deep, angry stab wound from Clesandra's knife. *He has Clesandra's knife. I have to get it back.* Both men eye me nervously, as if waiting for me to unleash another tidal wave at any second. Pattison is the most vulnerable, so I climb up behind him. Finding no place for my hands to grip, I wrap my arms around his waist, making sure my grip on him is tight enough to be uncomfortable.

I can feel the tension in Pattison's body as he fires up the engine. Rustin takes the lead, and Pattison and Sirval throttle forward after him. The aircraft shoots ahead beneath us with a surprising amount of force and speed. My previous thought of knocking Pattison out of the driver's seat and taking control seems ludicrous.

The men weave their aircrafts between trees with

ease as if they've been practicing for years. *They have probably been doing practices under Smith's watch since we came to the planet.* I think with disgust. Pattison doesn't seem to be looking forward most of the time either. He's focused on the screen between the hand consoles. The blue screen displays the current topography of the forest, as well as capturing any animals in the trees or on the ground as bright orange-and-yellow shapes. There's a lot more life in the forest shown on the screen than there is with the naked eye.

Looking at the screen makes me dizzy, so I focus on the camouflage pattern in the middle of Pattison's back. Dropping my gaze down to his waist, I see just a tiny corner of Clesandra's knife poking out above the edge of his belt. I have to find a way of getting it back from him. I should also be trying to get as much information as possible from this man about what's going to happen to us next. I just don't know how to do it. I find myself wishing Lupète would give me some insight, a vision, something right now. He's been oddly silent since his last outburst to kill Clesandra.

Finding no guidance, I do my best to try to get Pattison talking.

"So Smith's got big plans for us, huh?" I yell over the drone of the aircraft.

Pattison doesn't answer.

"Plans on killing us, right?"

He remains silent.

"No? Planning on having one of you guys kill us in front of everyone?"

Pattison grips the steering console a little tighter, giving me the encouragement to keep prodding.

"That's it, isn't it?"

Pattison angrily throws the aircraft sideways around a tree. The movement sends me tilting violently to the right. I have to hug his waist with all my might to stay seated on the machine. I edge my hands down a little farther on his waist toward Clesandra's knife as he rights the vehicle and lets it level out.

"How many people has Smith made you kill already?" I can't see Pattison's face, but his jaw bulges from clenching his teeth. "Bet Smith's been making you practice," I say, thinking back to the horrific moment in the desert when Zap and the others were dropped at our feet. How many more were captured for target practice? How many were sacrificed so soldiers can get acclimated to shooting live victims?

"Shut up," Pattison growls.

"What have you done?" I use my best accusing tone.

"We're saving the human race," he answers flatly. The response sounds pre-programmed. Practiced, even.

"You really believe that?" His silence tells me he doesn't, but any response in opposition to Smith's mission would be met with certain death. I glance at Pattison's wristband and wonder if all Smith's soldiers are now outfitted with self-detonation chips.

"No, really?" I ask again, "How many innocent people has Smith made you kill?"

Pattison's hands grip the controls a little tighter. He acts like he hasn't heard me. "How many people have you watched get killed? Huh? How many did Smith force you to watch die?" I can feel Pattison's anger starting to bubble by the way his body shakes under my arms. "What's that? I couldn't hear you," I goad, trying to see how far I can push him. "Oh right, right, can't think for yourself anymore."

"Watch your mouth, kid," he hollers back.

There's a glimmer of hope. Pattison, like so many other soldiers, is just following orders. It's what we've been trained to do. Get an order, carry it out. End of story. But the world can't operate like that anymore. The old ways of following one or two leaders' commands has to change.

I keep pushing. "You really want Smith running the show when this war is over?" I shudder, thinking about what life will be like with Smith in charge.

"Shut your mouth, kid, before I shove you off the back." I can hear the edge in his voice.

"Ah." I'm almost laughing at him now. "You won't. You're too busy following orders, not thinking."

Pattison gives me a light elbow jab in response to my taunt. It's a warning blow, but I know he won't follow through.

"Who am I talking to anyway? You might as well be Smith's robot. A mindless, brain dead lackey who—"

"I'm not someone's lackey!" Pattison yells, throttling the engine to its max and weaving violently between trees, cutting in and out, and rolling the aircraft sideways, narrowly missing tree trunks. Branches and vines slap and try to grab at us. I tuck my head into the back of Pattison's shirt to avoid the brunt of the branches.

Pattison slows the aircraft and levels off. He shakes his head and rolls his fists tighter on the hand controls.

"You have no idea what you're talking about, kid. I'm the cleanup hitter," Pattison whispers. "Everyone on the team is needed. No matter how good a player they are," he says louder, very methodically. "Look, kid, not all players are good enough to hit a homerun. But if you can get some decent players on base, you can make a few damn good plays."

"What are you talking about?" His baseball jargon confuses me, and all I can think about when Pattison says everyone, is Jace being forced to the front lines. "Everyone? You mean for the war?"

"Everyone," he repeats. "Children too."

A chill runs the length of my spine. Uneasiness wraps its gangly fingers around my insides and crushes them slowly.

"My brother?"

"Don't know him," Pattison says. At the same time, he nods his head and I know his words are only for Smith's benefit.

I let out a slow breath that's half relief and half panic. Jace is alive. Pattison could be murdered for giving me this information. Even as cryptic as it is, anyone who cared enough to delete the aircraft noise interference from a recording might guess at the content of Pattison's message.

I lean into Pattison so that my lips are nearly brushing his ear. "Where is my brother?" I whisper.

"Everyone is where they need to be." Again, his response is cryptic. It's like he's been rehearsing answers to certain questions. I need more information. If Pattison is not acting like one of Smith's brainwashed soldier drones, then why is he following Smith's orders? If he doesn't agree with the war, then why deliver us on a silver platter?

Suddenly, I'm angry again. "What the hell are you playing at?" I growl over the aircraft noise. "If he was your brother, wouldn't you—"

"Shut your mouth!" Pattison screams and elbows me in the stomach. This time the blow isn't a warning. It's meant to force the air from my lungs so I can't talk. It's effective. "No more questions," he snarls and revs the engine faster.

In the few seconds it takes me to recover, all I can think about is my brother's safety. He's alive and that's a plus, but for how long? How many days does my brother have left to live? How long will it be until Smith orders us, *all of us*, to fight the natives? Well, maybe not all of us. I'm sure Smith wants me dead. He knows what Clesandra can do with the water. He'll use her. She'll be safe. Smith will make her do unthinkable things, but at least she's useful. She'll get to live. Lupète was right. I should've killed her. Even as I think it, I know I wouldn't be able to do it. What use could Smith have for me? I'm nothing to him. Just the carbon copy of a man he seeks vengeance upon. If that's all I am, he'll want nothing more than to kill me. Watch me die. Make me an example for other soldiers. Defy the mission and your people, be put to death. End of story. I hope he doesn't make Jace watch.

Jace, I have to get him out of Xinorsus.

"Where's my brother?" I shout again, feeling adrenaline and anger stir in me.

"I said no more questions," Pattison repeats.

"Tell me where my brother is!" I scream, and force my thumb into Pattison's seeping leg wound.

He howls in pain and tries to swat my hand away. The instant he lets go of the handgrips, the aircraft careens sideways out of control. We both topple to the left. Pattison grabs the hand controls and throws the machine hard right, narrowly avoiding a massive tree that would've killed both of us. He eases the aircraft level again and punches in code on the center console as he screams at me.

"You crazy son of a bitch, you're gonna get us both—"

I press the hot blade against his neck, and he throttles the engine down.

"You're going to tell me exactly where my brother is." Clesandra's knife shakes violently in my hand as I press the blade as close to Pattison's throat as I can get it without burning or cutting him. "Or I'll kill you." As

I'm saying the words, I realize I almost *want* to. I think how easy it would be to just slide the blade along his neck and open his arteries. He would bleed out in a matter of seconds. Not a bad way to go in comparison to other deaths.

"What am I doing?" I whisper out loud. I try to push the thought out of my head as quickly as it came. *Oh God, I am my father. Don't do this. You don't have to do this! Jace! Focus on Jace,* I tell myself. *Not your father. You're not him!* I pull an image of Jace's smiling, trusting face from my memory banks. I remember Clesandra's faith in me and what she told me last night. I hear Jeremy reminding me that I'll do what's right. I try to think about what he would do right now.

I take a deep breath and swallow hard.

"Easy now, kid," Pattison says as calmly as he can.

"You have to understand that I can't let Jace become one of Smith's soldiers. He's just a child," I say.

"I know. I know, kid," Pattison says.

"So tell me where Jace is and how to get to him."

This time I put the knife almost to his skin. He tilts his head back against the pain. "You want me to steer this thing or what?" Pattison growls, he's struggling to see the topographical map on the console and keep us from slamming into trees.

"Tell me what I need to know."

"Look, kid, you might as well put the knife down. Or kill me. If I tell you anything I'm as good as dead anyway when we get back."

"Or I can just kill you right now." Even as I'm saying the words I know they're a lie. I've already made up my mind. I can't do it. *Won't* do it. Killing him won't get give me the information I want. I squint in frustration and pull the knife away from his throat. Pressing a button on the side of the handle, the blade disappears.

He rubs a hand across his neck. "For what it's worth, I don't think the kids should fight either."

I tuck Clesandra's knife deep into my boot, and for the next several minutes we're both quiet.

"What does Smith want from us?" I ask finally.

Pattison shrugs. "Glowerbak got the order, not me. Just know we have to bring you and her back alive." He shrugs again.

I don't get to ask another question. The forest around us thins quickly. The rich, lush canopy above our heads turns brown and looks shriveled. In just a few short days the lack of water has taken a major toll on the landscape. I scan the screen on Pattison's console and see the outline of the massive pyramid of Xinorsus. We aren't far now.

Rustin and Sirval appear and pull their aircrafts alongside ours and Xinorsus comes into view. The ground leading up to the pyramid is dried and cracked. The plants that once grew on the building's sides for agriculture are gone. The grim reality of our situation on this planet hits me like a freight train. Xinorsus is a mere shell of itself. A few more months without water and this place will look just like Asik, but with slender, leafless tree trunks poking up out of the ground. No wonder Rustin and his men look so terrible. They're desperate. Staying at this base is not a viable option anymore. Staying is suicide.

Outside the pyramid, men are milling around large machinery and testing weapons. Every few seconds a flash of blue light appears with a loud boom and a small explosion of material. Men shout and cheer as they make sure their weapons, land and air vehicles are operating the way they should. A nervous knot forms in my stomach as I watch the tiny dots of men in the distance slowly grow larger. I don't like that the blue light resembles the same blue color of Clesandra's knife.

"When are we going to war?"

"Not soon enough," Pattison exhales. Seeing the state of the building, it's hard to believe they waited at all.

"Why are you guys still here?"

"You're our first priority, pretty boy," Rustin sneers, overhearing my question. He puts his wristband to his mouth and says, "Approaching the landing entrance, Commander." He gives me a wicked look and speeds past us. Sirval guns his engine after him. Pattison grumbles something under his breath but doesn't change our aircraft speed. I get the impression that he has no desire to come back to this place either.

As we approach and the people come into better view, I spend every ounce of energy searching the faces for my brother. Only older soldiers are outside the pyramid. They stop their weapons testing to watch us fly in. The soldiers look just as bad as Rustin and his team, and they don't look happy to see us. Thin and gaunt, they've lost muscle mass. Visible trace marks decorate their inner arms from the water substitute Davinic and Francine have been giving them.

Commander Smith steps into the glass landing tube to greet our arrival. He's got a maniacal grin painted on his face that makes my insides practically turn to stone. Just the fact that he can smile while the rest of his men are suffering makes me loathe him even more. Rustin, Sirval, and Pattison land the aircrafts down in front of the commander.

Smith's grin fades slightly when he sees Clesandra unconscious.

"I trust you didn't hurt her too badly? We need

her to be conscious," he says, approaching Rustin's vehicle.

"No, sir. Not badly," Rustin says, dismounting the aircraft and hoisting Clesandra's limp body up under her arms. She moans but doesn't regain consciousness.

"I always knew there was something special about you." Smith reaches a hand out to tilt her chin up so he can see her face better.

"Touch her and I'll—" I start in as menacing a voice as I can manage.

"You'll what? Kill me?" He doesn't even turn to look at me. I can feel my cheeks flush red with anger. "I'll take my chances, Evericon."

"Where's my brother?" My anger suddenly mingles with anxiety.

Smith smiles maliciously and doesn't answer my question. "You're lucky I still have a use for you," he says sarcastically. It feels like someone stomped the life out of me.

"You wouldn't," I say in disbelief. "If you've hurt him, so help me—" I start to advance on him, but Sirval grabs my arms. I shoulder him off and face the commander as four armed guards appear and point their rifles at me.

"Wouldn't I?" Smith counters, showing the whites of his teeth like a snarling wolf. He waves the guards off like they're an annoyance. "I suggest you do as you're told from now on, Soldier 134."

My insides burn with hatred at his arrogance, and I want nothing more than to rip him to shreds. But I hold my temper.

Smith, still staring me down, asks Rustin, "Where's Culchanter?"

"Wasn't with these two," Rustin responds. "Probably dead."

"Interesting," Smith says. "Interesting that she

would survive and not Culchanter." The statement is directed at me, but I keep my mouth shut, grinding my teeth to prevent me from saying something in anger that I shouldn't. "And her weapon? Where is it?" Smith holds out his hand in front of Rustin, whose smug expression drops.

"I don't have it." He turns to Sirval, who shakes his head. My stomach does a back flip when Rustin looks at Pattison. "You had it last," he accuses, and points to Pattison's leg wound, which is still oozing blood. "She stabbed you with it."

Pattison pats his pants pockets down like he's searching. "Sorry, must have lost it in the water," he says apologetically.

I try to keep the shock off my face.

Smith looks at Pattison suspiciously. "A shame," he says, disappointed. "Good thing we took samples. Glowerbak, Sirval, take the prisoners to the holding room. You go to the hospital ward," he says to Pattison. "Make sure Davinic knows they're here, they'll need hydration injections."

"Yes, sir," the men respond.

"Tomorrow is going to be a big day for the two of you," Smith says cruelly.

Rustin heaves Clesandra over his shoulder and leads the way out of the tunnel past Smith. Sirval tries to act as nasty and in-control as Rustin by grabbing my shoulder and guiding me by force, but I angrily twist out of his grip.

"Get off me." I scowl. Sirval is no more than a year or two older than me. Him actively following Smith's orders like a puppet, on top of trying to mimic Rustin's ugly demeanor, fuels my anger.

Pattison, who only walks with us for a short way before branching off in the direction of the hospital ward, exchanges a glance with me. I know he's thinking about the imminent war. I wonder if he's torn about what's about to happen. I also know he may be so desperate for his own survival that he'll follow anyone who promises a better future than the hell they're living right now. If I had to guess, Smith planned it that way. Use our escaping so he could prolong the battle and wait until everyone is near their wits end with starvation and dehydration. Soldiers were nearly at each other's throats, fighting when Clesandra, Sheol, and I were taken away. Holding everyone back from fighting the Mizuapa this long is like restraining a starving dog from a scrap of meat. If you aren't careful, you're eventually going to get bit. But, if you wait just long enough, and hold a glimmering scrap of hope in front of the animal and tell them what to do to get the food, you've got a lethal weapon.

We're his lethal weapon. A part of me doesn't blame them, either. The deep black-and-blue trace marks from the synthetic water solution and Pattison's sunken cheekbones are only a small reminder of the suffering these men have endured while wasting precious time searching for us. I don't agree with the war, and I know it's not right to destroy an entire race of people. At the same time, when it's a live or die situation, what do you choose? On Earth, I would have traded everything I owned if it meant my family could have enough water to live, even if it was just for one more day. Life is too precious. But *kill* for it?

The haunting sounds of painful moaning coming from farther down the tunnel brings me back to reality. Sirval and Rustin are leading us down the same tunnel Sheol and I were in the first night at Xinorsus, when we were looking for the hospital. It's not long before we come to a pair of guards blocking an entrance with large sliding metal doors.

I recognize one of the guards immediately. It's Marty. He's standing with another man around his height and build. The response would be contradictory to the situation right now, but when our eyes meet I still expect a warm greeting from him. Maybe it's because he spoke so fondly of Jeremy. Maybe it's because he seemed in such opposition to the war. I half expect him to wave the other guards away and whisk us all to safety, at least to somewhere other than here.

Instead, he eyes me reproachfully from his one good eye. The other guard has his arms folded across his chest, cradling his rifle nonchalantly.

"'Bout damn time you found his sorry ass," Marty grumbles to Rustin in his deep, rasping voice. Marty gives him a complex handshake like they're best buddies. My heart sinks. Marty, good friend of Jeremy's, has changed sides.

"Now we can get the hell out of here," the other guard mumbles in agreement.

"I wish," Rustin says. "This one here," he adjusts Clesandra roughly on his shoulder, "will make it so we can still use Xinorsus."

"How?" Marty asks.

Rustin shrugs. "Who cares? As long as we get the water and I get to kill junior here." He tips his head in my direction.

"Smith's going to let you kill him? Kill the son of the world's greatest war general?" Marty says, rolling his eyes. The four men share a laugh while they watch my cheeks flood with color. It's taking everything in my power to bite my tongue and not lunge at them.

"Son of the greatest war general, his family line is a joke." Rustin scoffs. "Please. Killing him will be as easy as pulling the trigger of a gun." He makes an imaginary gun with his hand and fires it right at my forehead. "Besides, who said anything about *letting* me kill him?" My hands ball into tight fists. All I can do is try to look threatening. Rustin laughs at me. "He thinks he has a chance in hell of fighting me and winning." The four men laugh again.

He turns back to Marty. "You got an empty holding cell for us?"

"Yeah, 4D is open," the other guard says. He punches in a code. The doors slide open and Rustin steps through. Sirval points his gun at me and motions that I should follow.

The tunnel seems to stretch on forever. Instead of the natural stone and dirt walls of the previous tunnels in Xinorsus, this one looks like a manmade extension. It's poured concrete and stone that's been whitewashed and infused with fluorescent lighting. It hurts my eyes. To our left and right are rows of square holding cells. I can't help glancing into some of them as we walk past. What I see shocks me.

The moment our feet cross the threshold, an eerie moaning mingles with screaming. The noise is coming from captive prisoners.

A single prisoner or groups of prisoners occupy each cell. All are natives. Those in groups huddle together against the farthest corner of the room. They've been forced into thin, sterile garments like the ones we saw on Zap. Some of the natives are strapped down to tables in the center of the room while groups of soldiers stand around taking notes or poking and prodding their bodies. The fear I see on the natives' faces rocks me to my core. These are not the faces of heartless killers. I'm glad Clesandra isn't awake to see this. I'm starting to lose my composure.

A sudden explosion and scream from farther down startles me. Instinctively, I dive flat onto my stomach in the middle of the tunnel.

"Get up, idiot," Rustin growls. I can't understand

why they don't look concerned. I creep carefully to my feet and continue to follow, but the native in the cell to my left catches my eye. He looks like Zeekir. When I look more closely I'm relieved to see it's not him. The young boy is standing shirtless at the far end of the room. I can see the outline of every rib and know that he's been starved for quite some time. Two soldiers are standing on the opposite side of the room from him. One is holding a handheld recording device while the other holds a small grenade in the palm of his hand. I take a step closer to the window even though Rustin and Sirval are threatening me to come with them.

The native boy, who has no idea the soldier is holding a weapon, reaches out his hand for the grenade. They regard each other with curiosity. The boy makes a confident motion with his hand to his mouth. It's a simple gesture of asking if the grenade is food. The soldiers across the room smile. Without thinking, I'm suddenly pounding on the glass trying to get the boy's attention away from the men. It doesn't work. Sirval makes a grab at me, and I backhand him in the face. He shrieks something unintelligible while I watch the soldier press a button on the side of the grenade, making it flare to life with a brilliant shade of blue. He gently tosses the grenade to the boy. To my horror, the native steps forward to catch it willingly. I'm screaming my head off and pounding on the glass, but it's too late. Both of the boy's arms and part of his right shoulder are blown off.

The soldier with the handheld device feverishly punches in notes while the other stands speechlessly as a fresh grenade materializes in the palm of his hand. The ridges of the grenade glow a vibrant blue, the same blue as Clesandra's knife. Whitewashed cell walls are coated with an appalling layer of fresh blood while the wounded boy writhes on the ground in agony. Blood is pouring out of his body. He struggles to his feet despite the fact that he probably has only moments left to live. No one is doing anything to help him.

Automatically I'm on the door, trying to yank it open. There isn't a doorknob, only a keypad that I don't have the numbers to. I rush to the cell window again, banging my fists against the protective layered glass, and screaming obscenities at the soldiers, but no one does anything. Neither one turns to look at me except the native. His pale, iridescent eyes lock onto mine, pleading with me to help him. Tears stream down his face. Then he looks at his mangled body and resumes a wail so shocking and mournful that I know I'll have nightmares about it until the day I die.

The two soldiers finally glance over in my direction. The one with the grenade makes eye contact with me. Shock and fear mingled with an unmistakable glint of excitement crosses his face before looking at the grenade in his hand, then lobbing it at the back of the boy's head.

It hits him square in the middle of his back and explodes. The window I'm pounding on reverberates under my fists but holds strong. There's nothing left of the boy but blobs of body parts. My ears ring from the sound of the explosion and my own screaming. The grenade the soldier threw re-materializes in the palm of his hand. He looks at it and smiles like it's Christmas day and he's just opened the best present of his life. I'm hardly aware of the fact that I'm being dragged away from the cell. All I can see in front of my eyes is the face of the boy who could have been Jace's age. Who could have been a brother of Zap or Zeekir or Niteg. I see his eyes begging me to help him, and it's Jeremy being shot mercilessly. I did nothing. I could do nothing to help him, either of them.

I'm thrown roughly into a cell of my own with

Clesandra a minute later. Sirval and Rustin stand in the open doorway, annoyed.

"Don't know why you're so upset. They're only aliens," Sirval comments before the door slides shut, blocking them out.

In a rage, I rush the door, pounding it with my fists. Kicking it with everything I've got. *They're only aliens.* The phrase strikes a discord with me.

"Aliens! Aren't we the aliens?" I scream, moving to the glass window and striking it repeatedly as they disappear down the tunnel. Clesandra moans on the ground behind me. She's starting to come to, but there's nothing I can do to help her right now. I collapse to my knees, sobbing. I feel like I'm dying. I wish I could die. For the first time on this planet I allow myself to really cry. It's the kind of crying that makes your whole body ache. It's the kind that encompasses a lifetime of pain and suffering, amassing it into one huge deluge.

I embody the pain of everyone I've watched suffer on Earth and here. Mourn the boy who was just murdered. Pray, though I'm sure there's no God to pray to, for the ones whose suffering voices fill the walls around me. Beg forgiveness for the ones who will suffer at our hands in the coming days, and long to see my brother's face one more time.

Chapter 27

With my body finally spent and aching, I draw my knees into my chest, smear tears away on my arm, and tuck my head down to block out the light. Block out everything like it never happened. But I know better.

Passage of time no longer matters to me. I sit there on the cold concrete floor, not knowing if it's day or night, wishing Jeremy could take my place. He would know what to do. He would be able to come up with a plan of action. After a while, I hear Clesandra stir and feel her come sit beside me. She forces her hand into mine and we sit together, listening to the frightening sounds of natives being tortured and killed.

I flinch as another piercing scream echoes through the tunnel.

"What's happening out—" She makes a move to stand up and go to the window, but I pull her back down.

"Don't."

She must see the sadness on my face because she doesn't argue. "Did you find out anything about Jace?" she asks.

I shake my head.

"We'll get him," she reassures me.

I nod even though I can't block out the doubt that says she's wrong.

"How's your head?" I try to change the subject.

"It kills."

Turning to look at her, I wince at the swollen mass on the left side of her temple that has turned a nasty shade of black and blue. A corner of the lump has swollen so much that its split open. A path of dried blood blends into her hair. I reach over to wipe the dried blood away.

"I'm sorry," I tell her quietly.

"Don't worry. We'll get him too." She drops her head onto my shoulder and shuts her eyes.

"I know. I know. And we'll get out of this," I whisper, kissing her head. "I promise."

I stare at the metal door, overwhelmed by the fact that there's a good chance we won't make it out of this. That Jace may already be dead. The minute the thought crosses my mind I force it out. Jace is still here. He has to be. Smith is holding him captive somewhere too. Maybe even in one of the cells of this tunnel.

We sit in silence for a long time until we eventually hear the harsh sounds of solider boots marching down the tunnel corridor away from us. It's almost too much to bear listening to them joke and laugh, as if killing and torturing people is great fun.

The intermittent sounds of screaming fade into sad moaning, sobbing, and hushed conversation in a language neither one of us knows, yet can still understand.

Suddenly, tired of sitting around doing nothing, I get to my feet and stride purposefully toward the door.

Like the other doors in this tunnel, there's a keypad with numbers and symbols. I don't have the code, but I start punching in random numbers and letters anyway.

"Not gonna work," Clesandra grumbles.

"I have to try. Can't sit here anymore."

"There's a million possible combinations." She points out.

"Thanks for the vote of confidence."

She sighs heavily and stalks over to where I'm standing. "If we're gonna do it this way, we have to keep track of the combos."

"Nothing to write with," I mumble, punching in

another random code.

Clesandra is silent for a moment. "Here."

I turn toward her and she's got a stray rock from the floor. She scrapes it along the wall, making faint gray marks in the white paint. "This'll do. Start with three number combinations."

I tell her the numbers and symbols, and she scratches them into the wall. It's busy work and will probably prove futile, but it's better than doing nothing. So we painstakingly begin to work through every set of possible combinations.

Surprisingly we haven't been working long before there's a subtle click and the sound of gears shifting in the wall. We're about to celebrate our dumb luck when the doors open, revealing Lupète.

I'm not sure if I should be happy to see him or concerned.

The look on his face makes me lean more toward concern. He steps into the room, carrying a pair of needles filled with an amber liquid, and the doors grind shut behind him.

"Lupète," I say his name cautiously. "What's going on? What is this place?"

He locks eyes with me, and I feel that same pulsating pressure in my head that comes with his gaze.

"This is a testing facility." He verifies my worst fears. *You should have followed my directions*, he speaks in my mind.

"I couldn't do that."

"Do what?" Clesandra asks.

Lupète ignores her and looks at me with disappointment. "You have no idea the trouble you have created. Now I have to fix it." His voice is filled with sadness.

I shake my head. *Fix it?* What's that supposed to mean? "Where's Jace? Is he okay?"

I watch his expression carefully. Even if this man never cared an ounce for me, I know he had a fondness for Jace. His nostrils flare at the question, and his golden eyes glaze over. My stomach drops.

"Where's my brother?" I ask accusingly. "Tell me where he is."

"Jace," he says my brother's name with anguish that confirms my fears. "You should have listened to me." *You didn't listen. Now he'll have to—*

"No. You're lying." I interrupt, knowing what he's about to say.

"What's going on?" Clesandra sounds concerned, but I can't focus on her now.

I've seen how it ends. Jace won't survive. You know I wouldn't lie to you.

The ground feels like it's falling away beneath my feet at his words.

"You can't know that for sure. How the hell? What the hell are you?" I scream. "You act like you're helping us, by giving me these visions." I pull at my hair in frustration. "Are you on Smith's side or ours?"

"There are no sides anymore. The choices the two of you have made together make taking *sides* implausible. Both will take equal damage."

Lupète turns to me. "You have to understand, we both want what's right. We both want what's best for everyone. We aren't that different, you and me."

"We aren't that different? You aren't even human!" I finally say the assumption aloud. Though he has a human body, his golden glowing eyes and perfect shimmering complexion is neither human nor alien.

My racism should have more sting, but Lupète isn't offended.

"I was born on Earth. Just like you," he says.

"But you're not—"

He holds a hand up, stopping my words. "I was

conceived on Panacea. My mother was from the first group of scientists on the planet. She had an...indiscretion. It started a small civil war between the scientists and the Mizuapa people who deemed such an act...unforgivable."

I scrunch my face, regarding him as if he's crazy. "You have to understand," Lupète continues, "that the Mizuapa are not primitive murderers. They can perceive things better than humans. They see, or more so feel, the long-term effects of decisions far before the actions are carried out."

"Like your visions?"

"Similar. I'm not the same as the Mizuapa. I can literally see parts of the future before they happen. Call it a mutated gene created between the two species. The future, though, is not always perfect. People still have free will," he says sarcastically, implying disgust at my execution of free will. "My communication with you was an attempt at bending the rules of free will for everyone's benefit." Lupète ignores my look of repulsion.

"The Mizuapas' ability is more like instinct. It's almost like they can see what a person is, but their curiosity is their biggest vulnerability. Humans can't afford to have indiscretions here. It changes too much. The mixing of genetics creates beings with too much power."

"Like you," I say to him.

"No. Like me." Clesandra interrupts from behind me. "I control the water," she whispers.

"But she isn't one of them. You're not one of them. You're from Earth," I reassure her.

"She is...one of them," Lupète tells us. "The female genetics adapt the instant they arrive on Panacea."

Clesandra runs her hands down her arms, across

her tattoos.

"How else would the human race survive and reproduce?" he says. "My mother adapted as you did, Clesandra. Perhaps she fell in love with a native here, or maybe she was raped. I know nothing of the background of my father. But, the Mizuapa could tell that what she and my father *created* would have consequences. Perhaps not good ones. They started attacking the science research base, looking for her. While the Mizuapa are a generally peaceful people, they are not without military skills."

A chill runs the length of my spine, remembering how quickly Zap and the others were able to disarm Clesandra.

"My mother, along with several other scientists, requested immediate clearance to return to Earth. Not all of them were military-trained scientists. They didn't sign up to be slaughtered. Most of the team came back to Earth. It wasn't until they arrived and were taken out of cryogenic sleep that she realized she was pregnant. You can imagine the reactions from scientists and doctors on Earth. That's where Smith intervened. You have no idea the things your people would have done to me. The horrid experiments, tests—"

"Like the ones going on in these cells?" I fume.

His jaw clenches. "I don't condone it."

"But you're letting Smith allow it to happen." His silence confirms my accusation. "So his side then?"

He looks at me quizzically. "I have a debt to him. You should understand this. It's just like you have a debt to your brother Jeremy."

The name rolls so casually off Lupète's tongue. The way he says it boils my blood and my hands ball into fists. "Things would have been very different had Jeremy allowed you to travel with your father overseas. Would you like to see?"

"Shut up," I snarl.

"Do you think you are more like your brother or your father?"

"Shut up! I had to stay back! Jeremy knew...someone had to take care of Mom and Jace and Caileen."

Had to? Lupète almost smiles at my anger. "You fight so hard to find Jace, to keep him from facing the same fate Jeremy enlisted into. *The one you were a coward to face yourself.* Who is Jace looking after?" He peers at me knowingly.

I don't want to consider that Lupète's right. If Jeremy hadn't broken my leg, and if I had gone to war with Jeremy, would I have accepted war is a part of everyone's existence and simply allow Jace to suffer the same terrifying fate?

"Smith," Lupète continues, stole me away from the quarantine facility where I was born. Even as a child I had visions. I wasn't able to control them. I could give them to people with a touch as I can for you. They just...happened. Perhaps the commander saw a vision of something that he wanted when I was a baby. He saved me. He raised me. He gave me a purpose in medicine and research. So yes, my *side,"* he says, "has always been with him...for his benefit and success."

"Then why help us? From the beginning you've been giving me visions, asking me to protect her." I take Clesandra's hand. "Even after Smith ordered us dead. Why bother?"

"Success could still have been had without exterminating a whole race of people. They would have adapted. But not now. Not with what has become."

"The water?" I ask.

"But I don't even know how I'm doing it," Clesandra adds.

"That's because it's not you controlling it," Lupète says with an edge of frustration. "Your child is."

Chapter 28

The two of us stand in shocked silence.

"What?"

"Not possible." Clesandra's shock turns to anger. "You lying son of a..." Her voice trails off, and I wonder if she's thinking about last night. "It wouldn't be possible." She searches my face for confirmation. "It was only one time, one day...even if...*it* wouldn't be formed."

"No. It's not possible," I agree. "Don't listen to him."

"You know so little," Lupète starts. "For instance." He turns back to me. "By your standards, I'm roughly your brother's age, but mentally and in appearance I'm probably closer to thirty. Growth and development for people like me is much more rapid. The only thing that appears to prevent development is death and cryogenics."

"Not possible," Clesandra is still murmuring.

Lupète and I regard each other for a moment while Clesandra mutters to herself.

You made a mistake, but there is one way we can still fix this, he says in my head.

I shake my head, knowing what his suggestion will be.

It's the only way. Smith will still get what he wants. Just not by using her. Jace will get to live.

"There has to be another way," I whisper.

We have to kill her if you want Jace to survive, he repeats.

I close my eyes, feeling like my whole existence is slipping away from me. *Jace. I have to save Jace.* He's the only family I've got left. It was bad enough knowing that he might have to fight in the war and what the implications of that would be for him. But kill Clesandra? I love her.

I love her deeply, madly. Sure, I'll survive her death physically. But Jace...

Lupète stands silent, observing me. I know he can see my internal debate, can probably hear it, too. His frown deepens the longer he watches me.

"I can't." Giving Clesandra's hand a squeeze, I beg him to understand.

"I see," he says. *She is more important to you than your own flesh and blood.* His words compress my insides like I'm being crushed from the inside out. "I can see your mind will not be changed. Here." He holds out his hand for Clesandra. "Just one quick shot and I'll leave you to your fates," he says with contempt. *Just know that you are not only murdering your brother with this choice, you are murdering an entire people. It won't be a fair fight. Smith will use her to take the water. And what about the Mizuapa? Those that aren't brutally murdered will starve. Waste away completely. You're aiding a murderer with this choice.*

Clesandra tucks her arms behind her and takes a step back. "What's in it?" she asks warily.

"Synthetic hydration solution," Lupète responds automatically.

I block her.

"She doesn't get the synthetic water," I tell him. He should know this. He has all the specs on every one of the soldiers on the base from working with the hospital team. Clesandra and I exchange a look.

"This is a different mixture. It won't hurt her," he replies. *Tell her it won't hurt her. You have to help me do this. It's the only way.*

Still torn, I try to work through the possibilities of

what life will be like if Jace or Clesandra are dead. Who to save? Which life means more to me?

Tell her!

"He's right." I'm hardly aware of the words coming out of my mouth. Clesandra looks at me suspiciously. "Pattison did say they would be giving us a hydration solution to make sure we're good to go for tomorrow." My insides compress a little more. I wonder if she can read the lie on my face.

"Now give me your arm," Lupète commands more forcefully and steps toward her again. I glare at him, looking at the two needles, both filled with an equal amount of liquid. He holds one in each hand, his thumbs hovering precariously over the syringe pumps. Little beads of sweat are forming on his brow.

Why are there two needles? I think the words in my head. *You never intended to let us live, either one of us.*

Lupète bares his teeth.

Now, to clean up this mess, he says, and lunges at Clesandra. I yank her out of the way just in time.

In the distance, boots ring on the pavement. There's shouting and what sounds like scuffling and slamming coming toward us. He's coming fast. Lupète shrieks something that I don't understand and makes another lunge at Clesandra. I step between them and slap his arm out of the way. He manages to maintain his grip on the needles and readies himself for another attack.

The doors to our cell slide open again.

"Stop! What are you doing? Lupète, stop!" an angry voice from the entrance of our cell yells.

Lupète flinches like a puppy that's just been caught wetting the carpet. Smith stands in the doorway with a 9mm handgun pointed at him. The commander wipes a trail of blood away from his freshly split lip.

"We need them...alive." He mops sweat from his forehead with the back of his hand.

Lupète turns slightly to face him and slowly shakes his head. "I'm sorry," he says apologetically. "But you don't *need* them." His thumbs are still on the tops of the syringes. "You can still get what you desire."

"Well, that's the interesting thing about desires, isn't it? Sometimes they change."

"You can't have her." I put myself firmly between Clesandra and the two men.

Smith laughs. "I'll *have* whomever I want. Lupète leave us," Smith commands.

Lupète dips his head in submission and takes a small step away from us. Smith lowers his gun.

The moment the gun's aim is dropped, Lupète lunges at us again.

"No!" Smith yells.

I shove Clesandra as far away as possible. Smith whips his gun around on Lupète and fires at him blindly. The bullet misses and ricochets off the cell walls. He fires again and the ricocheting bullet nearly hits Clesandra.

"Stop shooting! You'll kill us all," I scream. Before Smith can fire another round, I plow into him like a linebacker.

We spin backward, grappling at each other. The gun goes off again and again and again amidst screams from both Smith and I. There's scuffling in the background from Clesandra and Lupète. I send a silent prayer that she can hold herself against him.

The gun's clip is empty in seconds. When nothing but clicking happens we both drop the gun. Smith reaches for something tucked in his belt. I manage to get a solid punch in while he's reaching. The blow nails the commander dead center in his face. My fingers break. Blood erupts from his nose, and he wheels on me with his own fists. In the time it took me to hit him once, he comes back with three of his own strikes—two to my head, making me see stars, and one to my stomach, stealing the air from my lungs. He shoves me to the ground and straddles me.

"Stop! Don't want to hurt—" he yells.

"What do you want?" I gasp and throw another punch.

Smith smacks my fist away and smashes my head into the concrete. "...could kill you now...need you—get to...Evericon—" he grunts.

His words and broken phrases don't make sense. Despite my inability to see straight or breathe, adrenaline forces me to lash out again and again. I know my hands make contact, but I struggle to see where I'm hitting.

Suddenly, Smith shrieks and his weight is thrown off me. I struggle to my feet and wipe blood out of my eyes. A huge bald man with a jagged scar on his face is swinging Smith into the concrete walls.

"The girl!" Marty yells. "Get the girl!"

I don't think twice. I run back to the cell. Clesandra and Lupète are dancing around each other. Every few seconds Lupète makes a lunge at her.

I rush to get between them and he turns on me. Holding both needles like fencing swords, he lunges at us.

Lupète is centimeters from making contact with Clesandra, but by some miracle, I'm able to tug her out of the way just in time. Lupète tumbles to the ground, tripping over Clesandra's leg. We both take defensive stances, ready for him to get back up and attack us. Strangely he doesn't. An odd sound comes from his body like air slowly escaping a balloon. He rolls himself over. Both needles are lodged in his chest. His gold eyes regard us with surprise.

"I was so sure," he whispers. "It wasn't supposed to happen this way. This wasn't how I saw it. You were going to let me..."

"I would never let you." I bend down so my face is an inch from his and yank the syringes out of his chest. He gasps, and I throw the needles into a corner of the room.

"Where's Jace? Please tell me," I beg.

"Not here. Gone." He starts to gasp and convulse, foam frothing from his mouth.

"Gone? Gone where?"

He doesn't answer me. Lupète's body shudders on the ground violently, his head smacking a sickening rhythm on the concrete before all movement ceases. In disbelief I shake his shoulders repeatedly.

"Where is he?" I shriek. "Gone where?" What little bit of liquid left in my body forces its way out of my eyes. Clesandra wraps her arms around my shoulders in a bear hug. I shake her off, but she locks her arms around me again like a vice until I turn into her.

"We'll find him."

Suddenly a high-pitched wailing of sirens interrupts us. The florescent white lights in the corridor change to flashing red.

"We have to go!" Marty's suddenly standing in the entrance to our cell. He's breathing heavily and a deep forehead laceration dribbles blood into his eyes.

Clesandra and I get to our feet, ready for another attack. Remembering her knife, I quickly dig it out of my boot and toss it to her. She flips the blade open.

I stare him down fiercely, putting myself one step in front of Clesandra.

Marty looks surprised. "I came to get you out." He gestures to Smith's body behind him.

"Is he dead?" I ask.

"We don't really have time to worry about that. Put it this way...if he's not dead, he probably won't walk the same ever again. And if we don't get moving we'll end up the same way."

"Why should we trust you?" Clesandra asks warily.

"Look. I'm on your team. We don't have time to debate this. If you're coming, come. If not, suit yourself. Evericon?" He waves me toward the exit.

Clesandra and I exchange a nervous glance. My brain says not to trust the man, but my gut says the opposite.

"Let's go." I grab Clesandra's arm and drag her toward the entrance of the cell.

The three of us step into the tunnel corridor. As I step over Smith's body, I turn back and give him a swift kick in the ribs.

"What the hell?" Clesandra yells, her voice echoing in the open space.

Both of us wince at her outburst. She's peering into a cell a few steps ahead of us and seeing the horror I witnessed hours earlier. I don't even want to know what she's seeing inside. "What the hell's going on in this place!" she yells, jogging to another cell farther down.

I sprint after her, grabbing her arm. "Don't look," I warn. She wheels around on me, breaks my grip, and then makes a run at Marty. "What the hell have you guys been doing to these people?"

Marty blocks her fists.

"What gives you the right? Let them go! All of them!" she shrieks.

Violent shouting and the sounds of gunshots ring in the tunnel behind us.

"Gotta go!" Marty screams.

"Not without them," Clesandra yells, pounding on a nearby cell door.

Marty and I both pull her away. She fights us for a few seconds until a bullet bouncing off the tunnel walls nearly hits her.

We sprint past cell after cell after cell, hundreds of them. I catch haunting glimpses of Mizuapa natives, some dead, others with their faces pressed up against the window glass watching us run past. I try to keep my eyes focused on the tiny, black dot at the end of the tunnel that's getting bigger with each step. I glance at Clesandra. Her face is stony, emotionless, trying to hide the hurt and pain she feels for the people we're abandoning.

"When we get close to the end of the tunnel," Marty yells, "there will be an escort waiting for you."

"Where are we going?"

"There's a group...a few of us. You'll be safe."

"My brother. Is Jace with them?"

Marty shakes his head. "Taken!" he yells.

"Where?" I yell back, panic flooding my bloodstream again.

"Not sure. We're still looking for him."

Out of breath, we've reached the end of the tunnel and sprint out into the darkness. It's almost pitch-black outside. There's an empty aircraft idling in the distance. No one is near it. The three of us come to a halt a few feet from it. It's too late before we realize it's a trap. Clesandra curses. My body involuntarily convulses as Tasers immobilize me. Out of the corner of my eye, there's a flash of blue, a face I think I recognize, and an immediate explosion. The ground shakes. The Taser darts are ripped off me, and Marty's gruff arms pull me back up to my feet.

"Get up!" he yells. There's another explosion and flash of blue. There are voices of soldiers yelling.

Clesandra is next to me again. She's on her feet, unharmed. Her knife blade smeared with blood. Marty drags me toward the aircraft. I'm running, though I'm not sure how. My arms and legs feel weak, and my heart feels like it's about to burst from the jolt of electricity it just received.

We climb onto the back of the aircraft, Marty in the driver's seat, me in the middle, and Clesandra clinging to the back. These aircrafts were never meant for more than two passengers and it groans angrily as it struggles to get into the air.

Marty flips a switch somewhere and the center console screen lights up a vibrant green, displaying the topography of the area despite the darkness. He yells something to us that I can't quite make out over the sound of the engine and the people yelling around us.

We hurtle forward into the night as soldiers bark orders to each other. Gunfire and flashes of blue pop and sizzle around us. Something hot whizzes past my head and mist drenches my face. Startled, I try to think of where moisture would be coming from out here.

"Oh God!" Clesandra curses repeatedly from behind me. A second later, I realize it isn't rain. The left side of Marty's head is gone. His body tips sideways, taking the controls and the aircraft with him. In the split second it takes me to realize the man who saved us is dead and we're going to crash, I somehow knock his hands loose and take control of the machine.

Time slows down. Marty's body tumbles far below us, his lifeless form seeming to take forever to hit the ground. The bullets travel in slow motion. I can see each one as an individual tiny, blue orb. The explosive sound takes an eternity to reach my ears. When it does, it sounds distant and much quieter than it should. Somehow I manage to weave in and out of trees as I angle the machine upward. I see the trees coming at me as bright-green slow-motion beams and narrowly avoid each one of them. Clesandra's fingernails dig vicious half-moon craters into my sides. It's her screaming voice that causes time to speed back up.

Trees whip past us.

"Duck!" Clesandra screams. I dip my head just in time to avoid being decapitated. Leaves and branches slap and gouge us, tangling around the frame of the aircraft. Just when I'm absolutely convinced we're going to crash and die, that the branches are going to swallow us up, there are no more trees. We punch through the canopy into open sky. Purple light from a star in the distance is starting to creep up and light the planet. I make the rookie mistake of taking a quick look straight down and feel my stomach rise into my throat. We're so incredibly high off the ground. If either one of us falls off this contraption, we will definitely die. I feel dizzy.

Screen, eyes on the screen, I tell myself. I look away from the ground and stare only at the screen in front of me. The circles of green and topography of the landscape distract me. I take huge gulps of the thin air until the tingling feeling in my head, arms, and legs starts to fade.

"You must be lucky. Thought for sure you'd crash us into something and it'd be over," Clesandra breathes behind me.

"Thanks for the vote of confidence," I say, still breathless. "Wish I would've taken flight lessons on base."

Clesandra and I take a second to glance behind us. The canopy covers any sign that Xinorsus and the men firing at us even existed.

"How long until they come after us?" I ask.

"Not long. They are probably already coming."

I curse under my breath. Eyeing the topography on the screen, I carefully tilt the controls right. The aircraft responds with ease.

"Where are you planning on taking us?" she asks.

I don't even really know how to take us anywhere on this thing, but I tell her the only place I can think of.

"The village." I point to the large grouping of mountains rising ominously in the distance. "To get Jace."

"What if they're not as friendly as Zap?" Her voice is neutral, but I know she's thinking about how the natives immobilized her and nearly left her die in the desert.

"It's the only other place Jace would be," I tell her. "We're just going to have to take our chances."

Chapter 29

I take a few seconds to get better acclimated with the controls, trying to remember and recreate every movement Pattison did. Unfortunately, he knew code and configurations for the screen that are completely foreign to me. The most I can figure out is left, right, up, down, fast, and slow. Hopefully that's all I'll need.

I power the machine as fast as it can go. Hurtling it toward the distant mountains, I'm fueled by the panic to find Jace before Smith, or the rest of his army, catches up to us. I wish I knew if Sheol and Zap made it safely to the village. I have trust that Zap will keep Sheol safe, and that her people are not savage murderers who will kill us as soon as they see us.

I imagine what it would be like if roles were reversed and an alien species showed up on Earth. There would be no mercy with people like Smith and my father in charge. Shoot first, ask questions later. Whoever took Jace hopefully doesn't have that mentality.

I look behind us one more time to make sure no one is coming. At best we'll only have a few hours lead before Smith's minions can mobilize a strong force. For the moment, it's just the two of us hovering in the sky, with the sound of the aircraft engine ringing in our ears. Clesandra clings to my waist, burying her head into my back to avoid the wind. I push the machine a little faster.

With the aid of the center console screen to help see where we are going, it only takes about thirty minutes of flying before the landscape below us changes dramatically.

In our first flight on Panacea, we were flown over

a part of the planet rich with lush-green tropical foliage. Though I can't see any source of water, no rivers or lakes below us, there has to be water deep below ground. Enough water for the trees surrounding Xinorsus to grow. When we get closer to the mountain range, the trees thin and almost completely disappear, leaving in their path miles of vibrant pink and gold sands that butt right up to the edge of the mountain range. Only small patches of green that run away from the base are any indication that water flows above or below ground.

The moment we crest the mountain range, I understand why Smith would want control of this area.

"Look." I nudge Clesandra, who picks her head up and readies her knife. A stone village built right into the sides of the mountain emerges below us. An enormous, fast-moving river flows along the inner edge of the mountains. It looks to form a complete and perfect circuit, but on closer inspection, branches of the river break off and flow into the mountains, disappearing from sight.

I slow the aircraft, hovering just above an expansive valley in the middle of the mountain range. Miles of farmland stretch out below us. Parts of the ground look sectioned off and are dotted with vibrant colors that must be fruit trees. Specks of people moving far below on the ground seem to stop and look up at us.

I tilt our aircraft right and start to follow the circular path of the river and mountains, looking for a safe place to land. I'm also searching for Sheol or Zap even though we're too far above ground to make out anyone's face.

"What do ya think is out there?" Clesandra points beyond the mountains across from us. A roiling, undulating wall of dark mist stretches up to the sky.

Rich dark foliage in front of the mist tells me that water, fed from the river, spills out on the other side of the mountains into that area. I'm reminded of Smith's warning about the "dark spots." Is that what he was referring to? The wall of misty, dark, fog looks ominous and forbidding. Nothing goes in and ever comes back out. Edging the aircraft a little closer to that side of the mountain range, we can see paths in the ground cut by numerous wide branches of river that flow right into the mist. Where those rivers spill out has to be the other source of unattainable water Smith was talking about. If he found a way of damming the flow of water leaving the natives' village, he could have his own permanent oasis. The moisture in the air would be forever trapped within the mountain range, constantly circulating water within the village. Not to mention the mountains provide practical coverage from ground attacks. This area would be easy enough to turn into a fortress, especially since none of the natives appear to have flight capabilities.

"That has to be the dark area Smith was talking about," I tell her, circling the aircraft back toward the center of the village. "Well?" I reach back and touch her arm. "Now or never, right? You ready?"

She doesn't answer, just holds her knife up next to my face. I give her a nod and start to ease our hovering aircraft down into the center of the valley below.

"Maybe you should put that thing away. Don't want to seem threatening," I tell her.

She mumbles something that I think sounds like, "You're kidding, right?" But she warily tucks the blade into her belt.

I carefully attempt to spiral the aircraft down like I've seen done a hundred times by air force pilots landing on Asik's military base. But having never flown or landed a plane, it's hard for me to keep the aircraft even and level on my approach. The machine's controls are so sensitive that just a simple turn pitches us sideways. Clesandra digs her fingers into my sides to stay on the machine with me. From the ground, my maneuvers probably appear amateurish. Hopefully the Mizuapa see our approach as just that and take pity on us.

Individual faces of the natives come into view as I gradually slow the aircraft. Their expressions and the way Clesandra digs her fingernails in a little deeper makes me start to reconsider landing. *You're crazy. You know they're going to kill you, right?* The thought bores into the back of my mind so strongly that I almost turn the aircraft around and fly away in panic. *What if Jace isn't here, either? What if they kill you outright? Who will find and protect him then?*

I tighten my fists around the hand controls, forcing myself to ignore the adrenaline pumping through my veins that's telling my body to run away. I picture Zap's curious face at our window the first night. I picture Zeekir attempting to help keep me alive by trying to feed me camel bugs. *Not murderers.* I keep looping the phrase in my head as the aircraft crunches to the ground.

Not a pretty landing. Clesandra and I are jostled right off the machine. It bounces repeatedly on the ground and starts to spin out, cutting massive circular paths in the Mizuapa's fields before grinding and sputtering to a stop.

We're surrounded in seconds. I catch a glimpse of a tall, silver-eyed lady when I roll myself over. She's neither curious nor friendly looking. In fact, she's just the opposite. I get an immediate feeling of despair. This was not the right choice. We shouldn't have come here. We're not welcome. We will die. Her massive palms grab my face before I can even put my hands up to block her. Everything goes black.

Chapter 30

The images come instantly. There are flashes of everything that's happened to me in my whole life. There are flashes of everyone I've ever spoken to. Every feeling, emotion, and thought I've ever had. Good or bad. They resurface in bursts. At first I'm certain I'm being killed. That my life is literally flashing before my eyes. Then, somewhere in the depths of my consciousness, I'm aware of what's happening. I hear other people's voices. Voices I don't recognize. A language I think I know, but that's still completely unfamiliar.

Terrified, I realize my entire life, who I am as a person, is being evaluated. I struggle even though it's pointless. Once they see who I am, who I come from, the thoughts I've had, what I am inside, I'm as good as dead.

Out of nowhere, I hear a voice I recognize.

"Let him go! All of you! Get off them!"

The images fade as quickly as they came. My eyes roll forward and refocus. My heart swells at the sight of a slim boy, his aqua-green eyes and sandy-colored hair bobbing in front of my face.

"Sheol," I breathe his name.

A lopsided grin tugs the side of his face. He extends a hand for me, and I realize I'm lying on the ground in a large, ornately designed stone room surrounded by people. I take his hand. He hauls me to my feet and grips me in a massive hug, pounding my back hard. All around us are hundreds of faces, most of which are not focused on me anymore. They touch each other's arms and shoulders, muttering. Sharing what they've learned from me with each other. I wince, wondering what they must be thinking.

"They're going to kill us. Aren't they?"

"Don't worry about them," he says casually, though his eyes say the opposite.

"Shouldn't I be worried?" I ask nervously.

"Yeah, sort o...they did it to me too. That weird 'sight' thing." He waves his arms about. They didn't kill me. They haven't killed you yet, so you should be good. Just don't do anything stupid. I was just trying to convince them to come save your sorry asses too," he says, pushing me backward. He sidesteps away from me and folds his arms across his chest. "And you. I have a bone to pick with you, sister," he says with a scowl.

Clesandra is up on her feet, too, glaring at a few female natives who look at her with interest as they share information among themselves.

Clesandra narrows her eyes at Sheol. "You know I couldn't let him go alone."

"Yeah, yeah, you're both madly in love. Blah, blah, blah."

She purses her lips, annoyed.

"Relax. I woulda done the same thing with this one." He points over to Zap, who's standing in a crowd with the others. She's heatedly discussing something with the silver-eyed woman who originally stole my memories. Neither one of them looks happy.

"I get it. Trust me. You did what you thought was right. But you didn't have to knock us out. My head had a lump the size of an orange."

"No other way." She scowls.

"Yeah. Whatever." Sheol scowls right back, but I know it's with fondness. A second later he opens his arms wide, inviting her in. "Admit it," he says with a smile. "You missed me." She glares at him but steps forward. He hugs her around the neck, and then turns back to me.

"Where's Jace?"

He does a quick scan of the area. "I didn't see him, just the two of you guys."

It's like Sheol just stabbed me in the gut.

"He's not here?" I suck in a haggard breath, feeling the room suddenly get smaller.

Sheol's jubilant mood drops. "No. He's not with you?"

Clesandra and I shake our heads.

"He was taken," I tell him. "I assumed these guys," I gesture in a circle angrily, "took him."

Sheol shakes his head. "No. He's not here. Taken? Taken where?"

"I don't know!" I shout, my voice echoing off the stone walls. "Do you think if I knew I'd be standing here right now?"

The room around us goes suddenly silent. All eyes trained on our small group. Zap slips away from the silver-eyed woman and sidles up next to Sheol protectively.

"Okay. Okay. Relax, buddy," Sheol says soothingly, and eyes the natives uneasily.

"For God's sake! Please don't tell me to relax right now. My brother is gone and I don't know where he is. Smith's men are coming here right now. They're coming with weapons—weapons like you can't imagine and Jace is gone!" I feel the emotion welling up, constricting my chest, making it hard to breathe. The room continues to get smaller.

The natives move in around us. Clesandra and I take defensive stances. Zap touches my arm. I want to pull it out of her grasp, but something inside stops me. A chain reaction occurs as Zap touches me, and someone else touches her, and so on until the entire room is connected. The only one who stands apart is the silver-eyed woman. She doesn't join the others. Instead, she glares at our group reproachfully.

It's the most powerful feeling I've ever experienced. Voices and words that are as clear as day come in snips, then unite around my pain. "Smith, war, death, suffer, brother, Jace, hurt, taken, lost, must find, save..." like the hum of electricity coming from a high-voltage cable. I get the overwhelming feeling that these people understand, that they want to help.

Zap's hand floats away from my skin. "Will find," she says in her high-pitched, sing-song voice.

"It's too late. You can't help. Smith's men are coming. He's going to destroy this place," I say, looking around at all the faces. I grip Sheol's shoulders. "They have to leave. You have to get Zap to convince them to leave. Smith will kill them. You have no idea what he's been doing...the kinds of tests." I can't even vocalize the horrors I've seen.

"Calm down, Avery. You're safe here."

"You don't understand!"

"He's right, Sheol," Clesandra says. "These people are no match. Smith has hundreds of 'em captive."

An uneasy murmur ripples through the room.

"They've fashioned weapons from her knife," I whisper. "It's going to be a bloodbath."

Out of the corner of my eye I see the tall silver-eyed woman approaching us. She's much older than the majority of the people here. Her long, flowing, white hair and rough, angular features make her appear cold as stone and sinister. She looks at Zap with a mixture of pain and disappointment.

"We will not find this boy, Jace," she says coldly. Her voice is firm and assertive. I take a quick look around the room. No one is moving. All eyes are on this woman. She speaks easily, not straining to search for the correct words of our English language. She speaks out loud and deliberately so that Sheol, Clesandra, and I can understand. This woman, who stands judging us in a way that is only fitting for the atrocities my people have committed, must be in charge.

Zap looks hurt.

"Like your father, you trust too easily." She reaches out a hand to touch Zap's face. Zap pulls away and steps directly in front of Sheol. She says something angrily in her native language that I don't understand. Murmurs of dissent from the other natives fill the room.

The woman's expression darkens. "Your father is dead because of it, and so is the half-child he helped create with *them*," she says with a tone of hatred and irony. She turns to face Clesandra and me. Her silver eyes are the color of cold slate, boring knowingly into mine.

Lupète. She could only be referring to him. I cast a sideways glance at Zap. She's cautiously looking at the other Mizuapa people from the corners of her eyes, but still standing protectively in front of Sheol.

"You should have done what was asked of you," the silver-eyed woman says to Zap. "Your job was to bring back the half-child. Instead, you bring us this boy." She gestures disgustedly at Sheol. "And others are now here. These people are dangerous. Can you not feel it, child?"

Murmurs of agreement drift up from others in the room.

So Sheol was just an accident she stumbled upon. Zap wasn't there to see him the first night we arrived. She was looking for her brother. Her half-brother. I wonder if she could feel something when Lupète arrived on Panacea again. Was that what drew her in?

"You should not have come," the woman says. "Your people bring only death and pain."

"Came to warn us. Help us," Zap spits back.

The old woman shakes her head.

"They came only for the boy," she says to me.

She's right. I feel like I should look away ashamed. I'm *only* here for Jace. Sheol, though I love him, he's practically my brother, is secondary. Warning these people is the right thing to do, I'm glad we did it, but it's not why I came. This woman, with just one touch, knows who I am and all my motives. I should be ashamed and disappointed. I'm only thinking of myself. How the loss of Jace will kill me. How I won't be able to live with myself if I let him die like I let Jeremy die. Even knowing this, I force myself to hold her stare.

"Where's Jace?" I say, trying to match her tone.

"The boy is gone," she states.

My world crushes inward a little more. *Why does no one know where he is? Why does everyone insist that he's simply gone and say it as if it's unchangeable fact?*

"No," I say sternly with a shake of my head. My hands are balled into fists. "You people know where he is."

"Yes, we do," she agrees.

"Then tell me where he is!" I yell, taking a step forward. I don't care what happens to me. Don't care that the other natives assemble themselves in a wall around the woman. Don't care that even Zap looks concerned and moves in.

"Avery, chill," Sheol warns. His voice, though I can feel the vibrations echoing off the stone walls, sounds like a whisper in my ringing ears. I feel Clesandra's tight grip around my arms. I also know that with all the adrenaline pumping through my veins

I can break her hold easily.

The old woman's expression doesn't change.

"No one can help him where he is. Not our people. Not yours. The boy is gone," she says again. She gestures behind her to an enormous opening in the stone. This room, tucked high in the side of the mountains, overlooks the river and the farming valley below. In the far distance where the woman points is the other ridge of mountains, and beyond that, the dark mist that rises ominously like thick, toxic smoke.

"No." I shake my head in disbelief.

The woman nods. "He is gone. No one is permitted to enter. No one can help him where he is," she repeats.

"No. You're lying to me!" My knees crack violently together, no longer willing to hold my weight as I realize Jace is lost. If what this woman is saying is true, if he is indeed in the dark area, there is no hope for him.

"Jace. Oh no, Jace," I say his name as my knees buckle and make painful contact with the stone floor. I rip my arms out of Clesandra's grip and bury my face in my hands.

For a moment it's just me. I'm alone in the room. No one else. It's quiet except for a horrible sound coming from somewhere. *Where is that sound coming from?* I realize it's coming out of me. The shock of losing every single person in my family settles like a heavy boulder on my chest.

"Avery."

My voice is being called, but it sounds so far away. So easy to ignore it.

"Avery!"

"Let her go!" Sheol says, panicked. I know I should care, but my whole body feels numb. Zap's voice joins Sheol's, and something hard hits the middle of my back.

"Snap out of it, man! Help us!" Sheol yells.

The pain is intense, like the sensation of being shocked with a Taser. I gasp a huge lungful of air and another blast hits me again.

"Up!" a commanding voice yells at me. It's no longer just me in the room. A wide circle of Mizuapa surrounds me. I'm lying off to the side in the circle. Zap is crouched next to me with her hand forming a claw, ready to strike me. With Sheol's hand on her shoulder, her outstretched fingers dance with flashes of static electricity. Zap and Sheol are staring down the silver-eyed woman. She has Clesandra, limp in her grasp. Clesandra's eyes are rolled so far back that only the whites show.

The woman grips the top of Clesandra's head so tightly that her body levitates off the ground. The other hand holds a simple-looking bone knife that's painted with ornate yellow flowers. The end of the knife is tipped with a long, black barb. I recognize the flower design and the black barb from Dr. Albero's agricultural training. The painted designs are Nexmors flowers. I can only guess that the black barb was painstakingly extracted from a mature flower. The venom inside will kill in seconds, and the old woman is holding the blade precariously near Clesandra's heart.

Seeing Clesandra in trouble revives me. Even if there isn't anything I can do for Jace, I can still try and save her. The woman I love.

"Put her down," Sheol says again. The three of us move to stand directly in front of the woman.

"Please let her go, we'll leave. I promise we'll never come back here," I beg.

The woman looks at Zap. "Too late," she says with a tone of sadness.

"No," Zap says strongly. "Let them..." She struggles for the last word. "Leave," she says finally.

"He may go." She points the tip of the knife to Sheol and begins to bargain with her daughter. "If you stay. He can go."

"Where I go, she goes," Sheol says defiantly. The look on the woman's face turns bitter and angry.

Zap intertwines her fingers with Sheol's and gives his hand a squeeze. "He go," she says fervently. Sheol starts to protest, but Zap continues. "Others go too."

The old woman shakes her head. "Both of them must die. They have created another." She places her closed fist that grips the knife against Clesandra's abdomen. A hum of agreement rises from the other Mizuapa people.

"What's she talking about?" Sheol asks. Zap turns to him with sad eyes and must transfer information to him because he looks at me shocked.

"All the more reason to let them live!" he shouts angrily.

"Not good." Zap tries to tell him. Sheol won't hear it. He takes another step toward the woman. I follow. The crowd of Mizuapa erupts with warnings and angry tones. The woman places the tip of the blade to Clesandra's skin. A surge of adrenaline spills into my muscles as I prepare to rush the woman. She's less than thirty feet away, and I could tackle her in seconds. I also know that even if I do, and succeed, the rest of the Mizuapa will swarm and kill us. But I see no other options.

As I ready my muscles, there comes a sharp metallic sound in the distance. *They're here.* My knees feel weak again.

"I told you they were coming. If you're smart, you'll lead your people as far away from here as possible," I say to the old woman.

The woman doesn't say anything. We regard each other in tense silence. Little beads of sweat are forming on her brow and above her upper lip.

Zap says one faint word in her own language and looks at the silver-eyed woman. Pure panic is in her eyes. I don't have to know her language to know she called her mother's name. The old woman casts fleeting sideways glances at her people. They turn nervous eyes to the open-air side of the room. The sound of Smith's aircrafts are getting louder. A few seconds later the explosions come. The bombs are being dropped in the valley, killing and scattering those people who are not in the room with us. Thankfully, we're too high up to hear their screams.

"They're clearing the area," Sheol says solemnly. The mountain shakes, and tiny bits of stone and dirt rain down from the roof of the building. The Mizuapa in the room look terrified, but they hold their ground, waiting for instructions from the silver-eyed woman.

She knows this is the end for her people. If she doesn't get them out now, everyone will be lost. Even so, she narrows her cold, gray eyes on me. She takes the tip of the knife and angles the blade into Clesandra's chest. I think I can see a bead of her blood form beneath the cloth. The muscles in my legs contract, and I spring forward without thinking.

Just as I reach the woman her silver eyes grow wide and unfocused. She coughs, and a fine red spray of liquid bursts from her lips and nose. A splash of crimson appears from the bullet hole in the middle of her chest and blossoms, saturating her ornate clothing with blood.

Zap shrieks, and the old woman's legs give out. I catch her arm and pull the knife away from Clesandra's skin as she falls. There's popping and banging coming from all around us. Flashes of blue streak past us, and bodies fall, hitting the stone floor with a sickening sound. The room erupts with panicked screaming. Six or seven aircrafts hover around the entrance with soldiers shooting haphazardly into the room. Clesandra, who is no longer under the grasp of the old woman, is starting to regain consciousness amidst the chaos.

Panicked, she yells for Sheol and I. Clesandra starts to get up and I instinctively tackle her back down and cover her head. The Mizuapa scatter, disappearing down corridors and through gaps in the stone walls that I didn't realize were there. Zap is one of the few alive Mizuapa who remains. She gathers her mother's lifeless body into her lap, wailing so loudly it's surprising the mountain doesn't collapse from the mere vibrations of her sorrow.

The room is nearly clear. We have to get out. We have to follow the Mizuapa, otherwise we'll be captured again.

"Sheol! We gotta go!" I yell.

"Working on it!" he barks back. Clesandra and I crawl our way over to him. He's next to Zap, trying to pry her fingers off her dead mother. The three of us work her fingers free and literally drag her to a gap in the stone walls.

It's too late.

"One more step and you're dead, Evericon." Rustin's cruel voice comes from behind us.

Clesandra and I both wince. We stand up and turn toward him, our hands in the air. Zap, not sure what to do, follows our lead. Even with her hands in the air I can see her body convulsing with sadness. I look around the room. Dozens of bodies lie dead or dying in pools of blood. A few Mizuapa people are moaning or gurgling as they take their last breaths. I swallow a hard lump in my throat. We did this. These people were not prepared, and we led Smith's army right to them. For what? So I could get Jace back? He isn't even here! All these people died for nothing because of my selfishness. *My selfishness.*

"Kill me then." I take a step toward him.

"Shut up," Clesandra hisses from behind me.

"Yeah, Avery. Shut up," Sheol agrees.

I turn and look at them. "No, he should kill me. I deserve to die." I take another step toward Rustin and hear the hammer of his gun click.

"I'm warning you," Rustin says.

"If you had the balls you'd have already done it, Glowerbak," Pattison's voice cuts in. He steps off his aircraft, letting it idle at the entrance. "Besides, you have specific orders *not* to kill him."

Three more men on different aircrafts step off their machines to join Rustin and Pattison. All men have their guns pointed at our hearts. The tiny red laser lights drift slightly on our chests as the men inhale and exhale.

Rustin's expression is wild and angry, his pupils dilated. Tiny beads of perspiration dot his paper-white forehead. Rustin was never a stable person to begin with, but he looks like he's lost his mind completely.

A native on the ground moans painfully, and Rustin swivels and puts a bullet in his head to stop the noise.

Zap shrieks and rushes toward Rustin, but Sheol catches her arm and yanks her backward. "No!" he yells.

Rustin turns on her and fires blindly. The bullet catches Zap in the shoulder, tearing a massive chunk of flesh and muscle away from her arm. She collapses to the ground, writhing in agony, kicking her feet while Sheol cradles her head and yells obscenities at Rustin.

"I can shoot the two of you, no problem," Rustin

says, chambering another round, and pointing the gun at Sheol's head. His finger is on the trigger, but he doesn't get to pull it. Pattison shoots Rustin before turning and shooting the rest of the men in his group. All but Rustin's is a lethal shot. I'll never be able to get the shocked look on their faces out of my head. Pattison shot Rustin in the identical spot to Zap.

"See how it feels to suffer with no one here to help you," Pattison says, stalking over to Rustin, and digging the heel of his boot into the gunshot wound.

Pattison turns to look at us. "Well, kid. You ready to go?" he asks me.

"What's going on?" Clesandra asks suspiciously.

"Not everyone is who you think they are." Pattison lowers his gun and limps toward us.

"Traitor!" Rustin howls in pain.

"You guys coming or not?" Pattison asks again.

"Where?" Sheol asks.

"Only one place left to go. We don't have time to debate. Either you're coming or not."

Clesandra and I exchange a glance, grab Rustin's weapon from the ground and join Pattison.

"Why are you helping us?" I ask.

"I got tired of being a pinch hitter. It's my turn to try and hit a homerun. Get their guns," he says. "Smith's army's not going to just let you guys walk out of here with me."

"What about Zap?" Sheol asks. He's doing his best to tie his shirt around her upper arm to stop the bleeding.

Pattison looks torn.

"I'm not leaving without her," Sheol says through gritted teeth.

"If she can stay on the aircraft while you fly it, she can come too."

"Fly? I don't know how to fly one of those

things!" Sheol yells.

Pattison is getting frustrated. Cursing under his breath, he looks at the aircrafts like he's trying to decide something. "You and the girl fly with me. We'll just have to hope the machine can handle the extra weight. The two of you can manage on your own, I guess?" he says to me.

"We got here on our own, didn't we?" I say sarcastically.

"Judging by the road rash on your arms, I'm guessing just barely." He turns and limps over to Sheol. They help Zap up. "We'll wedge her between the two of us."

The five of us mount our aircrafts and power them up. Pattison groans under the extra weight and picks up speed slowly.

"Get ready," Pattison yells.

We rev the engines and push them as fast as they can go out of the mountain above the valley. The scene that unfolds before us is startling. I don't know exactly what I expected to see. Something less gruesome, I guess, but it's a true bloodbath. It looks as if all of Smith's men are here. Some of them flying aircrafts, while others are on the ground using grenades and guns to kill any native they come in contact with. As predicted, the natives, though they are excellent and skilled fighters, are no match for the types of weapons the invaders bring. Smith's men take them by surprise, and the weaponry allows the soldiers to fight the natives at a distance. The Mizuapa are most lethal at close-range fighting. I am happy to see that even with our army's weapons, there are still many casualties on our side. I should feel guilty hoping the Mizuapa win. I don't.

The moment our aircrafts leave the stone mountainside, our center console lights let us know other aircrafts are following us and engaging their weapons. I don't know why that information surprises me. We make obvious targets since all the other aircrafts in the sky are occupied by only one rider.

Seconds later, flashing red lights and a whooping siren lets us know something is wrong. Pattison's aircraft, only one hundred yards or so ahead of ours, is blaring wildly too. An automated message booms robotically at us.

"Land immediately. This vehicle is being deactivated. Land immediately." The phrase loops along with a frantic, high-pitched beeping. All around, other aircrafts close in.

"They're going to catch us!" Clesandra screams.

"Shoot at the machines," I yell back. Clesandra and Sheol fire multiple rounds. Bullets ricochet loudly off the metal frames.

"You can't aim at the machines!" Pattison yells. "Aim at the people." He's pushing his aircraft as fast as it will go toward the dark mist in the distance.

People are starting to fire at us from the ground level too. A bullet hits the rear end of our machine. A new siren and set of warnings lights illuminate the console screen. The bullets hit our fuel line. The engine strains to take us over the mountain ridge. Aircrafts behind us are closing in fast.

"I can't get enough speed! We're not going to make it!" I yell back to Clesandra. "How many bullets you got left?"

"None!"

"Shit!" I lean my full weight on the controls, trying to keep them level. "Don't suppose you can make another water crystal thing appear?"

"Doesn't work like that. I don't know how to do it!"

"Now would be a good time to learn!"

I feel her tight grip on my waist release, and I swivel my head around to look at her.

Clesandra's right arm extends toward the water in the river. Nothing happens at first.

"I can't!"

Panic grips me. The other aircrafts are so close I can make out the outline of people riding them. Just when I think we're done for, Clesandra's whole body lights up like the fourth of July.

"Oh God," she curses. She's turned completely around, straddling the seat with her knees, both arms now outstretched wide. There's a deep rumbling like the sound a building makes as it collapses in on itself. I think I hear people screaming, even though I know we're too far above the ground to hear anything like that. Even though it's the most dangerous thing a rookie pilot can do, I look straight down.

A wall of water is rising from the river into the sky. It's frothing, foaming, tumultuous power comes straight into Clesandra's open hands where it begins to crystallize in a gorgeous baseball-sized droplet.

The aircraft pilots blast through the wall of water rising from the ground and continue their pursuit. Clesandra closes her fist around the crystal. The remaining water flowing toward her ceases and falls back down from the sky as a torrential rainstorm. The glowing tattoos on her body fade, and she comes back into herself.

"I did it," she says in disbelief.

Smith's soldiers start firing on our aircraft.

"Throw it at them!" I scream at her.

"What?" she shouts.

"The crystal! Throw it at them."

Without thinking, she hurls the crystal at the soldier closest to us. The crystal hits the aircraft frame and explodes in a massive tidal wave that takes out that soldier and three others. Terrified, the remaining pilots veer off and break formation.

Clesandra laughs and shouts victoriously, "That'll teach 'em."

I shake my head, looking at the flight controls nervously. "That's great, but we're still going to crash!"

She looks over my shoulder at the screen. The moment she does, the hand controls jam up and the engine cuts out.

"Oh God! We're really going to crash!" I yell.

"Hold the hand mounts level!" Clesandra barks. "We're almost over the mountains. Maybe we can glide!"

I peek down again and see she's right. We're halfway across the mountain range headed toward the mist. Pattison's aircraft is a mere speck that seems miles ahead of us now. Clesandra wraps her arms around my waist again and we glide forward.

We make it over the mountain range only to discover a new problem. We're speeding up. Our bullet-shaped vehicle is not the greatest for long-term gentle gliding. We're losing altitude rapidly and speeding toward an imminent crash.

"We're still going to crash," I say.

"No. Gonna land. Just faster than we want," Clesandra answers.

Oh good. We're still going to die.

"We're gonna have to bail!"

"As in, jump off?" I scream incredulously.

"Unless you want to blow up with the machine when it hits the ground!"

A new siren on the screen lets us know that we're approaching the ground faster than we should. It's telling us we're going to crash and die with an alarming amount of numerical statistics. *Three percent chance of survival. Great.* The ground is coming straight at us, and we're about two or three miles from the giant wall of mist. I look ahead just in time to see Pattison's vehicle, with Sheol and Zap in tow, whiz inside and disappear from view.

"Remember to roll when you hit the ground!" Clesandra shouts. "Get ready. One... two..."

My muscles tense. I don't hear her say three. Our minds and bodies become one as we forcefully launch ourselves off the side of the aircraft.

Again, time slows down. I have enough conscious thought before the moment of impact that it seems like we are falling for minutes instead of seconds. I can see every detail of the ground I'm about to hit. How it doesn't look dry and hard. It doesn't look sandy like a desert, either. The ground is a dark color I don't really recognize. Stray branches and soft, green plants poke up out of the ground. I hear our aircraft exploding in the distance, but the sound doesn't seem as sharp and hard as it should. It's more like a dull *thump*.

When Clesandra and I connect with the ground, we don't land on hard-packed earth at all. We land in slime! It's thick, squishy slime. We sink deep into it, and for a moment I panic, flailing my arms wildly until I feel hard bottom beneath the layer of slime. I plant my feet and stand up. The muck comes up to my chest. I check myself over, surprised that nothing is broken or hurt. Then I look for Clesandra. I don't see her anywhere.

Dread washes over me.

"Clesandra!" I call her name. "Clesandra!" I swirl my hands through the muck and brine, trying to find her. There's a thick splashing three feet in front of me. A dark form rises out of the mud. "Clesandra!" I shout, relieved. I try to rush over to her, but the thick stuff slows me down.

When I finally get to her, I throw my arms around her neck.

"Wait, wait, wait." She pushes me off and swipes at her face with her mud-covered hands. I brush her hair back from her face.

"We lived."

"Of course we did," she says, annoyed. "I told you before I'm not gonna lose you."

Mud or no mud, I pull her in and press my lips to hers. She doesn't let me kiss her for long before gently pushing me backward.

"You taste like dirt," she says, and smears mud away from her mouth. Our eyes lock and she smiles. "We lived," she echoes.

I point at the dark mist a half-mile in front of us. "Pattison took Sheol and Zap straight in there," I say. "He's right, it's the only place left that Smith is afraid to go. He won't chase us there."

"Didn't Smith say that no one ever comes out of there?"

"No one has ever come out. Alive or dead," I confirm.

She bites her lower lip and looks at the mist. "At least that we know of."

"It's the last place Jace might be," I tell her.

"Are you sure? Aren't you afraid?" she asks.

"Of course I am." I balance my chin on top of her head and hug her so she can't see the anxiety on my face. "But I can't live with myself unless I know what happened to my brother."

She nods.

"You're not afraid? Tough girl like you?" I smile down at her.

She doesn't answer, so I pull her in again and kiss the top of her head. "It'll be okay."

"If we live or die in there maybe it'll be for the

best anyway," she says quietly.

"What do you mean?" I ask, stepping back so I can read her expression.

"I'm afraid of what will happen to these people if we don't go. And Smith can't have him," she adds with a serious tone.

"Him?"

She looks down at her stomach and back up at me. "Him," she repeats. "It's better this way. You know...if I die."

"Don't—"

Clesandra gives my hand a squeeze. "It ain't right, you know, one person having full control."

She's right, and if we don't go, Smith will find a way of exploiting her somehow.

"I have to do this to make sure Smith doesn't get him," Clesandra says.

"You mean *we* have to do this."

Her expression turns sad and distant as she looks from me to the dark wall of mist in front of us.

I tilt her chin up gently with my fingertips so she's looking directly at me.

"You don't think you're going alone? I said I was never leaving you alone again." Her beautiful green eyes shift back and forth between mine. "And I meant what I said." I pull her to me and kiss her deeply and passionately, feeling that same overpowering, primitive desire never to stop.

The distant sounds of Smith's men coming after us make us come up for air. They've reassembled, and the deep rumble of hovercraft engines straining under the weight of soldiers and weaponry isn't far off. The vehicles, shimmering in the heat waves, crest the mountain. They can see us now, too, and I think I can almost make out the commander's angry face. I guess he's not dead after all. I smile at Clesandra, knowing that he won't have the satisfaction of winning this war.

She smiles back, and I know she's thinking the exact same thing. Whatever happens, good or bad, we have each other. Clesandra laces her fingers in mine and we trudge into the black mist together. For once, I feel confident that I'm doing something right. I know Jeremy would have done the same thing.

ABOUT THE AUTHOR

Andrea Perno writes futuristic science fiction. She divides her time between being a full time art teacher in Baltimore and writing. With very little "sit down" time to herself, she creates most of her writing through voice notes on her phone while driving to and from work. She grew up in Florida and Pennsylvania and now resides in Maryland where she enjoys the company of her husband, family and friends. In her spare time she can be found writing, creating artwork or on the back of a horse soaking up the sunshine outdoors.

Stop by and say Hello to Andrea on Facebook:
https://www.facebook.com/pages/Andrea-Perno/629019327187343

Find more books by Andrea Perno from Beau Coup Publishing:
Amazon http://amzn.to/1eXtxp0

The Last Drop Series
The Last Drop

Made in the USA
San Bernardino, CA
21 March 2016